THE
PERFECT
BOYFRIEND

S. E. LYNES

BOOKS BY S.E. LYNES

Mother

The Pact

Valentina

The Proposal

The Women

The Lies We Hide

Can You See Her?

The Housewarming

Her Sister's Secret

The Baby Shower

The Ex

The Summer Holiday

The Split

THE
PERFECT
BOYFRIEND

S. E. LYNES

bookouture

Published by Bookouture in 2025

An imprint of Storyfire Ltd.
Carmelite House
50 Victoria Embankment
London EC4Y 0DZ

www.bookouture.com

The authorised representative in the EEA is Hachette Ireland
8 Castlecourt Centre
Dublin 15 D15 XTP3
Ireland
(email: info@hbgi.ie)

ISBN: 978-1-83618-196-5
eBook ISBN: 978-1-83618-195-8

To Bridget McCann, my fathomlessly generous friend, with much love.

PROLOGUE

If you could turn back time, you would not have come. But here you are.

The north-east wind howls through your coat. From the black sea, brackish spray whips your hair into your eyes, trickles water down your neck. It's so bitterly cold out here, it makes you want to cry.

His arms are rough beneath yours. He is all that's holding you up. Your head spins. Vision comes and goes. The word *sweet* comes to you as you struggle to recall the cloying smell on the cloth he pressed over your mouth.

North Pier. That's where you are. You know it like the back of your hand. Security lights glow in the restaurant, empty now. The Silver Darling. You always meant to go but never did. So many things you meant to do and never did. You always loved the name. *Silver Darling. O, my darling. O, the sands, o, the shore, o, the waves, o, the sea.* Your child, your precious child. All you have lost. It is too late to change your life's mistakes. Too late to change any of it now.

Your knees buckle. Blackness clouds in, blood pressure in free fall. He tightens his grip, but your legs have collapsed like a puppet's. He pulls you up, groaning with the effort, fingertips fat blocks through your thick winter coat. Your vision clears. You're stumbling again now – staggering on the glittering stones of the jetty. Your wrists are bound together with soft nylon stockings, your fingers clamped in an imitation of prayer. The pitiless wind bites into your skin. Behind the tape, your teeth chatter; the vibrations skitter through your body. How terrified you are, how helpless, how hopeless. North Pier. The harbour. The ghoulish familiarity. The horror of knowing exactly where you are and why you're here. He has told you why. He has told you everything, and you understand that this is why you need to go.

'I need you to shut your damn mouth,' he whispered, before. 'I need to live the life I've earned. Surely you get that?'

You gulp, once, twice, as if something has stuck in your throat. It is only regret, rising bitter on your tongue. Your regrets are infinite, enough to vomit on the frosted ground. You have bitten them back all these years, swallowed them down, but no more. They are all you have now. There will be no turning back the clock. There will be no doing it all differently. It is too late to change what you have done.

The North Sea explodes against the seawall. Like fireworks, you think. Like shooting stars. Your head is as heavy as a cannonball. You try to turn, the instinct to run still the tiniest ember within you. But his grip is too tight. He is so much stronger than you. If you break away, you will fall. Even if you could run, he is faster. You sink. He pulls you up. Your vision clears, your feet staggering pin-steps once again. This dance you do; a dance of death. Warm tears run down your neck, soak your collar. You are crying for the past, for the present, for all of it. All your mistakes. So many mistakes. If only...

Sirens wail in the distance. You twitch with hope. From the esplanade, you think, though you can't be sure. But they are not for you. Even if they were, they are too late. You have reached the end: the end of the pier, the end of your story, the end of your life. The North Sea is sharp black blades. It is hellish depths. It will be quick. You have that, at least.

'Please,' you whisper. 'Please don't.' But your words are feathers in the wind.

He unties your hands, his face grim. The stockings have left no mark, which was his intention. He cannot afford to leave a trace.

'I feel bad,' he says. 'But success takes sacrifice, especially for someone like me.'

'Please,' you plead, your eyes sticky.

He turns you roughly by the shoulders. Deftly he wets the cloth and presses it over your face.

Sweet, you think. The smell is sweet.

ONE

KIRSTY

Kirsty Shaw/transcript #1 (uncut)

My name is Kirsty Shaw.

What, so – just go for it, like?

OK. Right, so.

So the shift that day pretty much started with an emergency. I was in the delivery room with my trainee, Debbie St John. Debs, we call her. Mum was a lady called Lauren Coolson. I see thousands of faces and hear thousands of names, as I'm sure you can imagine, but Lauren stayed with me – maybe because of what happened later.

I took Lauren's hand because I could see she was transitioning into the final stage of labour. Mums need a lot of encouragement and reassurance, especially if it's their first. I told her to breathe for me and that she was doing great, and I gave her fingers a squeeze. I can still remember the way her frightened blue eyes fixed on mine and how I gave her what I suppose I'd call a gaze of professional reassurance. *I've got you*, the gaze says, and it doesn't waver. *You'll be safe with me. Your baby will be safe with me.*

We were our own world at this point, Debs, Lauren and me, the three of us locked together in our task. When I stop to think, which I suppose is what I'm doing now, our world is so ordinary and so extraordinary at the same time. What we have in that delivery room is symbiosis; the symbiosis of delivering new life.

You can tell I've had a good think about it, can't you?

Anyway, I can remember the weak morning sunlight filtering through the high windows. It had been minus five when I'd come in, according to the temperature display on my trusty old Ford Focus. But in the maternity unit it was warm as toast.

Lauren was doing her breathing as she'd been shown in her NCT classes. Her hand was tight around mine, our eyes meeting now and then. At this point, all the antenatal theory had come crashing down. I could see it in her face, the realisation that none of those classes can quite prepare you for the reality. That reality was only a few short weeks away for me obviously, but I wasn't thinking about that then. All I was thinking about was this woman and her baby, of keeping them both safe.

'Check dilation,' I said to Debs quietly but firmly.

'Don't go,' Lauren said. Her voice was full of anxiety.

'I'm not going anywhere, love,' I said, re-establishing eye contact, keeping my voice super neutral. 'I'm staying right here until we get this wee bairn out, all right?'

Lauren nodded several times, briskly and bravely; you can probably picture what I mean. Two big tears squeezed from the corners of her eyes and ran down the sides of her face like raindrops. She was flushed with exertion, her teeth clamped. I told her to relax her jaw if she could, to remember to take the gas and air when she felt the contraction coming. You time it, you see, so that the nitrous oxide will take full effect at the peak of the contraction.

'Nine centimetres,' Debs said, but she looked doubtful, so I knew I should double-check.

'I'm going to see where we're up to,' I said to Lauren. 'Just a sec.' I let go of her hand and had a quick glance before mouthing *Good* to my young colleague, whose face softened with relief.

'Okey-doke.' I took Lauren's hand once again. 'You're nearly there, but don't push until I tell you to, all right? Remember your classes. Just keep breathing through those contractions for me... That's it, you're doing really well. Brilliant. That's it. Soon have this baby out for you. Not long now.'

Another load of nods; sweat was pouring from her forehead, her smile stoic behind the air mask. Her eyes closed. She groaned.

'That's it,' I said. 'Get that lovely nitrous oxide down you. Better than Prosecco, that stuff. Breathe through it – that's right. Make like Leona Lewis and keep breathing for me, OK?'

It's good to use a little bit of humour. I think so anyway. It shows you're comfortable and that everything's going smoothly. I carried on telling her she was doing brilliantly, that the baby would soon be here, stuff like that. And then I told her I was going to check her cervix again but that I was right there with her.

Lauren closed her eyes as the contraction subsided. I needed no more than a second to see she was fully dilated. I gave the merest nod to Debs, our shorthand for *Stand by*.

'Hold Mum's hand just now for me,' I said to Debs, who did as she was told while I positioned myself as best I could. I'm not going to lie – my thirty-five-week bump was pretty bloody awkward against the end of the bed.

'Now, my love. With your next contraction, I want you to push as hard as you can for me, OK?' My voice will have been louder and firmer by now. Not to be bossy or anything like that, just because Mum needs to know you're in charge. 'Hubby'll be here soon, but we don't need him, do we? We can do this. Girl power!'

In reality, hubby was stuck in a traffic jam at the Brig O Dee, but right then wasn't the moment to tell Lauren that.

Lauren's body reared up. She let out a really loud moan, in the grip of the shuddering I knew so well but had yet to experience myself.

'And push,' I said. 'Push like your life depends on it. That's it. Thaaaat's it. Brilliant. That was brilliant. And breathe. Breathe it out. Excellent.'

Debs and me just did our job. Not like it could wait, is it? There was no pause for thought as to the miracle of it all. That would come later. It always comes later. For now, there was only this. This woman, this baby. Their well-being in my care, their lives in my hands. Really, it's all you think about, if you're even thinking at all. I suppose my training has long passed into reflex.

Baby's head crowned, black and slick. Shifting my bump out of the way, I called out: 'I can see the head.'

Debbie wiped Mum's brow with the cold cloth. I could feel my belly heavy underneath me, the ache at the base of my back. It was a killer, that last week on the ward. I can admit that now. A real killer.

'Baby's head is almost out,' I said. My heart had quickened, but on the outside I was calm, as I always am. 'Can you push again for me? One more big push and we'll have this wee one out.'

Lauren gave an animal roar, teeth bared in a grin of pain. Baby's head emerged fully then, face pink, eyes screwed shut, and I let myself exhale.

But a moment later, the head receded, its pink complexion flushing blue.

Instinct kicked in. Immediately I took a step back and pulled the red alarm cord to signal an emergency.

'McRoberts,' I said to Debs. 'You know your McRoberts manoeuvre?'

She nodded. She looked terrified.

The door opened to Donna, a colleague.

'Shoulder dystocia,' I said.

She nodded and disappeared back into the corridor.

'Take the right leg,' I said to Debs. 'Do not do anything till I tell you.'

I moved my bulk around Lauren's left leg and gripped her hand while I lowered the bedhead.

'OK, pet,' I said. 'I need you to lie down flat, OK?'

'What's the matter? What's happening?' Lauren's voice was high and trembling.

'Everything's all right.' I kept my voice low, though my heart was beating hard by now. 'Baby's shoulders are stuck. We need you to be flat so we can get baby out, OK? We're going to push on your legs to free baby up. Let yourself move with us, all right? Don't push against us, even if it feels a bit strange. Everything's going to be fine, but you need to do exactly what I say.'

The door swung open again, this time to reveal the strawberry-blonde hair of Wendy, the midwife in charge, then Emma, the duty paediatrician, then Donna again, armed with pen, paper, a stopwatch, ready to be what we call the scribe.

'Go.' I nodded at Debs, who pushed against Lauren's right shin. With all my strength, I leant against her left. She gave a loud cry and kicked out like a horse, sending me staggering backward.

I went in again, trying to shift my bump away from her foot as it jerked wildly.

'I need you to relax your body for me, Lauren,' I called out. 'Don't kick out, love, all right? We need you to let us push your legs so we can get baby's shoulders out from behind your pelvic bone. Don't kick, OK? Relax for me, pet, that's it. Work with us.'

'Two minutes and twenty,' Donna said, her voice grave.

Lauren stopped kicking. The room was electric, suspended in hyper-focus. The adrenaline that moments ago had fuelled that strange, specific mix of joy and pain had mutated into terrible concentration. Midwife in charge, scribe, duty paediatrician, trainee midwife and me, senior midwife, all of us cogs, interlocked and turning now towards one thing only: the preservation of this precious little life.

'Two minutes and forty.'

The baby's face was violet, sunken. I gave the signal to Debs and together we pushed with all we had.

'Two minutes fifty.'

There was a shift.

With a howl, Lauren's legs splayed frog-like on the bed. Baby's left shoulder popped, square and dark as a storm cloud. Gently, I freed the right shoulder, and the rest slithered out. A bruised plum. A girl.

'Apgar score low,' I called out. I knew it immediately, without needing to run the checks. Quickly I secured and cut the umbilical cord before passing the infant to Emma. She turned away to the resuscitaire, her elbows moving back and forth as she massaged the newborn's tiny body.

'Lauren.' I was back with Mum, holding her hand while the bedhead slowly rose. 'You have a beautiful little girl.' I was fighting to keep the emotion out of my voice. 'She's had a tricky time getting out, so the doctor's just giving her a little rub to wake her up, all right?' Though my voice was cool, my heart was racing still, my ears trained to what was going on behind me: the silent industry of saving a life. There was a chance the bairn would not survive. There was a chance she would have complications. I found myself counting the seconds in my head: one, two, three...

A mewling cry, full of rage.

'There you are!' The relief in the paediatrician's voice was as clear as the collective sigh that followed. 'That's a grand pair of lungs.' The entire delivery room seemed to slouch, as if the walls were letting out a long-held breath.

A minute or two later, baby had been wrapped in a blanket and was being lowered to her mother's breast. The infant's tiny face was pinky-red now, her rosebud mouth pouting, ready to suckle. I helped Lauren latch her on before standing back, smiling at this new mother and baby, reunited after what must have felt like forever.

Lauren looked up and met my eyes.

'Thank you,' she half sobbed. She kissed the top of her little girl's head before laying her cheek against it. Her eyes were still on mine. 'Thank you so much.'

What could I do but smile? And smile I did, as my heart slowed, my eyelids going nineteen to the dozen, blinking back tears. 'Nothing to thank me for. You did all the hard work.'

'Well done, everyone,' Wendy said in her soft north-east burr. She was already making her way back out into the labour ward. 'Kirsty, pop in and see me when you finish up here, all right?'

A moment later, the door swung open yet again to reveal a frazzled-looking man in a suit.

'I'm Rob Coolson,' he said, breathing heavily. 'Am I too late?'

I knocked on the door of the midwife in charge's office, blinking back a couple of the rogue tears that were coming to me more and more lately, and focused on the name plate in front of me: *Ms W. Burman.*

'Come in,' called Wendy's voice from the other side.

I pushed the door open. 'You wanted to see me?'

'Aye.' She was sitting behind the desk, a pile of paperwork in front of her. 'I'm taking you off labour ward as of now until after your mat leave, OK?'

'OK.' I hesitated. 'Did I... did I do something wrong?'

A perplexed frown crossed her face. 'Just now? God, no! Why would you think that? That was excellent work. Exemplary.' She nodded to my stomach, her eyebrows shooting up. 'But I can't have you being kicked on my watch.'

Understanding dawned. This was not about my handling of the situation. It was about the bump.

'You'll be in Postnatal now till you leave,' Wendy was saying. 'When is it? Next week?'

'Aye. Few more shifts and I'm out of here.'

'Tough, isn't it, at the end?' She sat back in her chair, twiddling her pen. 'I remember that. I was absolutely knackered with our Holly.'

I smiled. I *was* knackered – absolutely. Everything hurt. Every part of me weighed a ton, and there wasn't enough barrier cream in the world for the chafing on my inner thighs.

'It's OK,' I said. 'I lose track of time when I'm here.'

'Well, look after yourself. Check your ankles. Watch your blood pressure. Make sure you put your feet up every moment you can.' Wendy peered at me over her glasses. 'I mean it, missus. Every moment. Promise me.'

I made a cross with my fingers. 'Guide's honour.'

'Good. And well done again for today. You're an excellent midwife, Kirsty Shaw. A real credit to the profession.'

The tips of my ears were burning. 'Everyone's amazing here,' I said. 'It's a great team.'

'It is. Now, it's quiet for once, so I want you to put your coat on, get yourself outside in the fresh air and take some deep breaths, all right? If I see you back in here before fifteen minutes is up, you'll be in big trouble.'

'But I'm not due a break until—'

'That's as may be. But I'm telling you to take a breather, and I'm in charge. Now off you go before I change my mind.'

At the lockers, I threw on my dad's coat – one of the few

things that still fitted me – over my scrubs, then pulled on Dougie's ski mittens and my old bobble hat before heading out through the main hospital. In Aberdeen in winter, you don't just pop out, even for five minutes, without giving it the full Scott of the Antarctic.

Outside, the air was crisp and cool after the heat of the delivery room. It soothed me like an ice pack to a fevered forehead. I lifted my face to the weak winter sun hazing in the blue day and made myself breathe deeply. It was still only a little after eight in the morning.

What was I thinking about just then? Well, the baby obviously. Its wee face. I was running through everything I'd done, reassuring myself I'd done it all correctly. Apart from that, it was just another day in the job I loved. Life and death. That poor baby's face would come back to me later because that's what happens every time you have a close call like that – and I've had a fair few over the years. The what-could-have-beens. But at the same time, I knew I needed to compose myself, that I owed it to my team, to the women who came in and to the babies yet to be delivered.

So that's all I was thinking about really as I walked back to the maternity ward.

And that's when I saw him.

And my heart stopped dead.

TWO

KIRSTY

KS/transcript #2

Hughie Reynolds had been my close friend. And then my boyfriend. It's not too much to say that he became part of my family, back in the day. My parents loved him like one of their own. Even my kid brother thought he was the bee's knees. But the day we got our exam results, he disappeared, leaving nothing but a nasty note and an ever nastier taste in all our mouths. All these years, I'd thought he was dead, even thought he must have killed himself. But now here he was – alive and well and very real.

He was with a female doctor, heading in the direction of the main theatre. They were deep in conversation, oblivious to me frozen like a statue, one hand on the corridor wall. Two doctors discussing a case, barely noticing the world around them, isn't unusual, but I was panting with shock at the sight. Really, I couldn't get my breath at all. Her I didn't recognise, but I knew him all right, from that very first glance. I knew him from when he was a boy and I was a girl, but even though I could see him plain as day, I couldn't believe my eyes.

My body prickled all over with heat, my breath still shallow. I told myself it couldn't be him. There was no way. Next thing, I was arguing against myself: it *was* him. Definitely. Then no, it wasn't. Yes, it was. On and on like that. There was something about the swing of his arms, the forward tilt of his head, the way his left foot turned ever so slightly inwards. Funny, you don't realise how much you've noticed about a person until you see them from a distance – in this case physical distance and, I suppose, the distance of time. You think you've forgotten all but a foggy impression, but in reality they've just burrowed deep inside you. They're right there, in all their details, crouching in the darkness, waiting to unfurl.

They came closer. My throat closed. I made out the word *biopsy* but no more. Instinctively my hand came up to rest on the bump, fingers spread. All I could think was: *he must not see me*. My heart was hammering fit to burst. Dread – that's what I felt. Pure dread. This was the guy who had robbed me of something I couldn't even name but that had taken me years to get back. I didn't trust myself not to shout at him or fly at him with clawed hands, or worse, burst into tears.

For a second, I worried they'd see me leaning against the wall, fighting for breath, and think I'd gone into labour. But as it was, no sooner had their soft rubber soles squeaked by on the buffed vinyl floor than I was kicking myself. I was gutless. I should've said something. I should've challenged the bastard. But I was still shaking, eyes closed against the sight of him, gripped by a childish instinct to make myself invisible. Their mutterings faded. I heard the squeak of the swing doors. Then nothing.

My armpits and the palms of my hands were damp with sweat. Disappointment flooded me at my own reaction. *Really? I told myself off in my head. After all these years? Really, Kirsty? You're a grown woman, for Christ's sake. You're married. You're about to have a child of your own. Hughie Reynolds is not worth your oxygen. You're better than this. You're bigger than this.*

But at the same time, I was thinking: *What kind of coward are you? Why should he get away with the world's most selfish vanishing act? Go after him and demand an explanation!*

Thinking about it, the whole arguing-with-myself thing began there. The self-doubt that had started years before returned that day.

I made myself do some yoga breaths: in through the nose, out through the mouth. Seeing Hughie after more than a decade had caught me off-guard, that was all. If I felt like I'd seen a ghost, well, that was because I had. And of course the emergency delivery had rattled me. I could still feel the tears at the back of my eyes, the tightness in my chest. But Hughie Reynolds had no power over me anymore. I didn't need his explanation. I would never grant him the satisfaction of giving it. No, I didn't need anything from him. He was nothing to me. No one. I should get back to the team.

But then I thought: *no.*

No.

So, I pulled myself tall, which, admittedly, isn't very. And I went after him.

He and his colleague had gone past the main theatre suite by then, heads still bent together. Taking care to hang back, I shuffled silently behind them. He walked like Hughie. I can't tell you exactly why I say that, only that this was the way Hughie Reynolds put one foot in front of the other, his body leaning to the right and left with each pace with a kind of slow, flat-footed jollity. They were heading for the Aroma Café. I followed at a distance, nauseous by now. They didn't stop for coffee but headed instead down the corridor towards the anaesthesiology department. I stayed with them, half crouching, braced to react should they turn around. But they didn't. They disappeared through the double doors.

I stopped dead. I couldn't follow any further, but I was one hundred per cent convinced it was him. Bald, thicker-set these days, but him. He never did have much hair, I thought, even back in the day. Back then, the front was all thin and wispy due to fire damage, but now what little was left was grey and cropped close to his head.

Anaesthesiology. I stared up at the department sign like a goon. Was he an anaesthetist then? If so, he'd achieved his dream after all. So why had he never been in touch?

Beneath the sign was a list of over fifty consultant anaesthetists. I ran my finger down to the Rs – Rathbone, Richards, Rogers. There was no Reynolds. I placed my hand flat against the door but hesitated. This was not my department. I wasn't sure what I'd say once on the other side, who I would ask for. If he wasn't Hughie, then I had no idea who he was.

With no real clue what to do next, I kind of skulked in the corridor. I hated it, hated myself for waiting like that, like a groupie hanging about a stage door for an autograph. I hated the desperate feeling that had filled me. It was humiliating and felt somehow like he'd got one over on me yet again.

Two minutes ticked into three, every one of them spent in silent argument with myself. I had to get back to Maternity. Wendy had given me fifteen minutes; it had been kind of her to do that, and to take more would be wrong.

The door swung open. My heart raced, my skin heating quicker than a stove. Every muscle in me tensed for danger.

But it was two women, both in scrubs, marching back towards the main theatre suite.

I turned away, feeling completely ridiculous now – an obsessive, mad, hugely pregnant stalker. I was losing my mind, and for what? Some stupid lad who'd behaved like a pig to me and my family years ago. Someone I had trusted so deeply that years after his sudden disappearance, part of me still couldn't believe there hadn't been some sort of misunderstanding, some joke I'd never got.

Head down and feeling like a total loser, I walked away. I didn't need this nonsense. It was a waste of my time and energy. My baby was almost on the way. I was about to be a mum for the first time. Within days, I'd be out of here; I had more than enough to think about.

But that's the thing about unresolved history. It's the moth, isn't it? That damn flame, so bright, so dazzling, so warm until it's not warm any more, it's hot, too hot, and all you know is your wings are on fire and you're completely buggered.

Behind me, a hinge squeaked. *Do not turn around*, I told myself. *Rise above it and walk away while you still have your dignity.*

Well, of course I turned around. And I did not keep my dignity.

Hughie Reynolds was strolling out of Anaesthesiology alongside the same female colleague, who I saw now was much younger, fresh-faced, pretty. Both in blue scrubs. Lanyards swinging.

'Hughie?' His name left me in strained, airless syllables. 'Hughie Reynolds?'

He faltered, came to a stop and looked at me. Our eyes met. I swear my heart was audible, a big banging drum. He blinked once, twice. I didn't blink at all. It was as if there was no air, and yet we were both breathing. I could feel my chest heaving up and down, as if I'd run a race. Something flickered across his face – panic, maybe fear – but it was only a moment and then his expression flattened, his head twitching almost imperceptibly.

All this played out in a matter of seconds before, without even acknowledging me, he resumed walking, as if he thought I'd been speaking to someone behind him or something, like when someone shouts a name and you stop but then you realise they weren't shouting your name but someone else's. Like that. His colleague glanced at me, then at Hughie, her brow furrowing before she too carried on her way, colouring a wee bit, as if embarrassed for me.

But he didn't get to embarrass me. Not again. I was standing in their path, just a couple of metres away. He would have to damn well push me out of the way if he wanted to get past. And there was a lot of me to push.

Hughie Reynolds, I know it's you, I wanted to shout as he approached with painstaking slowness, his gaze fixed studiously on the floor. My legs were shaking. I opened my mouth but couldn't find my voice. He came closer still, drew level.

'Hughie,' I managed at last. 'Hughie!'

He didn't stop. Didn't even slow down. He was so obviously pretending not to hear me, it was actually quite sad. I reached out, tugged his sleeve, forcing him to look at me.

Beside him, his colleague's gaze was bouncing all over the place, as if she was trying to figure out how she should be reacting. Maybe she was looking for a way out. She looked more uncomfortable than I felt, and my skin was crawling.

'I'm really sorry,' I made myself say. 'But you are Hughie Reynolds, aren't you?' To my confounded annoyance, my eyes pricked, and when I next spoke, my voice was all bubbly, like it was full of water. 'It's me,' I trembled. 'Kirsty Shaw? From school? We were... friends. We... went out? Do you not... do you not recognise me? I mean, I know I've changed.'

I gestured to my swollen appearance. A laugh escaped me, betraying the sob I was trying to stifle. With a wild feeling, I switched my gaze to his colleague, as if to say: *Help!* But her eyes were still flicking between us and a blush was backwashing her freckles with dark pink. I sensed she was mirroring my own rising humiliation. My face was raging hot.

Hughie frowned, half puzzled, half amused.

'I'm sorry,' he said. 'I didn't realise you were talking to me.'

He shook his head ever so slightly and stared right at me, driving the lie home with his steely eyes, pale blue and alive with the hint of mischief I remembered – mischief that could slide so easily into cruelty. But he didn't sound like him. He sounded... English. English, not Scottish. Doubt filled me. Maybe it wasn't him after all. And now I'd made a complete arse of myself. My face burnt fiercer as he side-eyed his colleague, a benign smile fixed on his lips, as if to say, *Excuse me a moment while I humour this woman who has clearly lost her mind*, before turning back to face me.

'Hughie?' His name was little more than a whisper. Certainty had fallen so far from me, I began to clutch at it. 'It *is* you. I *know* it's you. Come on! It's me, Kirsty!'

Still with the benevolent smile of a minister, he said, half to me and half to his colleague, 'I'm afraid you must have me confused with someone else.' The words were polite, but the tone made me feel as small as a church mouse.

'But...'

It was all I could say. My head was shaking almost of its own accord: *no, no, no*. And I couldn't seem to stop the tears, despite me willing myself with everything I had not to cry.

'I'm s-so s-sorry,' I stuttered. 'I-I thought...'

'I hope he's a fine-looking fellow, whoever he is,' the man who wasn't Hughie joked in his educated vowels. You might think my humiliation was complete, but it had one more kick in the gut in store, because at that moment, I remembered what I was wearing – my dad's coat, Dougie's stupid ski gloves, my stupid, stupid bobble hat of shame.

But whoever he was, he was no longer looking at me. For the second time, he was continuing on his way.

I have no idea why, and frankly, I feel mortified even remembering, but I found myself walking alongside him, faster and faster, to match his quickening steps. I don't know what I thought I was going to achieve, how I thought I could revive the dead duck that was my dignity. My back ached. Everything ached actually. Meanwhile, his lanyard swung about like a childish taunt. My breath was running out. I couldn't walk any faster. I couldn't...

On the lanyard, I made out a B. Near gasping by now, I tried to block out the sound of them talking as if I weren't there running beside them like a demented servant, as if I were a mad person on the street you lose by steadfastly ignoring them until they go away.

The lanyard spun. A, I read. R.

BAR.

They were striding away now, away from the crazy pregnant lady in the bonkers hat. I slowed to a breathless stop.

'I'm so sorry,' I called out, a metallic taste flooding my mouth. 'You look exactly like someone I used to know, that's all. Used to go out with actually. It's... uncanny.'

'I'm afraid I have to dash,' he said over his shoulder, addressing me only now he'd made his escape. 'Good luck finding him!'

Defeated, I watched helplessly as he inclined his head to say something I couldn't catch to his young colleague, who guffawed like the acolyte she was. I stared at the blank refusal of the doors shuddering to a close. Confusion filled me from toe to head. The vision of myself as a deranged nuisance flowered before me. A madwoman calling after a stranger in the middle of a hospital. How must I have looked? Humongous and jabbering, aggressive and swaddled in an ill-fitting coat, hat pulled stupidly low against the Aberdeen winter cold, a cold that overrode all vanity, all sense of fashion. How ridiculous. How bloody ridiculous I was. How mortifying.

But I had the first three letters of his name now. All I had to do was match it to the department staff list.

THREE

HUGHIE

Hughie Reynolds/audio recording/excerpt #1

When you shouted my name across the hospital corridor, Kirsty, I'll admit, I almost failed to keep it together. It took every drop of sangfroid in my weary soul to dig out some charm and smooth the whole thing over. An impressive abuse of power, even for me. Your anxious bewilderment was an absolute picture. In the face of my flat denial, there, in front of my colleague, in our place of work, there was nothing you could say. You looked like a child who'd been told that Christmas had been cancelled because Santa had blown the gift budget at the bookie's.

You must have been so shocked to see I'd become a consultant anaesthetist. Consultant anaesthetist. Worth a repetition, I think. Two words that convey so much status, so much power. *So* much power, Kirsty, you cannot even begin to imagine. I got there in the end, blood under my fingernails, teeth edges worn smooth from the grinding. Maybe that should be my life's motto: *He got there in the end.* Ironic, for someone who always loved a shortcut. But back when we first met, I was trying so hard to play the long game for once, go the correct way, and guess what? It didn't help me one bit. Where I come from, where I *really* come from, we bend the rules.

Being caught. That's the only deterrent I've ever known, the only thing I fear. Rules serve only people like you. They're made for people like you. We're not all born into cosy wee nuclear families with a mummy and a daddy, central heating, regular meals, cocoa and a story at bedtime. If you'd ever really known me at all, you would know that I had nothing of the sort growing up. The start I had in life would literally make your hair stand on end. It would make you weep, sensitive soul that you are.

If you'd only thought for five minutes about the lengths to which I must have gone to get here, you might have seen why there was no way I was ever going to acknowledge the connection between us – in front of my colleague, for God's sake. You would never have expected me to give it all up for some girl I had a brief thing with when she was a kid. Because, let's face it, that's all you were. In your eyes, I might not have earned my place in the world, but trust me, I have. The problem with people like you is that you're so easily scandalised. You sit on your high horse, convinced that following the rules makes you virtuous, righteous, good, but you're not nearly as good as you think and more wrong than you will ever know. You have no idea how you would be, how you would act, what choices you would make, if the circumstances were different.

But none of that is important now. We are where we are. While you're alive, I can't be who I want to be. You don't get to take that away from me. You're the reason we're here, Kirsty. No one else. You've pushed me to this.

I hope you have the grace to remember that at the end.

FOUR

KIRSTY

It was a long moment before I was able to move. Slowly I turned and walked back to Anaesthesiology. I pushed open the door, not caring now who saw me, prepared to field any questions that came my way. From beneath my coat, the blue trousers of my uniform would at least tell whoever saw me that I was staff, and that would give me enough time to check the roster.

It was on the wall just inside the door. I ran my finger down the names, mouthing Bar, Bar, Bar to myself like a sheep. Sweat joined the mess of sticky tears on my face. Just to top it off, my nose was running. I sniffed, pushed the moisture into my hair, wiped my hand on Dad's coat. Bar, Bar... Bar-ry. Barry. My finger came to a resolute stop. Dr Barry Sefton, Consultant Anaesthetist. I ran down the rest of the list, to be sure, but there was no one else with these letters in their name. The man I had just seen was called Barry Sefton.

Except he was not Barry Sefton, or so my thinking went at the time. He was Hughie Reynolds. I knew it like I knew my own bones. I was *convinced*.

'Hughie,' I whispered. 'What the hell have you done?'

On feet I hadn't seen in months, I made myself walk back to the maternity ward, a shower of questions raining down.

Was it him? How was that possible? Was he a figment of my imagination? If not, why had he come back? Why now? What did he want? And why was he pretending to be someone else?

Because yes, at that point I was still totally convinced it was him.

There was a time I saw him everywhere. Afterwards. He'd be in the big Asda at the Brig O Dee, or up at the arcade at the beach, or in the Saturday crowds milling about on Union Street. Later, I'd see him in the faces of shop assistants, uni lecturers, fellow students. Later still, when the months had become years, I'd see him in other women's husbands and partners come to hold their wives' hands in the maternity ward. For one flashing second, I'd be convinced. My body would heat with whatever it was that would flare up inside me like wildfire, just like it had a moment ago. That familiar burn. Half fear, half fury.

When that happened, I'd play my mum's words in my head, repeat them over and over. *There is nothing he can do to you now. He is nothing. He is no one. He is not fit to breathe the same air.*

That was what passed for therapy back then. And anyway, then I'd look closely, and whoever this guy was, his features would rearrange themselves in front of my eyes. A nose would shorten, a lip would thicken, an eye colour change from blue to green. It was never him. Of course it wasn't. Over time, the expectation dropped away, and with it the visions or flashbacks or whatever they were went too. Until that day in the hospital, I hadn't seen Hughie Reynolds in someone else's face for years.

Is that what had happened?

I imagined Dougie might tell me the shock of the emergency had caused it. Dougie's more into all that psychology stuff than me, but I've done a fair amount of digging into it recently, as you can imagine. But even then, I knew that flashbacks were the stress whiplash after the necessary calm of high-intensity situations. They were part of my job, just as staying calm in the moment was. You can't hold on to all that tension without it finding a release afterwards. Normally, the flashing visions would be of the emergency delivery itself. They would wait until the evening to spook my waking dreams. But maybe that day they'd transformed into something from my youth: the boyfriend who disappeared.

So my thoughts ran.

I did consider that it might be my hormones. Not that I'd have let anyone else say that. God knows, pregnancy had treated me to some strange dreams by then. It had only been the night before last that I'd been on a roller coaster with Taylor Swift.

But *if* it actually was him...

He wasn't wearing his glasses, I realised. Must have had contacts or laser surgery or something. Looked a bit jowly round the jaw, to my eyes. A few stone heavier too. Gone to seed. Let himself go.

Good.

God knows how I got through that shift. All I know is, by the time I came out of the hospital at seven, I'd completely forgotten where I'd parked. Thankfully, when I clicked my key fob, my trusty little Ford Focus flashed its orange lights and I made my way slowly towards it, huffing and puffing and wincing a bit at the pain in my lower back.

As I got into the car, I wondered how long Hughie had been back in Aberdeen. A week? A month? How long was it since I'd last seen him? We'd left school in 2013, so that made it, what, ten, eleven years? Where had he been all this time?

I arranged my great bulk with even greater difficulty behind the wheel. Hughie Reynolds was all I could think about. *Hughie Reynolds, Hughie Reynolds, Hughie Reynolds*, on a loop. I considered calling Tasha, who would freak. *What the hell is that bastard doing back here?* she would say. But I was starving hungry and desperate to get out of my work clothes and have a shower, so I started the engine, pulled out of the space and drove slowly towards the car park exit.

I suppose it was only natural that I was thinking back to old times. Hughie Reynolds had made such an impression on both Tasha and me back in the day, me especially. What you have to understand is that when he showed up that September, he was the most adorably vulnerable boy I'd ever met. But then, when he got his wings, he swiftly became the most exciting. It was 2009, the year we started our Standard Grades. With his newfound confidence came constant suggestions of fun stuff to do, stuff we'd always had on our doorstep but never bothered with. Hughie Reynolds was something else, all right. He didn't so much change the city we lived in; more like he changed the way we lived in it.

I pulled out of the car park and headed towards North Anderson Drive, my head filled now with the gangly sight of Hughie aged fifteen in his brand-spanking-new Aberdeen High uniform, his tired eyes that wouldn't stop blinking behind his glasses, his thin brown hair falling foppishly forward over his high forehead. Standing in the corner of the yard, he looked absolutely terrified.

'Hiya,' I said. 'You look a bit lost.' I'd only arrived in Scotland a few years before and could still remember Tasha looking after me, so it was my turn to pay it forward, I guess.

'Hello. Yes. I'm sorry. I'm new.' A soft Edinburgh accent, an accent to melt a girl's heart.

'That's OK,' I said. 'I'm Kirsty Shaw. Pleased to meet you.' I stuck out my hand, which he shook. His was dry and warm.

'Hugh,' he said, still so formal and shy at that point. 'Pleased to meet you.'

'Hugh!' It was Tasha, rubbernecking at my elbow, not wanting to miss out on the new boy. Surreptitiously, she elbowed me in the ribs, and a split second later we were both stifling a fit of the giggles. 'No offence, but if you like your face the way it is, we'll be calling you Hughie, OK? No arguments.'

I cringed at her bulldozer approach, but the boy didn't seem too fazed.

'Hughie,' he said, as if trying it out. He was so serious, I wanted to pull him into my arms and give him a big hug. 'All right. If you think it's better.'

'Trust me, it is,' Tasha said. 'Where are you from, Hughie?'

'My parents are from Edinburgh.' He looked down at his shoes. 'Were.'

There in the car on that freezing Aberdeen night, I wondered if he'd known back then that he was blowing our minds with the sheer scale of the tragedy, the dark romance of it breaking our teenage hearts. Through his tortoiseshell glasses, his eyes were blue – the blue of bathroom tiles rather than Wedgwood, if you know what I mean.

'I'll take you to the office,' I said. I'd spoken to him first; he was mine, not Tasha's – that was just the rules. 'And you can come to ours for tea later if you want.'

And like that, we took Hughie Reynolds under our wing and laid claim to him. He was our shiny new thing, our trophy: the posh laddie with the even posher name. By the end of that day, we'd introduced him to everyone, which guaranteed no one beat him up, because Tasha's big brother was the hardest lad in the school. Together with Gus and Callum, the five of us fell into hanging out. We went to our first parties together, took our first drink, smoked our first cigarettes, our first joints. Rites of passage. Teenage kicks. Dreams.

He did come home with me, but not that day. It was the

next day or the one after, I can't remember. Around the table with my family that first time, I think we all fell for him a bit. He'd told me on the way to the school office that his parents had died in a house fire back in Edinburgh. He'd been placed with a foster mother in Aberdeen because that was where his parents were from originally. I can remember swooning a wee bit. I was so young, the romance of it hit me before the sadness did. The romance was tied up with the sadness, if you get what I mean, the idea of myself as a romantic heroine, there to soothe and heal this broken boy. With his soft, educated accent and his tragic past, Hughie was like a character from a book or a film. Not good-looking, not exactly, more *charismatic*. He had the *rizz*, as the younger midwives say now. All about the rizz, was Hughie. But he wasn't like that to begin with. The rizz came later, as his confidence came back, and I used to like to think I had a part in returning it to him.

That evening, while we were having tea, we gave Hughie a thorough lesson in all the Aberdonian phrases we'd learnt since we'd got here.

'Foos your does or fit like the day,' my kid brother Billy said, his accent stronger than ours since he'd only been six when we moved up. 'That means how are you and how are you today. And you say affa fine, which means really well.'

I laughed. 'Don't say that. Honestly, don't. You'll sound ridiculous if you're not from here. But if someone says it, at least you'll understand.'

'A quine is a girl,' Billy said, getting overexcited already. 'And a loon is a boy. A bonnie loon is a nice-looking lad. An affa bonnie loon!'

'A... really good-looking lad?' Hughie asked with a smile.

'That's it! You're a natural.'

'Pack it in, Billy,' I said. I turned to Hughie. 'Sorry. My brother's a right nosy parker.'

'The burger all right for you, love?' Mum joined in,

changing the subject and wrestling the monopoly of the conversation from our Billy. 'I got them from Herd's so they should be OK.'

'It's delicious, Mrs Shaw,' Hughie said, with perfect manners, even though he'd barely had two bites. It occurred to me that he'd almost lost his Edinburgh brogue and was already starting to sound Aberdonian.

Mum beamed. Dad asked Hughie if he liked the football, a man's answer to avoiding emotion if ever there was one.

'My father was a Rangers fan,' Hughie said.

'Well, that can't be helped.' My dad grinned to show he was joking. 'I'm Liverpool myself, but now we're up here, I support the Dons.'

'The Dons?'

'Aberdeen. I'll take you to a match if you'd like?'

'I'd like that. Thank you, Mr Shaw.'

'Call me Keith. And Mrs Shaw is Gail. You're welcome here any time, lad.'

Back in the present, the traffic was at a standstill coming up to the Kingsgate Roundabout. Rain was sheeting down, the sky was black and all I could think about was Hughie. Honestly, if memories were water, it was like someone had turned on the tap.

I turned off the engine and blew into my gloves, thoughts turning now to our fortnight in Tossa de Mar. That would've been the summer of 2012. Hughie organised the whole thing, pretty much. The rest of us wouldn't have known where to start. It was Hughie who rented the villa, paid the deposit with money from his Saturday job, chivvied us all along to book our flights. It was Hughie who helped me fill in a passport form, drove me to the big Asda by the Brig O Dee to have my photo taken in the booth.

And when we stepped off the plane at Barcelona... God, the heat! I'd never known anything like it. Like walking into a gas oven – literally – the smell of sun cream and black tobacco, hot tarmac, garlic. Burning days. Red skin. Games of Uno and nightclubs and rum and Cokes you could stand your straw up in. And somewhere in that boozy haze, we shared a kiss, Hughie and me. It was awkward, drunk, but somehow we ended up together.

The traffic edged forward. I restarted my car and pulled forward, ground to a halt only to pull forward again, and so on as I crawled my way home.

That holiday was the last hurrah for all of us. After that, it was straight into sixth year and we buckled down to get our remaining grades for uni. I was determined to get into midwifery at Edinburgh; Hughie was dead set on medicine. His dream was to be an anaesthetist, but towards the end he started smoking more than a few puffs at the weekend. Often, when we'd talk on the phone, he sounded out of it, and in the end, his results weren't good enough. And that's when he disappeared off the face of the earth.

I'd always wondered if that was the real reason. But at the time he made me believe I was, and I was too young to know any better.

The traffic loosened finally. I took a left onto the Great Western Road, and as I passed Mum and Dad's flat, I decided to give Mum a quick ring on the hands-free. I'd taken her in for a cataract operation the day before and I wanted to know how she was getting on.

'Just calling to check you can still see,' I said when she answered, turning left again, almost home.

'I can indeed,' Mum said, her voice bright. 'I've still got the patch on, but it's absolutely great. Are you calling in? I'm just having a glass of wine. Your dad's gone to Pilates.'

'Thanks, but I'm away home for my tea. Just wanted to make sure you're OK.'

'I'm grand, love.' Down the line, I heard the telltale sip – that'd be the Picpoul going down red lane, the sun long since disappeared over the yardarm. 'Thanks again for taking me. Did I tell you the surgeon put in a lens?'

'You did, aye.'

'Twenty-twenty vision! My glasses are in my bag. I suppose I'll give them to the charity, won't I? Honestly, the things they can do these days!'

'That's amazing! Listen, do you remember that guy I went out with in sixth year?'

'Hughie? Of course I do. Bastard. Why?'

'I saw him. Just now, at the infirmary.'

'What?' Mum's voice was electric. 'Hughie? Just now?'

'Plain as day. Strolling around like the cock of the walk. Well, you know Hughie.'

'Did he say hello? Did he see you?' Mum's voice was rising, incredulity increasing with every word. 'What the bloody hell was he—'

'He'd passed me before I realised, and by the time I got my breath back, he was gone. He's bald now – if it was him, I mean... Anyway, I followed him to Anaesthesiology.'

'So he did become an anaesthetist?'

'Looks like it, only...'

I told her the whole story, about me in my yeti get-up pretty much forcing him to talk to me, about him denying it was him.

'So it *wasn't* him?'

'Apparently not. It was some guy called Barry Sefton. I mean, close up, he was older, but I can't shake the feeling it really was Hughie, you know? His eyes! Even with the English accent. I was convinced. Honestly, I thought I'd seen a ghost.'

'Well, if he is alive, it's a good job I didn't see him. I'd have put my hands round his skinny neck and strangled the bastard.'

I laughed. 'He's not that skinny any more. He's filled out.'

We took a moment, sharing a smile neither of us could see but both knew was there. A minute later, Mum muttered, 'As I live and breathe. An imposter, eh?'

'If it was him, yes.'

'That figures. But if he's pretending to be someone else, why would he come back here where folk know him?'

'I know, right? It doesn't make any sense.'

That was it exactly. It didn't make sense. And if it didn't make sense, it was probably all in my head.

I was getting worked up over thin air.

Over nothing.

FIVE

KIRSTY

I took the final left turn into Ashbury Gardens, my street. In front of me, a flashy red sports car was pulling up outside the Kellys' place, more or less opposite Joan's. Joan's curtains were closed, her white Polo on the drive where it always was at this time of day. I made a mental note to pop the stew over to her as soon as I got home. Meanwhile, there were no lights on in my house and no van on the driveway. I felt myself sink a bit, I have to admit. I'd so wanted Dougie to be home.

To top it all, the house was freezing. It even smelt cold, you know? Like wet stones. Dougie had forgotten to put the heating on, or maybe had left it off to save a bit of money. I knew we wouldn't get the place warm now until late, by which time we'd be in bed. Teeth chattering, I flicked the switch on the thermostat but kept my hat pulled low over my ears, my scarf wound tight and my coat zipped up. I filled the kettle. It would have been coming up for quarter past seven or so by then. On the stove was a pan of pasta sauce, acid red, still warm. I dipped my finger in and sucked. Sweet tomato, peppers, basil. Yum.

Dougie would have made it after work, probably in a coat and hat, before heading to the gym to stave off the stomach rumbles. Despite my shifts, we always tried to eat together when we could.

While I waited for the kettle to boil, I googled Hughie Reynolds on my phone. There were two, but neither was him. One Hughie Rainford, who looked about eighty, and a sheep farmer in Orkney called Hugh Raynor. If Hughie was still alive, it looked like he didn't use social media. I tried LinkedIn. Not there either. Why was I even looking? What did I care? He was best forgotten. I'd thought I'd seen him, but I hadn't. Simple case of mistaken identity. End of.

I made a brew and carried my mug up to the nursery, which looked derelict, with no carpet and the walls still only half painted. I kept meaning to finish it, but those last few months, I was always so tired after work, and my days off were spent getting my strength back for the next shift.

I crossed the landing into the bedroom, warming my hands on my drink. My stomach was still tight. I was thinking about how when Hughie and me took those passport photos, we did a second lot with the two of us pulling daft faces, thinking we were cool and original, little realising teenagers had been doing that for... well, as long as there'd been photo booths. After he vanished, I tore up those photographs into a thousand pieces, threw them out of my bedroom window and watched them flutter away like so many snowflakes.

On my dressing table was my jewellery box, which I think now was why I'd gone into the bedroom in the first place, subconsciously or something. I fetched it and sat down on the bed, held it a moment on my knee, which was jackhammering. My jewellery box is white leather, with two layers, like a chocolate box. You can buy extra layers to stack up as you acquire more necklaces and earrings and what-have-you. Dougie had bought it for me for Christmas, handed it over with the usual embarrassed shrug... *I didn't know what you'd want, so...*

I love that box even though I'll never be able to fill it with finery, let alone need more layers to stack. I love it because Dougie chose it for me. I always say I'd love anything, anything at all, even a flower cut from the garden, and I would, if it was from Dougie, even if it was terrible, which sounds mad but it's true.

Inside the box were my odds and sods: a signet ring I'd had as a teenager, a silver chain Tasha had given me when we were thirteen, a year after I'd got to Aberdeen; it had gone black a long time ago, but I'd kept it anyway. A badge in the shape of a trophy with the words *Dancing Queen* on it, an old fake gold medal for breaststroke from the Aberdeenshire swimming championships 2008. Apart from my wedding ring, which had become too tight now I was in my third trimester, there was nothing in there of any value other than sentimental or funny – which for me is the highest value there is.

I lifted the top layer, knowing fine well what I was looking for. The tray beneath has three compartments. In one of the smaller ones was a clear plastic wristband, impossibly tiny – my name tag from when I was born: *Kirsty Georgina Shaw, 16/12/1994.* My mum gave it to me along with her childhood jewellery box on my seventh birthday. I still had that too some-where – in the loft probably. As a kid, I used to love the wee ballerina that popped up and pirouetted when you opened the lid. I used to press my eyes to the gap between the lid and the box whenever I closed it, desperate to see the moment she stopped dancing and lay down, but the gap was always too small, the darkness too deep. She remained a mystery.

In the larger compartment of the lower tray was a white envelope, folded in half. I dug it out, a dark cumulus of anxiety blooming in my chest. The sense that I was doing something wrong simmered inside me. I should not have kept this note.

Should at least have shown it to Dougie. But I hadn't. I'd missed the moment. And then Dougie and me were getting married and I guess I thought it was too late.

I should have burnt it. I hadn't done that either.

Why not? I honestly don't know. Maybe I'd kept it as a reminder of what one person can do to another, a warning against trusting anyone too readily. Whatever, the note had continued to exist, hidden and secret like shame itself. It still had the power to take me back to that frightened eighteen-year-old girl who'd believed she was loved, only to discover she was not loved at all.

On the envelope, in Hughie's flowery handwriting, his nickname for me:

KK

No stamp, as I remembered. The looping letters had been written in the same hand that had filled the huge, padded Valentine's card full of cheeky verses I'd kept at the back of my teenage wardrobe, little poems full of hints about what he wanted to do to me, hints I'd laughed at to hide my fear.

In the cold, empty house, I took the note from the envelope and read the words over again, with no better understanding than I'd had eleven years before.

> *Dear Kirsty,*
> *Just to let you know, I'm out of here. You'll never see me again. I'm sure you'll be upset, but that's because things don't usually go wrong for people like you. You're not used to disappointment, you see. I'm sure I should have told you face to face and all that, but tearful goodbyes aren't really my style. And besides, I don't really follow rules. Only people like you follow*

rules because rules are made for people like you. They're not for me, not for my kind.

You and your family were good to me for a time, granted, but that time is over. Don't take this person-ally, but I didn't love you. I didn't love any of you. You think we had something because that's what you wanted to believe, but we didn't, not really. I went along with it because it was easier and because I'm good at pretending. So please don't waste your time looking for me. I never existed, in a way. Life is just one big mirage.

H

There in the chilly bedroom, it was as if I was reading that letter for the first time, my smile falling away, all hope for what it might have contained curdling in my belly, all joy at my exam results crumbling to ash. My eyes swimming. The ball that had formed in my stomach swelling and hardening with every line. Tears of hot confusion spilling over as I looked up at Mum, who was staring at me with concern. Her smile too had fallen away.

'What's the matter, lovey?' she had asked gently, but I heard the hint of an edge, her protective hackles already on the rise. 'What is it?'

'I don't know. I... It's from Hughie. I think it must be a joke. It's a joke. Only it's not. It doesn't...'

Mum took the letter from me and read, the furrows in her brow deepening. She was still pink-faced from her joy at my exam results. As I watched, the pink deepened. But it was no longer joy.

'What?' She looked up, her frown mirroring my own.

'What's he on about? A mirage? Didn't love... What? You'll never... What's he planning to do, fly to the moon?'

'I don't know,' I whispered. 'I don't know, I don't know, I don't know.'

'What happened? Did you have a fight?'

'Oh, Mum.' I burst into tears.

She sat with me at the kitchen table, her arm around my shoulders as I wept into her chest. I told her how, when she and Dad had been out the night before and Billy had been downstairs on his Xbox, Hughie and I had been fooling around in my room.

'He wanted to...' I sobbed. 'He wanted to, y'know... But I... I...'

'Oh, love. Oh, my baby, my poor baby.'

I dissolved into tears, too mortified to say what had happened, even while it flashed back, fragmented and dreamlike, unreal. The panic when Hughie had tried to undo the buttons on my jeans. The black glaze in his eyes, his alien urgency, his snarl when I said no, his disdain when I tried to explain that I hadn't really seen him while we'd been studying for our exams, that it didn't feel right.

That I didn't want to.

'He tried to...' I managed. 'But when I tried to stop him... I... All I did was suggest we wait, you know? Till we got to uni. I said it was only a few weeks away, but he... he just turned like a... like a vicious dog.'

'Bastard,' Mum muttered. 'I'll kill him.'

The image of Hughie flashed: eyes like slits, lip curled, enough to show the white fang of his canine.

'You don't love me,' he'd spat.

'I do!' My body had flared with heat, with a kind of fear.

His laugh then made me feel like I was going to be sick.

'If you loved me, you'd want to,' he said, his tone dripping with the cold hate of a stranger. 'And don't start crying. It's me who should be crying.' He picked up his jacket from the floor, shook his head at me, his face set in an expression of disgust so complete I would never be able to forget it. 'You're pathetic. You're nothing.'

He left. I cried myself to sleep, turning over excuses for him in my mind, excuses I repeated now to my mother through choking gasps of shock.

'He's been smoking a lot of weed lately,' I said as she rocked me from side to side, kissing my hair, murmuring soft sympathies. 'He's been really stressed about the results. He's not been himself.'

'Oh, my love,' Mum soothed, holding me tight.

'He wanted...' I sobbed. 'He wanted... but I didn't want to... I said no.'

'And that's your prerogative, love. No one should force you to do something you don't want to. Ever.'

'He said I was pathetic. He said I was nothing. And then he... he just... left.'

Mum leant back a little and took a breath, visibly processing her shock at the boy who had become so much part of our family we referred to one of the kitchen chairs as Hughie's seat.

'Well,' she said after a moment. 'If that's how he's going to behave, you're better off without him, aren't you?'

'But now he's just... gone? How can he have just gone?' I picked up the letter and shook it. 'And I'm nothing? We're all nothing? He's not even going to say goodbye?'

'I have to say, I'm very surprised. He had me fooled. Had us all fooled, didn't he? You say he's not been himself, but maybe he has been. Maybe this *is* who he is, love. And if it is, then good riddance.'

'He said I was nothing.' I collapsed into a fresh bout of broken-hearted tears.

Mum shifted again, took hold of my face in both hands and looked into my eyes. 'Listen to me, Kirsty Shaw. You are not

nothing. If he says that, it's because that's what *he* is, all right?'
She returned me to her embrace, stroking my hair, tucking it
behind my ears with a tenderness that made me cry all the
more. '*He's* the nothing. You are a very special person, do you
hear me? You're beautiful inside and out, and he doesn't deserve
you, OK? One day you'll find your person. You'll find someone
who'll walk over hot coals for you, and when that day comes,
you'll see Hughie Reynolds wasn't fit to clean your boots.
Bastard. Treating you like that. I'll kill him.'

Later, when I'd drunk the sugary tea Mum had brought up
to my room, I texted him. It felt like I was capitulating in some
way; he didn't deserve anything from me, but I couldn't help
myself.

Is this some sort of joke?

When there was no reply, I swallowed what was left of my
pride and called him. He didn't pick up. I called again. Again
and again, hating myself a little bit more each time. I was so
confused and so ashamed. It's hard to think of it even now, that
shame. I was too young to know it didn't belong to me. All I
wanted was to hear him say he hadn't meant it, or take it back,
or give me some reason why, because I couldn't believe we
could end on this unfinished note. It felt cruel, darkly tantalis-
ing, like a song without its ending or a question met only with
silence. The change in him had been so sudden, so violent, the
letter so cold, so utterly, inexplicably horrible. Really, it was like
he'd become someone else.

Where was my friend, my boyfriend? Where the hell had
he gone?

When Dad got home from work, he read the letter while I
sat at the table with my head bowed and Mum filled him in on
what had happened the night before. It was embarrassing as
hell, but my parents were always cool about stuff and Mum
didn't need many words to get the meaning across.

'That boy sat at our table for years,' Dad said in a low, trembling voice, the letter funnelling and shaking in his fingers. 'He sat there and ate our food and drank our wine and he...' Lost for words, he pushed his hands through what remained of his hair. 'I took him fishing! I paid for his football tickets, and he turns round and...' Eyes flashing at me, he plucked his car keys from the kitchen table. 'Come on.'

'What?' I was by now a puddle of fresh tears.

'He can look me in the eye and tell me what the hell he thinks he's playing at.'

'No,' Mum chimed in. 'Leave it. There's nothing to be gained...'

'Dad,' I sobbed. 'Please. It's OK. I can go myself.'

'Well, you tell him from me that if I see him, there'll be words. You don't treat people like that. Especially not people who've been good to you. I've never heard the like. Never.'

I took the keys and left. I hadn't dared admit I had no idea where Hughie lived – it was too mortifying. In Dad's car I drove around and around the city streets, eyes on stalks, searching for him. I texted Tasha, Gus and Callum, checked the pubs, the bars, Duthie Park where we used to hang out, the beach, Codona's funfair and the arcade, the harbour. All our places, with all our memories held inside them, every one of them spoilt, soured.

And even after I'd been to Tasha's and showed her the note, after I'd burst into yet more tears and dried them again and we were smoking the doobie that was supposed to be for celebration purposes out of her bedroom window, there was no way I thought I'd *never see him again*. Like, literally, never. Someone must have seen him – rumours were already going around that his results had been disappointing. Tasha had heard it from Callum.

'He'll be raging,' she said. 'All he wanted was to get into medicine.'

'Maybe he's had a breakdown,' I said, still clutching at

straws. 'The note did read like that. Maybe he'll show his face once he's nursed his bruised pride and say he's sorry.'

Tasha blew a long grey jet out over her back garden. 'Maybe.'

'Maybe he's been hurt.' Another straw falling through my fingers. 'Maybe... Oh my God, do you think it was a suicide note? It was pretty final. He could be in hospital. Unconscious. An overdose.' I took the joint from Tasha, had a wee puff and handed it back. 'Maybe someone else copied his handwriting.'

'Maybe he's joined the secret service,' Tasha said, heavy on the irony. 'Maybe he's been kidnapped. By aliens. Local Laddie Lost in Alien Abduction Shocker.'

'Maybe we should call the police,' I said, only half joking.

But Tasha shook her head, pushing the dog end against the jar lid she used as an ashtray. 'He's a wee gobshite. Honestly, hen, there's no mystery here. We thought he was the big man, but he's just a prick, pure and simple. Lesson best learnt sooner rather than later. He hasn't gone. No one just goes like that; it's all for the drama – you'll see. He'll turn up soon enough and we can all tell him what we think of him.'

But he didn't turn up. He really did vanish. Over the following days, as I took to my bed, Mum and Dad built the myth that we'd effectively become his adoptive family and that he'd run away rather than have to face us after his poor showing in the exams. I wanted to believe them, but as the days turned into weeks and the weeks into months, Hughie's shitty behaviour, the horrid note and what I thought must be temporary insanity turned into something darker, sinister and completely unfathomable. I began to wonder if he really had taken his own life, if that's what the note had meant. But there was no body. Had he been abducted, coerced into some cult or other? But there was no phone call from a worried foster mother asking if we knew where he was. Which meant he must have told her he was leaving, as, at eighteen, he had every right to do.

He hadn't gone missing, since there was no article in the *Press and Journal* asking for information, no missing person investigation, no police enquiring after his last-known whereabouts. There was nothing. He had used us and had walked away without a backward glance. We had believed him to be part of our family, our friend, my boyfriend. I had believed he cared for us – for me especially. Hughie Reynolds had dropped into our lives like a stone into a pond. But whatever ripples he had sent circling had completely vanished, leaving only an eerie flatness, an absence such that you wondered if he'd ever been there at all.

SIX

KIRSTY

Back in the present, a heavily pregnant woman re-emerged from her memories and found herself still sitting on her bed, an old letter she should have destroyed long ago quivering in her hand. To think I'd been so naïve as to imagine this vile, arrogant note might have been an apology for his appalling behaviour the night before, the switch in him that I could still remember all these years later, the shock I could still feel, the disillusion. I had hoped that he might have written something cute, something that didn't include the actual word *sorry* – which wouldn't have been his style – but would have conveyed how mortified he was at his treatment of me – *me*, his KK.

But no, it wasn't an apology.

The radiator clicked as it warmed. I pulled my coat tight around me and closed my eyes against the tears that had come despite myself. I was crying at everything in that last trimester, and Hughie Reynolds was one of those things. It wasn't about him, not really. That's what I tried to tell myself. It was about the day I'd had, that wee baby all blue, the bone-deep tiredness of late pregnancy, and, I'll admit, the childish disappointment not to have come home to Dougie, the one true love Mum had promised me I'd find all those years ago, my person, the one who would walk over hot coals if it meant keeping me safe.

I crumpled the note into a hard ball and drained the cold dregs from my mug before taking it, along with the crushed letter, into the kitchen. I put the mug in the dishwasher. In the sink, I set light to that letter like I should have done a decade earlier and stood transfixed, watching it burn.

Minutes later, it collapsed to ash against the stainless steel.

And that's when I remembered Joan.

In all the turmoil, I'd forgotten to take the stew over. It was a bit late now, but if I didn't go, she'd wonder where I was. I was surprised she hadn't texted to ask me where I'd got to; she would usually. I'd pop my head round the door, I thought, give her the stew and stay for ten minutes, fifteen tops.

The kitchen clock told me it was after half past seven. Dougie would surely be on the way home by now.

I scribbled a note and left it on the kitchen table.

Just bobbed to Joan's quickly. Back in a jiffy. Get the pasta on! Love you, K xxx

I grabbed the Tupperware from the fridge and lumbered down the drive, a stitch needling at my side. That'd be the stress of seeing Hughie, I thought. That or the tea, giving me acid reflux. The joys of late pregnancy.

I rang Joan's doorbell. The living-room curtains were drawn. The air was bitter, the sky black. On the grey pavement, street lamps splashed their fuzzy haloes. Further into the close, light glowed amber from between curtains, illuminated frosted glass panels in front doors, striped Venetian blinds with yellow. Folk were home from work, kids from school. Everywhere, in these granite boxes, the people of the city were fixing supper, chatting about their days.

I checked my watch. What was taking Joan so long? She

was usually at the door in seconds, her regular walks keeping her fit enough to put me to shame. Mentally she'd always been sharp as a tack, if not always in good spirits – although lately she'd not always been one hundred per cent on the ball. Nothing I could really put my finger on, but just occasionally she appeared to struggle to know whether to say hello or what she was going to say next. It was only ever a moment, and on days like those, I'd either prompt her or make small talk until she found her way back again. I'd often wondered if she suffered on and off from depression. But something in her manner always made me feel like to ask would be to pry. Still, as proud and private as she was, I'd been starting to think I should maybe broach the subject. At eighty, it was sadly possible that dementia was on the horizon. The problem was how to raise it without offending her. But Joan had no family, so far as I knew. There was her friend Reeny, but she was of a similar age, so when it came to next of kin, I reckoned that was probably me.

She appeared finally, a Picasso in the fluted glass pane of the front door.

'It's only me, pet,' I called. 'Sorry I'm so late.'

At this, the distorted features shifted forward and the door opened a crack. One pale blue eye appeared, magnified in a spectacle lens.

'Joan? It's me.' Why was she not opening the door? 'Everything OK?'

'Kirsty,' she said breathlessly. The door opened wider. The one eye became two above a fine, straight nose and a faltering smile. Joan's tall, thin frame appeared then, her white hair pulled back into her trademark French pleat. 'Sorry, dear.' Her smile faded. 'I thought you were... someone else.' She turned away, erect, her shoulders square, knowing I'd follow her indoors without her having to ask.

I straightened my own shoulders. Dad had been on at me about my posture since he started Pilates, enthusiasm bordering on a lecture, like every fitness evangelist who ever lived. I closed the front door behind me and made my way down the tiny hallway, making small talk all the while – how cold it was, how short the days, how we hadn't to worry though; it was getting lighter now and spring would soon be here.

In the living room, Joan settled into her high-backed chair near the gas fire, her perfect spine lending her something of the Sphinx and making me want to suck in my stomach – an impossible task, if ever there was one.

The room was warm and clean and smelt of the lavender furniture polish Joan loved. She had no cleaner or any kind of help and was as elegant as ever in her bright pink cashmere sweater with matching cardigan, the fine navy silk scarf with pink polka dots she often wore, dark blue jeans and cream sheepskin slipper boots. But the television wasn't on and there was no evidence of a book or a newspaper, which meant that she'd been sitting here in silence.

There was something twitchy about her, I noticed then, as if she were searching for someone hiding in the room. She wasn't looking at me at all, so much so that I actually glanced behind me to see if there was someone there. But no, there was no one.

Unsettled, I turned back to Joan, whose hand was now hovering shakily at her chest, the fingers half curled as if something precious had dropped from them and she hadn't yet realised.

'Everything all right?' I said, unnerved.

She passed her trembling hand across her forehead but said nothing.

'Joan?' Concern flared in my chest. Her apparent confusion could be a stroke, I knew that. I took out my phone, ready to call 999.

'Joan,' I said. 'Can you see me OK? Joanie, darlin'? Can you tell me what you're seeing? Have you a headache at all?'

Her gaze flickered. She met my eye finally, hers round and

red-veined with what looked like pure fear. 'I canna tell,' she whispered, her eyes brimming. 'I canna tell you... He'll... he'll... I canna tell you.'

A hot slick of panic shot through me from head to toe. My heart thumped.

'What can't you tell me, love?' I asked, my voice high with anxiety. 'Who is he? Has someone been here?'

Instinctively, I looked about, into the shadows at the back of the room. There was no one. I wondered then if there might be someone elsewhere in the house. I knew I should investigate, but I couldn't leave her like that, so I took hold of her hand and spoke again.

'Joan? Can you hear me? Who was here, love? It's OK. You can tell me. I won't tell anyone.'

Her head shifted almost imperceptibly, and she stared up at me, blinking as if seeing me for the first time. 'Did you come before, dearie?'

'No, love,' I managed, heart still banging in my chest. 'I'm a bit later today, that's all. Got... held up. Was someone here just now? Can you tell me who it was?'

She didn't answer.

'Joan,' I tried again. 'Was someone here?'

'Lachie,' she almost cried out. 'Lachie doesna know. He doesna know about the...'

'Lachie? Do you mean Lachlan? Do you mean your husband? Lachlan's passed on, love. He passed a long time ago, remember? A long time ago now.'

Joan's shoulders slumped a little, her face relaxing. 'It was so sad. The cancer took him.'

Silence settled between us. My heart was slowing, but anxiety had made a tight fist in my belly. It was Lachlan she had seen. Grief had sent her a phantom, a memory made flesh by old pain.

'Have you been for your walk today?' I asked after a

moment, an attempt to rouse my dear pal out of... was it some sort of fugue? Whatever it was, it was much worse than her previous wanderings, which had only lasted a second or two and had never involved seeing dead husbands or folk who weren't there.

'This morning,' she said, the colour returning slowly to her face. 'Along the harbour. Affa chilly the day. Icy wind on the pier. Have to walk regularly. Blow away the cobwebs.' She smiled, her daily routines offering up grips for her to climb back to herself.

'It is awful chilly,' I said as brightly as I could manage, putting my phone back in my bag. Whatever it had been, the crisis was over, but I still felt fraught. 'They're saying it'll be minus five again tonight,' I gabbled on, talking myself down as much as Joan. 'I'll check your blanket's on the timer before I go, will I? Good for you for going out though. I don't think you'd catch me out in this weather, not at eighty.'

'Eighty-one.' With her mischievous smirk, Joan appeared to be one hundred per cent back in the room. 'Five thousand steps a day. Sudoku. Crossword. Have to stay active.'

'You're not wrong about that.' I walked over to the window and peered out from behind the curtains. Joan's frightened outburst had compounded the day's nerves, and I couldn't seem to shake them off. I looked up and down the close, thinking I might see someone skulking about the place. I didn't think about the flashy red car, not then. There was only Joan's white Polo parked on the driveway. She'd driven that car every day since I'd known her, always to the beach for her walk. I suspected she'd done it for years, and that it helped her to fight off the old black dog, or whatever it was she couldn't, or wouldn't, talk about. But now, I shuddered to think what would happen if she were to experience an episode like she'd had just now while at the wheel.

'You still taking the car up to the beach?' I asked, making my way back to her. It was not as direct as I needed to be, but Joan could be as prickly as a prickly pear sometimes.

The old woman huffed, no flies on her. 'Why wouldn't I? I'm nae blind, for goodness' sake. I'm an excellent driver, I'll have you know.'

I threw up my hands and smiled. 'Only asking. Shall I make you a cup of tea?' I held up the Tupperware. 'I've brought you some chicken and chorizo stew. Dougie made it.' At that point, it occurred to me there was no lingering aroma from an evening meal, which was odd. 'Have you eaten?' I asked. 'Do you want me to heat this up for you?'

Joan shook her head. 'No thank you, dear. I'm nae hungry.'

'Are you sure? You should have something. You have to keep your strength up, you know. You'll not walk far on an empty stomach.' I hesitated, the plastic box still in my hand. Really, I wanted to heat it up then and there and stay to make sure she ate a good hot dinner. But if there was one thing I knew about Joan, it was: good luck to anyone trying to get her to do something she didn't want to do.

'It'll be fine for tomorrow,' I said, after a moment. 'I'll plate it up and put it in the fridge, then all you have to do is microwave it, all right? Your appetite will've come back by then, I'm sure.'

'There's nae need to bring me food.' The tone was brusque, but barely were the words out when her face softened. 'But that's affa kind, thank you, dear. And thank Dougie for me, won't you? You're too good to me, so you are.'

Satisfied she was settled for the moment, I left her and checked the rest of the bungalow. There was no one hiding in the bedroom or behind the shower curtain, as, by then, I knew there wouldn't be, but I was still pretty jittery.

Fifteen minutes later, Joan was sipping tea the way I knew she took it – strong enough to slice, with two sugars and a passing glance of milk. God only knew how the woman slept.

Her dinner was ready to go in the fridge. The electric blanket was set to come on at nine thirty and go off at ten.

'Do you need anything picking up from town tomorrow?' I asked. 'You're low on eggs and you've only half a packet of Hobnobs.'

'No thank you, dear. I'm going to the big Asda with Reeny the morn.'

'I'll see you tomorrow evening then, OK? Usual time.'

'Usual time, aye. Lovely.'

Just then, I winced as an almost square lump appeared at the top left-hand side of my hot-air-balloon belly.

'Oh, would you look at that!' Joan reached up, her face alight with a joyful, questioning expression.

Understanding, I took her warm, papery hand in both of mine and placed it on the protruding limb. 'A knee or an elbow, I reckon.'

Her eyes brimmed. After a minute or so, she asked me if it was a loon or a quine – a boy or a girl.

'Remember, I told you,' I said. 'It's a surprise.'

'A beautiful surprise,' she said and laughed for the sheer wonder of it all. But her laughter gave way to something melancholy I couldn't quite read. She pulled a tissue from her sleeve and dabbed at her eyes. 'New life.'

'New life, aye,' I said. 'New life, new hope, eh?'

For a moment, we stayed like that, the two of us in the silence, her hand on my swollen belly. I remember it so clearly, how quiet we were, how close. After everything that happened, I hold that memory tight in my heart.

SEVEN

KIRSTY

KS/transcript #6

Outside, the sky was cloudy charcoal. Not one star. Dougie's van was on our drive. At least there was that. I walked slowly, dizzy with hunger and out of puff, the baby pressing on my lungs. It could've been Hughie, the emergency delivery, exhaustion or hunger, I don't know, but the visit with Joan had flooded me with an apprehension I could not seem to quell. I'd never seen her so frightened and confused before – not inside her own home, where she was always at her best. It was as if she'd been looking for someone, or expecting someone, or someone had called in unexpectedly and left her discombobulated. A man – real or imagined, it was hard to know – had been in her house.

Did you come before, dearie? What was that about? She'd never mentioned Lachlan before either. When she had just then, her face was full of confusion. *Lachie doesna know about the...* Know about the what? Could she have seen her late husband as clearly as if he were alive, her mind's eye playing cruel tricks? Or had a real, solid, living man inveigled his way into her home, pretending to be him? I'd watched enough documentaries in my time to know there were some terrible folk out there ready to prey on the vulnerable, and if Joan's mind had started to come and go...

I was glad then that I'd persuaded her to let me have a spare key cut a couple of years previously. I would never use it unless I absolutely had to, but now I was thinking, if something bad were to happen in the night, she was all alone in that house, no one there to look after her. In an emergency, she might never get to her phone in time. I resolved to look into getting her a pendant alarm so she could alert me or Dougie at any time.

As I squeezed past the van, I remembered the burnt paper in the sink. Dougie would have seen it. I would have to rake up things I didn't want to talk about or want Dougie to hear. I would have to admit to keeping that note and I wouldn't be able to explain why. It might hurt Dougie's feelings, something I never, ever wanted to do. Hughie flashed in my mind's eye – back then and as I'd seen him this morning. Joan's confusion and alarm just now. That tiny baby, blue as a damson, sinking, sinking, sinking.

I slid the key into the lock, searching for how to broach the subject of the letter. It had taken me a long time to get over it, Hughie disappearing like that, the nastiness of our last encounter. For a long time I couldn't get rid of the idea of myself as something discarded, worthless, the victim of a mean confidence trick. Guilt too, from the impact on my whole family. I was the one who'd brought him into our lives, after all.

In time, I recovered and managed to go to uni, albeit as a diminished version of myself. Over the three years of the course, I did my best to repair the damage. Even made myself go on a couple of dates with guys who were nice enough. But nothing really came of them, nothing felt right. Instead, I threw myself into my training. My training was how I finally grew back the brutally pruned stem of myself into some sort of wonky flower. Nothing takes you out of yourself like the delivery room.

Nothing makes the world seem like a better place than putting a healthy newborn into the arms of an ecstatic new mum. That was where I set my focus; it was what saved me.

A year after graduating, when I'd started as a trainee midwife at the infirmary and was saving up to buy a wee flat, I recognised Dougie in a bar in town. We got talking, made each other crack up laughing, shared a few shy glances and eventually swapped numbers. A day or two later, we arranged to go for a hike up to Lochnagar. There was no game-playing, no stressful dance of who likes who more, just the simple, easy rhythm of two people who loved to walk in nature and stand silently in old clothes and scuffed boots before its breath-stealing beauty. Dougie was so nice to talk to, so funny, so clever despite not pursuing any kind of further education, preferring instead to crack on with a trade. Dougie was the first person I could even imagine being near, let alone close with, and something inside me, something I'd been resisting for a long time, clicked.

I was about to push open the front door when I heard my name being called. My heart sank. Moira, my next-door neighbour, was standing at the waist-high fence that separates our front gardens, fag in hand. That cigarette is like the Olympic torch – always burning, never going out.

'Have you seen Zip-Zip?' she asked. She was wearing a teddy bear onesie, a brave choice in her sixties and so near to a naked flame.

With a sigh of resignation, I pocketed my key. 'Gone AWOL again, has he?'

'Not seen him a' day.' She bit her lip. 'Put his tea out for him and banged the pan, ken? Usually brings him back, but nothing.'

'He'll be up by the heating vent, will he?' I replied. *Because that's where he always is*, I did not add, instead pulling open the garage door and throwing down my big handbag, which Dougie loves to tease me about on account of it being so enormous. In it are all the usual things you'd expect to find, such as a purse, a compact mirror, lip salve, keys, a telescopic umbrella... but there are also bandages, a miniature first aid kit, a Kindle, a torch, collapsible scissors, disinfectant spray, antiseptic wipes, a mobile phone charger, butterfly plasters and a stapler. Tasha reckons I could deliver a baby at the side of the road.

She is not wrong.

But back to the cat.

With some effort and more than a pinch of overtired insanity, I pulled the stepladder from the garage and set it up. Getting up the ladder was a challenge. Not only because by now Moira was wittering on about how I shouldn't be doing that in my condition whilst simultaneously not moving one centimetre from her spot at the fence. I was so dizzy I shouldn't have been anywhere near that stepladder. My belly was so big I could barely reach the sides to hold myself secure.

I reached the third step but didn't dare go any further. My head was spinning and my stomach was growling like a bear. But it was OK, because sure enough, when I shone my iPhone torch, two glassy eyes caught the beam, *What the hell do you want?* in their expression. Before I'd even called his name, Zip-Zip stood up, arched his back and slunk down the skeleton wisteria to the breathy soundtrack of Moira gushing over his reappearance, over my *genius, hen* at finding him in the place in which he had been found at least a dozen times since he was a kitten.

A moment later, Zip-Zip sashayed over to the cat flap and disappeared inside, his erect tail and round black arsehole a final *fuck you.*

'Thanks, hen, you're a wee doll,' Moira called, giving me the thumbs-up before following the cat indoors.

'No problem.' I jumped the last two steps down and promptly rolled my ankle.

. . .

In the kitchen, Dougie looked up from a big pot of boiling water, a bunch of spaghetti half submerged and sticking up stiffly like a bad fright. 'What've you done to your foot?'

I pulled out a chair and sat down at the table. 'I was helping Moira's cat down from the gutter. *Again.* Except it didn't need any help; it was just waiting for me to climb the stepladder so it could come down by itself. Bastard. Hello, by the way.'

'You should have told her to fetch her own bloody cat for once. She knows fine well where it is.'

'Aye, but she's in her sixties, so—'

'Sixty is no age! You're eight months gone!'

'It's not a disability! I can do everything I could do before. Except maybe pole dancing.' I smiled, to make the peace.

'You couldna pole dance before.' Dougie leant over to kiss me on the cheek, one warm hand resting on the bump. 'You have to be *careful*, darlin'. Precious cargo.'

'I know, I know. Precious cargo.'

'I'll put the stepladder away.'

'I've done it.' I stood up. 'But if you're taking care of dinner, I might grab a quick shower.'

'Sure.' Dougie glanced at the pasta box. 'You have nine minutes. Eight and a half, to be precise.'

'Fab. You're a star.'

'What was all that burnt paper in the sink by the way? Tory party been leafleting again?'

I'd made it as far as the doorway. My stomach flipped, but I forced a jolly laugh, which came out hollow. 'It was just some old papers.' I turned away but could not make myself take one step. Instead, I found myself drumming on the door frame before turning back to face my darling Dougie, who was looking at me with an expression that carried no doubt, no doubt whatsoever, that what I had just said was the truth. Gah.

'Do you remember that guy I went out with at school?' I asked, shame burning hot in my cheeks.

'Hughie Reynolds?'

The way his name slipped out so immediately made me feel even worse.

'The very one. Only, I think I saw him today. At work, like.'

'Bloody hell. Seriously? At the infirmary? Bad penny or what?'

'Except it wasn't him.'

'Right. Hang on, what d'you mean, it wasna him?'

'Well, it looked like him, except older, but his lanyard said Barry Sefton. Which is weird because I'm sure it was Hughie. I'm gonna check the staff database tomorrow.'

'Did you... did you speak to him?' A blush gave Dougie away. 'I mean, could he have been wearing the wrong name tag?'

Heat kindled at the base of my throat. I needed to drop the subject. Hughie should not be allowed to infiltrate our home like this.

'I thought of that, but... I said his name. Called out to him, like, but he... Well.' I was too embarrassed to go into the gory details. 'Anyway, when I got home, I remembered... I mean, this is silly, but I remembered I had this stupid note he left me, so I—'

'He left you a note? You never said anything about a note.' Dougie's blush deepened, causing the heat in my own face to intensify – in sympathy or shame, it was hard to tell. Not having told Dougie before felt acutely like a betrayal, which was not my intention.

'No. Well. Yes.' I looked about me, flustered. 'It was *not* a nice note. I don't know why I kept it... It really messed with my head at the time. I sort of had to take to my bed for a few weeks. GP gave me some meds.'

'To your *bed*? You took, what? Antidepressants? Oh God, I didn't...'

I shrugged. 'I was very young. It was just so... violent, in a way. I don't really like talking about it. Anyway, Dad went mad. Both my parents did actually. Hughie was all at sea when he first arrived and we kind of adopted him. He was part of the family, had his own key, everything. So when he just disappeared, it was big, you know? Shocking. The note was... it was pretty nasty.'

'I knew he'd done a bunk, but...' Dougie's voice was quiet.

'I didn't really want to relive it, you know? At first I could talk about nothing else, but then I realised that every time I talked about him I felt worse, so I... I stopped. Put him in a box and closed the lid, I suppose. I don't know why I kept the note, to be honest. Maybe because when he left, it was like he vanished, you know? I hadn't looked at it in years, but when I got home, I just had this need to... to get rid of it. Like burning sage or something. Purifying our home before the baby comes, I don't know. Anyway, that's what the mess was. I just don't want that guy anywhere near us.'

Dougie's face was unreadable – absorbing what I was saying, maybe, wondering why I'd lied, how best to react.

'Hormones making me crazy,' I joked, despite feeling incredibly miserable. 'Seeing folk who aren't there, burning letters... Whatever next, eh?'

'What did it say?' Dougie's voice was still so quiet it made me want to cry. That quiet was hurt, and I knew it. 'The note. What did it say?'

I shook my head, cutting the wire after the bomb had exploded. 'It was... mean,' I managed before making myself repeat the contents of the letter, realising as I did so that I knew every word by heart.

For another long moment, neither of us spoke. I didn't know what Dougie was thinking, but I was back under my duvet in my teenage bedroom, burning with humiliation, thinking the world had ended, that I'd never be able to go to uni, never become a midwife, never love anyone ever again. That's the lunacy of youth, I suppose. The intensity of those black-and-white feelings, the fact that it's the first time we're feeling them. We have no clue how to get through and out the other side, or even that others have suffered the same or worse. At the time, I couldn't see any way out of the hole I was in. How young I was, how shattered my sense of reality, my illusions of love. It was Mum who took me to the doctor's, who held me in her arms night after night and told me I would be OK. Dad put all his sympathy into fury at Hughie, a failed campaign to find the bastard and bring him to account.

I could not look up. More than anything, I wanted to fold myself into Dougie's arms, but I wasn't sure how to cross the space between us. So I stayed by the door, holding on to the frame, feeling nothing more complicated now than aching sadness and the desire to lie down in a warm bed and fall into a deep sleep, Dougie by my side stroking my hair and telling me we were still us and always would be.

'Must've been a terrible shock to see him,' Dougie said, so softly I felt tears prick. 'Or whoever it was. Brought up some bad stuff, eh? Triggering.'

'Ach, it's ancient history.' I tried to brush it off, convincing no one. 'It was the note more than anything. And no sooner had I seen him than I was wondering if I had, if that makes sense. I don't know. I don't know what's going on. And then Joan was really out of sorts. And on shift there was a baby, the wee soul was suffocating and...' I had begun to cry properly now. 'Sorry. I'm not making sense.'

'Hey.' And like that, Dougie answered my silent wish, arms warm and enveloping and full of generous-hearted love. 'Don't upset yourself, darlin'. Don't think about it. It's OK. It's all OK.'

'I should've told you before,' I sobbed. 'I didn't want to upset you. It was... humiliating. It was done on purpose, you know? To hurt me. And my family. I felt guilty that I'd made them suffer, you know? Like it was my fault Hughie had even been in our lives. Even telling you now, it's like I can feel it all over again. It was just so confusing. And then everyone was talking about it, asking me why, what did I know, weren't we supposed to be a couple, and I didn't know anything except that he'd pretty much denied I'd ever been anything to him.'

'The shame is all his,' Dougie whispered into my hair. 'All of it. None of it was your fault, and you were just a kid. I'm so sorry he did that to you.' There was no reproach, only kindness. 'And I'm sorry I wasn't here to watch you burn that letter. We could've had a proper wee ceremony, like a wicker man thing. The guy sounds like a total arsehole.'

I laughed, wiping my eyes and my nose, recovering. 'He is. Was. I should never have let him in my head the first time, and I sure as hell won't let him back in now.'

EIGHT

HUGHIE

HR/audio/excerpt #2

Did you know I wanted to be an anaesthetist even before we met? Oh yes, months before I came to Aberdeen, actually, I saw a real, live consultant anaesthetist in action. Edinburgh Royal Infirmary, 2009. It was like my life had been leading up to that moment, watching that man do his job and feeling everything fall into place. It was the way everyone deferred to him, the way the nurses looked at him, the reverence. And the patient – it was a woman, I remember, a woman of about thirty, who looked up at him like he was a *god*, like all her trust was in him, and in his eyes I saw the power he had over her. It was the most thrilling thing I'd ever witnessed. Without blinking, I watched as he put her under, and I thought: that is what I shall use my education for. No more looking over my shoulder. No more scraping an existence. *That* is what I want.

And you couldn't let me do it, could you? You had to shout my name. You had to challenge me right there, where I worked.

When I took this job, I did wonder if I'd see you, but I never thought you'd recognise me, not in a million years. Nor in eleven, for that matter. Make no mistake, Kirsty. I know I've aged disastrously – don't think I don't. Some folk, you look at them and they're just the same – a wrinkle here and there, an attractive peppering around a still thick hairline, a belt that fastens on the same damn hole. Others, like me, you'd never pick them out in a line-up, so dramatically have they deteriorated. If the hair loss and lack of spectacles weren't enough, there's the vastly expanded waistline and resulting salmon face, the product of too many takeaways, too many bottles of Merlot and too many attacks of the munchies on long, lonely weekends. Too much of everything really. So yes, sadly, I know I've changed a great deal.

But you. You saw through it all. You always did notice people. Tell me: how did you know me so instantly? You can't have laid eyes on me for more than a couple of seconds before you blurted out my name. But then I suppose I recognised you too, didn't I? How was *I* so sure it was *you*, right? I'd had you in my sights for no longer than you'd had me, and it wasn't as if you looked the same either, heavily pregnant and bundled up like the Abominable Snowman. If my shift hadn't gone on longer than scheduled, I might never have seen you at all.

Maybe we're both incredibly good with faces.

Maybe we knew this moment would come, sooner or later.

Maybe we're still stuck on one another after all these years.

I couldn't get out of that hospital fast enough. I was already keeping my fingers crossed it would be the last time you'd lay eyes on me. I knew immediately and instinctively you could be a problem and felt the seed of irritation even then. If I'd left work a minute earlier, I could have got on with my life in a calm fashion. But if anyone was likely to blow my cover, it would be you, and by the time I'd left the infirmary, any trace of calm had dissipated like so much smoke.

What were you doing anyway, walking around the hospital wearing all your outerwear?

It was almost as if you were looking for me.

Were you? Were you on to me even then?

I guess you can't answer me, can you?

NINE

KIRSTY

KS/transcript #7

Sometimes it doesn't start with something big but something small, something that seems almost insignificant in the grand scheme of things – a guy who looks like someone you once knew or an old friend who appears frightened and confused. Sometimes it's about putting those things together. At least, that's how it is in the documentaries I like to watch. But at that point, there wasn't enough to get me thinking along those lines. I'd just had a bad day.

When I hobbled downstairs the next morning, the smell of coffee drifted towards me – decaf for me, the hard stuff for Dougie.

'Hey, you,' I said, as I always did.

'Hey yourself.' The response to my call. Dougie turned to plant a kiss on my head. 'Sleep OK?'

'Not really. I was too worried about Joan.'

'What are you like?' Dougie had already fetched a bandage and was crouching down to strap up my ankle. It wasn't so bad, but better safe than sorry, and my arms weren't long enough to reach around my big dome of a belly.

The night before, over late dinner, we'd discussed Joan's confused state and I'd felt a bit calmer. Joan was getting older, Dougie had reassured me, and confusion was simply part of that process. But lying awake in the small hours, the feeling that my friend's fears were not just the visions of a deteriorating brain but something real and solid had grown out of the darkness and reached for me with long, clawed fingers. When I finally banished those phantoms, I was in the delivery room all over again, the wee bairn's head sinking, purpling, myself stuck fast, unable to move, unable to shift my enormous bulk, to help, unable to save that precious life.

'You need to worry about yourself for a change,' Dougie was saying, breaking into my thoughts now the ankle was well and truly secured. 'Joan's a feisty one. She'll be fine. Precious cargo, remember.'

I sipped my coffee. 'Precious cargo. OK, boss.'

A silence drifted down. With it, an almost imperceptible note of tension.

'How about... the other thing?' Dougie was cleaning the work surface with what you might call excessive vigour. 'Seeing that guy and stuff.'

'Ach, he's nothing,' I said. 'He's no one. Honestly. Wasn't even him, right?'

My shift went OK, but I was getting more and more tired and thinking my mat leave could not come soon enough. A little after seven, I pulled into the street and immediately noticed a red sports car parked almost opposite our house, nearer the mouth of the close. It looked like the same one I'd seen the day before. I drove past at five miles per hour, rubbernecking to see who was inside. But the car was empty.

Did I think that was strange? Yes, I did. Straight away. As I said before, it's not the big things necessarily, it's the little things, the wee shifts and changes not everyone notices. I knew I'd never seen that car before, and in a cul-de-sac, it's not like we saw a lot of traffic. So to see it twice in two days seemed unusual, and I did wonder if it belonged to the person who'd been to see Joan and frightened her. But I told myself not to jump to conclusions, that it was just a flashy car and that there were billions of flashy cars in the world.

Joan's white Polo was out front, so I parked on our driveway before doubling back. My ankle had started to throb, but I ignored it. I was keen to see Joan, hoping to find her in brighter spirits. I knew I wouldn't relax until I'd checked in on her.

As I walked stiffly back past the empty red car, I had to fight the urge to cross the road and look inside it. I was about to go and have a peek, but then I thought the owner could be in any one of the houses and might be watching me from one of the windows, so best not. Instead, I looked all around me: up towards Stephanie and Carl on the bend, the McGilvery family opposite us, the Kellys opposite Joan, Andrea and David Robinson at number 15, the Sweeneys at number 20. There was no one about. It was bitterly cold and so, so dark. Folk were either still at work or at home with a fire in the grate and something hot on the stove.

I was breathless again. Wheezing. The baby must have been wedged against my lungs so that I couldn't fill them properly. It was continually surprising to me to go through all the things I'd learnt about in theory but only ever experienced by proxy. And the birth was almost upon me. I hoped the whole experience would make me an even better midwife, able to understand exactly what women went through and say exactly the right thing in their moments of need. Already I knew I'd never again lecture a woman on what not to eat, not after sending Dougie out to the twenty-four-hour garage for an almond Magnum the other night, the entire packets of ginger snaps I ate daily in the first trimester. If the heart wants what the heart wants, well, the pregnant belly is no different, and hell hath no fury like a pregnant woman in need of a posh choc ice.

I rang on Joan's doorbell and gave a friendly rat-a-tat on the glass pane. Waiting, I glanced back occasionally towards the red car, which looked a bit like a roller skate. For the second time, Joan was slow coming to the door. I rang again, waited, already starting to worry. From inside, no hint of movement, only the silent stillness that comes from an empty house. But her car was there, so she was obviously at home.

Heart quickening at the thought of her having had some sort of fall, or even a stroke, I took a few steps over to the sitting-room window and peered in, expecting to find her nose-deep in the *Press and Journal*, or perhaps asleep. But her high-backed chair was empty. Her favourite china mug with the William Morris floral design stood on the coffee table. It occurred to me that if I could see in, that meant the curtains were wide open despite it having been dark for hours.

The fluttering in my guts returned, stronger now. It was nothing, less than nothing, but Joan was so tidy, almost militarily tidy, if you know what I mean. Shipshape. She would never have left a mug there like that. She would have taken it with her when she left the room and washed it up. This mug must have been there since lunch, because Joan only had one tea in the morning and one after lunch, plus the one I made for her after her supper when I was on days, since I could only pop in in the evenings then. She knew I was going to check in today. She was expecting me.

So where was she?

I turned a slow circle. It made no sense for her to be out if her car was here, none whatsoever. If she went walking, she drove to the beach. If she went shopping or to Reeny's, she'd go in the car. Whoever owned the red car opposite was clearly not her visitor, otherwise they would be here, in the sitting room, chatting with her.

With a faint pang of concern, I scanned the crescent for life before ringing and knocking again. Minutes passed. I thought of how she'd been the day before, how she'd thought I was someone else. The man who may or may not have been in her house. Her dead husband. The thing she couldn't tell me. The fear in her eyes.

Cautiously, and with a sense of intruding, I wandered round to the back of the house and peered through the kitchen window. There was no one, no crumbs, no plate, no sign of any food having been prepared.

A rustling came from next door's garden. I swivelled around, almost losing my balance.

'Hello?' I called out. 'Joan? Is that you, darlin'?'

I listened. There was no response, no more movement. A squirrel, perhaps, or a bird.

After a minute or so, I returned slowly to the front of the house and glanced back towards the road. The red sports car was still parked at the kerb, only now there appeared to be someone inside it. My heart raced and heat rose from my belly. Who was it? What were they doing?

I was about to go and ask if I could help them at all, but before I could get anything more than a glimpse, the car pulled away. I stood rooted to the spot on Joan's front path, watching as it drove slowly past and vanished around the corner. The driver was a guy or possibly a tall woman in what looked like a woolly hat.

With a huff of exasperation, I rang the doorbell for a third time. Joan couldn't be far away. But where would she be at this hour, and on foot? She walked in the morning, always in the morning, and would have been shopping with Reeny in the late morning. She was never out in the afternoon in winter and liked to be home before dark whatever the season. I tried to recall if she had ever been out when I'd called in before. Never was the answer to that. I'd told her yesterday I'd call by this evening. She hadn't texted to say she'd be out. She would have texted. Definitely. She was simply that kind of person.

'Weird,' I half whispered to myself. 'Where are you, Joanie?'

It was edging towards half past seven. The temperature was plummeting. Aberdeen winters are not for wimps, and definitely not for elderly women with not much meat on their bones. Concern grew into anxiety. Really, this was so odd. Could Reeny have come to pick her up and taken her somewhere? Supper out? The cinema? It was perfectly possible, if unusual, but Joan's manners were old school. She would always have texted with a change of plan, even if it meant she'd be no more than a minute late.

'Joan,' I muttered to the empty air. 'Where are you, darlin'?'

At the sound of a car engine, I looked up, expecting to see Reeny's yellow Nissan, my friend smiling from the passenger seat. But it was the flashy red car – the same one – its nose at the exit to the crescent. I attempted to jog down Joan's drive, but I was far too heavy, my body unwieldy and my ankle protesting, so I downgraded to an awkward waddling limp. I was a wee bit spooked, but it was more of a general feeling and it certainly didn't cross my mind that whoever it was might be watching me specifically. I thought they'd simply visited a friend on the close then perhaps taken a wrong turn and had to double back. I thought if I could speak to them, I could help point them in the right direction or at least put my own mind at rest. But as if in response, the car eased across the mouth of the close and drove away.

I limped the short distance home, a hard knot in my belly, chest tight. Despite all my arguing with myself, instinct told me something wasn't right. Yesterday I'd seen Hughie after eleven years, walking along as if everything were normal, only to find out that it wasn't him even though every cell of my being told me otherwise. Then Joan had appeared to be suffering some sort of episode that same evening, and now she wasn't in at a time she was always, always at home and hadn't let me know she'd be out. Thirdly, a sporty red car I'd never seen before was lurking about and driving off then returning before driving off again. That was weird. Wasn't it?

Yesterday Joan had spoken about someone being at the house. Could that someone drive a red car? Had they come back thinking to intimidate her again, only to find her not at home? But that didn't make sense because there was no one in the red car when I'd first seen it, and the only explanation for that was that the driver had been visiting someone else.

I didn't know. It was like trying to herd kittens in my brain. What would anyone want with Joan, an eighty-one-year-old woman who kept herself to herself? More likely was that she was lost somewhere, confused and anxious, catching her death. The idea of it fair winded me. It was a terrible, terrible thought.

I pulled out my phone and called her, but there was no reply. I texted:

Only me. Just called in to say hello but you weren't in. Just checking everything is OK. Let me know when you get this. Xx

Dougie's van wasn't on the drive yet. The drive itself felt steep. My legs ached as I walked up the short rise. When I got inside, the house was so cold I could see my own breath fogging in front of me. Muttering curses and making a note to set the heating to come on at five, I flicked on the thermostat and lit the wood burner, where Dougie had left a small wigwam of dried twigs over a firelighter. Shivering, I crouched as best I could, feeding in the smallest bits of kindling, making sure the fire was good and hot before I slid first one then two small logs inside and closed the window.

Still in my coat, I went into the kitchen and set about preparing the mince. Alone in the silence, my thoughts looped:

Hughie who wasn't Hughie, Joan's anxious state, her empty house, the red car, Hughie not being on the staff system when I'd had a sneaky look earlier. Of course he wasn't – because it wasn't him; it was a man called Barry Sefton.

Somewhere deep down, I knew that was the only explanation. My brain was in conflict with my gut and my gut was putting up a good fight, but it wasn't him and that was that. It was silly to get myself into such a state, weeping and burning letters like a schoolgirl. I'd done a real Kirsty special, seeing one thing and making it into another. Whoever this Barry guy was, he'd put a bee in my bonnet, that was all.

But now my neighbour was missing and there was a strange red car hanging about.

The mince hissed in the oil. I stirred it, watching it brown. My neighbour wasn't missing. That was far too dramatic. She was out, that was all, and had forgotten to tell me. I shouldn't let myself spiral.

The radio – good idea. Music to take my mind off things. I found a tune but almost wished I hadn't. 'Diamonds' by Rihanna. We used to sing it in sixth year at the tops of our voices. By then, Hughie was well and truly out of his shell. He was the life and soul of the common room, used to stand on a chair and lead us all in ad hoc karaoke whenever a favourite song came on. It was a great laugh, a real tension diffuser as exams got nearer and everyone got more and more stressed. I used to look up at him, his cheeky smiling face, his strong singing voice, and feel myself swelling with pride. That's my boyfriend, I used to think. We're like best friends. He really gets me and I get him.

I turned the dial. Depeche Mode were singing 'Just Can't Get Enough', a tune my folks would still bop around the kitchen to even now, their young selves bursting from them like hidden identities they only let out when they thought no one was looking. The music made me smile, even got me swinging my hips

and singing along. Slowly my breathing settled; my chest loos-
ened. Joan was an independent woman, not an invalid. She was
out with Reeny, that was all. Not like she had any other pals.
All I needed was for her to text me back and tell me she was
OK. That, and for Dougie to come home and give me a hug.
Then I'd be right as rain.

But when I checked my phone, I saw Joan had replied:

*I am quite well, thank you, Kirsty. There's no need to come to
the house. Regards, Joan.*

TEN

KIRSTY

It was too early to call in on Joan on my way out to work at 6.30 the next morning. Like most folk, she wouldn't be up for a good hour or two. The night before, I had stared at her message, eyes brimming, which was, I suspected, the third trimester hormone cocktail making me hypersensitive. Joan could be prickly, brittle sometimes, but she didn't mean it. That's all this was: Joan being Joan. She was simply of a generation that didn't go gushing about their feelings. And besides, tone was hard to read over text – that's why they'd invented emojis. Joan hated emojis; she thought they showed a lack of vocabulary.

I'd taken a deep breath and fired off a reply:

As long as you're OK. Xx

Once home, Dougie had allayed my fears again, told me it was very probably as I thought – that Joan and Reeny had gone out on a wee jaunt, an octogenarian Thelma and Louise. The idea did at least make me laugh.

After a thankfully shorter shift in Postnatal, I drove home to find Joan's car gone. No sign of the red car either. I felt my chest deflate with relief. At the back of my mind, I'd been worrying about her all day. It was unusual for her to be out in the late afternoon, especially in winter, but at least it meant she'd been home and gone out again. She was probably over at Reeny's or had popped into town for something.

Dougie was going out with some of the lads from the site that evening, so I took advantage, ate an early supper and tucked myself up in bed early with a true-crime drama on the iPad: the incredible story of a young lassie who disappeared late one night aged twelve and was found seven years later in a Spanish holiday resort working in a nightclub. Turned out her biological father, who no one knew existed on account of her mother never admitting that her husband wasn't the real dad, had got in touch and coerced the girl into fleeing the country. Once there, he had forced her to work in his club, and not only serving drinks.

His own flesh and blood, I thought, turning off the iPad. Such terrible things happen in the world and no one ever sees the clues until it's too late.

The pillow was soft. That lovely fresh bedding smell. Dougie had changed the sheets. What a star. I let myself drift into a field of flowers and felt it all fall away.

The 6.30 alarm on Saturday morning was brutal. Beside me, Dougie groaned. The bedroom stank of alcohol and stale garlic. I was almost overcome by a wave of nausea, but I kept it to myself. Dougie had been doing overtime on a project in a big house on Rubislaw Den to make some extra cash for the baby and deserved a night out. The fact that I couldn't go out on the ran-dan wasn't anyone's fault, and no one likes a judgemental Judy, do they?

Half an hour later, we were eating scrambled eggs in the kitchen. I didn't need to be out the door, but I was on call so I was dressed and ready to go should the hospital need me.

'Good night?' I asked, but Dougie, whose eyelids were

tombstones, was trying not to admit to being hung-over and said only:

'Few drinks, nothing too wild.'

Sensing Dougie just wanted to be quiet and eat, I chatted on about the documentary I'd watched, about Joan not being home the previous afternoon either.

'There's some weird things happening,' I said with a flourish. 'First Hughie, then Joan not being in the other night when it was zero degrees out, then the red car hanging about – did I tell you about that? Don't you think it's weird?' When there was no reply, I added, 'Only, on those documentaries you can never believe people didn't spot what was happening, d'you know what I mean? It's like there's always so many signs and no one sees them until it's too late. You're literally shouting at the telly sometimes. But I suppose none of us think we're in a documentary, do we? You don't think you're in some sort of crime drama; you're just living your life. But the signs are all around.'

Dougie looked up. 'Sorry, what?'

I threw a piece of kitchen roll across the table, but I was laughing as I teased, 'Honestly! I waste my breath!'

Once Dougie had left, I threw on Dad's puffer coat and wandered down to Joan's. Only to put my mind at rest. After that, I'd leave well alone. My ankle felt all but better, but I knew I should keep the weight off it as much as I could, especially while no one needed me up at the infirmary. Wendy's words came to me, my promise to rest and keep my feet raised.

Ah well. Wendy wasn't looking.

It was still dark out, and colder than a witch's tit, as the saying goes. Shivering already, teeth chattering, I checked I had my phone on me in case work rang. There were no messages, no missed calls. Secretly I hoped they wouldn't call me in. I could open one of my many unread books and put my feet up for real.

Joan's car wasn't on the drive again. I looked at my watch and saw it was not yet eight, early to be up on a Saturday, let alone out and about, even for Joan. The curtains were open. Had they been closed last night? I didn't know, hadn't thought to check.

A nervous feeling started up in my belly. The previous night, Joan's car not being there had been reassuring. That morning, not so much. Her behaviour was erratic at best; at worst, worrying. Had she even been home?

I wandered up the driveway and, without ringing the bell, peered in through the window. The sitting room looked the same. No, wait. It looked *exactly* the same. The same William Morris china mug that had been on the coffee table on Thursday was still there, in the exact same place.

I returned home feeling a bit sick and unsteady, unsure if I was overreacting or what. With Dougie out earning overtime and Tasha either at work or having a long lie like a normal person on a Saturday, I had no one to talk to, no one to tell me I was getting worried over nothing. Tasha didn't even know about fake Hughie yet. I wished I had Reeny's number. I would wait an hour then call Joan, just to be on the safe side. I checked my phone, in case I did have Reeny's number. But no, no Reeny. The number would be in Joan's address book in her hall table. I'd have to let myself in with the spare key to find it, and at that moment, letting myself into Joan's house without her permission felt like a step too far.

Back indoors and too antsy to settle, I decided to go to the beach. There was no way I could be pacing around my house like a hen on a hot girdle; I'd drive myself mad. Some fresh air and a change of scene would do me good. I'd take a walk and see if I could spot Joan's car at the harbour. Who knows, I might even see the woman herself, walking tall along the promenade, oblivious to her heavily pregnant neighbour having kittens on her behalf. Plus, one of my new mums lived in Footdee – Stella, who had fled an abusive relationship down in Glasgow shortly before having her baby and was still vulnerable. I could call in and see how she was getting on.

So my thoughts ran.

I hit the Esplanade and followed it down the length of the bay. To my left, the frigid North Sea reflected the low, rocky sky. To my right, the parade of cafés with Codona's fairground behind, memories of the waltzers, the roller coaster, milkshakes, ten-pin bowling, burgers and chips, Coke floats, hysterics, cheeky cigarettes, sticky toffee pudding, illicit swigs of whisky from Hughie's hip flask, candy floss, kisses. It all seemed so innocent now. It was, I supposed. I'd believed it was.

There was no sign of Joan's white Polo anywhere abouts. At that time on a winter's day, there weren't many cars at all. Not like it was sunbathing weather. Later, there would be some brave loon surfing the waves, but not for a while yet.

I took the road down the length of the promenade and round, left into New Pier Road at the back of Footdee, the collection of low houses that stood in two squares at the very edge of the land. Stella's house was in North Square and backed onto this road. I kept my eyes peeled, but Joan's car wasn't there either. A dull pang of worry tightened in my chest. Why was it, I thought, that my life was trundling along quite happily until I saw Hughie Reynolds' double, and since then, it was as if the world had tilted, making everything lean ever so slightly to one side? None of it was enough to shout about, but it still felt... well, odd.

I parked up and went to knock on Stella's door.

'Kirsty!' The pink in Stella's bleached-blonde hair had faded along with her bruises these last months, and pregnancy had left a layer of much-needed flesh on her bones. Without her heavy kohl and the foundation she used to cover the traces of her ex-partner's violence, she looked childlike, freckled, pretty. Her eyes were a beautiful green, with flecks of amber, gold and turquoise. Snug in a papoose on her chest, six-week-old baby

Luna slept. *The moon to my star*, Stella had whispered through tears, moments after the birth, gripping my hand so tight I thought my fingers would break.

'I was just passing,' I said. 'I'm on call but I thought I'd drop by and see how you and the wean were doing.'

Stella had been discharged weeks before, but she was one of those patients who'd got under my skin, and I didn't see the harm in visiting.

'Come in, come in,' she said, still beaming. 'It's great to see you, so it is.'

The small house was sparsely furnished with second-hand stuff, much of which I'd begged, stolen or borrowed from pals and brought over in Dougie's van when I heard about Stella's situation. On the wall in the sitting room hung a large square tie-dyed cloth Stella told me was called a mandala. The house was clean, the smell of fresh laundry in the air. I refused her offer of a coffee, not wanting to cause her any work, but she insisted and, sensing she really wanted to make me a drink, that it was a question of pride, I agreed to a decaf if she had it.

'Of course! It's what I drink these days too!' She was so bright with her new happiness, chattering on about baby Luna, how well she was doing, how she was right at home in the papoose. 'I can get everything I need done just by clipping her in and carrying her around the place!' she chuckled.

'That's great,' I said. 'But be careful you don't exhaust yourself, OK? Your health visitor will tell you the same. Your job is to sit about...'

'... like a cow and make milk.' Stella laughed. There weren't many years to separate me from this woman, only the tracks that ran across the landscapes our lives had dealt us. 'Don't worry,' she went on, 'I've got milk coming out of my ears. Well, not my ears obviously, but you know what I mean.'

We shared a wee giggle and settled with our coffees. It was such tender work, this. The work of women looking after one another – quietly, calmly, without fuss or judgement. I couldn't help but think of the welcome that awaited my own baby, the community of women that would be clucking around us like so many hens – my pals, my amazing colleagues in Maternity, my mum – even Joan.

'I was out looking out for my neighbour actually,' I said. 'I've been a wee bit worried about her because she was really out of sorts the other day... When was it? Wednesday, I think. And then Thursday, her car was there but she wasn't, and yesterday her car wasn't there, and it wasn't there again this morning. Only, she's religious about her daily constitutionals, as she calls them. Her five thousand steps, taking the sea air, rain or shine, so I thought I might see her hereabouts. Only she's quite elderly now and—'

'Wait.' Stella put down her mug on the white square IKEA coffee table. 'Is that the old lady who walks by the sea?' In her Glasgow accent the words sounded wistful, poetic, like the title of an old novel.

'Might be. Tall. Thin. Long, I mean. Walks very straight, like... like someone's holding her head from above by a string.'

'Aye, that's right. Does she drive a white car? A Volkswagen?'

'She does, aye.'

'I know her! She parks just here behind the house. I see her sometimes when I'm out with Luna. She always stops and passes the time of day.'

My heart quickened. 'Have you seen her this morning?'

Stella shook her head. She stood up and wandered over to the back window. 'If she was here, her car would be on this road. I wave at her sometimes. Thursday morning I think I last saw her, but definitely not yesterday. I was in town doing my messages.' She frowned, coming back to the sofa and sitting down.

'So you saw her Thursday? You're sure?'

'Yes, Thursday, right enough. She seemed a wee bit agitated. Out of sorts, like you said.'

'I'm sure it's nothing to worry about.' I tried not to let my voice betray my quickening pulse. 'It's just, she doesn't have family and not that many friends either. She has me and her friend Reeny and that's about it, so far as I know. I suppose she might have relatives she's never told me about. She's not exactly a chatterbox, you might say, but I suppose you get to know folk over time, don't you? You pick up bits and pieces, often from what they're not saying. I saw a picture of a lassie once in her bedroom when she was in bed with COVID the other year, but I didn't like to pry because, well, because the photo wasn't in the sitting room, so I assumed... and of course she wasn't well, so I...' I stopped, aware that I'd started to blether on. 'I might call by her friend's house,' I said. 'Reeny's round the corner from me in Gray Street, though I'm not sure which number. I'll go there now.'

But as I stood to leave, my phone buzzed. Work.

'I'll go later,' I said, to myself more than Stella, as I texted my reply. 'That's me being called in.'

ELEVEN

KIRSTY

The shift was long. Every time I thought I was going to be let away, I was pulled back in. One poor lassie had had to have an emergency C-section after twenty hours of labour when the cord became tangled around the baby's neck. She arrived at Postnatal shattered and pale, but by the time I left, she was sitting up in bed with a strong cup of tea and a couple of Rich Tea biscuits, baby out for the count in the crib beside her.

'Thanks for everything,' she said when I stopped to say goodbye for the day.

'There's no need to thank me,' I said. 'Just doing my job.'

I grabbed Dad's coat and my bag and headed for the main entrance. By this point, I was fantasising about a hot bath, supper with Dougie and bed.

But as I crossed the threshold, the man who looked like Hughie passed me on his way in. This time he was dressed not in scrubs but smart jeans, a woolly hat and a black North Face puffer coat.

My chest tightened. My skin burned.

'Hughie?' His name came out in a strangled whimper. I'd said it aloud even though I knew it wasn't him and despite my humiliation only days before. But I couldn't help myself. And another thing: I could've sworn he hesitated. It was a second, less than, but I saw it – at the sound of his name, he faltered. But he'd already gone by and now he was heading into the body of the infirmary.

I couldn't move. All I could do was stand on the pavement outside main reception, quivering, unable to go to my car, unable to follow him inside, unable to do anything at all.

I don't know how much time passed. It might have been minutes, it might have been seconds, but eventually I unglued the soles of my shoes from the tarmac and shambled into the foyer. I lumbered past reception, deliberating at the T-junction before continuing in the direction of Anaesthesiology. At the lift, the floor numbers lit up. I pressed the call button and waited. The numbers counted themselves down, electric green, painfully slow. Ground floor. The lift pinged. The doors rolled open. I stared into the empty metal cube. Another ping and the doors rolled shut. The numbers ascended once again. I was still standing on the shiny linoleum, muttering curses.

What was the point? What was I going to do, track him down and embarrass myself again, this time in front of a crowd of my colleagues? Why had I even followed him? His name was Barry Sefton. He wasn't Hughie. He. Was. Not.

Except he was. I knew it. Even if I didn't understand it, I knew it in my bones.

My heart was still battering in my chest when I called Tasha. I was marching towards my car, phone clamped to my ear.

'Kirsty,' she said, sounding pleased to hear from me. 'How're you getting on? How's the bump? How's Dougie?'

'Fine, all fine. Something super weird has happened. Actually, it happened on Wednesday, but it's just happened again. Do you remember Hughie Reynolds?'

'Of course. Wee shite. Why? Come back from the dead, has he?'

'Well...'

I told her about the first sighting, gave her all the embarrassing details.

'He's using the name Barry Sefton,' I said finally. 'He's an anaesthetist.'

'Barry Sefton?' Tasha asked, gratifyingly incredulous. 'So it was him or it wasna?'

'I've just seen him again. I called after him and I swear to God he stopped. But then he carried on, and I didn't want to make a show of myself a second time. I'm up to high doh with it all. Honestly, if you'd seen him... Do you think I'm a stalker?'

She laughed. 'Listen, I'm at work.' As if to prove her point, a telephone rang in the background. 'Hold on and let me have a wee lookie on his LinkedIn. Barry Sefton, you said, yeah? Hold on.'

I'd been so fixated on Hughie that I hadn't thought to google Barry Sefton. While Tasha searched, I called myself an idiot a few times and got into the car. It was an effort to slide behind the steering wheel. Really, I needed blocks on the pedals. Down the line, I could hear Tasha's fingers tapping on the keys.

'I know this has got nothing to do with anything,' I said, 'but my elderly neighbour's gone missing.'

'Your who now?'

'Joan... you know Joan, who lives in the bungalow next-door-but-one? The one I call in on most days.'

'Hair like Grace Kelly except white?'

'Aye. Except I haven't seen her since Wednesday.'

'And she's definitely missing?'

'Not definitely, no. She just wasn't in on Thursday evening even though her car was there, and she wasn't in yesterday either. A girl I know saw her Thursday morning, but her car has come and gone at funny hours. Plus, she sent me a weird text. Well, not weird, but rude. No, not rude, more... brusque. But she can be quite brusque, to be honest...' The more I spoke, the more I wondered if I was worrying about nothing.

'Old folk are a law unto themselves. My gran's always going AWOL, and she never takes her phone. Maybe if you don't hear anything over the weekend, call social services? Does she have any rellies?'

'Not so far as I know. She has a pal called Reeny. And me.'

'What's her name again?'

'Joan Wood. She's eighty-one.'

'I'll keep my ear to the ground, but try not to worry. If you've heard from her, she's probably just being a wee bit dotty. She's bound to turn up with some tale or other. I'll let you know if I hear anything, OK?'

'Thanks. Maybe we should get Gus and Callum out for a drink next week?'

'Aye, let's do that. We can reminisce about Hughie Reynolds and his mystery disappearance. Unless you don't want to? Sorry, that was tactless.'

'Not at all.' I half laughed. 'Water under the bridge. Did you ever go to his house, by the way? I've been thinking back and I realise I never did. He always came to ours.'

'I canna remember. I just remember we all thought he was the bee's knees, didn't we? I was a wee bit jealous when you and him got together.'

'Were you?' I'd had no idea.

'I didna fancy him exactly, but...'

'... he had something about him,' I filled in. 'The whole air-of-mystery thing.'

'And he could roll a doobie one-handed like a rock star. We thought that was so cool.'

'Funny what you think's cool at seventeen. These days I'm

all about someone who can make a decent casserole and fix a leaking tap.'

'I know.' Tasha giggled. 'Scott reset the boiler the other day and I was putty in his hands.'

'What I can't get over,' I said, 'is how someone so cool can be so fusty by the age of thirty. You shoulda seen the jeans, Tasha. Stonewash. Like something my dad would wear.'

'Your da is one very stylish gent,' Tasha said, giggling again but almost immediately stopping. 'Hang on. I've got him. Dr Barry Sefton. He's on LinkedIn.' A pause extended down the line. 'I'm nae sure,' she said quietly, as if to herself. 'Something around the eyes, I suppose, but like he hasn't slept in weeks. I can see why you thought it was him, but nah. Let's see...'

'Could it be him?' I asked after a moment, my chest tightening.

'Ah... nah.'

My heart kind of dropped. I don't know how to explain it even now, but I felt... disappointed.

'Nah,' Tasha went on. 'Let's see. Nah. Nah.'

'Tash? Are you going to keep reading it to yourself and saying nah?'

She gave a chuckle. 'Sorry. So. You ready? Medical degree from UCL, practised at Edinburgh Infirmary 2007 to 2009 and then the American Hospital in Dubai from 2010 to 2023. Aberdeen Infirmary December 2023, two months ago. It's not him, doll. Not a chance. If he graduated before 2007, he'll be well into his forties by now. I can't really see Hughie in him, to be honest. Maybe he just reminded you of him.'

I had been so sure. I had no idea where this information left me. It wasn't news though, was it? I already knew it wasn't Hughie. It wasn't. It just wasn't. After all that stress, it wasn't him.

And yet...

'Hormones playing tricks,' Tasha said.

'I'll pretend I didn't hear that.'

It was after six by the time we ended the call. I was still dejected. I suppose I had a sense of anticlimax. It wasn't that I'd wanted Hughie to be back in town, more that I'd wanted the instincts I'd worked so hard to trust again to be right. Ironic, that the boy who'd blown my confidence in my own judgement the first time had turned up in the form of a man who'd shattered it all over again.

And that man wasn't even him.

I found Barry Sefton on LinkedIn and pored over the photograph. To my eyes, this was Hughie – fatter, older and bald, but him absolutely, one hundred per cent. But I could see how Tasha could have looked at that image and not seen the resemblance. To cheer myself up, I sent a message to my school pals WhatsApp group:

Anyone free for a drink next week before I pop?

It'd been a while since we'd seen each other. They were all obviously bored, because the replies came in almost immediately and were variations on the theme of *Hell, yeah!* We settled on Tuesday evening, seven o'clock in Under the Hammer.

It felt like the first normal thing to have happened in the last couple of days.

Of course, I wasn't to know then how the evening would end up.

TWELVE

HUGHIE

HR/audio/excerpt #3

Let's roll back the years. Just for fun. We've got time to kill and it won't take too long, my little KK. I can picture you as if it were yesterday, with your pint of sweet cider, sharing a girly giggling fit with your feisty sidekick Tasha. Kirsty Shaw, queen of the Coke float and champion consumer of sticky toffee pudding at the Inversnecky Café. The girl I taught to blow smoke rings in the dunes at Balmedie Beach, helped get her first passport, roll her first joint. The girl I taught to kiss.

When I saw you, swollen and rosy with late pregnancy, I have to admit the memories came gushing in like the rapids on Codona's log flume. Like that, I was back in the school yard. My first day, beside myself with nerves, longing for all the world to turn and run; and you, so curious, asking me where I was from, what my name was, did I know anyone. Me, with the elegant Edinburgh vowels that would fade by the hour, telling you about my parents dying in a house fire. A backstory straight out of a Gothic novel, save for the fact that I'd been pulled from the inferno. I had the fire-damaged skin and hair to prove it. Little did I realise that girls are suckers for a sob story.

And there I am, four years later, a jealous rage rising up from my feet as I compare your grades with my own, knowing that after four years of hard work and mind-bending stress, I was back in the mud where I belonged while you, you, the less intelligent, if you don't mind my saying, were off to uni to follow your dreams. Everything was always so easy for you and you didn't even know it. I bet Mummy and Daddy were delighted. I bet they took you out to celebrate with your snotty little brother. I'm guessing you went to Edinburgh because that's where you'd set your heart.

It all went to plan for you, didn't it? As it was always going to.

I just wish you'd been a good wee lassie and left me alone. Why couldn't you have left the past where it was? Why couldn't you have let me be? We had some good times, back in the day. I mean no offence when I say I wish I'd never seen you again. I never wanted to, we both know that, but I did. It's almost enough to make me feel bad for everything that's happened since.

Almost.

None of this is my fault, after all.

No, Kirsty. This one's on you.

THIRTEEN

KIRSTY

KS/transcript #10

Driving home, progress was slow, the sky black above the orange haze of the city. My eyelids were drooping. Every time I thought I couldn't be more tired, I hit a new point of exhaustion. My head felt like a bowling ball, my neck a matchstick. The worry over Hughie and Joan had hardened now to a rock of anxiety inside me. Maybe all it was, I thought, was my body announcing that I needed to rest in readiness for my baby to come along. My life hadn't turned upside down, not really.

But it was about to.

On Union Street, the traffic was at a complete standstill. I huffed and turned off the engine, unable to stop myself mulling over that guy looking so like Hughie, even if Tasha hadn't been able to see it. But even if it had been him, there'd never been any need to react in the way I had. It wasn't as if he was here to harm me, was it? And there was nothing to say I had to have anything more to do with him. People were easily avoided, if you wanted to avoid them. I needed to stay calm and keep my

mind on Dougie and the baby. I had lost focus, and I felt bad
about that now. Two more shifts, that's all I had to do, and I
could put my feet up and wait for this bun to come out of its
oven.

I called Dougie.

'Hey, babe. What you up to?'

'I'm making Douglas Saturday Stew.'

'That's a thing?'

'It will be. I got sausages from Herd's. It's a... OK, so it's
basically a sausage casserole.' Dougie laughed.

'We need to get on with the nursery,' I said, humourless,
sharp – blurting it out for reasons lost to me. 'I can't order the
carpet until we've painted the walls.'

'Good God, give me a chance, woman.' Dougie gave another
laugh, softer this time.

'I'm sorry. Sorry, that was... naggy. I'm a bit... I saw that guy
again.'

'Hughie Lewis not the news?' Bless Dougie, trying so hard
to keep my spirits up with a lame dad joke.

'Hughie Loser and the News,' I drawled.

'Damn. Yours was better. So you saw him?'

'No. Yes. I mean, no.'

'Glad we got that cleared up.'

I gave an exhausted laugh. The car in front moved. I
restarted the engine and pulled forward.

'Tasha looked him up on LinkedIn,' I said.

'What, Hughie?'

'No, Barry Sefton.'

'Right.'

'He's in his forties, for Christ's sake. He graduated while we
were still fighting acne.'

'Well, at least you can relax now.'

'I suppose.' Except I hadn't, not by a long shot. 'By the way,
you've not seen any sign of Joan, have you?'

'No, sorry. I'm only just back myself.'

I sighed. 'I dropped in on one of my mums today. She lives up at the beach and she sees Joan every day.'

'Wait, what? I thought you were supposed to be putting your feet up?'

I felt myself blush. Busted.

'I was,' I said. 'I mean, I did, but I was at the harbour and...'

'And what were you doing at the harbour?'

I said nothing. I couldn't think of anything to say.

Dougie gave an exasperated sigh. 'Please tell me you weren't...'

'I just thought I'd have a wee look for Joan's car, that's all. And then I saw Stella at the window, so I... I called in for a chat.'

'But she's a patient! Honestly, that's so above and beyond, it's—'

'Anyway,' I interrupted, 'Stella, that's her name, she hasn't seen Joan since Thursday morning, and she said she seemed agitated. I told you she was agitated, didn't I? When I saw her on Wednesday? I'm starting to think something isn't right.'

'Bee...'

'I'm not being Bee, I promise. There's no bee and no bonnet, just me worrying about my elderly neighbour, that's all. With genuine reason at this point, I think. Have you seen a red sports car driving about?'

'Kirst, stop! Stop, OK? There's no red car. You're stressed. You're hormonal and you must be absolutely knackered. You've been on the go since half six this morning and you're doing all of that while carrying another human being around the place. Don't start putting two and two together and getting five.'

'I'm not. Honestly I'm not. Only I looked into Joan's sitting room and her mug was in exactly the same place on the coffee table as it was on Thursday. Like, *exactly* the same place! That's weird, isn't it?'

'Oh, darlin'.' Dougie sighed. 'A mug on a coffee table doesn't mean she's been... I mean, what is it you think's happened to her? She's been abducted by aliens? Whisked into a black limo by the Aberdeen mafia?'

I thought of Tasha, all those years ago, taking the mick. Why was it always aliens who did the abducting? 'Don't,' I said. 'Please. I don't know what I think, only I...'

'I'm not taking the piss, I promise. I mean, I am a bit, but only to get you to take a step back and see you're winding yourself up. Remember that time you called the police about the squatters at number thirty-nine?'

I felt the heat of another blush climbing up my neck. I did call the police. And it turned out the neighbours had gone abroad for a year and rented out their house. The 'squatters' were in fact tenants.

'I get it,' I said. 'I'm tired. I am. I thought I'd have some time today to chill. I went to the beach, OK, maybe a wee bit to find Joan's car but also to clear my head, and I just happened to see Stella, and then I got called into work and it was really busy and now the day has gone and the traffic is gridlocked and—'

'Hey. Hey. It's OK, babe. You don't have to account for yourself, OK? I just don't want you worrying over nothing, that's all. I don't want you stressing yourself. Joan will be fine. The red car is a red herring – see what I did there, red car, red herring?'

I rolled my eyes, but I was already smiling. 'Groan.'

'If the car was anything,' Dougie went on, 'I'd have seen it again. Do you know what I think? I think seeing that bastard has flipped you out. You've not been yourself since. You've been jumpy. Paranoid, like. I understand. It sounds horrible, what he did. And you're sensitive. It's why I love you so much. But you're with me now, and I'm not going to just up and leave, OK? Believe me, I know how lucky I am. You are one in a million, and I will never, ever leave you, Kirsty Shaw. I promise. Do you hear me? There is no mirage here. There's us. And we're as real as it gets.'

Tears were dropping off my chin. 'Maybe I am a bit jumpy.'

'Come home.' Dougie's voice was full of kindness. 'You need a hot supper and a good long sleep.'

'OK. I'm two minutes away. Love you.'

'Love you too.'

I rang off and wept with sleepy gratitude. Dougie had understood things I hadn't understood myself, seen the deep fear at the heart of me, a fear I now saw so clearly. It was obvious. The whole thing with Hughie had left me shell-shocked, numb and afraid back when I was little more than a kid. I thought I'd moved on, and I had, but somewhere deep down, something had festered inside me. Fear. Fear of history repeating itself, maybe. Was it possible that without really knowing it, I'd been afraid Dougie too would just up and disappear, leaving only a cruel note? After all, I knew from bitter experience that it was possible for a person to do that to another person. And if it had happened once, it could happen twice, couldn't it?

But Dougie wasn't Hughie. And now I thought about it, maybe my fears had been made so much more intense by the loss of control I felt over my own body. This life growing inside me I had to protect at all costs. In that moment, it seemed to me that pregnancy was the first lesson in giving up control. It was chaos, physically and emotionally, and learning to submit to it was surely a kind of training for the greater chaos to come.

Yes. It made sense. Lookalike Hughie had freaked me out – that's what this was. I'd been blindsided at the precise moment I found myself truly vulnerable again. Let's face it, I thought as I pulled into the close: huge as I was, I wouldn't be able to run for my life or help anyone in a crisis. But I needed to trust that

Dougie would be there for me and our child. I had to believe that, Joan's memory not being what it was, she'd simply gone to see friends or family, had forgotten to mention it and would in all likelihood be fine. And that the flashy red car was just some random person who had got lost.

Joan's car was still not on her driveway.

I drove past, staring at the empty space as if to magic the white Polo into being. And despite Dougie, despite all my rationalising, the car's absence brought a flutter to my chest. I parked at the end of Joan's driveway and waddled up to her front door. I rang on the doorbell, knocked, called through the letter box: 'Joan? Joanie, darlin'? You in there, pet?'

There was no sign of life. I walked over to the window. In the sitting room, the mug was still exactly where it had been. I gasped. It was Saturday night. Where the hell was she? And why weren't the curtains closed now that it was dark? Throat thick, I walked as fast as I was able round to the back of the house. I narrowed my eyes and peered into Joan's shadowy bedroom. It felt nosy to do that, weird, but I stared in anyway. Inside was nothing but dark shapes. I could make out the bed, perfectly made. Empty. I tried the back door, but it was locked.

Back around the front, I rang at Joan's next-door neighbours, Rab and Nancy. Rab answered, in his slippers, one shirt button popped open, an ellipse of pink, hairy belly. He hadn't seen Joan for a day or two, he told me. A few days, come to think of it. No, he hadn't seen any visitors come to the house. I thanked him and wandered back down to the road. Hands on hips, I looked up and down the crescent, searching for what, I didn't know. An old lady. A showy red car. Hughie Reynolds swaggering along, whistling a tune. Something. Anything. An end to this weirdness.

Did I think about calling the police? I did, but it was all still too flimsy, so I rang Joan instead. When there was no answer, I texted:

Hiya, Joan. It's only me, Kirsty. Not seen your car for a couple of days so perhaps you've gone away for a day or two. Can you let me know you're OK when you get this?

I was still standing on the street outside her house, still nailed to the spot with worry, when her reply buzzed in:

Everything is fine, thank you.

FOURTEEN

KIRSTY

I read that text three times. It wasn't that the message was rude. It wasn't that Joan had said anything outlandish. But it just wasn't *right*. There was no explanation as to her whereabouts, no attempt to reassure me, no acknowledgement of Thursday's arrangement, nothing, just that robotic *Everything is fine, thank you*. I couldn't put my finger on anything other than to say: it just wasn't like Joan.

Pressing my lips tight, I composed a reply:

Joan, I'm sorry if you feel I'm being nosy, but you weren't in when I called the other day and usually you would let me know if you were going to be out.

I read it back. Texts are so hard to get right at the best of times, and this one sounded aggressive. I deleted it before replacing it with:

As long as you're OK, I'll leave you in peace, but you can't stop me keeping an eye on you! X

Better. Lighter. I'm used to keeping my own feelings out of situations and I knew I had to do that now. Joan was feisty, clever, funny, physically fit, but she was on her own, she was in her eighties and her mind wasn't what it was. As such, she was vulnerable. This wasn't about me; it was about safeguarding. I couldn't afford to forget that.

A text from Dougie chimed in:

Hey. Where've you got to? Tea ready.

I texted back: *Soz! There in 2. Xx*

I got back into the car to drive the few metres to my own house. From inside, the sitting-room lamp gave out a soft vanilla glow. I couldn't see indoors, but I could imagine Dougie pottering about, setting the table, after going to the butcher's earlier specially in order to make something warm and comforting for us both. For all three of us, I thought, giving the bump a wee stroke and turning off the engine. In the well under the dashboard, my phone lit up. I picked it up, saw a text from Joan and sighed with relief. Whatever the cranky old bird had to say, at least she was alive. I opened the message and read:

There really is no cause for concern.

I frowned, fighting back the urge to cry. I felt like I'd been told off. Tried to think if I could have offended her in some way I hadn't even been aware of. Maybe that comment about her driving had really hacked her off. Maybe she was sick of me calling in all the time, treating her like an invalid. If not, what had got into her? All these years, we'd been more than neighbours; we'd been friends, real friends. In case it isn't obvious, I loved that grumpy old stick. But this? It was as if we were strangers, as if I were some pain in the neck she was trying to shake off.

Tears came. Wiping them roughly aside, I trudged wearily towards the house. I was halfway in with my key when the door opened. I fell into Dougie's arms and wept.

. . .

The house was toasty but I couldn't stop shivering. A delicious savoury smell filled the kitchen – meat, spices, buttery spuds. Dougie poured me a small glass of Guinness and told me to drink it, that it was full of iron, that it wouldn't do me any harm at this stage. I sipped, my hands shaking, tears still trickling down my cheeks. Brushing them away like the annoyance they were, I went through all the latest events while Dougie listened, without once interrupting. Together we read Joan's recent messages.

'I can't believe I'm getting so upset about some stupid old woman,' I said. 'I don't mean that. You know what I mean. Joan's not stupid. And she's not just some old woman either. I'm just cross and a bit gutted, if I'm honest. I can't believe she'd respond to me like this.' I grabbed some kitchen roll and mopped more tears away, blew my nose.

'Dementia is a cruel illness,' Dougie said, loading the steaming stew onto my plate. 'And loved ones always end up in the firing line unfortunately. It's because you're so close that she's being so blunt. Have some mash. Come on – you need to eat.'

The stew was hot, too hot. Mouth watering, I held my head over the steam, took a forkful, blew as cool as I could, impatient to eat.

I took my first mouthful and closed my eyes, almost bursting into fresh tears, this time of gratitude. I know I keep saying it, but I really was so tired, so, so tired. 'This is the best stew I have ever eaten. Thank you, darlin'. You're the best.'

Dougie smiled and winked. 'Eat.'

For a moment, we were silent, focused. I could feel the fuel hitting my system, raising my blood sugar, bringing me back to life.

'It must be so hard for the families,' I said once I'd eaten almost half my plateful. 'Like, if I were her daughter. I mean, I feel like her daughter sometimes and that's why it's so... shocking. But at least I know she's OK. OK physically at least. Still doesn't answer where she's got to though. It's so weird.'

'Sounds like she's becoming a wee bit paranoid. Like she's forgotten how much she relies on you or how often you drop in.'

'Did I tell you she was talking about seeing someone? In her house?'

'You thought it was her late husband? Lachlan, was it?'

'But what if it wasn't in her head? What if it wasn't Lachlan at all? What if someone *did* come to her house that day? A man? Could – and don't dismiss me on this – could whoever was at Joan's be whoever was in that red sports car?'

Dougie frowned, chewing slowly as if figuring out how to respond.

'Because I'd never seen that car before,' I added, before there was any mention of bees or bonnets. 'The only car I've ever seen at Joan's is Reeny's yellow Nissan.'

'The red car wasn't at Joan's though, was it? It was parked in the road.'

'I know but it was kind of opposite, and it just seems too much of a coincidence that Joan was in a state that day and there was a red car lurking about outside her house. I've seen her distracted, yes, but not going on about someone else, not telling me she'd seen Lachie's ghost.'

Dougie gave a slow, pensive nod. 'I think you're right. In that it is a coincidence. But that's all it is. We've nae seen the red car since, have we? And it wasna opposite Joan's; it was opposite ours. Joan's proud. Old school. Perhaps she knows she's losing her marbles and doesna want anyone seeing her like that. She could be poorly. Have you checked she's not up at the infirmary having a procedure or something? I reckon, wherever she is, she just doesna want you to see her not at her best.'

'But she's not even there to see, best or no!'

'Well, perhaps she doesna want to be a burden. She might've taken herself off somewhere to be looked after. You

said she's affa private. She might have pals out of town you
dinna know about. I know you know her and you love her, but
how much do you know about her really? She's of that generation, isn't she? They dinna like to hang out their dirty laundry
for all to see. Maybe you *should* back off a wee bit. Don't go
round if she doesna want you to.' Dougie reached over the table
and took my hand. 'You're exhausting yourself trying to help
everyone all the time. You took your mum up to have her eye
done the other day. You call in on clients on your days off.
You're up ladders getting lazy bollocks' cat for her...'

A laugh broke from me, despite it all. 'Lazy bollocks!'

Dougie's grin softened, flattened. 'Do you think maybe...
with the texts... maybe it's about that note from Hughie? Like,
the note is maybe fresh in your mind?'

'How do you mean?'

'Well, that letter made you doubt things, didn't it? Back
then. Made you doubt your judgement. And these texts from
Joan...'

I nodded slowly, understanding dawning. 'I see what you're
getting at. Like, the texts are making me doubt my friendship
with Joan? Like history repeating? That's clever. You should be
a therapist!'

Never one to accept a compliment, Dougie gave a sardonic
eye-roll and pulled a silly face. 'So, maybe thinking you saw that
bastard up at the hospital and coming home and reading that
note again, you've subconsciously put all the random things
together and you're trying to find a connection.'

'Well, it did all start happening at the same time.'

'It did. But in reality, it's completely separate. This consultant guy, Joan going AWOL and an unfamiliar sports car...
they're three different things. I don't see any link, but someone
more spiritual, say, might see signs. Maybe Joan disappearing' –
Dougie made air quotes around the word *disappearing* – 'got
somehow connected in your brain with that prick *disappearing*

back in the day. And now she's sent some texts that are a wee bit strange or not like her or whatever, well, it's back to the letter, isn't it? Making you doubt things. Like you say, your understanding of your friendship, who you are to one another.'

'I'm making a connection to something that floored me when I was younger and that's why it's getting me so rattled.'

Dougie smiled tenderly. 'You're tired. Hormones buzzing about all over the place. The baby'll be here soon and you're coping with all that too. It's scary. I'm scared! But you need to look after yourself and the bump, OK? You can't be everything to everyone. You can't be everyone's best friend.'

Everything Dougie had said made perfect sense. But still, without really knowing why, I wasn't one hundred per cent convinced.

'Tell you what,' Dougie said, heaping another dollop of stew onto both our plates. 'If the old bird's texting, she has to be somewhere, so you can at least stop worrying about that. What are we, Saturday? OK, so if we don't see her by tomorrow night, we'll call her again. And if she doesna pick up, we'll use the spare key and make sure she's not in, and if she's not in, we'll call the police, OK?'

'That's what Tasha said.' I searched Dougie's face, wondering what the reaction would be to what I was about to say. 'But will you come over to Joan's with me later tonight? I just want... I'd feel better if I checked inside the house tonight rather than tomorrow. Just in case she's unwell or something.'

Eyes closing, Dougie visibly suppressed an exasperation that was, at its core, affectionate, protective.

'Doug? Douglewoogs? Light of my life? Star of my sky? Diamond of—'

'All right! All right.'

Despite it all, at least we could make each other laugh.

FIFTEEN

KIRSTY

After dinner, Dougie went upstairs to grab a shower, feet heavy on the threadbare stair carpet we'd start saving to replace once we'd sorted the nursery. I lay on the sofa and put on a true-crime documentary on Netflix. It was called *Delivering Death* and was about a serial killer in the Cotswolds. I drifted off, woke up as the mystery was being revealed. No one suspected the milkman, no one at all, until the police made a vital connection: all the victims had their milk delivered. They arrested the milkman, but it turned out it was actually the postman, who got caught on one of those ringtone doorbells with a hidden camera. The postie was injecting the milk on the front step with fatal quantities of opioids harvested from his late mother's sleeping pills.

No one noticed the pinprick in the foil tops.

'Evil,' I whispered to myself as the programme ended. I would never get milk delivered, not after seeing that. Or letters, for that matter. I checked my watch. It was quarter to ten. I'd let myself doze off and now it was late. Where the heck had Dougie got to?

Rousing myself, I called up: 'Dougie? I'm away to Joan's. Are you coming?'

No reply. Unease flashed, so near the surface of me. But when I got upstairs, I found Dougie asleep on the bed still dressed in work scruffs and snoring like a lawnmower. I laughed softly, but at the same time, I was kicking myself for panicking like that. What was wrong with me? I seemed to be swithering between panic attacks and bursting into tears like a teenager. It was a good thing I was finishing work very soon.

Back downstairs, Dougie's words came back to me. *Maybe it's about that note. Seeing that guy.* There was some truth in it. I did feel very like I had back then: sad, scared and confused, the sense of what was real sliding about, the same protectiveness of my family, this time my family-to-be.

I grabbed Joan's key from the spare key drawer. I have a key for all but two of my neighbours, all of them with sticky paper labels with their names attached. Dougie used to tease me for getting too involved with folk, but it's me they come to when they need their plants watering or their cats feeding – or helping down from the drainpipe. *They* come to *me* – not the reverse!

Joan's car still wasn't on her driveway. My breath caught. It was almost ten at night. Surely not even Dougie would tell me that was normal? It was midwinter. Joan was practically a hermit. I didn't think I'd seen her with anyone other than Reeny. The only explanation now was that she was staying with friends she'd never mentioned to me, or...

Or what? Did I think she'd been kidnapped? Yes, I did actually. I did. I shook the thought away before it could form, but it formed anyway: Joan, bound and gagged, eyes wide with terror, thrown into the boot of a car. I shivered.

From inside her bungalow, the pale light of a lamp shone out. The light was on – yes – but the curtains weren't drawn. OK, so it wasn't a dead body in the bathroom, but the feeling of panic tingled all over my skin. You don't put the lights on and leave the curtains open, do you? At least you don't when it's properly dark out. Scalp prickling, I walked slowly up the driveway, wondering now if I should go back and get Dougie to come in with me. There was so obviously someone in Joan's house. But I wasn't sure it was Joan.

I was almost at the front door when the light went out.

A squeal of fear escaped me. My heart battered fit to explode right out of my chest. I was halfway home before I remembered Joan had a security lamp. I swore out loud. I'd set the timer myself to go on at seven and off at ten if she wasn't there to override it. That explained why the light was on but the curtains were open – it had come on automatically. I made myself breathe out, but no sooner had the air left me than I stopped again in my tracks. I could feel the creasing of my brow, another roll of nerves in my belly. The lamp shouldn't need a timer, should it? Not on a winter's evening. Joan was always at home on a winter's evening. She would have drawn the curtains. And overridden the timer.

There was no one in that house.

I had seen her car come and go, but I hadn't physically laid eyes on her since Wednesday.

As fast as my swollen feet would take me, I waddled back up her driveway. I was wheezing, my heart beating much quicker than I would've liked. I should be in bed, I thought. I should have been in bed hours before, but I couldn't rest. How could I with all that going on? Steeling myself, I pressed a hand to the glass and peered through the living-room window.

At the sight of the mug still in exactly the same place, I yelped.

I checked the back. But Joan wasn't in her bedroom. She wasn't in the kitchen. I couldn't see into the bathroom, but unless she was peeing in the pitch-dark, then she wasn't in there either. A flashing image: Joan collapsed on the bathroom floor, cold, dead for days. I gasped with fear. It felt so wrong to go in, but if she'd had a stroke or a heart attack, it could well have happened in the bathroom – it was very common.

I returned to the front, let myself in and switched on the hall light. Listened. To silence, absolute silence. I headed straight for the bathroom and opened the door. I didn't need to go in to see there was no one there. I hesitated. To snoop around the rest of the house felt intrusive. I could see well enough from the windows to know that the other rooms were empty. Dougie had said we should wait out the weekend before calling the police.

But still. I was here now.

I pushed open the bedroom door. I didn't go in, just looked in from the hallway. The bed was made, as I knew it would be. I went back up the hallway. The living-room door was already open. I peered inside. The chair, the coffee table, the mug: all as it had been. I retraced my steps and let myself out.

Outside, the night was starry. My fingertips were ice cold and had gone deep pink in the sub-zero air. I walked home disconsolate, as if I, not Joan, were lost to the dark night. My premonition of her collapsed was just that: an instinct, a sense of foreboding, a *feeling* – nothing more.

SIXTEEN

KIRSTY

KS/transcript #13

It was after four the following afternoon. Sunday. Dougie was just home from a fishing trip with my dad and some of the lads from work, kitbag slung over one shoulder, rods clutched in the opposite hand.

There had been no sign of Joan this morning when I'd called round, but I didn't text for fear of annoying her. I was keen to call the police but had hung back on that too. Better to let Dougie get in the door and clean the fish and wait until we were settled with a hot drink before broaching the subject. Looking back, I realise that calling the police was a step I didn't want to take. There was erratic behaviour and a certain brusque tone in her texts, but at the same time, nothing in Joan's house had been taken. There was no sign of any kind of struggle. When I imagined telling the police about a William Morris mug on a table, it sounded beyond stupid. And something else too: if I called the police, I would be admitting that Joan wasn't simply out of town, and that felt too dark for the reality I was living in just then.

'Good catch?' I asked as I filled the kettle.

'Not bad. Cod. Five pounds or so. We can have it tomorrow.' From its plastic sheath, the fish slithered into the kitchen sink, mercury bright. Dougie traced the tip of the gutting knife down its silver belly. A line of blood leaked thick and red.

I made the tea and took mine over to the table to sit down. Dougie was quiet, I noticed. Quieter than usual.

'Did you have a good day?' I asked. 'Any craic?'

'There was a floater today actually.'

I almost didn't catch the words because Dougie's back was turned towards me. It took me a moment to grasp the sense. When it hit, I stood up, too shocked to sit, and moved back to the sink.

'Doug?' I said, nausea rising, the feeling that I was choking. 'Did you just tell me there was a body in the water? In the sea, you mean?'

'I did, aye. Off the harbour.' Guts oozed silently, piling crimson and slick against grey steel.

'What?' The word was little more than a breath. 'You can't come in and tell me there was a... a body and just carry on!' Hysteria chimed a shrill note in my voice. I had spent the entire weekend fretting, wondering whether to text Joan again or call or check her house more thoroughly or go round to Reeny's or go to the police or do any damn thing, only for Dougie to placate me, to tell me to wait, and now I was being told there was a *dead body* in the water?

Poor, shrinking Dougie turned to face me and leant against the sink, knife in one hand, the fingers of the other coated in blood. 'I'm sorry. I shouldna have said that. As soon as I said it, I realised. I didna mean to upset you, babe. I'm sorry I said floater – that was... it was insensitive. I shoulda said body or person or whatever. I shoulda kept it to myself, with you being like this. I shouldna have told you.'

'Being like what? Shouldn't have what? Told me there was a

dead body in the water when my friend is missing?' A pang of fear left me almost breathless. I pressed my fingertips to the worktop, watched them whiten. The butcher's block blurred. 'Oh,' I said. 'Oh no, no, no. It wasn't... it wasn't Joan, was it?'

'Joan? What? Why would you think that?' Dougie's face was screwed up, perplexed.

'I just thought... Sorry, I thought...'

I had no idea what I thought. Outside the window, stars hovered over the hedge, diamond bright in the black velvet sky. I could feel hot tears running down my cheeks. Dougie was looking at me with such pained sorrow, and all I could feel was frightened and cross and confused. I lowered myself shakily onto the kitchen chair, but immediately heaved myself back up and returned to the counter, to arms open and ready for me to collapse into, a warm and living body for which I was endlessly, endlessly grateful. In the sink, the bearded cod stared up glassily from wet raspberry guts.

'Please,' I whimpered. 'I know I'm being irrational, but can you just tell me it wasn't Joanie? I just want to hear you say it.' I searched Dougie's gaze. My poor darling looked like literally anywhere else in the world would be preferable to right here, right now. 'Doug?'

'I... She was ten metres away, like, ken? We called the police. We didn't go any nearer or fish her out because it was clear she was dead and one of the lads said about crime scenes and that. It was a woman though. A woman rather than a girl, I should say. The police are there now. Suicide, the lads reckoned.'

'So it *wasn't* Joan?'

'Pete said she'd have to have been in the water for at least three days, and Joan has been in contact more recently than that, so no...'

'Oh thank God.' I stood back, brushing tears into my hair.

My cheeks were sore, chapped from the last icy months and from crying all the time. 'But it's so cold out,' I said meaninglessly. 'The sea will have been freezing. That poor, poor woman.' Still weeping, I pulled at the drawer handle. The collection of keys swished forward and crashed against the front. I rootled out the one with the paper label marked *Joan*.

'I'm going over,' I said.

Dougie nodded. 'Do you want me to come?'

'No, it's OK. You sort the fish. I won't be a sec.'

'If you're sure.'

A minute or two later, I was on Joan's driveway for what felt like the tenth time. Her car still wasn't there. Light leaked through the gap in the living-room curtains. It was a little after five. The light must have been turned on manually, I thought. The automatic timer was set for seven. And this time the curtains were closed.

Panic abated. I let out a long, shuddering breath of relief. Joan was home. Her car must be at the garage, for a service or something. I pushed the heel of my hand to my forehead and sniffed. Why the hell hadn't I thought of that?

I think I must've been on automatic pilot with the shock or something because I slid the key into the lock and opened the door a crack. Hesitated. What was I doing? I wasn't thinking straight. If Joan was home, I had no right barging in like this. I'd give her a terrible shock. With the door ajar, I backed up a little and rang the doorbell once, twice, three times.

From inside the house came movement – a soft brushing sound of fabric, a click.

'Joan? Jo-oan! Are you there, pet?' I stepped into the hallway and touched my hand to the radiator. The heating wasn't on. The house smelt closed up, musty. Chilly. Usually it was cosy, toasty and smelling of lavender and whatever Joan had had for her supper. 'Joanie, are you there, darlin'? It's only me, Kirsty. Just wanting to check you're all right, love. Not seen you for a day or two.'

I stayed dead still, holding my breath so I could listen for the smallest noise. The house was silent. I'm not sure how to explain it, but I had the *sense* of someone breathing. I flicked on the hall light and screwed up my eyes against the glare.

'Joan?' I could hear the quiet fear in my voice, but I made myself take a step, two, three, and then I was at the living-room door. There was no one, only the standard lamp in the corner casting a pink glow from beneath its tasselled shade. The flowery mug was still on the coffee table. I waited a moment, listening harder than I had in my life. All I could hear was my own blood thrumming in my ears. There was no one here.

But there was, a voice inside me replied.

Softly, as I took my first step into the room, I began to murmur a lullaby Mum used to sing to me at night: *Go to sleep, my baby*. It was my only comfort in a house I knew had been empty for days. *Close your big blue eyes*, I sang, barely above a whisper, the melody trembling as I took another slow step. Painstakingly, I crossed over to the mug. I picked it up. Stared at it as if I had never seen it before. *Angels up above you*, I half wept, *keeping the-eir wa-atch over you*.

I put the mug back. Cursed myself. My fingerprints would be on it now. The thought came so quickly as to be little more than instinct. Another followed: *This could be a crime scene*. Another argued against it. *This is not a crime scene. Joan's not here, that is all. There is no sign of a struggle.* And then: *But there was a body in the water: a woman. You haven't seen Joan for four days.* And then again: *You are conjuring disasters out of unrelated events. You are weaving conspiracies from the air. You are tired, you are pregnant, you are stressed, you are scared, you are seeing people from the past who are not there, you are losing your bloody mind.*

Hand to my chest, I forced my breathing to slow, blowing

out jets of air like a runner after a race. At the base of the mug, dark brown crusted speckles had formed – the last drops of instant coffee evaporated away over hours. This mug hadn't been touched in days. No one had been here in days. Today, a dead body had been found in the sea. If, *if* this was a crime scene, I could tell the police I'd come into the house, and that I'd touched this mug. They could take my fingerprints and elimi-nate me from their enquiries.

How could I have thought like that? I wondered later. How could I have gone straight to *crime scene*? Now, I think it was because despite Joan having been in touch recently, despite Dougie telling me bodies take days to surface, despite the fact that I couldn't conceive how it could possibly be her in the water, I couldn't completely rule out that it wasn't. It was like Hughie's appearance as Barry Sefton – a gut feeling against which all logic, all evidence, argued to the contrary. It simply could not be Hughie. There was no scenario in which it could be. Nor could the dead woman be Joan. But my gut had told me it was Hughie just as it was telling me now that the woman lying face down in the sea was not some poor woman I didn't know but Joan, my dear old Joanie.

It occurred to me then that given her mental state last time I'd seen her, she could well have decided to take her own life. I don't know if the thought was as solid as that, as tangible. But in viewing her home as a crime scene, maybe I was already subconsciously reaching for alternatives to something so terrible as suicide – namely, murder. How could murder be less awful than suicide? Did it mean I preferred to think of my dear old friend having been killed rather than face up to her feeling desolate and lonely enough to throw herself into the cold North Sea? I didn't know. I don't want to think about it, even now. I can't. What I will say is that no one can predict where their mind will go in these situations. I try to remind myself of that and not judge myself too harshly.

I was still standing at the front of her living room. In better possession of myself now, I turned to survey the back half of the room, where the mahogany dining table with the fluted edge stood surrounded by four ornate mahogany chairs. It was then that I saw it: the drawers in the matching sideboard were open, their contents half spilled out.

I let out a cry. My hand flew to my mouth. Breathing quickly now, I crept over to look more closely.

Had these drawers been like this before? Had they been like this on Thursday? I didn't know. I didn't think I could have seen so far into the room from the front window, and even if I could have, my focus had been trained on Joan's empty chair, the flowery mug abandoned on the coffee table.

I approached the sideboard. My hand hovered over cloth napkins, silver cutlery, postcards, bills, old letters. It didn't look like anything had been taken; more like Joan – or someone – had been searching frantically for something.

What was it? A passport? Money? Did she – or they – find it? And did that mean she was in danger... or worse? Or better? An impromptu trip abroad, maybe even with Reeny? No. That didn't chime with the Joan I knew at all. So – what then?

I made my way back to the hall with the intention of checking the other rooms. There was no one in the bedroom. The bed was still made, but this time I allowed myself to trespass further into Joan's private space. As in the sitting room, the chest of drawers was open, the contents disturbed. The wardrobe doors had been flung wide and there was an empty shoebox on the floor. Again, I had the impression nothing had been taken but that someone had been searching frantically for something.

On the bedside table was the photograph of Joan and the young girl I remembered from nursing Joan when she had COVID. Without touching it, I leant forward and examined the fuzzy image more closely than I had been able to do when Joan was ill. The girl looked about twelve. She had blonde hair and was wearing a T-shirt with three stripes across the chest, pale red shorts, long white skinny legs. Joan was much younger here, early thirties, perhaps, definitely no more than forty. Her paisley blouse had the telltale long collars and trim fit of the seventies. She was good-looking, tall, what people used to call a handsome woman. Despite the fashionable cut of the clothes, she looked traditional, respectable, like a minister or doctor's wife, someone who went to church, made jam, sewed lavender into little cloth bags.

I wondered who the girl was. A neighbour's child? A friend's? A niece? The girl was skinny, with long legs, like Joan. And now I looked closer, there was a resemblance in the eyes, their colouring, the shape of the brow. Could this girl even be her daughter? A daughter she never spoke about, one who, for some reason, had not been allowed to grace the mantelpiece? Perhaps the girl had died, which would explain why Joan never talked about her, why she never talked about herself much at all, why perhaps she kept this photograph here, so that she might wish her lost daughter goodnight.

My eyes pricked. I blinked to clear the fog of tears. On the dressing table was a wooden jewellery box inlaid with intricate pieces of mother-of-pearl, a hairbrush and comb set, an old-fashioned glass perfume dispenser, the pump covered in gold knit and adorned with a gold tassel. The jewellery box was closed. I didn't open it. That would have felt too much like violating my dear pal's privacy, and besides, it was no longer in my imagination now; I knew I could very possibly be walking around a crime scene, leaving trainer prints over those of the intruder, if there had been an intruder.

In the kitchen, I flicked the light switch with my elbow and waited for the long fluorescent ceiling tube to strobe into life. The hard white light bleached the kitchen with its surgical wash. Every drawer and cupboard had been opened, though they didn't appear to have been ransacked as in the other rooms. The back door looked odd. As I neared it, I saw it wasn't closed properly. I pulled my coat sleeve over my hand and closed it, making sure the catch clicked. There was no key in the lock, no key on the worktop, no key that I could see in any of the open drawers, and I didn't want to rifle through anything. As the seconds ticked into minutes, I was feeling increasingly wrong in that house. Gingerly, I made my way out, switching lights off with my elbow as I went and closing the front door behind me.

Outside once again, sadness flooded me, so overwhelming I had to stop a moment and close my eyes, one hand against the door for support.

'Joan,' I whispered. 'Where are you, darlin'?'

A minute or two passed. I blinked open my eyes. It was so dark out. Winter days here are so short, the debt for the long summer nights. I heard a low purring sound. At the exit to the crescent, a car was crawling away around the corner, head- and tail lights off.

My throat closed. Was that the flashy red car? Had someone been watching Joan's house? Who the hell drove without their lights on, unless they didn't want to be seen? Who was in that car?

Stressed to the roots of my hair, exhausted to the marrow of my bones and God knows what else, I lumbered home, my body cumbersome, huge, my lower back aching. On the driveway, there was barely room for me to squeeze past Dougie's van. Anger was flaring now. Frustration at the impossible twin conundrums of Hughie not Hughie and Joan's weird behaviour, at my condition, my heaviness, my helplessness. I felt like the damn drummer in the Salvation Army band, my belly a solid rotund protrusion in front of me: bang, bang, bang. Alone in the close, I squeezed my hands into fists and let out a stifled groan.

The porch light was on. Dougie must have put it on for me. I wondered what I would say when I got in. Joan was missing. That was a fact now, pretty much. The inside of her home didn't look right... although she might have been searching for something to put in her suitcase. She hadn't been spotted in the close since Wednesday last week, but her car had come and gone, she had been texting and Stella had seen her. The body of a woman had been found floating in the North Sea, but Dougie said it couldn't be Joan because this person had been in the water for the best part of a week.

But that didn't mean she wasn't missing. It didn't mean she wasn't in trouble, and it didn't mean someone wasn't driving away from her house in a car with no lights on. The ransacked drawers, the dirty coffee mug, Joan's agitation, the visitor she'd spoken of, who I of all people had dismissed as a figment of my friend's tired old mind.

My phone buzzed in my pocket. I pulled it out – a text from Dougie:

Fish all done. Where u? If u not back by time I've had shower, I'ma comin for ya! X

I smiled at the obvious attempt to cheer me up, even though it made me feel sad.

As I reached the house, the front door opened and Dougie was standing there, almost imperceptibly sagging with relief at the sight of me.

'Any sign?'

I shook my head and burst into tears. 'We need to call the police.'

Inside, we hugged one another tightly and for a long time. I felt the warm touch of a kiss on my head, the lovely press of Dougie's hands against my back.

'You're sure you didn't get a look at the woman in the water?' I asked when we finally stepped back from one another. 'Even what she was wearing?'

'Well, no. I mean, jeans and a coat, I think, but it won't be

Joan. It won't be. Looked younger. Young, I'd say. Don't think about it, darlin'.'

'There was evidence of a break-in.'

'A break-in?' Dougie sounded reassuringly alarmed.

'Well, the drawers were all open, as if someone had been rifling through them. The back door was open.'

'Was there a window smashed?'

'No.'

'Was anything broken? The lock bust? Any furniture turned over?'

'Well, no, but—'

'That's not a break-in, darlin'. Messy drawers are most probably Joan trying to find something. It points much more towards her going out or going away. Like looking for a passport or something, ken? You said she'd not been herself lately. Maybe she decided to get away.'

'But she wouldn't leave her house open like that.'

'Was it locked last time you went?'

'Yes. But—'

'So that means she's been back there, doesn't it?'

'But the back door key wasn't there. And I saw that red sports car again.'

'When?'

I sighed, trying to think. 'Thursday?'

'Was it definitely the same car?'

'I don't know. I couldn't tell, but it was suspicious! Really, Dougie, I think I should call the police. What if the woman in the water is Joan?'

With a slow shake of the head, Dougie sighed. 'Don't mix things up in your mind. Joan behaving erratically does not mean she's gone and drowned herself.'

'Drowned herself? What, so now you're *sure* it was suicide?'

'No! She maybe slipped and fell, got blown in by a gale.

Whatever. It's not her, babe. They'll identify the body soon enough. Let's see what tomorrow brings, eh?'

'I think something's happened to her.'

My phone vibrated in my hand. At the sight of Joan's name, my blood ran hot through me. I opened the message and stared at the words, barely aware of my mouth falling open.

How dare you go into my house without my permission? Stay away.

SEVENTEEN

KIRSTY

KS/transcript #14

When I looked up, Dougie was making a crazy face.

'What are you goofing around for?' I snapped, horrified. 'It's not funny. I'm like a daughter to that woman, you know I am, and she sends me this?' Tears fell. 'First she just jaunts off without so much as a cheerio, and now she's sending me these messages like I'm some sort of irritation to her. Why is she being like this?'

Dougie's palms came up in a stop sign. The stupid smirk was still there, and I felt fury rise. 'I'm sorry, babe. I didna mean to laugh, but you canna deny it; she might be a grumpy old bat, but she's definitely alive.'

But I couldn't laugh. I didn't want to be the one to say *after all I've done for that woman*, but... after all I'd done, it was like a slap in the face.

'I heard a noise,' I said, grudgingly letting myself be persuaded into the sitting room to watch the news. 'As I went in, I definitely heard what sounded like someone moving about, and then a click. I told myself it was the heebie-jeebies, but when I got to the kitchen, the back door was on the latch. That's so weird, isn't it? Isn't that weird?'

'It must have been Joan, sneaking out the back.'

'But that's mad. Isn't that a mad thing to do? She was so terrified when I saw her on Wednesday, going on about Lachie not knowing this thing she couldn't tell me, and then she hears me coming in and runs away like she's scared of me? I'm beginning to worry she's lost her mind. I mean, where is she going on these trips in the middle of winter? It's bitterly cold, Dougie! It's so bitterly cold!'

'You're right. It's mad. Bonkers.' Dougie was frowning at the remote, bringing up *Reporting Scotland* on the iPlayer.

'It's so cold out.' My voice was as small as a child's. 'I hate to think of her in her back garden, shivering, waiting for me to go. How could she see me as a threat? It's too awful. Her mind must be playing tricks. Do you think I should go back and check on her? If nothing else, just to lock the back door for her?'

'No.' The reply was firm, almost angry, and it shocked me into silence. 'No,' Dougie said again, more softly, reaching out to lay a comforting hand on my leg. 'You might end up locking her out. More likely is she left it on the latch. It's probably been banging on and off like that since she went out. Let's just watch the news, eh? And try not to take it too personally. When folk get old, they get grumpy and rude sometimes, but it's got nothing to do with you. I promise we'll call social services in the morning, OK? But it's not a police matter, I don't think. Here it is. Let's see if they say anything.'

'But...' I stopped.

Dougie paused the TV and sighed. 'But what?'

'Well... first there was Hughie who wasn't Hughie.' I was searching for what I meant, rootling through the words like coins in a drawer. 'And then Joan saying *Lachie doesna know* about... something. And then the flashy red car. And now this. A body, for God's sake.' I gestured towards the TV. 'Why now?

And what's going to be next? I'm supposed to be having a baby in a few weeks. I can't afford to be getting this stressed. You didn't see her on Wednesday. You didn't see the fear in her eyes.'

'Try not to make this into a conspiracy, OK? Let's not have Squattergate all over again. Or the time you thought that woman at work was having an affair and you almost told the husband and it turned out it was her brother. You care too much. It's why I love you, but you've got to wind your neck in.'

I was about to argue, but Dougie pressed play, and as the theme music faded, the pristine presenter delivered a headline that made the blood freeze in my veins.

'On *Reporting Scotland* this evening, police are asking for information concerning the body of an elderly woman found off Aberdeen Harbour earlier this afternoon.'

In shocked silence, we listened to the bulletin, delivered in grave tones.

'Aberdeenshire Police believe the woman to have entered the water earlier this week and are investigating all possibilities...'

When the report finished, Dougie turned off the television and turned to hold both my hands. 'Look at me. Kirsty. Look at me. Breathe. Dinna stress. Dinna panic.'

'They said elderly.' I almost couldn't get the words out for the sobs racking through me. 'Elderly, they said. Oh God, it's her! It's her – I know it is. They're asking for anyone who might know her. They can't identify her. Oh my God, it's so cold out. It must have been so cold in the water. What if it's Joan? I can't bear it. I just can't.' Tears were running from my eyes and nose, darkening my lap in fat wet spots. 'We need to call the police.'

'But it canna be her, darlin'.' Dougie spoke with the kind of placatory calm we use for tricky patients. 'It's *literally* impossible. I told you. One of the guys I went fishing with volunteers on the lifeboats and he gave us all the details. It takes days.

Days. They even said that just now. Earlier this week, they said. The body sinks before it floats. It's heavy. Pete said it's the bacteria in the gut that causes gas to form and that's what makes the body rise to the surface and it takes four to five days sometimes, especially in winter. And Joan literally just texted you.'

'So where is she then?' I asked, teeth bared, flitting between devastation and simmering rage. 'Eh? Answer me that. Where's Joanie?'

'I don't know. But we're not going to help the police by clogging up the phone line with a wild goose chase, are we?'

'No, but—'

'Kirsty, look at me.'

Despite my flailing, I did as I was told. Dougie's eyes were soft and blue, and they were pleading with me. 'Whoever it is, her family need to know as soon as possible. It's not Joan, OK? It's not her. It cannot be her.'

'I'm sorry,' I whispered. 'I'm just so worried.'

'I know. I know. Because you care about folk more than anyone I've ever known. But you need to sleep, darlin'. You need to get your rest. Precious...'

'... cargo, I know. Precious cargo. I'm so tired.' I yawned like a dog.

'Baby aside, *you're* precious – to me. To your folks, to my folks, to your pals, your team up at the infirmary. To this wee bairn you're carrying for us. For once in your life, you've got to look after yourself, Kirst. You're not thinking straight.' Dougie lifted my hands and kissed my knuckles, one at a time, first the left hand, then the right, so carefully, so tenderly, before meeting my gaze once again. 'You're not on day shift tomorrow, are you? So in the morning, you can have a long lie. I'll bring you some toast and tea in bed, and you can chill out for once, OK? Doctor's orders. If they haven't ID'd the body by then and you still feel the same, I'll take you to the police station myself when I get home from work. But let's let the cops do their job.'

Dougie's words must have hypnotised me or something. I nodded, yawning incessantly now. I needed to rest as much as possible, that much was true. I had to get my strength back if I was to have any chance of making it into work. My exhaustion was thick, soupy. I could barely keep my sticky eyes open.

'Sleep,' I whispered. 'We'll call tomorrow if they don't ID her. OK. It's a plan.'

EIGHTEEN

KIRSTY

KS/transcript #15

After a troubled night watching minutes grow into hours on the red digital display, I threw on some clothes and left Dougie sleeping. I was going to be in bother, I knew, but for reasons I couldn't explain even to myself, I had to go to the harbour. It was where Joan had walked. It was where Stella had seen her on Thursday morning, the last sighting anyone had had of her. It was where the police were saying the woman had entered the water last week. The small amount of rest I'd managed had returned me to my senses. Logic pointed to Joan being alive – I could see that now. I couldn't quite let myself believe it, but I was holding on to it with all I had.

Joan's car still wasn't parked outside her house. Ignoring the temptation to let myself into the bungalow for the third time, I drove instead to New Pier Road, scanning the streets for her white Polo all the way there with a sense of frenzied desperation.

Did I see a parallel with the past? Only when I parked up

behind Stella's cottage. I think Dougie's words from a day or two earlier must have sunk in, because at that point I realised this was exactly what I'd done eleven years before, searching, searching, scanning the roads, pit in my stomach, tears in my eyes, scouring the city for Hughie's blue Renault 5. And yes, here once again was the unexplained disappearance of someone I loved, plus the odd, hurtful notes, this time in text form but with the same message, that of a close relationship denied.

Stella's house was in darkness, the kitchen blinds closed against the night. The thought of mother and baby sleeping safely inside brought me a moment's warmth, something pure amidst all the ghoulish unpleasantness revolving endlessly in my mind. In the night's waking dreams, eighteen-year-old Hughie had read his note aloud with scalding scorn before laughing at me and tearing it to pieces, the pieces becoming snow falling thick on the ground, myself trying to get through the drift, only to find myself too big, too swollen to move, getting ever slower, heavier, feeling myself fall but never land, an endless falling as I perished in the freezing blizzard.

I shivered. It was only 7 a.m., the sky black felt. I was so wrapped up, I looked like a human marshmallow, my eyes all that was visible to any onlookers – not that there were any at that time. According to the car thermometer, it was minus four out. I texted Dougie, who would wake to an empty bed and the note I'd left to say I couldn't sleep, that I'd gone for a drive and not to worry. *I'll rest when I get home. I promise. Love you.*

I heaved my enormous bulk out of the driver's seat and waddled, stiffly at first, pain in my sciatic nerve easing slowly. Along the backs of the dark and sleeping houses I headed towards the quayside, then up past the lighthouse, home to the Silver Darling restaurant for as long as I could remember. I wondered if they'd identified the body yet, whether the verdict would be an accident, suicide or something more sinister.

Beyond the North Pier, the sea was spiky smoked glass, the

headland a black cut-out against the charcoal sky. I cupped my hands against my face and blew warmth into them. My nose was a cold, wet pebble. I thought of that poor woman in the sea, hoped she didn't suffer, but at the same time, I knew this was unlikely. Suicide. It was such a big thought, too big to wrap my head around. Who would take their own life in such a cruel way? In what depths of despair would they have to be swimming that they felt there was no choice but to drown? I was crying again, wondering how much was sadness, how much was hormones, whether these constant tears would stop once the baby was born or if they were part of me now. I'd hoped to see a policeman, to try and get some information, but seeing no one, I headed back towards the car.

As I approached my trusty old Focus, I saw Stella at her kitchen window, the baby in a pink velour onesie against her shoulder. Spotting me, she grinned and waved, gesturing at me to come and say hello. A warm familiar feeling of community spread through me. Stella always seemed so pleased to see me. Like Joan always had.

What had changed that?

'What are you doing here at this ungodly hour?' she asked, stepping back to let me inside. 'I thought there was only me and Luna up in the whole world.'

'I bet it feels like that sometimes, doesn't it?' I replied, half thinking that once my baby arrived, these lonely wee small hours would be mine too.

Stella made us some decaf coffee, and I let myself be soothed by her chatter.

'I came to see the harbour,' I said when we sat down together in the tiny living room. 'Couldn't stop thinking about the woman who threw herself off, you know?'

'Is that what happened?' Stella's eyes were plates. 'Was it suicide?'

'No, sorry, I shouldn't have said that. That's just me imagining, you know. Although I have to say, I *can't* imagine it. You saw it on the news?'

'Heard it on the radio, aye. Terrible. Poor woman. Some poor family's going to get a terrible shock, so they are.'

'I was thinking about Joan. She's still missing. I've not seen her since Wednesday.'

Stella's mouth dropped open. 'Your neighbour? The woman who walks here? You think it could be her?'

I shrugged. 'Dougie says not. But I don't know. I feel it. Inside, you know? That's why I'm here, mad as that sounds. I just felt the pull to come and see for myself. But then I often feel things and I'm often wrong.' I frowned and met Stella's eye. 'You saw her Thursday morning, didn't you? It *was* Thursday, wasn't it?'

'It was, aye.'

'Thing is, she's been texting me. Texted me only last night, as a matter of fact.' I didn't mention the strange, almost rude tone. It felt too much like I'd be betraying a friend.

Stella sipped her coffee and for a moment stared vacantly at nothing before coming back to herself with the merest shake of her head. 'Actually, she said something really weird. Well, not weird exactly, more intense, like.'

'On Thursday?'

'Aye. She sort of looked at me, like, deep into my eyes sort of thing, and she said, "Whatever you do, keep your daughter close."'

My skin prickled all over. 'Joan said that?'

'Aye. I didn't know how to react, so I just smiled and said I would, nae bother. I remembered her saying it about two minutes after I'd seen you the other day. I was going to call and tell you, but I didn't want to pester you with it. I thought she'd have turned up by now. But... she's still missing?'

'I don't know. I mean, I'm not her keeper, but it's just that they've found this woman. Dougie says I join too many dots, but I'm not so sure. I'm thinking I'm definitely going to call in on her friend Reeny.'

As I left Stella and baby Luna to their day, I felt my jaw set. I was going to find Joan, whether she wanted to be found or not.

NINETEEN

HUGHIE

HR/audio/excerpt #4

Maybe you suspected even then, back when we were together, that my origins were more humble than I claimed. I know my accent slipped from time to time, that Leith vernacular sneaking in. You'll notice now, by contrast, I use words like *vernacular*. An education will do that for you, no matter how you scratch and cobble it together. I used to wonder if you thought the dropped consonants and the odd expletive were just me imitating a rough ned for the sole purpose of entertaining you. See? I use words like *expletive* now too, but I can still swear like a Glasgow docker if the need arises.

Did you ever notice the details of my backstory didn't always match up? Depends how hard you were listening, I suppose. I can remember fluffing my lines occasionally, the panic that would overtake me in those moments. But no one noticed. You never noticed. Maybe you learnt not to take people at face value only after we parted. If that's true, at least I gave you the gift of suspicion, a necessary tool in life, I have found. For people like me, trust is danger. It can be death.

And I'm used to hiding things. I've been hiding things all my life, KK, in ways you have never had to. Some of us, like you, get to live. Some of us merely get to survive. The difference is everything. Funny how the easier it is for you to live, the easier it is to judge those who survive. The people I work with, the educated elite, my God, some of the things they come out with. How it's all about hard work and good choices. What I want to say is, *Many people work hard in ways you cannot imagine, but in order to make good choices, you have to have those choices in the first place.* But I keep my mouth shut, of course. I bite it all back. I do not drop my guard. I do not relax. Relaxing is not, has never been, for people like me.

Anyway, when you met me as a sweet little laddie, I had come up the road to start a new life, embrace new opportunities. I worked so hard to free myself of the stamp of nature, but four years is a long time, and here's another theory for you as to why it all went wrong: when it finally came down to it, maybe I faltered because I was scared of real, genuine success, success that was based on hard work, on merit, on *me*, instead of short-cuts, scams and gambles. I don't know. I'm sure a psychologist would have a field day, but the long and the short of it is that I messed up as I was pre-programmed to do, and when I saw those crappy grades, I knew it. I'd had my golden chance, my only chance, and I'd blown it like the trash I was. It was in my DNA.

But I didn't give up. As I said in my wee note, rules are not really for my kind. So. I ignored them and went back to what I knew: the old life, old opportunities, old me. Turns out, you don't need Highers to learn everything you need to know about anaesthesiology. You don't need Highers to buy textbooks, study, even attend lectures. Honestly, Kirsty, when I used to look about the lecture theatre at my fellow students and calcu-late how much their degrees were costing them, it made me laugh my head off. There was I, getting it for free. No one –

absolutely no one – asked me who I was, what I was doing there. No one. Scary, eh? London is a big city, big enough to swallow a person, render them anonymous. UCL has no passport office, no border control. Just one more young face in a sea of young faces, hungry to learn. Just like Aberdeen High, for that matter.

Tell you what, though, much of it was pretty boring. Some of those anaesthesiology classes were enough to put you to sleep.

Oh, come on. Don't look at me like that. Wouldn't be your old Hughie without a wee joke, now, would it?

The rest of my illustrious career you'll have read on my profile. Except you won't think to question the data. You'll have seen my qualifications and believed they were real. They are real, to me. Just because a certificate is faked doesn't mean I didn't do the work, doesn't mean I didn't attain the grades. Just because a LinkedIn profile has... inconsistencies doesn't mean there isn't some truth in it. I did the work. I made new opportunities, another new life, another new me – older, wiser this time. Lesson learnt.

Life is just one big mirage. It really is. The truth is up for negotiation.

And so now I'm consultant anaesthetist Barry Sefton, sucking up all that glorious reverence. Hard beginnings and time have lost me what little looks I had, but I still get laid occasionally. Do you know why? Because people respect me. They admire me. Women admire me. I have a great bedside manner, if you'll forgive my flippancy. Seriously, though, most consultants have their standard patter – where are you going for your holidays? What do you do for a living? That kind of stuff. Me? I go for storytelling. Which is, I suppose, what I'm doing right now. Telling you a story. The story of young Hughie, who set out on the road like Dick Whittington and sought his fortune.

All I wanted was a way out, Kirsty. All I wanted was to be

revered. Like the guy I'd seen in the hospital just before the police came to tell me my mother and her boyfriend were dead. That was the day I realised no one could even see me, with my hospital porter's mop and my overalls and my air of humility. No one was looking at me at all.

To not be invisible, perhaps that's all I ever wanted; to cross the chasm between surviving and living, to finally be one of the lucky ones.

But last week I bumped into you. And my luck ran out.

TWENTY

KIRSTY

Before I got back in my car, I retraced my steps all the way along North Pier Road. For my own peace of mind, I needed to double-check. But there was no sign of Joan's white Polo, and I couldn't get my head round that at all. If she were at home, went my thinking, the car would be on her driveway. If – God forbid – she'd driven here to throw herself off the harbour, it would be here.

So where was it?

Where was *she*?

What did her words to Stella signify?

Whatever you do, keep your daughter close.

That wasn't life advice; that was something much more urgent. Regret? A warning? Did it have something to do with the photo in Joan's bedroom? Joan had never mentioned a niece or a daughter, but to have a photo by her bed suggested the girl was important to her. Was I right in thinking there could be some family connection? *Could* that girl be her daughter? If she was, why, in all the years we'd known one another, hadn't Joan said one word? Why not mention her once my own child had started to swell and kick and elbow? I remembered the way her hand had risen in silent request to touch my pregnant bump and feel the life move inside. The way her eyes had watered. *A beautiful surprise*, she'd said. *New life.* I had to find out more about the girl in the photo.

I had to find Reeny.

A text buzzed in. Dougie.

Where are you, you mad woman? X

I smiled, replied:

Needed some air. On way back now to put my feet up. Have a good day at work! X

OK. See you later. Love you. X

Love you too 😊

I walked slowly back to the car, determination pressing my lips tight shut. I didn't know which number Gray Street Reeny lived at, but I was hoping her yellow Nissan would be parked outside her flat. It didn't much matter. At this point, I was prepared to knock on every single door if I had to.

The traffic had built up since the post-apocalyptic deserted-ness of the city in the pre-dawn. The Great Western Road was busy, but not too busy heading back into town. I made a left into Gray Street and halfway down recognised Reeny's car, bright as an early daffodil in the row of greys and blues. I slowed to five miles per hour, searching for Joan's white Polo. There were two white cars, but one was a Mondeo, the other a Fiesta. Muttering curses, I parked up fifty yards from Reeny's car, walked the short way back and rang on the nearest doorbell – a ground-floor flat. My stomach growled. No breakfast. Dougie would give me a row, after giving me a row for going AWOL in the dark. I checked my watch. Only a little after eight. There was no movement from inside the flat. No one in, or no one up at least.

I flushed with embarrassment. It was far too early to make a house call. Reeny was in her eighties. What was I thinking? I backed away. I should have thought this through. With a pit of guilt in my belly, I resolved to go back later.

Back in the car, frustration chewed at me. No matter how calm Dougie had been the night before, we had agreed to call the police today if nothing had changed. And despite the facts Dougie had given me, nothing had changed in terms of the way I felt. I couldn't wait until this evening – I could not. I didn't need Dougie or anyone else to come with me; I'd go by myself.

TWENTY-ONE

KIRSTY

KS/transcript #17

The desk sergeant, whose pre-stubble chin fuzz made him look about twelve, led me through the security door and into an interview room.

'Wait here,' he said, eyes drifting over my bump with mild terror. 'My colleague will be with you in a moment.'

'Righto.'

Ten minutes later, another male officer, also about twelve, walked in and gave me a fake smile into which I read his innate sense of superiority. A smile you'd never tire of slapping, I thought, as he took the seat opposite, placed his notepad on the table and told me his name was Tod. Tod, who was just passing through on his way to detective inspector, no doubt.

'You have information pertaining to the woman found off Aberdeen Harbour yesterday?' he asked in his English accent after we'd exchanged rather stiff greetings.

'I don't know. I suppose I might have information that might *pertain*,' I said. I can't usually tell, but right then I did notice the lilt of Scottish that had infiltrated my vowels over the years. At the same time, I couldn't help but observe the sardonic rise of the young man's eyebrow. Really, I thought. Does his mother know he's working at the police station?

'Sorry.' He frowned like you do at a kid who's trying to get one over on you. 'You do have info or you don't?'

'If you'd let me finish,' I said, already beginning to regret ever coming here. Wasn't there someone older I could speak to? Someone who did their own laundry perhaps?

Plod Junior showed me the palms of his hands – a sarcastic apology. I wanted, with a force that almost overwhelmed me, to bid him lean forward so I could poke him in both eyes. But I didn't. Obviously.

'I don't know if my information *pertains*,' I repeated, slowly and with excessive care, 'to the woman found, because they've not said who she is yet. But the thing is, my neighbour Joan, Joan Wood...'

I told him everything that had happened, coffee mug and all. I didn't mention the texts. I wasn't sure why, only that this loon was already eyeing me like he didn't take me seriously, or like he took himself far too seriously, one of the two. If I mentioned them, I had the feeling he would tell me, as Dougie had, that this meant Joan was merely out of town. I didn't want that. I wanted him to tell the team to get the sirens on pronto and race down to Joan's house.

To give him credit, he did at least take notes. Asked if I was related to the *elderly lady*. No. Was I Ms Wood's carer? No. Did Ms Wood and I have the kind of relationship in which we told one another our movements day to day? No, but...

'So you're saying you think she's the woman found in the water?'

'I'm not saying anything of the sort. I don't know what I'm saying. But on the news, they said the woman who drowned was elderly, and I'm saying I've not seen my elderly neighbour since Wednesday evening and my friend last saw her on

Thursday at the harbour, and she was behaving oddly on both occasions. And now there's an elderly woman in the water. You're the policeman, not me.' I sighed with pointed exasperation and leant back against the chair.

'Gotcha.' The boy stood and thanked me for coming in, his hand outstretched for me to shake. I picked up the subtext: *Get lost, I'm busy.* But I obliged politely, saving it all for Dougie when I got home. Tapping his yellow pencil on the pad, he told me with an air of great self-importance that he'd pass on the information to the team, but not to worry, most of these cases were simple misunderstandings.

In your long experience? I refrained from asking as he escorted me out into the foyer and through the main door, possibly to make sure I left. I thanked him despite myself and stepped back out into the crisp January day. The impression that I'd been humoured and dismissed lodged inside me like indigestion. But at least I'd done something. I had alerted the police to Joan's odd behaviour.

Joan could have family out of town, I supposed, family she'd never mentioned. She'd never mentioned the girl in the photo, after all. She was a funny old stick sometimes. I'd done all I could. Maybe Dougie was right. If Joan didn't want me coming round all the time, it was better to respect that. Maybe my almost daily visits were overbearing, intrusive. Nosy, even.

It was possible. But something darker was also possible.

This I knew of old.

TWENTY-TWO

KIRSTY

KS/transcript #18

After a quick trip into town with Mum to buy essentials for the baby – a decent enough diversion, but I was too superstitious and too preoccupied to buy anything much – I returned home to an empty house.

Did I tell Mum what was going on? No, I didn't. Why? Because she'd already told me my ankles were looking shiny and had given me a row for having black rings under my eyes. I love the fact that I live near my folks, don't get me wrong, but when Dougie and me got pregnant, I think I felt the wheel turn. I was becoming a parent now and I needed to protect Mum and Dad as they'd once protected me. And sometimes that meant not sharing every last thing like I used to. So when she said I was looking tired, was there anything the matter, and asked if I'd seen Hughie again, I told her I was soon to finish work, not to worry, that I'd found out it definitely wasn't Hughie after all, and did not divulge my trip to the police station. As for Joan, I was glad I hadn't mentioned her to my mum and I didn't that day either, because I knew if I did, I wouldn't be able to stop myself running through my endless theories.

'I'm heading home,' I said, the yawn that followed the most authentic thing that had left my lips in the last few minutes. 'I'm going to make a nice brew and put my feet up.'

Which is almost what I did. I went home – that I did do. I put on the heating and made myself a herbal tea, googled the news and waited for the kettle to boil. There was nothing new about the woman in the water and nothing about Joan's disappearance either. Of course there wasn't. A quick glance out of the window told me there was no flashy red car either.

Which left only Hughie-not-Hughie.

I brought up Barry Sefton's LinkedIn profile on my phone and reread the impressive credentials Tasha had summarised for me on Saturday evening. Looking at the photo of the man I knew in my bones if not my head was Hughie Reynolds, I shivered with the creeps. How could Tasha not see it was him? Why did I think it *was* him?

I googled Hughie and Hugh Reynolds again, but there was nothing, not even a Facebook page. The police interview was beginning to weigh heavy, the instinct that I hadn't been believed, that the young boy had seen only a hugely pregnant woman, a human being he couldn't relate to at all and who didn't know her own mind. To be honest, I'm not sure I did.

I looked about the empty house, anxiety crawling over my skin. Antsy must come from the word ants, I thought, because ants were what it felt like. I knew I should rest, but how could I? I had to find something to do to keep my mind from fizzing like an Alka-Seltzer in a glass of water. Those true-crime documentaries were full of people who appeared to be sleepwalking through their own lives. I didn't want to be like them. I wasn't like them. I was wide awake on no sleep.

The facts looped in my mind like a song you hear and can't stop singing even though you don't like it. Joan had been unusually anxious and now she was missing. A man from my past was haunting me but it wasn't him. A woman was dead in the water. A fishy red car was hanging about the close. I knew something was up even if the dunderhead cop did not. How could I rest until I knew what had happened to my Joanie? And frankly, at that point, I was beginning to think I'd never relax until I'd spoken to Barry Sefton on his own, just him and me, face to face, no witnesses. I wanted to look him right in the eye and hear him say he wasn't the boy I used to know. So maybe I did know my own mind, in terms of what was inside it – but not enough to recognise its contents as the stuff of madness.

I called Joan's number again, but there was no reply. I thought of her car, missing, then here, then gone again. What if she'd got into a state at the wheel? She could have come off the road. Her car could be in a ditch somewhere, her broken inside it. The police would need helicopters, drones. It could take them weeks.

It was no good. I had to find something to do before I started climbing the walls. With new determination, I took my tea upstairs, stripped off the cheap men's XL hoodie I'd bought three weeks earlier and stood in my thermal underwear and stretch maternity trousers. In the wardrobe mirror, I saw a cartoonish version of myself, a superhero whose power was to bounce back up if ever she fell over.

'Boing,' I said to my reflection, clutching my belly with both hands. 'Boing, boing, boing!'

Where would all this skin go afterwards? I wondered. I'd have to tie it up with a hair bobble round the back. Might be useful for hanging my house keys. I'd be sure not to lose them that way, right enough.

My eyes drifted across the landing to the nursery, the half-yellow wall framed in the doorway. That was it. I would finish painting the nursery. Paint the walls rather than climb them. It was something.

Sliding open the wardrobe door, I realised I had nothing big enough to cover me while I worked, so I opened Dougie's side and found an old checked shirt screwed up in a ball by the pile of shoes. When I shook it out, I found it had a hole where the breast pocket had come away and the fabric was already splashed with pale grey from when we'd painted the living room. Perfect. I put it over my thermals and decided to brave taking off my socks so as not to ruin them.

I fetched the radio and tuned it to Radio Scotland so I could catch the news after *The Afternoon Show*. Feet shoved into an old pair of hospital Crocs with a split in the sole, I took up arms: a wide paintbrush and the tin of pale yellow paint.

I'd almost finished the entire first coat when I heard the theme tune for *The Afternoon Show* fading, followed by the familiar sting for *Drivetime*, which I knew would have the news at the top. I lowered the paintbrush and listened with all my attention. I could hear my heart beating, the pulse of blood in my temples. I felt like I couldn't breathe.

'On Radio Scotland this afternoon, the woman found off Aberdeen Harbour has been named as Mrs Joan Wood of...'

The paintbrush dropped onto the bare boards. A great yellow splash across my Crocs, up my bare shins. My knees banged against the floor, tears already in free fall, sobs racking, curling me over. 'Oh Joan. Oh no, oh God no.'

'... believed to have entered the water sometime between Thursday evening and Friday morning. There is to be an inquest. Police are keen to talk to anyone who might know or have spoken to Ms Wood recently.'

'Oh God. Oh Joan. Oh my poor darlin'.'

'... a solicitor's secretary from Aberdeen, a former colleague described her as an intensely private person but a hard-working, decent woman who never missed a day.'

. . .

Music was playing – a traditional Scottish reel. I found myself in the middle of the nursery, the dirty old floorboards pressing into my knees. My back was aching and I was shivering from head to toe. The heating must have clicked off, I suppose, while I was away with the shock, if that's what had happened. All I knew was I'd lost fifteen minutes. And I knew I had to stand up. I had to get up off the floor and get warm quickly. But I couldn't move. It was like I was set in position. Genuinely, I couldn't think how to connect my brain to my limbs.

Slowly, painstakingly, I managed to raise myself to a standing position before hobbling stiffly out onto the landing and switching off the radio. I don't know if I was aware that my finger had left a yellow print on the power button or if that was something I discovered later. As it was, I took the stairs down one at a time, gripping the handrail tightly, afraid I might pitch forward and tumble headlong into the dark hallway.

At the bottom of the stairs, still dizzy, I threaded my arms through Dad's coat sleeves and pulled on my hat. I could hear myself moaning like a child. I had a sense of being outside my body. Like I could hear my breathing, my footsteps, the swish of my clothing when I moved. Outside, the sky was darkest blue. In the house opposite, my neighbour Shona McGilvery was giving her kids, Isla and Duncan, a snack while they watched the telly. On the pavement, my paint-splashed Crocs moved one in front of the other. I couldn't see them, could only hear them squeaking over the glittering black frost.

'Joan.' I whispered her name over and over. A patrol vehicle was parked outside her bungalow, incident tape all around. 'Joan!' I tried to run, but my knees felt loose, like the bones weren't properly connected.

Joan was dead. Not missing. Not forgetful. Not away on a jaunt. Not fed up with interfering neighbours. Dead. I would never see her again. The fact of it was astonishing. I could barely grasp it. I *couldn't* grasp it.

I stood helplessly on the road, staring up at my friend's house. I couldn't stop saying her name. Her hand on my belly, her eyes shining: *New life*. My own eyes were dry of tears. How could I not have seen? Why hadn't I pressed her about the thing she couldn't tell me? Was it this? Had Lachie been calling to her to join him? Is that what she hadn't been able to admit? If only I'd realised, I could have stopped her. I could have stayed with her. I could have alerted social services, told someone, told Reeny.

I could have saved her. I could have saved my friend, and now...

Something was edging towards me, something I couldn't quite see. I stood stock-still while it crept out from the shadows of my brain and presented itself.

They said the woman had entered the water on Thursday night or Friday morning. That's what they'd said on the news.

But if Joan had drowned late on Thursday night, who had been sending me those messages?

TWENTY-THREE

KIRSTY

'Sometimes texts come in a few days after they've been sent,' Dougie said.

This was later on. We were sitting together on the sofa. Dougie had come straight home, lit a fire in the stove, put a blanket around my shoulders and made me an emergency Cup-a-Soup. But still I couldn't stop the juddering that was passing through my body in waves.

'But her car was missing,' I said, not for the first time. 'And the coffee mug was on the table. And the curtains weren't drawn that time. And her car wasn't at the harbour.'

'How do you know it's not at the harbour?'

'Because I drove around searching for it this morning! And the other day. Saturday, was it?'

'Oh, darlin'.'

A silence descended, heavy with unspoken reproach. I was fighting the same feeling I'd had at the police station: that of being humoured, dismissed, seen through the fish-eye lens of pregnancy.

'And why did it all start happening the day I saw that Barry Sefton guy?' I said, not caring how mad that sounded. 'Who I still think is Hughie, by the way. Eh? Answer me that.'

'It wasn't Hughie. *You* told me it wasn't.'

'Well, it wasn't Joan in the water either, was it? Except it was. And it wasn't fear in Joan's eyes, was it? It wasn't despair. Oh no, it was dementia or confusion or old age, something to be dismissed and ignored like... like a pregnant woman in a police station. I'm telling you – I *told* you she was afraid! She was scared and I... I stopped seeing her as a person and started seeing her as an old lady. I thought I was better than that. She was my friend. I loved her. If I'd taken her seriously, if I'd treated her like I'd treat you or Tasha or my mum, I would've called the police right there and then. If I'd treated her as a person.'

'Don't beat yourself up.' Dougie reached out and smoothed my hair. 'You weren't to know.'

'But I did know!' I half turned away, not ready to be touched. 'I felt it.' I banged the heel of my hand against my chest. 'I felt it in here. The same way I knew that guy was Hughie Reynolds.'

'Except he wasn't.'

'Well, no, but...'

'But what?'

'He said life was one big mirage. In that letter. He said he didn't play by the rules or the rules weren't for his kind or words to that effect. Maybe he changed his name.'

'Kirsty. Darlin'. Why would he change his name and then return to a place where folk know him? Come on!'

'Don't tell me to come on! You're doing what I did to Joan. You're seeing me as a pregnancy, not a person. I'm not just hormones and emotional outbursts. Just because I can't stop crying doesn't mean I don't have something to cry about. Just... just believe me, can't you? I know it sounds crazy, but there's a connection – I know there is. Hughie turns up. Joan goes missing. That red car—'

'For God's sake, that red car has never been seen again.' Dougie's voice rose, almost to a shout.

'I know, but what if whoever was in it took Joan?' I was shouting too now. We never did this, never. 'What if he took her and threw her off the pier? Is that something else that can't have happened because I've said it? Why else was the sideboard all open and rifled if someone didn't take her? Eh?'

'Stop!' Dougie stood up, began to pace about in front of the fire. 'She must've been looking for something. You said she was anxious. She was probably in some sort of hyper state. Why would anyone kidnap an old woman who keeps herself to herself and throw her off a pier? It makes no sense. Why?'

'I don't know! I don't know, do I? That's what I'm trying to figure out!' By now I was standing up too, meeting Dougie's eye with my own defiant gaze. 'I'm going to the police station. Right now.'

'No!'

That shocked me. I took a step back. 'What do you mean, no?'

Dougie's face fell into sorrow, eyes closing momentarily in a bid to stay calm. 'Joan had been showing signs of dementia for months – you told me that yourself. The guy at the hospital is just a middle-aged bloke who reminds you of some bastard you went out with who messed with your head. Worse than messed with your head – sorry, I don't mean to trivialise it. But Joan must have sent those messages on Thursday night, and they will have been sent posthumously because they'll have been stored on the server. She won't have had her Wi-Fi or her 4G on or whatever. She's old, Kirst. Was. They're not clued up on tech. They don't even know what 4G is.'

'She did know what 4G is! She knew her way around an iPhone better than I do. She ordered clothes on it! She did her

Sudoku on it! Those texts were in response to mine, to things I did! Now *you're* being ageist.'

'I'm not! I'm trying to get you to see that it seems like it's all connected but it's not. It's just... not. It's sad, is what it is. Really, really sad. And I'm not just seeing you as a pregnancy, but the truth is, you *are* hormonal and tired, and you *are* facing the birth of our baby in a few short weeks and that must be scary, and all I want to do is to look after you. God knows, I'd be scared out of my wits if I had to push out a whole human being, and I'm so grateful to you for doing this wonderful job for us, putting yourself through it all so that we can have a family.'

I sniffed, felt my heart rate slow a little.

'Hey.' Dougie stepped forward and took my hand. 'You've *got* to let the police do their job. You've already told them what you know. There's nothing else to say. You need to look after yourself now, if not for yourself then for our baby, OK? Precious cargo. For us? For me.'

'I've got to go. I have a night shift.' I knew I was being brusque, but I couldn't help myself.

'Can't you ring in sick?'

'You know better than to ask that.'

'I know, but you're upset. You're totally exhausted.'

'Me being exhausted won't stop the babies coming,' I said, as kindly as I could, and planted a kiss on Dougie's cheek. Everything was getting on top of me, but I didn't want to leave on a sore note. 'I won't sleep now anyway. It'll do me good to get out of myself and forget about all of it. I'll see you in the morn. Love you.'

TWENTY-FOUR

KIRSTY

KS/transcript #20

So this would take us to the Tuesday, I think. Tuesday morning. I can remember stirring at the sound of Dougie getting up for work. I'd only been in bed for half an hour by then. Nights are a killer. A double killer when you're heavily pregnant. But I had the day off and I only had one shift left, and Postnatal was way easier than the delivery room.

I rolled over and closed my eyes, letting the familiar noises wash over me: the shower running on Dougie's lovely shoulders, the wardrobe door opening and closing, the rustle of work jeans and shirt being pulled on. A kiss on my head, a warm whisper in my ear:

'Bye, darlin'. Try and rest, eh?'

'I won't move from this bed,' I muttered, opening one eye. 'Promise.'

'There's some tuna mayo in the fridge and soft rolls in the bread bin. Make sure you eat. Bye then. Love you.'

'Love you too. Have a good day.'

Minutes later, the front door closed with a soft click. I

redoubled my efforts to sleep, closing my eyes tight and snuggling further under the duvet. I tried, I really did, but Hughie Reynolds swaggered into my mind, an intrusive thought in human form.

'Hey, babe, fancy a spin out to the loch?' He was holding up the green canvas rucksack he used to have, grinning. No one looked at you the way Hughie did. No one had ever looked at me like that anyway, like I was the only person on the earth, the only one who mattered. It was always fleeting, a second, maybe two, but the intensity of it made my insides melt.

I squeezed my eyes shut tighter still. Muddy kaleidoscope colours popped and vanished into hazy, purplish black. But still he came; I couldn't stop him. There he was, sitting in his little blue Renault, one long, thin leg out, foot on the pavement, the cheekiness that radiated from him, the capability, the confidence. Something about him, something you couldn't put your finger on, something that stuck. He had brown hair and round tortoiseshell glasses, thin nose and lips, small eyes. Really nothing special – a cocky sixth year calling at his girlfriend's gaff to show her his new wheels.

But to me, at seventeen, he was the coolest person I had ever known. And somehow, maybe because I'd found him at his lowest ebb, taken him into my home like a wee bird with a broken wing, maybe because my family had fussed him and helped nurse him back to his dazzling self, maybe I felt like he belonged to me.

'That's never yours?' There I am, walking towards him down the front path of my old family home. I'm giddy with excitement and full of it, and I feel so light in my body just thinking about it, it's like I'm walking on air. I'm thinking, someone I know has actually bought an actual car. 'Did you buy it? Did you really? I can't believe it.'

'Told you I would. Get in. I'll take you for a spin.'

Did you love him? Dougie had asked me once, early on in our relationship.

I did. I had. I loved him as a friend and as a boyfriend, but he was more than that. He was part of our family, almost as if he and I had been married or something. I don't know, I can't explain it. Little things, like he'd take his turn making a brew, or one time he and Dad cooked the fish they'd caught for our tea. I can still remember the two of them in the kitchen, riffing like they were a double act on some dumb mid-morning cookery show.

And so afterwards – it was heartbreak, yes, but more, somehow. Confusion. The burn of betrayal. Humiliation. Grief. And something else, something that had always lingered, that seeing him again had made me realise still lingered: an unfinished story, a note missing from the end of a song, a last conversation I never got to have. If you'd asked me in that moment to put what I had to say to him in one word, one word only, I would have replied: *Why?*

Now, of course, the person I loved was Dougie – mind, body and soul. Hughie was a younger love, intense – infatuation in the mix, for sure. He was banter, teenage messing. Nicknames. KK, he called me. I called him Reynolds or Specky. Sometimes he called me Titch, on account of me not being very tall. Pushing and shoving, throwing and being thrown shrieking into the shallows at the beach, all for laughs. I loved him because I trusted him, I think. I loved him because my whole family loved him, though we never said it out loud, not at the time and not afterwards. The love was part of the grief, the shock. Everything we'd shared, everything we were together – from the first shaky notes of his devastated orphanhood to the raucous laughter at the beach – these things were real to me. And I truly believed they were real to him.

Outside, a car alarm went off. Moments later, it stopped. I'd tried hard to get back to sleep, but I was wide awake now, and like a rock in my chest, it hit me. My friend was dead. My friend had drowned in the winter sea. I had known it before I knew it, and now I knew it for sure. What had been tension, shimmering and fizzing inside my chest, was now solid, heavy in my guts. I sat up, eyes sore, gritty, yawning so hugely I felt faint. I reached over to the nightstand and turned on Radio Scotland. Poor Joan replaced Hughie with her lifeless and floating form, grey-fleshed, dead-eyed, lost.

At eight o'clock, *Good Morning Scotland* went to the news. I listened with a terrible concentration as a police spokesman read a prepared statement asking for information about Mrs Joan Wood. Who she might have seen recently. Where she might have been on Thursday, who she might have spoken to. I knew I had to go back to the station, and that I would go that morning, that I would not wait for Dougie.

As I lay in bed, bones so heavy against the mattress it felt like they were half submerged, I wondered if Stella had contacted the police. Her encounter with Joan put her in a specific place and time, didn't it? With her viewpoint over the back road to the harbour, she might have been the last person to see her alive.

But then Joan was back here on Thursday night, wasn't she? Wasn't it Thursday her car was on the drive? Or was that Friday? I needed these facts for the police now. Should have written them down. Would have, if only I'd had faith in my own sense of things.

But as I showered and dressed, something began to strengthen within me, as last night's conversation drifted in and out, certain words repeating themselves, rephrasing themselves. In the clarity of the morning, and after at least some sleep, Dougie's theory about Joan's messages coming in after she'd died seemed flimsy, as did the dismissal of the lurking red car, the rifled drawers. These were exactly the kind of things that folk in true-crime documentaries didn't take any notice of until it was too late: the strange car seen only once or twice, the mug in the same place for days, the funny mood the victim was in that day, the guy that looked like your ex.

Dougie had been trying to get me to calm down, I knew that, to stop obsessing enough to get to bed and rest. This precious cargo belonged to us both. We were both nervous, both wanting all to be well. Just because I was entering my thirty-sixth week didn't mean it was all done and dusted. I knew that more than anyone. This new life that would be our joint responsibility would change our relationship forever. How was anyone ever ready for such a thing? What would it be like afterwards? What would *we* be like afterwards? I didn't want to let this thing with Joan come between us, but at the same time, I had to go to the police right now, without telling Dougie. I knew if I rang, Dougie would try again to dissuade me, and I didn't want that, not again.

Downstairs, I made some toast and a decaf coffee, took them into the sitting room and stared out of the window, eating standing up while I gathered myself to make my move. Joan's place was just out of sight, but I didn't need to see it to envisage the bleak flicker of its impromptu fence. At the thought of the cops scouring my old pal's home for clues, the ache of tears came to my throat. Poor Joan. So private in life, so exposed in death. I couldn't get the thought of the freezing water out of my mind. Her last moments must have been filled with such fear and despair. If it was suicide, what on earth must she have been going through to throw herself to such an icy death?

I wiped away tears with the back of my hand. Whatever Joan had been worried about, no matter what, I could have helped. If I'd followed my instincts that first day, or on Thursday evening, maybe I could have saved her. But instead, I'd waited. I was called into work. I'd let myself be persuaded by Dougie to leave it. And now it was too late.

You can't help the dead, can you?

Except I could help her now. Her messages on my phone might provide some clue as to what had happened to her. Because they hadn't been sent posthumously – I was now more convinced than ever – and that *proved* foul play. And if Joan's death wasn't suicide, the police needed to look into it properly. They needed to find her killer.

Dizziness overtook me. I had to lean for a moment against the windowsill. *Killer.* The word was outlandish, impossible. People like Joan didn't get murdered. They just didn't.

An accident then. Joan goes walking. She stumbles. The cold water causes her to gasp. The water floods her lungs. There would have been no surviving. But that still left the question of the texts.

If, if by some fine thread of a chance, she had taken her own life, I needed to know why. Because there had to have been a specific reason, something that happened the day Hughie Reynolds' doppelgänger appeared in my life like an unwanted guest at a party. And whilst it was hard to see a link, I thought of those documentaries again, how full they were of unrelated events, which turned out not to be unrelated after all. Who was to say Hughie or Barry or whoever he was wasn't part of the picture? What if... oh my God, what if that red car was *his*?

No. That was too far-fetched. But hormones or no, suspicious death or no, whether it was murder, suicide or a tragic accident, I had to stop turning it over in my mind and turn it over to the police. Whatever Dougie said, I had relevant information, and this time I was going to demand to speak to someone old enough to tie his own shoelaces.

TWENTY-FIVE

KIRSTY

KS/transcript #21

I was shown into the same room by the same laddie who'd been on reception the day before. After a few minutes, a female officer came into the room and smiled.

'Thank you for waiting,' she said, sitting down opposite. She was older than me, about forty, I would have said, with dull dyed brown hair tied into a thin ponytail and big brown eyes ringed with the telltale dark smudges of tiredness. A new mum, I guessed, or she suffered with insomnia or was maybe just up too late. 'I'm Angela,' she said. 'Pleased to meet you, Ms Shaw.'

'Kirsty. Pleased to meet you.'

'Kirsty. Great. You have some information concerning Joan Wood, is that right?'

'I came in before. Yesterday, in fact. Joan is my neighbour. Was. My good friend actually. Yes. She was my pal.' Tears pricked. I tried to blink them away. 'Sorry. I'm still...'

'It's OK. Take your time.' The cop slid a tissue across the table, a small act of kindness that threatened to melt me into nothing but water.

'I came in yesterday,' I started again, once I'd composed myself. 'Joan had been missing since last week, only I didn't know if she was missing or not because her car came and went but she was never in, and her curtains were open at funny times and her back door was unlocked one time, and... Sorry, I don't know where to start.'

'You're the lady who came in yesterday?' Angela asked. 'Your information was incredibly helpful, thank you. We acted on it immediately. I'm afraid my colleague didn't take note of your name otherwise we would have called you back in.'

My mouth fell open. Tod hadn't done his job properly, the arrogant wee sod. But he had done something. 'Is that why you were there? At Joan's house? Because of me?'

Angela nodded. 'We went straight there. Quicker than waiting for dental records. There were photos, ID. It was very helpful.'

'And was it suicide?'

'I can't tell you that at the moment.'

'That's OK. Only I didn't tell the laddie, but she sent me some messages. On my phone, like. I didn't tell him because I thought he wouldn't take me seriously if I'd had messages from her. That's why I didn't come in before yesterday. But I knew something wasn't right, you see. And now... now it's even more strange because if she entered the water on Thursday like you said on the news, that means she sent me those messages after she died. Which means... well, it means someone else sent them, doesn't it?'

I showed the messages to Angela, explaining what had happened prior to each one.

'How did she know I'd been in her house?' I asked. 'If she was already in the water? Or more to the point, how did whoever it was know, unless they'd been watching? And that car driving away with its lights off could have been the red car, couldn't it? Something funny's going on. I think she's either been frightened to her death or... or murdered.' I made myself stop despite wanting desperately to add that I'd seen my ex from eleven years ago on the day this all started. I needed this woman to take me seriously. And in the cold space of the police station, I could see more clearly that mentioning someone who looked like Hughie Reynolds but was actually some guy called Barry Sefton might have risked her seeing me as a conspiracy theorist.

'Can I take your phone a moment?' she asked.

'Sure.'

She noted down Joan's number and gave the phone back. 'This is very helpful, thank you.'

'The last time I saw her,' I said, 'I had the impression she'd seen someone. She was scared. This person had scared her. She was talking about her husband, but he died way back so I thought she was just, you know, having a bit of a senior moment, but later, I thought maybe she *had* seen someone and she was confusing him with her late hubby. Lachlan. She said he didn't know... something. She said she couldn't tell me whatever it was. When I asked her what was the matter, like. "I canna tell you," she said, exactly like that. Like she was scared. But whoever the person she took for Lachlan was, maybe it was him who took her? Maybe it was him in that car? Maybe he took her to the harbour and—'

'Let's not get ahead of ourselves.' Angela's smile had cooled. I knew I'd said too much.

'Did he tell you about the coffee mug?' I asked quickly. 'The laddie? Tod? The coffee mug in the exact same place? Oh, and the drawers were rifled.'

But Angela was already standing up. 'He did, thank you. But we have to go through the correct procedures, and it's best to avoid speculation.'

'It's just that if she didn't send those texts, then who did?'

'We'll look into it.'

'And if she'd driven herself to the harbour, her car would still be there, wouldn't it? So where is it?'

'Ms Shaw.' Angela held out her arm towards the door, and I felt the heat of a blush climb up my neck. 'Thank you so much for your time.'

TWENTY-SIX

KIRSTY

KS/transcript #22

Once again I found myself outside the police station, the heavy blue door shut firmly behind me like a slap on the arse. The cold wind bit with sharp teeth. I pulled my hat down low, buried my chin in my scarf and shoved my hands into my pockets.

What now?

I didn't know. On the way back, I took the roads like a game of snakes and ladders, end to end, up and down, zigzagging for Joan's white Polo. Nothing. Where the hell had she parked and how the hell could she have walked all the way to the harbour? It was impossible.

I couldn't face going straight home, so I stopped in town and treated myself to a sandwich and decaf coffee in a café. I tried to read a magazine someone had left. I suppose I was pretending to be someone who reads magazines in coffee shops and whiles away the hours wondering which look she should choose for the coming season. But my budget would never have stretched to any of those looks, and it didn't matter anyway because I couldn't trick my mind into relaxing. My mind was having none of it. The conversation with the policewoman played and replayed. I gave up, paid the bill and left.

I still had no idea where I wanted to go or what I wanted to do.

Inevitably, I ended up back at the close. The police car and tape had gone. I wondered if the officer had taken my information seriously; if she had listened or had just been humouring me.

I felt like I was running around in circles, getting nowhere. In front of our house, I stopped the car but I didn't get out. Frankly, the thought of being stuck at home made my skin itch.

A text landed. Dougie.

Are you resting? X

Yes, I replied. *Feet well and truly up xx*

Staring at the lie I'd just told, the words *trust your gut* came to me. I hadn't trusted my gut so far, and now Joan was dead. But trusting my gut wasn't the problem. The problem was getting anyone else to trust it. Frustration at Dougie, at the police was hardening into a nut of resentful determination. Wendy and Dougie would shake their heads at me failing to stay at home with my feet up on cushions, but I didn't care. I'd rest when the baby came, but right now, I had to find out what the hell was going on. And a good place to start was Reeny.

Reeny's car was parked on the opposite side of Gray Street from last time. I sighed, taking in the multitude of brightly coloured doors in the blocks of pale grey granite. The only thing to do was try one and hope whoever answered knew which number Reeny lived at. I parked up, swearing at the effort it took to get myself out of the car. No one tells you it will be like this, I thought, resolving to be sure to warn my pregnant mums about what was to come. I had first-hand knowledge now of what the three stages Dreary, Cheery and Weary really meant.

I rang the doorbell of the ground-floor flat nearest Reeny's car. After a minute or two, a woman with strong prescription glasses that made her eyes look like wee stones answered and told me that Reeny lived two doors down. I thanked her and made my way to the yellow front door. I should have guessed. Reeny, it appeared, liked the colour yellow. As I reached for the doorbell, I wondered if she might be the only person who wouldn't dismiss what I had to say as hormonal conspiracy theories. I rang the bell. From within came the yap-yapping of a small dog.

After a minute or two, the door opened an inch. There was a snuffling sound, a growl, and a black nose wedged itself in the crack about a foot from the floor.

'Kirsty,' Reeny said. She opened the door wide and almost immediately her eyes filled. 'Oh, Kirsty. Isn't it dreadful? Come in, hen. Come in.' The little dog – some form of terrier, I reckoned – barked loudly whilst at the same time backing away.

'Dinna mind Sergeant,' Reeny said. 'He's a' gob and nae troosers.'

'Hello there, wee man.' I bent as best I could to pet the dog, who calmed down quickly and trotted away into the interior of the house.

I followed Reeny inside. Where Joan was tall and regal, Reeny was stocky and brisk, her silver hair straight, almost oily with shine and cut long on one side and short on the other. She was wearing patterned harem pants, what looked like a hand-knitted jumper made from multicoloured wool and a coral-coloured silk scarf. On her feet – the only similarity in their styles – were the same sheepskin boot slippers Joan wore.

I imagined them choosing these slippers together on one of their shopping trips to John Lewis and felt myself choke.

Reeny looked exhausted, with black shadows under her eyes. She asked after the bump and told me she'd been as sick as a dog with her son, Fergus, but that her daughter, Laurie, was *nae bother at a'*. Her voice still had its brightness but she was more quietly spoken than usual – the stuffing knocked out of her, no doubt, by shock and grief.

'When are you due?' she asked, and, 'When are you finishing work?' and, 'How much time are you taking off?'

I answered on autopilot, explaining that Dougie and me were both going to take parental leave.

'Very modern,' Reeny said, brushing her hands over her trousers. 'So different these days and a good thing too.'

We were being brave, but we'd both been emptied out by this terrible loss – Reeny more than me. It must be so hard to lose a friend of so many years, I thought – so suddenly, so sense-lessly – and my hard, sore heart broke for her.

She insisted on making coffee and disappeared into her kitchen at the back of the house, leaving me to settle on the spongy velvet sofa, which was the colour of soft-boiled egg yolk. The dog, Sergeant, sniffed at my ankles a moment before deciding there was nothing of interest scent-wise, turning his back on me and curling up in his tweed doggy bed. The room was cosy, the walls covered in photographs of Reeny and the generations of her family – school portraits of grandchildren in uniforms, holiday snaps, a picture of Reeny and what must have been her late husband, him in a kilt and sporran, Reeny in an elegant ballgown of creamy yellow silk. In the tiny window of the wood-burning stove, orange flames danced about. I fought an overwhelming sleepiness, the urge to lie flat and cry in that nice warm room.

'Here we are.' Reeny was carrying a tray loaded with a coffee pot, a milk jug and two delicate china mugs. 'You need your strength,' she added as she slid the tray onto the low wooden table. In addition to the coffee there were some thickly buttered digestive biscuits, the sort of snack Dougie would have called a heart attack on a plate. Reeny sat down in the armchair and sighed. 'Tuck in now. Don't be shy.'

I helped myself to a buttered biscuit while Reeny poured the coffee, not caring if it was decaf or the real thing. I suspected women of Reeny's age had little time for decaffeinated anything. She bustled about pouring milk, adding sugar. In the few times our paths had crossed, she'd always struck me as a bundle of positive energy. Her friendship with Joan was one of opposites attracting – I saw it in that moment. The two women shared what many of their generation do: they were power-houses that ran on the batteries of stoicism, brisk daily walks and a total refusal to let anyone do anything at all for them. But today, even Reeny appeared diminished, her shoulders round, her mouth struggling to maintain its usual upturn.

'I saw it on the news last night,' she said, lifting her mug and nudging the tray towards me. 'I couldna believe it. Couldna believe it. I knew something was up, but this...'

'Did you?' My skin tingled. 'Know something was up, I mean.'

'Aye. We went to the big Asda on Thursday morning and she seemed affa out of sorts. Affa out of sorts. Then on the Friday morn... Fridays we always meet, regular as clockwork, but when I texted to confirm, she didna reply. So I rang her and... well, she didn't pick up. I texted again to say I hoped she was OK, but when she replied, she was very brusque, I suppose you'd say.' She shook her head and gave a sad half-laugh. 'I know she could be a wee bit blunt, for want of a better word, but she was never rude. Not like that.'

The sweet biscuit had stuck in my throat, but I couldn't seem to coordinate my mug to my mouth in order to wash it down with some coffee. 'Wh-What did she say?'

'She told me to stay away basically. It was... well, it was rude, there's nae other way to say it.'

'Do you think she sent that message?'

Reeny frowned. 'What do you mean, dear?'

'It's just that by Friday, she was... I mean, she'd passed.'

'Well now.' Reeny's frown deepened; her biscuit hovered in mid-air. 'That's a fair point. I suppose I thought it must've been soon after that she...'

'They said Thursday afternoon or Friday morning.'

'Aye. I suppose I didn't think about that, no. But now you're saying it...'

I didn't add that I'd received blunt texts too. The woman was already shattered; I feared I'd only make things worse. Instead, I found myself reiterating Dougie's weak reassurances. 'Texts arrive late sometimes.'

'You're probably right,' she said softly, reflected flames from the stove wavering in her eyes. 'Fair took me back though, so it did.'

'Took you back? To what?'

'A long time ago, hen. See, Joan and I used to be best pals.'

'I thought you still were. I thought you went way back.'

'We were, aye. We do. But not always. After her daughter left, she...'

'Her daughter?' The hairs on my arms rose, but Reeny was looking around the room, searching for the word, as if she hadn't heard me at all.

'... withdrew,' she finished eventually.

I put my coffee back on the tray. 'So she *did* have a daughter?'

TWENTY-SEVEN

KIRSTY

KS/transcript #23

Reeny's expression was full of sadness.

'She never spoke about her,' she said. 'But aye. Rose. Rosie. Left school at fifteen. I probably shouldna be telling you this, but I canna see the harm now. She fell pregnant to a teacher at the school, you see. Aberdeen High.'

'Aberdeen High? Oh God, I went there!'

'Aye. It was quite the scandal, I can tell you. A horrible time for Joan, for Lachie, and of course for Rosie. Lachie was... he was a very traditional man. A judge. Old-fashioned in his way, ken? Rosie was the only child, the apple of his eye, and he came down hard.' Reeny pursed her lips and shook her head. 'She... took off.' She made a fluttering motion with her hand and looked up, blinking. The skin around her eyes was red. She met my gaze. 'They never saw her again.'

I felt a physical pain in my chest. 'Never? Not ever? Oh. Oh, that's so sad.'

'All hell broke loose. The teacher was fired. Nowadays he'd be locked up, but it was different times. I dinna know what became of him, but Lachie and Joan were devastated, absolutely devastated. Lachie never recovered. I don't think Joan did either, in many ways. They tried to find the lassie, but... she'd gone. I think it killed him, if I'm honest. And it changed Joan. She was never garrulous or one for gadding about, but after that...' Reeny shook her head. 'She was, I don't know how to say it except sad. Broken, like. Closed up like a book.'

'She had a photograph of Rosie. In her bedroom.'

'Did she?'

'I only know because I looked after her when she had COVID. But she never mentioned her, and I never felt like I could ask.'

'Aye, well. Joan did make you feel like that. They were estranged. Joan tried over the years, as I've said. I think she must've had an address because she wrote to her. Anyway, Joan dropped out of touch with all her friends. All except me. We were still close, in as much as anyone could be close to Joan, like, ken? But then, after Lachie died – this was, oh, a decade or so ago, maybe more – she suddenly stopped returning my calls. Just like that.' Reeny clicked her fingers. 'Stopped dead. I'd helped arrange the funeral, write the eulogy and a' that stuff, ken? I'd sat with her, cried with her. I'd held her hand in the silence, but she just...' She made a puff of smoke with her hand.

'I tried to keep in touch, but in the end, I had to let her go. I told her she knew where to find me and that I'd always be there, and I meant it. I knew it had nothing to do with me, the way she was, but I couldna keep banging my head against the wall, you know? As much as I cared for her, I felt like I was outside a room and she was inside, determined to cry all her tears alone. If someone doesna want to let you in, they dinna want to let you in, and to keep trying – well, it hurts too much. In the end.'

'I thought she'd had enough of me,' I managed.

Reeny shook her head. 'Oh no, lassie. She adored you. You were the daughter she'd lost.'

'Did she actually say that?'

'She loved the bones of you, dearie. She might nae have said it directly, it wasna her way at a', but she did. The angel up the road, she called you.'

'The angel up the... Oh.' I pushed my fingers over my eyes, throat aching with swallowed tears.

The two of us sat a moment, the hiss and crackle of the fire the only sound.

'So is Rosie still alive?' I asked, once I felt able to speak.

'She'd be in her sixties now. Early sixties.'

'And the baby?'

'Joan never said, but I think it was accepted that Rosie'd had a termination or had it adopted. Or lost it. Miscarried, like, I dinna ken.'

'No wonder she never spoke about her.'

Reeny raised her eyebrows. 'Personally, I think that was a mistake. Locking it all up in a box doesna take the pain away, does it? Talking about it won't either, I get that, but it can ease things. Anyway, a few years ago, we became friends again.'

'I had no idea. She always said you were an old friend. Her best friend, she said.'

'I was. Not that she'd ever say that to me. I didna see her for years after Lachie passed, but then I bumped into her up at the beach. She'd recently moved into your road. By then, I'd lost Logan, my husband, ken? We went to a café, her and me. Tea and scones. Old ladies together.' Reeny gave a brief laugh weighted with sadness. 'She still had that dour way about her, you know. Hair all done just so, everything just right. She was always turned out affa smart. Like she was going to work, even in her seventies. Anyway, she told me that shortly after Lachlan passed on, she found out Rosie had joined him in heaven.'

'Rosie *died*?'

She'd be in her sixties now, Reeny had said only a moment ago. I hadn't realised she'd meant...

'Aye. Four or five years had passed by then. As I say, Joan had moved out of the big house in Ferryhill to the close. I understood why she'd nae been able to see me or anyone for a time. Such grief takes too much from you, ken? And just like that, we were friends again, like before. I didna push her. I never pushed her. I let her tell me only what she wanted to tell me and left the rest alone.'

'You were a good friend.'

'I hope so. I think I realised eventually that even if she was alone in that room, it was enough for her to know I was sitting outside it. Anything else was about me and what I wanted, and if you care for someone, it's not about what *you* want, is it?'

It was late on that Tuesday afternoon and almost dark by the time I left Reeny with promises to keep in touch. I meant it. I had the sense of a new friendship that felt more like the work of years than a few hours by the fire, and it made me feel just a tiny bit better. There was someone else who had loved Joan as I did and who could keep her memory alive with me.

Reeny hovered on the doorstep. I can still see her, this bright, compassionate woman. She'd wrapped the rest of the biscuits in foil, and there on the step she pressed them into my hands.

'Keep your strength up,' she said. 'You're eating for two, so.'

'I'll be round next week once I've got my last shift out of the way,' I said, bending to kiss her soft cheek. 'You take care now.'

Outside, the air was wispy with the beginnings of the haar. I suppose if you're not local I should explain that the haar is the sea fret that locals joke raises the prices of properties further inland each time it rolls into the city. By the time I'd reached my car, it was so thick I could barely see ten metres. I got into my car and fired the engine, turned the headlights on full beam and pulled out very slowly. Visibility was down to five metres by now and I had to lean forward, as best I could in my condition, squinting. At the top of Reeny's road, I checked the rear-view. Edging out of a parking space about two metres behind were the headlights of another car. As it pulled out and moved slowly towards me, I recognised the trademark four silver rings of an Audi through the fog. And the colour: red.

My throat closed like a clam. I stayed at the junction, indicator clicking, straining to see who was in the driving seat. A man, I thought. Tall. Some sort of beanie hat. I was pretty sure the driver I'd seen the other time had been tall and had been wearing a woolly hat. The same driver, then. Had to be.

I turned right onto the Great Western Road. Heart beating fit to burst, I made myself drive slowly, gaze switching between the rear-view and the side mirrors. The road was like a funeral procession in the mist. The red car also took a right, as I'd known it would, keeping a distance between us. I tried to make out the registration – 32, I thought. Maybe an S. It was hopeless; all I could see were headlights behind, tail lights in front. Stomach lurching, I indicated left and slowed to ten miles per hour. A few seconds later, the Audi followed. My chest tightened.

I slowed down even further – five miles per hour now. The car behind also slowed, still keeping its distance. My breath was coming fast and shallow. The entrance to my cul-de-sac was ahead on the left. I couldn't decide whether to take it. But then, if it was the same red car, it had already been to our road. Most probably the driver had already seen me.

I took the turn, barely breathing at all now. Half of me was willing whoever it was to follow just so I could see who they were; the other half was praying they would continue on their way and leave me the hell alone. At Joan's bungalow, no more than five metres from the mouth of the close, I stopped dead.

'Come on then,' I said through gritted teeth, eyes glued to the rear-view. 'Come on, if you're coming.'

The Audi glided past the turn. A man at the wheel. Almost definitely, though it was hard to tell. But was he following me or not?

I pushed my head to the steering wheel and let out a roar. This was not my imagination. No way. I should drive back the way I'd come and chase this person down. But I was shaking with fear. In the end, I have to admit, I didn't dare.

Instead, I pulled onto our drive, shaking with fright. I wasn't expecting the van to be there as Dougie was going out straight from work. Fighting the urge to call, I heaved myself out of the car, legs trembling beneath me as I walked the short distance to the house. Once inside, I leant back against the front door, panting with a strange mix of fear and relief. I was home. I was safe. But if the red Audi had been following me, it must also have followed me to Reeny's. Which meant it had most probably followed me from the police station. Or to the police station. And now it had followed me home. Whoever was in it knew where I lived, and that I'd been to the police. I didn't know for sure that it was the same car as last week, but at the same time I did – in that gut of mine, the same way I'd known everything.

But who was in that car and what did they want with me?

In my pocket, my phone buzzed. Back still pressed against the door for support, I took it out and saw there was a text from an unknown number. Holding my breath, I opened it.

Keep your nose out of things that don't concern you. You have been warned.

TWENTY-EIGHT

KIRSTY

KS/transcript #24

A noise that was half-word, half-cry escaped me. My breath was coming hot and quick against the palm of my hand. It wasn't in my head. None of it was in my head. It was out there, and it was real: threat, danger, someone.

You have been warned.

Whoever was in that red car had sent that text, I was sure of it. Whoever sent that text had probably also sent the texts from Joan's phone. That was reasonable, wasn't it? It certainly didn't feel like too much of a leap. I closed my eyes and tried to trace a line of thought. Whoever was in that red car was linked to Joan's death – was that logical? I was no police officer, but surely it wasn't completely impossible? Logic or no, possible or impossible, I knew it in the very depths of myself. Someone was responsible for my old friend's death, and that someone was threatening me to make me stay quiet. Was that right? But why threaten me? I didn't know anything!

The only real information I had, I had already given to the police.

The house felt colder inside than it did out. It was as if the granite walls had stored the winter chill and were now radiating it from their huge grey bricks. My heart was quick, my chest still tight. I wished I'd left the heating on, even on low. It wasn't worth putting it on now; it wouldn't have time to warm the house through in the hour or two I had before I went to meet the guys, and besides, I reminded myself, we had to make economies, especially now the baby was almost here.

A deep, hot bath finally penetrated the cold in my marrow. It took a good ten minutes for my teeth to stop chattering. I let myself soak, tried to relax, but it was impossible. Joan's frightened expression wouldn't leave me, her eyes looking through me as if to find someone else. Joan and her daughter smiling from a photograph in happier times. The empty house that didn't feel empty. The daughter who died so soon after the husband. The mug on the coffee table, the news, the body in the water, the red car's four silver rings, the police, the man who wasn't Hughie. Barry Sefton. Reeny. The number plate hiding in the haar.

I climbed into bed, put on the electric blanket and pulled the duvet over my head. When I opened my eyes, two hours had passed and I was running late. I dressed quickly and went downstairs, microwaved some tinned chicken soup and ate it standing up, steeling myself to go out.

Outside the house, I scanned the close. There was no red car. No neighbours, no police officers, no one at all. Winter could be so desolate, and I felt it deeply in that moment. If Dougie had been there, I would have cancelled. We could have cuddled up, watched something mindless on TV, eaten chocolate. But Dougie wasn't there. No one was there. No one would pick me up if I fell, no one would call an ambulance or run for help. There was, quite literally, no one to hear me scream. The wind buffeted me, almost blowing the beanie from my head. The cold was liquid ice, the kind that ran down your collar no matter how tightly you tied your clothes to your shivering body.

I hugged myself, patting at my arms, and took a step towards the road. I needed to see people. I needed not to be alone. By the time I got back, Dougie would be home. It would be worth going out just for that.

I took another step, another, but stopped, my chest tight. And then it hit me: I was too scared to walk into town. It was as simple as that. And somewhere deep down, the promises I'd made to Wendy and Dougie called to me. *Rest up. Just chill out for once. Precious cargo.* For God's sake, woman, just drive. I pressed the key fob and the Focus bleeped into life. Dougie and Wendy would approve. But it wasn't the distance or the cold or my swollen ankles that scared me. It was who might be out there, waiting. Until I figured out what was going on, it was better to stay safe. It wasn't like I'd be drinking anyway. I'd park as near to the pub as I could, get there in one piece, and tell my old school pals everything that had happened since I'd seen Barry Sefton strolling down the hospital corridors like he owned the place.

I just had to hope they'd believe me.

TWENTY-NINE

HUGHIE

HR/audio/excerpt #5

I have to say, I was shocked to see who you'd married. I guess I would've imagined you with someone more... intellectual. Maybe someone from out of town. Less homely. By which I mean, I suppose, someone more like me. God, I can be so vain, can't I? But *Dougie*? From the year above us? Does *Dougie* make you laugh like I used to? Is *Dougie* exciting to be with? When you're with *Dougie*, do you feel truly alive?

You can't answer, I know that. But you always were so nice to talk to, so good at listening, so caring, and I've been so lonely. Being here with you feels... I don't know... like old times. Not that I ever would've tied your hands back then. Not unless you'd asked me very nicely.

I suppose loneliness is the price I've had to pay for success. OK, so I'm not simply surviving, I'm not scraping an existence, but I'm not *living*; my life still feels like a poor simulacrum of my aspirations. Simulacrum means a representation, by the way, not the real thing. What I mean is, my life is an imitation of everything I wanted, and despite everything, it still feels like it. Forgive me if that explanation was patronising, but yes, my life is like a really great forgery. From the outside, you'd never be able to tell the difference. But when I said I got laid, for example, that's all it ever is. I can do the restaurant, the gallantry; I pick up the tab. I'm *nice* about it. I'm not here to make anyone feel cheap, but none of it *means* anything. I suppose I have a reputation as commitment-avoidant at best, user at worst. But I can't simply hand over power just like that. Call it an occupational hazard. Most people's personal boundaries are either too low or too high, I've found, depending on one's particular brand of childhood trauma. Mine are too high, in case you're interested. This is often the case with survivors like me. And no, I have not had therapy. I read.

But now I have your attention and can be sure you won't – can't – stop me, I could tell you a little more about the real me: that anonymous hospital porter, the boy who stood with his head bowed as he heard that his mother and her lover had died a seedy little death in a seedy little flat where the Forth meets the frigid North Sea. The young boy who had tried so hard to transcend his beginnings, who was so determined to make his way honestly, painstakingly, slowly – to be everything his feckless mother was not.

Everything changed that day. Her death was my second chance.

And I took it.

THIRTY

KIRSTY

KS/transcript #25

'Here she blows,' Tasha called out as I walked into Under the Hammer. She was already standing, her dark blonde hair scraped into a thick ponytail. 'Ahoy there.'

'I'm a whale all right,' I said, laughter shaking reluctantly out of me. 'Can't wait for this thing to come out.'

'Nature's clever that way,' Tasha said. 'Makes pregnancy so shite that by the end even the prospect of childbirth is tempting. What can I get you?'

'Tomato juice, cheers. Can you get them to put a slice of lemon in it? And loads of Tabasco. And salt. And only two ice cubes. Sorry. It's the baby making these demands.'

Tash saluted the bump. 'Right you are, boss.'

I exchanged hugs and how-are-yous with Cal and Gus before unwrapping the winter layers from my weary body.

'Sit here,' Gus said, giving up the big chair for me.

'Cheers, Gus, you're a pal.' I took the comfy seat while Gus grabbed a wee stool I might have broken had I sat on it.

Tasha returned with the tomato juice and more pints of

heavy for her and the boys. We swapped chat, funnies, grumbles, settling into each other's company easily as we always had. Then Tasha set me up by asking if I'd seen the Hughie lookie-likie again.

'Hughie lookie-likie?' Cal's face was all question. He and Gus exchanged a brief glance. 'What's this about?'

So I told them. I started with the strange sighting of the man who turned out to be Barry Sefton, and then described the ensuing events, culminating in Joan Wood's suspicious death.

'So you knew her then?' Gus asked.

'Aye.' Tears welled. 'We were good pals actually.'

'I'm affa sorry.' Gus took a contemplative sip of his beer while my three dearest friends shook their heads in sympathy. 'Poor woman. Poor you.'

I carried on, glad of the space to talk without interruption, without having to face an expression of doubt, incredulity, scepticism. I have to admit, I felt a pinch of resentment towards Dougie, who could have listened like this, could have believed me completely, without all the caveats. I told them about visiting Reeny earlier that day, the discovery that Joan had a daughter who died.

'The daughter, Rosie, left town after she got pregnant by a teacher at our school.'

'You're joking.' Tasha's mouth was an O. 'Aberdeen High? Who was it?'

'I don't know his name. I don't think she did. Reeny, I mean. It was way before our time obviously, but Rosie was very young. Fifteen.'

'God, that's shocking. When?'

I could practically see Tasha's journalistic antennae twitching. It occurred to me that we'd started this conversation talking about Hughie and now we were talking about Joan, yet the two things weren't linked.

'I haven't worked it out,' I said. 'But if she was only fifteen, it was a long while ago. She'd be in her sixties now, if she'd lived.'

'That's scandalous.' Tasha shook her head. 'He should be in prison. Mind you, he'd be well into his seventies now, wouldn't he, if he's still alive? And what about the text messages? Can we see them?'

I dug out my phone and held it out while they all hooked their heads over the screen. 'These came after she'd gone into the water,' I said. 'Which to me means someone else sent them to throw me off the scent. I would've gone to the police sooner if I hadn't got them. I thought she was still alive.' I pulled up the text from the unknown number. 'Then tonight, I got this.'

Tasha took the phone out of my hand, read the message and passed the phone along to Gus and Cal.

'Shit, Kirst,' Cal said. 'You need to go to the police.'

'I've been,' I said. 'Twice.'

'But that's a threat,' he insisted. 'It's harassment. You should—'

'It's only one message,' I interrupted. 'If the police are dismissing the others as being from Joan, it's only one message, isn't it? Before I got that one, I was on my way back from Reeny's and I saw the red car again. An Audi – 32 something reg. I couldn't read it because of the haar, but it followed me all the way to my close. Then about five minutes later, I got that text.'

'You really do need to go to the police, doll,' Tasha said.

'They're useless.' I threw out my hands.

'I know, but this isna right. Even if you canna prove the car is linked to Joan Wood's death, that last text is evidence of foul play.'

The boys repeated the words, their expressions grim: *It's no right, no right at a'*. Like Dougie, Joan and Reeny, like most folk I knew, their Aberdonian accents were stronger than mine. I found comfort in them, and in the words they contained. These were my people. I felt safe with them.

'Didn't the news say she was a solicitor's secretary?' Gus asked. 'Might be some disgruntled client.'

'But that's ages ago surely,' I replied. 'She was eighty-one.'

'Her husband was a judge,' Tasha said. 'Could be something in that. Some revenge thing.'

'Again, ancient history.'

'And what about this lookie-likie?' Cal said. 'Has he got something to do with all this?'

'We checked the LinkedIn,' Tasha said. 'Unless Hughie Reynolds stole someone else's profile, it's nae him.' She pulled up the app on her phone and showed the boys, who narrowed their eyes and shook their heads.

'I canna really see it,' Gus said. 'I mean, maybe, if you add hair and those stupid glasses he used to wear.'

'The *je suis un French intellectual* ones?' Cal rolled his eyes. 'I wouldna have recognised him fae that photograph, to be honest.'

'If it is him,' Gus said, 'he's nae aged well at a', has he? He looks like shite.'

'How the mighty have fallen, eh?' I managed a smile, though my stomach had folded over. Just the mention of Hughie was enough to make me anxious, even without all the other stuff.

Cal was shaking his head, twisting his glass as if to position it carefully on the beer mat. 'I never liked him, to be honest.'

'*What?*' I met his gaze and scrutinised it. He was serious. 'Since when?'

Cal shrugged. 'There was always something weird about him. And it was terrible the way he left you like that. Shoddy, very shoddy.'

'Shoddy, aye,' Gus chipped in. 'I could never understand

why the girls went so mad for him. I always thought he was a wee bit creepy.'

Mystifyingly, I felt a pang of defensiveness. 'I wouldn't have called him a *creep*.'

Tasha was laughing. 'You canna say that, Gussy! He was our mate. Until he did the dirty on Kirst anyway.' She met my eye momentarily in silent question.

'I never told you guys at the time,' I said, glancing at the boys, 'but Hughie was pretty abusive to me the night before he took off. He got quite nasty when I wouldn't sleep with him.'

'Nasty how?'

I shrugged. 'Ach, just lairy, like, you know? And then he sent me this note. It was... pretty mean. Anyway, I ended up at the doctor's and stuff. I was on meds for a while.'

A silence fell.

'I wish you coulda told us,' Cal said after a moment, his face soft. 'We coulda been there for you.'

'I know that,' I said. 'Trust me, it was enough to know you guys were there if I needed you. I had Tasha. And my folks were really good about it. I got through it. It was a lot at the time, you know? But it's in the past. The letter he left was the worst of it, believe it or not... It messed with my head.'

'Do you remember when we went to Tossa?' Gus turned to Cal. 'He never let us see his passport, did he?'

Cal's eyes widened. 'I'd forgotten about that.' He turned to Tasha and me. 'We were comparing photos, having a laugh, ken, and he just went mental, like. We tried to nick his passport, but he got really aggressive, didn't he?'

Gus nodded. 'He turned pretty nasty.'

'I'd totally forgotten about that,' Cal said again.

My heart had started up, galloping like a wee horse in my chest. Hughie wouldn't show his passport. What did it mean?

'I never went to his house,' I said after a moment. 'Never once in all that time. When he left that letter, I went driving round town trying to find him, kicking myself. I couldn't believe I'd let him know everything about me and there I was, didn't even know his address. He always said it was too small, his flat. He said his foster mum didn't like noise.'

'He didna live in a flat,' Gus said.

'What?' The hairs on my arms rose.

Gus shifted his gaze between us and let it rest on me. 'I went there once to do some homework after school. He lived in a big house. Three floors. Posh, I'd say. Antiques and all that. High ceilings.'

'I always thought the whole parents-dying-in-a-fire was bullshit,' Cal added with the slightly self-satisfied gravity that comes with baseless opinions with a drop of hindsight. 'It was such a cliché, like something from an eighties film.'

'But that's why his skin was rough,' I said. Again, I felt almost like I was defending him. 'Not rough, but thick, like. The burns.'

'Probably eczema,' Cal scoffed. 'But a fire was more glamorous.' He picked up his ale and suctioned a good quarter of a pint.

'You can't say that!' Tasha was laughing. 'He'd lost his parents whatever, however they died. He must've been traumatised, and at fifteen, we all talk a wee bit of shite, don't we? He had nae pals, raging eczema and that funny wispy fringe thing going on. So he made something up, so what? It was pretty exceptional circumstances, to be fair.'

'He never talked about his home,' I said. 'Never talked about his parents. I just assumed it was too painful. When he said he lived in a wee flat, I accepted it. What was I gonna say, *no you don't*? I accepted everything he said. Why wouldn't I have done? We were either at mine or hanging out with you guys or in his car. Why would he lie about his house?'

'Maybe his foster mum wasn't very nice,' Tasha said. 'Did you meet her?'

Gus shook his head. 'She wasna there. But there were home-made biscuits and the fridge was full of food, so it didn't look too bad a deal to me. The house was big, I'm telling you. Maybe she took in orphans like, I don't know, some sort of posh lady charity thing. Giving back to the community.'

'Maybe it was that,' Tasha said. 'Maybe. Maybe he thought if we saw the house, word would get out that he was a posho and he'd get beaten up or something. We had to get him to change his name, don't forget. And he was pretty quick to change his accent, as I recall.'

A dozen new questions were crowding in, adding to the pile. His passport... his parents... his home... his name.

'I wonder why he never let me go to his house,' I said, almost to myself. 'I can't believe I never questioned it at the time. Why wouldn't he let you guys see his passport?' I glanced at the boys. 'Do you think he was using a fake name?'

'He can't have had a fake name,' Gus said. 'He was a kid, not some criminal mastermind. I think it was probably more like his photo was embarrassing. Passport photos can be a total cringe at that age.'

'Right.' I placed my glass back on the table. 'So why lie about his home? And why leave town like a thief in the night? What was he hiding?'

'Hang on.' Tasha's eyes were glued to her phone. She looked up, her face draining of colour. 'Breaking news. Another elderly woman's been found dead.'

THIRTY-ONE
KIRSTY

KS/transcript #26

Tasha held up her phone while the clip from the BBC Scotland
North East bulletin played out. The rest of us leant in. Micro-
phone in hand, a glamorous female reporter with curly black
hair was standing outside a granite house with a yellow door. I
felt like I was about to be sick.

'The woman, who has not yet been named, is described as
being in her eighties. Neighbours alerted the police after
hearing her dog barking.'

'That's Reeny's flat,' I said. 'That's Joan's best friend, Reeny.
I was just there. She has a wee dog. Sergeant. It's her – it has
to be.'

The clip ended. All four of us sank into our chairs, our
expressions dull with shock.

'I'll call the news desk,' Tasha said after a moment. 'That
was my pal Smithy. She'll tell me what's going on.'

We waited in silence while Tasha called her friend.
Through her *a-ha*s and *OK*s and *right y'are*s and *no, I won't tell
a soul*s, I tried to control my rising panic, my tightening heart, a

black sense of dread thick as oil in my guts. Tasha closed the call and looked up.

'Right, so.' She placed her phone on the table slowly, as if delaying what she had to tell us. 'Smithy says the woman's name is Maureen McMaster. One of the neighbours said they heard her dog barking off the scale late this afternoon. They found her apparently asleep on the sofa. Peaceful, Smithy said. I don't think it's being treated as suspicious.'

'But it *is* suspicious.' My voice was hoarse. 'I was only with her this afternoon and she was as sprightly as a kitten. That's Reeny. Maureen. He's killed her like he killed Joan.'

There was a long pause. Then Tasha said, 'I'm taking you to the police station right now.'

'I'll drive,' I said, once we were out on the pavement. 'You've had a drink.'

Tasha shot me a weak smile. 'I don't actually have my car.'

'But you're coming into the station with me?'

'Of course I am, ya numpty.'

'I'm scared they won't take me seriously. It's the bump. Everyone treats me like I've lost my marbles.'

Tasha's nostrils flared as she made herself tall and squared her impressive shoulders. 'Madame, I'll *make* them take you seriously.'

We drove out of Golden Square and turned right into Union Street, the wide mile-long artery that ran through the granite city. I took Craigie Loanings up the hill, where I made a right, the road sloping down Rosemount then towards the station. On the descent, the brake fluid light flashed red. A moment later, when I touched the brake, there was no response. The back of the car in front was coming closer. I pumped the brake again, but nothing happened. The car was gathering speed. On the other side, headlights flared.

'Tash,' I cried out. 'There's no brake. There's no brake!' I swerved left down to Belvidere Street, leaving the blare of a car horn behind us and pumped the brake uselessly.

'Fuck,' Tash whispered, leaning forward.

Belvidere Street too was a downward slope. The car was getting faster.

She straightened in the passenger seat, glanced behind her, in front. With every second, the car increased speed. 'Can you work down the gears?'

I changed to third, to second, the car engine fizzing in protest but slowing a little. The houses flitted by, too fast, too fast. The parked cars pressed in. The line of trees at the end of the road rushed at us.

'Victoria Park's at the end,' Tasha said, her voice high with suppressed panic. 'The wee road there is quiet. Just do what you can. Can you get into first?'

Over and over I jammed my foot to the brake pedal, but there was nothing. I shoved the gears into first. The car engine buzzed like a great metallic wasp, carrying us helplessly down towards the T-junction. I grabbed for the handbrake and pulled. We went over the junction, unstoppable now. Thank God, thank *God* there was no one crossing our path. We hurtled towards the park, the line of trees, the fence. From somewhere, someone screamed. An almighty crunch, like a bomb exploding. Fence railings, up close. The puff of a white balloon.

Blackness.

THIRTY-TWO

KIRSTY

KS/transcript #27

I woke up in a raised bed, a pillow soft against my neck. The smell of industrial cleaner and disinfectant was as familiar to me as my own home. I was in hospital – I knew that much without even opening my eyes. I remembered the crash. Being carried into the ambulance, the paramedic leaning over me, an upside-down face telling me I was going to be all right.

I opened my eyes, blinking to slow the flood of brightness, but the light was low. It was late, I thought.

'Tasha?' I strained to sit up but felt somehow held in place.

'I'm here.'

I followed the voice to where she was getting up from a chair next to the bed. Her brow was furrowed, her eyes enquiring, shiny. There was a large plaster over the right side of her forehead and her right eye was black.

'Hey, you. How're you doing?'

My hands found my belly. A flash of panic shot through me. 'Is the baby OK?'

'The baby's fine. Everything's fine. You're OK, just cuts and bruises, but they're keeping you in tonight until they rule out a concussion. Belt and braces, I think, with you being up the duff and that.' She smiled.

'What happened?'

'Your brakes failed.'

'He cut them. He cut the brakes.'

Tasha sat on the bed and took my hand.

'Whoever was in the red Audi cut the brakes. I'm telling you.' I could feel the dry stretch of my eyes, hear the scratchiness in my voice. I sounded mad. Probably looked mad.

'We don't know that.'

'We were on our way to the police station. He'd already followed me home. Tash, please. Don't you start!'

Tasha gave me a strange look, full of sympathy, but there was something else in there I didn't like.

'Don't look at me like that.' My pulse beat in my temples. 'Why is everyone looking at me like that?'

'I'm not looking at you like anything. The police are going to come and take a statement, OK?'

'When?'

'I don't know.' She stood but kept hold of my hand. 'They're coming, OK? They'll be here when they're here. Dougie's on the way. But you need to sleep, matey. Just try and get some rest.'

'He killed Joan and Reeny, and he just tried to kill me.'

Tasha closed her eyes, took a deep breath and opened them again.

'What are you breathing like that for?' I croaked. 'It's the truth.'

'I've spoken to Smithy. She says it's not public information yet, but your friend died of natural causes.'

'But she was completely fine!' Again I tried to get up, but it felt like I was strapped to the bed. 'There is no way she would have died just like that. I literally saw her a couple of hours before, and I'm telling you, she was fucking *sprightly*.'

'Maybe she was heartbroken? These things happen. It's just a horrible coincidence.'

'I don't believe it.' Tears slithered down my neck and into the hospital gown. Where were my clothes? Where was Dougie? 'She was fine,' I insisted. 'She was absolutely fine.'

Tasha lifted my hand to her mouth and kissed it. 'Maybe you're right. When the police get here you can tell them, OK? I'm nae allowed to stay, so I'm going to go home to my kids, but I'll see you tomorrow. I grabbed your bag by the way; it's on the floor. I'm going to do some digging. Unless you want me to stay till Dougie gets here?'

'No. Go home. Call me if you find out anything, anything at all, OK?'

'OK. I'm taking your clothes to wash. I'll see you later.'

I watched her walk away, her stride cautious, like she was hurting all over, a bin bag with my clothes in it swinging from her right hand. I was caught between love and anger. She was my best friend, had been since the day she'd taken me under her wing, just as we later took Hughie under our wing. We'd always looked after one another and now she didn't believe me. But maybe what I was saying couldn't be true. I didn't know. I didn't know anything really.

Once she'd gone, I looked about me, impatient for Dougie to arrive. Or the police. I needed to say my piece. Someone needed to catch this guy. I wondered what time it was.

As if in reply, a moment later, the lights dimmed, the signal that it was now bedtime. Eleven then. Thereabouts. The ward hummed with quiet. The odd beep from a machine. I tried to sleep, but there was no way. How could I fall asleep? Where was Dougie?

A doctor came through the double doors, in scrubs and cap, a stethoscope around his neck. He was striding with purpose, as if looking for someone. His head twitched and he switched direction. It looked like he was heading straight for me. A burning feeling spread slick over my skin. My heart thumped. I watched him walk slowly towards my bed, as if enjoying every step. It was him. It was Barry Sefton. He was looking right at me. He was staring into my eyes.

At the end of my bed, he stopped, and for a moment it felt like there were only the two of us in the ward. Everything hung suspended, as if the very dust was frozen in the air. And into that silence he smiled, slowly and with menace, and mouthed: *Hi.*

THIRTY-THREE

KIRSTY

I closed my eyes, braced for violence. Looking back, I think I must have been too scared even to scream. But nothing happened. After about thirty seconds, maybe a minute, I opened my eyes again and Barry Sefton was gone. All that remained were the muttered conversations of the duty nurses and my own pounding heart. But what had just happened was like a bomb going off. No one else had heard the explosion, no one else could see that Hughie Reynolds was Barry Sefton, that Hughie Reynolds was walking around the hospital pretending to be someone else. I had no doubt now, no doubt at all. Why else would he come in and greet me unless he knew me? Unless he wanted to frighten me?

But what did it mean? Why had he changed his name? Why wouldn't he show his passport to Gus and Cal back in the day? Why was he here now? Was he the man in the red car? And did he or did he not have some connection to Joan's and Reeny's deaths?

My stomach folded. Last week, he didn't, wouldn't acknowledge me. Just now, he'd said hi. He was telling me it was him who'd cut the brakes, him who'd sent me the messages, him who'd killed Joan and Reeny. I knew it.

Did I? Did I know that?

No. The only thing I knew was that this man was Hughie Reynolds. It didn't matter what it said on Barry Sefton's LinkedIn, since there was no reason to believe any of that was true. Barry was no more than a fake ID.

The question was why? Why go to all these lengths?

It looked like Hughie was a fraud back in the day too, with his lies about his wee flat, his noise-sensitive foster mother, his caginess about his passport. Maybe the boys were right; maybe his parents never did die in a fire but in something much less cinematic. Maybe his foster mum was some boring well-to-do woman of whom he was ashamed because she was just as normal as anyone else's mother, and at fifteen, permanently embarrassed, self-obsessed like we all were, he wanted to pass himself off as something special, something subversive to impress his new friends.

Everyone had a story, and it wasn't always the story they chose to share with the world.

But what about his qualifications? If they were fake, that meant there was an unqualified anaesthetist working in this hospital, holding people's lives in the palms of his hands, putting them to sleep with potentially lethal drugs.

I had to tell someone.

But who would believe me? Who the hell would believe me?

A familiar voice reached me. My name, whispered with urgency in a voice I loved. I looked up from the whirlpool of my thoughts to see Dougie running towards the bed, eyes wet, one arm out, the other holding a swinging supermarket bag.

'Kirst.' Just my name said aloud, so fraught with love and

worry, made us both cry. Dougie sat on the bed, awkwardly, and we wrapped our arms around one another. I could smell alcohol, other people's cigarettes. 'Oh my God, girl, you gave me a heart attack.'

'I'm sorry.'

Dougie's shirt fabric was wet against my face. I pulled back. My neck hurt, my shoulders ached, even my cheeks felt raw, scratchy to the touch. Everything felt fragile, like one light tap and I would crumble into a million pieces.

Dougie took my hand and kissed it, just like Tasha had, and spoke in a whisper. 'They said I could stay a couple of minutes. I think I got privileges what with you being a midwife here. I'm so sorry I'm late. I didna hear my phone. We were in the Prince of Wales and it was deafening in there. I couldna believe it when I saw five missed calls from Tasha. Some pretty salty texts too, I can tell you.'

'She's gone home.'

'Aye, I know. I spoke to her.' Dougie held up the bag. 'I brought you a change of clothes. There's my big cardi in there in case you get cold, and your favourite woolly socks. I put your best maternity pants in.'

That made us both laugh. 'Got to keep up appearances,' I said.

'Your cheeks need a bit of cream, darlin'. They're affa red. Will I put some on for you?'

'Reeny's dead.'

'I know, doll. I know. I'm so sorry.'

'She told me Joan had a daughter. Rosie. She got pregnant to a teacher at our school and ran away. She was only fifteen. Joan never saw her again.'

'You're joking?'

'And that guy I thought was Hughie?' I rattled on, even though I could see Dougie was still processing what I'd just said. 'I saw him just now and it's him. It's him, I know it. But it can't be.'

Our eyes met. Maybe I was giving out too much information all at once but I didn't like the doubt I saw there.

'You have to believe me,' I insisted, my voice hovering now above a whisper. 'He's a fraud. He was a fraud back in the day. Gus said... or maybe it was Cal... one of them anyway, said he wouldn't show them his passport back when we went to Tossa that time. Said he got lairy with them. Violent. Why would he do that if he was for real?' Doubt quivered in Dougie's bright blue eyes.

'And get this,' I pushed on regardless, relentless, 'he told me he lived in a tiny flat and that's why he never invited me, but he didn't. Gus went to his house one time and it was a big place full of antiques. It was all lies. All of it. And now he's back and he's lying again. He's posing as an anaesthetist, but he's not an anaesthetist. I've got to tell the police.' I tried to ignore the darting irises, the sceptical creases at the corners of Dougie's eyes. 'Don't look at me like that! I saw him!'

'When?'

'A minute ago! Doug, he was looking *right at me*. He stopped at the end of my bed and sort of stared me down and then he mouthed the word *hi*. Slow, like. Like he was toying with me. He was trying to scare me. And when I opened my eyes again, he'd just – poof! – disappeared. If that doesn't prove it, what does?'

'Prove what?'

'That he's... I don't know. Hughie. And he's up to something. Fraud. That he *knows* me.'

Dougie sighed deeply, with sadness as much as anything. 'He does know you. You asked him if he was Hughie Reynolds a matter of days ago and he told you he wasn't. He recognised you, that's all. You're pretty recognisable at the moment, you know? How many eight-month-pregnant women does anyone

see in a week unless they're in the actual maternity ward?'
Another heavy sigh, a slow shake of the head. It was infuriating.
'You've had a nasty shock. Really nasty. And you're probably
concussed right now. You don't *know* it's Hughie, darlin'. You
think it is and that's understandable. You're under a lot of stress.
You've got hormones buzzing about and your exhaustion levels
are off the scale. I know you've got... difficult associations with
this guy, but you can't interpret a look and a hello as proof that
someone isn't who they say they are. Accusing a consultant
anaesthetist of being a fraud is libellous, Kirst! These careers
take years. They're built on reputations. If he was a fake, he'd
have killed hundreds of patients by now. He'd be wanted by
Interpol. You've not seen the laddie since he was a spotty
teenager and probably nine stone wet through. At best, this guy
could be a cousin or a brother, but most likely is that he has
absolutely *nothing to do* with Hughie Reynolds but he looks a
lot like him. And in your condition, you've had a deep, visceral
reaction. This is stress talking, and I think you know it. It's grief
too. You've lost dear old Joanie just when you're about to have a
baby, and tonight you've found out her best friend has passed
away. It's... it's just very sad.'

Everything made perfect sense, every word. I hadn't
thought that Barry Sefton might simply have recognised me
from our embarrassing encounter a few days before. And of
course the slow *hi* could have been ironic, an acknowledgement
of the funny side of that encounter. But I think, looking back, I
was too far gone by then. It was like I could hear Dougie but at
the same time I couldn't. Something had me in its grip and
wouldn't let me go.

'Reeny McMaster was killed.' The words fair rumbled out
of me, low and quiet as the beginning of a thunderclap. 'I went
to see her and she was fine, absolutely fine. She made me coffee
and buttered biscuits and we chatted for hours. Then *he*
followed me home. Reeny was killed maybe an hour after?

Neighbours said the dog was going mental. It was the red car, Doug. The red car followed me to her flat, saw me go in, then followed me home before doubling back. Whoever was in that car killed her like they killed Joan and then came in here to taunt me, and I think that person was Hughie Reynolds because, well, because, answer me this: how come Hughie turns up on the Wednesday and by the Thursday Joan is gone? I think he must have some connection to her.'

You can probably tell that by this point, my theories were all over the place. But I couldn't stop. 'How come whenever I went into Joan's house, I got a nasty message?' I hissed. 'Even when she was already dead? How come when I land up in hospital after someone cut my brakes, Hughie Reynolds aka Barry Sefton appears at the end of my bed to jeer at me? Eh? Don't you see the link? I think Hughie was in that car. I think he killed Joan and Reeny. I just have no idea why. Or how.'

Arms folded, Dougie leant back and blew out a huff of air. 'Whoa.'

The need to scream almost overwhelmed me. But if I screamed the place down, who knew what would happen to me? I could be sectioned, carted off and given a shot of sedative. I could have my baby taken away. How maddening it was not to be believed. The more you're not believed, the madder you feel. Oh, and how vile it is to hate everyone. It's awful. When I think of myself reduced to that.

I have to say, in that moment I even hated Dougie. The way you hate someone you love, I mean. At that point, with as much calm as I could muster from the scrappy remains of myself, I told Dougie I needed to talk to the police.

'Immediately,' I said, feeling my jaw clench.

'But they won't discharge you until tomorrow morning,' Dougie replied. 'You can't just check yourself out.'

I felt my jaw tighten. I was so sick of people telling me what

I could and couldn't do. 'I want you to go now,' I said, barely getting the words out through my clamped teeth.

'What?' Dougie looked so horrified, so hurt. 'No! I'm gonna sleep in the chair.'

'You're not allowed,' I said. 'You literally just told me that.' My eyes filled. I closed them. 'I want you to go. I'm asking you to go. Actually, I'm telling you. Please. Go home.'

THIRTY-FOUR

KIRSTY

KS/transcript #29

What I needed most of all was sleep, but sleep eluded me completely. When I did finally drift off, the red Audi drifted in, flashing in and out of granite turrets shrouded in the North Sea haar, Hughie at the wheel, mouthing *hi* at me as the car glided slowly past my living-room window. Hughie a teenager, Hughie a man, the strange smile he always wore, now a leer, sarcastic, mocking. *I didn't love you. I didn't love any of you.* I was in my own car now, screwing up my eyes, squinting at the rear-view. The number plate was furred in the white mist – 32 S... The letters vanished, reappeared, blurred. 32 SA? 32 SA8, maybe?

Hi, Hughie whispered, his breath hot in my ear. *Life is just one big mirage.*

The rev of an engine. A cloud of exhaust. A haar. Hughie stepping out of its thick whiteness. Hughie had something to do with Joan. Joan had a daughter, possibly a grandchild. But Hughie couldn't be that child. Unless... unless he came later. He could still be Rosie's son. He could still be Joan's grandchild. It was possible.

I startled, fully awake now. The night had passed, that's the best I could say about it, but the morning had brought a potential revelation.

The ward was bustling into life. Wednesday, I thought. A whole week since I'd seen Joan, little knowing it was the last full day of her life. A nurse brought breakfast, helped me up, chattering like a wee sparrow on a branch. I smiled and said thank you, but took nothing in. I ate without hunger, for the baby, for strength. I had another cry caused by guilt at having forgotten about the baby in the midst of all the chaos, then one more about telling Dougie to go home the night before. But I'd had to be alone. Who knows what I might have said otherwise? I'd felt mad, properly mad, but now in the yellow morning, it occurred to me that madness was a perfectly reasonable response to all of it.

The coffee was thin and black. I wondered if it was decaf, wondered if I should worry, but drank it anyway. It was so weak it wouldn't matter. It was hard to know what mattered. I'd left work now, I supposed. No goodbye, no box of choccies, no cuddly toys, no good-luck card signed by the team, just a suspected concussion and a night in a hospital bed.

I needed to send Dougie a text, to apologise. Poor Dougie. I'd been so awful last night, but I could smell the alcohol from a metre away and I didn't need a tipsy lecture on why I was wrong about everything. Maybe I was being hysterical. Maybe I was demented by hormones and tiredness and stress and grief. Maybe Reeny did die of natural causes – someone had told me that, Tasha or Dougie, one of them. I couldn't remember.

Call Dougie.

Text.

Yes, text first.

With much grunting and heaving of limbs, I managed to put the tray to one side and found my bag. Inside, my phone had four missed calls, all from Dougie from before the visit, and a text, sent after midnight which said only:

I'm sorry. I love you.

The words swam.

I'm sorry too, I wrote. *And I love you too, of course I do, daftie.*

There was another text. A number, not a name. I was pretty sure I recognised that number. A wave of nausea washed over me. With shaking hands, I opened it.

I warned you but you didn't listen. And now someone else is dead because of you.

My heart was in my throat. I called the number. Someone picked up. Heart pounding, sweat prickling on my brow, I whispered: 'Who is this?'

There was no reply.

'Who are you?' My voice was tiny. 'What do you want?'

Down the line, someone was breathing.

'I said who are you? What do you want from me?' The questions trembled out of me, but there was no reply, only breathing, steady and slow. 'Hughie? Is that you? What do you want?'

The line died.

Eyes wide, I scanned the ward, for what or who, I had no idea.

A moment later, the phone buzzed. I choked.

What I want is for you to keep your nose out of things that don't concern you. You had a near miss. Next time, you won't be so lucky.

Who is this? I replied and watched the rolling ellipsis, hand shaking, breath caught. Until the answer landed like a rock:

Really?

I yelped. Called again. This time, no one picked up. It was as if whoever it was had become bored. *Really?* The word suggested whoever it was thought I knew or should know who they were. He was goading me. These threats were warning me off, knowing I could expose him as a fraud. And *if* there was a link to Joan through Rosie, he was terrified of me discovering that too.

All that was left was to figure out the link between Hughie and Joan. But what on earth did some lad from school have to do with an old lady who once had a daughter? When we were at school, Joan would have been, what, seventy? Too old to foster, let alone adopt.

I was like, *think, Kirsty, think*, you know? Joan was born in... I was too fuzzy for arithmetic. I pulled up the calculator on my phone. 2024 minus eighty-one is 1943. Joan was born in 1943. She will have been, what, twenty-five when she had Rosie? Maybe a little older or younger? Wait. Didn't Reeny say Rosie would have been early sixties, had she lived? I took sixty-one from 2024. Ballpark: 1963. Daughter Rosie is born in 1963, give or take. She's fifteen when she falls pregnant to the teacher. Add fifteen to 1963... that's 1978, maybe 1979. Rosie's kid from that pregnancy, if it survived, was born in 1978, a year either side, tops.

I fell back against the pillow and groaned.

Was Dougie right after all? Had I imagined Hughie appearing at the end of my bed last night as a result of head trauma? Or was it simply Barry Sefton, who happened to be on shift, recognised me and said *hi*, a perfectly reasonable thing to do since we'd shared a minor comedy of errors in a hospital corridor, his voice low because we were in a quiet ward? Maybe it was the opposite of what I'd thought. He didn't want to frighten me at all; he literally just wanted to say *hey, it's me, the guy you thought you knew.*

Could it be that simple? In my traumatised state, had I interpreted a gentle hello as something threatening?

So why the warnings? And why did neither of the two

people closest to me believe there was something sinister going on?

I was so alone. And now I'd fallen out with Dougie, who only wanted to protect me and the baby I was carrying for us both.

'Oh God.' My head fell into my hands. What a mess it all was. I was supposed to be staying calm. I really had to stay calm. At this rate, our baby would be born stressed to a mother in the middle of a breakdown. But it was so hard to stay calm when I had no idea who was sending the texts or why I should know who that person was unless it was Hughie.

What was I missing? I'd thought of every single possibility, and it was beginning to sound like a looping conspiracy even to me. There was no proof that the red car in the close the last time I'd seen Joan alive and the red Audi that had followed me from Reeny's were the same vehicle. But the sightings corresponded to the texts from both Joan's phone and the unknown number, and the person at the end of the unknown number seemed to think I knew them.

Everything led to Hughie.

Nothing could be Hughie.

Hughie was the conspiracy theory.

But I still had to get to the police.

THIRTY-FIVE

KIRSTY

KS/transcript #30

I was supposed to wait for the doctor to discharge me, but I knew fine well I had no concussion, just as I knew the doctor could be hours. Getting out of the hospital without permission would be tricky, but this place was more familiar to me than the mole under my left eye. Still, with my Salvation Army drum belly and my hospital slippers, I wasn't exactly inconspicuous.

I drew the privacy curtain round and dressed in the clothes Dougie had brought me the night before: one of two dresses that still fitted me and Dougie's big cardi. At least there were some clean pants and some maternity tights in the bag. There'd been no reply to my text, but Dougie would never send me to Coventry, ever. The phone had most probably been left in the van.

Putting it out of my mind, I dug around in my big handbag for the car key before exiting my cubicle, leaving the curtain drawn behind me, hoping any passing nurses might think I was either being examined or bathed or changed. Seconds later, I was smiling at the duty sister and telling her I was away to stretch my legs in the corridor for a bit. Seconds after that, I was in the lift, car key clutched in one hand, phone in the other.

Outside, sleet was falling from a sky the colour of thousand-wash underwear. When the automatic doors opened, the air rushed at me in a freezing gust. I gasped in shock, reversing without turning, lorry-like, back into the hospital. I had on no coat, no hat, not even any shoes, all left behind for fear of their absence giving me away; only the hospital-issue espadrilles and my tights. Something else too. Something else was wrong with this picture, but I couldn't think what it was. I opened my hand and stared at the key, trying to remember where I'd left the car. I must've stared at that car key for whole minutes before it hit me. This was the spare. I kept a spare in my bag along with all the other emergency paraphernalia, but I didn't have the car, did I? My trusty wee Focus was a write-off. The police had it.

I took an Uber to the police station, worrying now that I could never get back to the ward before anyone knew I'd gone, worrying that my pregnant state and maverick-style hospital break would further hamper my chances of being believed. But I was too far gone by that point to turn back.

As I passed through the station doors, I caught sight of my reflection in the window and almost shrieked. My hair was all over the place, my belly so huge it looked fit to explode. I looked, I thought, like a drug-addled Space Hopper.

Before I told the desk sergeant why I was there, I asked if it was possible to use the loo, gesturing to my pregnant belly by way of explanation. If I had to waddle around weighing three stone more than I usually did, then at least I could claim some advantages.

The mirror in the ladies' gave me an even sorrier picture. I had a black eye, and there was dried blood crusted near my left ear. I ran my hands under the tap and tried to push some sense into my wild-woman hair, then started to rub off the blood with a wet paper towel.

'Shit,' I whispered as I cleaned myself up. 'Shit, shit, shit.'

I managed to wash off most of the blood and flatten my hair some of the way. The black eye was plum-like. It made me look like I'd wandered out of a violent cartoon, like me and Dougie had been taking turns to beat each other round the head with frying pans, Tom and Jerry style. My face was puffy too, perhaps a bit too puffy, and the non-black eye was, now I looked at it, quite darkly shadowed. Balancing with one hand on the sink, I lifted my foot. My ankles were swollen, shiny, even after so little time upright. That wasn't good. I didn't want to end up on bed rest with my feet in the air for the next three weeks.

As I made my way back to reception, it occurred to me that whoever had sent the texts might have followed me here. Police station or no, fear flushed through me at the thought. I took a glance outside, but saw no one, no red car, no consultant anaesthetist who might or might not be someone I once knew. Perhaps it was a good thing my Focus had been written off. Hopefully the cab had lent me some anonymity.

For the third time in as many days, I was ushered into an interview room. An officer brought me a sweet tea and I sipped it gratefully, wishing I had a chocolate biscuit to go with it. I was shaky and light-headed and felt like I might faint. When I tried to collect my thoughts, they ran amok like sheep after a gunshot.

The door opened and the same laddie I'd spoken to the first time came in. Tedious Tod. My heart sank. I knew fine well how he must see me, especially right at this moment: pregnant and deranged, a coatless, black-eyed pea-brain with whom he had to go through the motions because his boss had told him to.

'I apologise for my dishevelled state,' I said before he was able to form an opinion. 'I was in an accident. I've come straight from the hospital. They said I'd to give a statement today, and I wanted to do so without delay. Tod, isn't it?'

'And you're Ms Kirsty Shaw.' Apparently satisfied with his clever announcement of the name he forgot to take the first time, he sat down, notepad and pen at the ready. 'So,' he said, tone patronising even in that one word. 'This is relating to the incident at nine thirty-three p.m. last night. Can you tell me what happened, in your own words?'

I took a deep breath before I told him about the brakes failing, about my attempt to minimise the damage by crashing into the fence.

'It was either that or hit someone else's car. Or, God forbid, a pedestrian. It was lucky no one was killed.'

He looked up from his scrawl. 'Is that it?'

'That's not really why I'm here,' I said. 'I'm here because I think someone tampered with the brakes, but I'll get to that in a moment. Just let me... Let's see... I need to tell you about the red Audi and the texts.' In that moment I decided to leave Hughie out of it. It was difficult enough as it was to get the police to take me seriously.

Tod looked like he'd been told he was going to be stuck there for the rest of the day without food or water, but I carried on regardless – jabbing at his notepad whenever he paused and telling him he needed to write down every word. The room was hot. I slid my feet out of the paper slippers and flattened my stockinged feet to the cool linoleum floor.

'I took a cab here,' I said, hoping I'd told him everything. 'I was too scared to let you come to my house. I didn't even dare get Dougie to bring me. He's watching me, you see.'

'Dougie?'

'No! The guy in the red car! If he sees me talking to the police, I don't know what he'll do. He's already cut my brakes.'

'How do you know it's a he?'

I hesitated. I'd steered clear of the conspiracy stuff and stuck to the facts, but Tod, to give him his due, had asked a good question.

'Joan said...' I began. 'That's my neighbour, the lady who drowned. She said she'd seen a man. That was on the Wednesday, when I went to see her. I think that was him. Red-car guy. And I think red-car guy might be my ex-boyfriend, but that's another story. I think there's some link between Joan and the red Audi. The number plate is 32 SA8. Something like that. I couldn't see properly because of the haar.'

Tod really needed to try harder to hide the flickers of scepticism that crossed his arrogant young face, the kind of look that suggested he was saving all of this to tell his mates in the pub later. It was so irritating. I wanted to grab him by the collar and ask him if he thought this was funny, to tell him that one day his own wife might be pregnant and need to be believed, or he might be old and alone and no one would take him seriously and the kindness of folk would be all he had left.

But I didn't obviously.

'... because of the haar,' he repeated, overemphasising the words as he wrote, making them and me sound ridiculous.

'I'm telling you, the person who sent texts from Joan's phone is the same person who sent me these threats.' I slid my phone across the table. 'I'm not saying it's my ex, but I am saying I think it's the man who killed Joan.'

'You have no proof Ms Wood was murdered, Ms Shaw.'

'Well, no, but you need to find out who sent these texts. If you find them, you'll find whoever killed Joan and Reeny, I guarantee it. Reeny is Maureen McMaster, the lady who died yesterday. She was Joan's best friend, and I think he killed her to stop her going to the police. She suspected foul play too, you see.'

'Do you know that?'

I stopped, brought up short once again. Did I know that? I tried to recall my conversation with Reeny, but nothing came beyond our shared sadness, the butter thick on the digestive biscuits, the fire in the stove. The wee dog, Sergeant.

'I don't know,' I admitted, feeling suddenly incredibly tired. In truth, I realised then, I knew little more than that an old lady not in her right mind had died in the cold sea. A man I thought was Hughie seemed instead to be a middle-aged consultant. A car that had followed me not quite home may or may not have been the same car that had been parked on the close one day last week.

There was nothing here but a loose net. The facts were free-falling through its holes, and I could only watch them disappear.

I steeled myself. I was right. Somewhere, deep down, I knew I was right. I straightened in my seat and cleared my throat. 'I don't know what Reeny thought, but I think the person who sent the texts from Joan's phone is the same person who sent these. It's a continuation, see? The tone is consistent. And I know there's a consultant anaesthesiologist...' I stopped. I had sworn on the way here not to mention Barry Sefton. He was too high up. Too powerful. *Libellous*, Dougie had said. *These careers take years*. I had to be sure, much surer than I was. I didn't have nearly enough to report him to the police. It could backfire, horribly. I could lose my job.

'Look,' I said. 'I'm not a detective, but I think these women might have been murdered. I think the person who did it is very clever and has disguised these deaths under a veil of old age. He's hidden Joan's car. If it was suicide, her car would've been parked by the harbour, wouldn't it? Joan always parked on New Pier Road. I've told you this before. And now, whoever killed Joan and her best friend is trying to frighten me and might even try to kill me.'

'Why do you think they'd want you dead?'

'Because I'm on to them?' I couldn't say anything about Hughie and Barry Sefton without getting into hot water. But if I didn't, I sounded mad. It was enough to make anyone grind their teeth.

'I appreciate you must be frightened.' The words sounded regurgitated from a manual or a training course or something.

'We will investigate the threats, of course. We take these matters very seriously. But you've had a shock and have sustained a head injury.'

'Minor head injury.'

'Yes. But in your condition—'

'Don't you dare.' I glared at him.

He had the grace to look flustered. 'What I mean to say is, forensics are investigating the brake failure on your vehicle. And I can tell you your friend's car has been found.'

'*What?*'

'Ms Wood's car has been found on New Pier Road. That's where you said, isn't it?'

'But... but I saw it at her home on Thursday.' Again I had to stop. 'I think... I'm pretty sure it was Thursday, if not Friday. I looked all around the harbour and it wasn't there then. It wasn't there on Saturday either. I checked.'

Our eyes met. His narrowed.

'Are you going to write that down?' I asked.

He averted his eyes, but the pen went nowhere near the paper. 'Ms Wood's death has been recorded as an open verdict.'

'*What?* What does that mean?'

'It means that while the circumstances could be seen to be suspicious, there's no definite cause of death other than drowning.'

'No definite cause? She was murdered! At the very least, he frightened her to her death! I checked those roads with my own eyes and I'm telling you her car was not there in the days leading up to her being found. Someone must have put it there after I looked. Someone had put the frighteners on her. Someone is threatening me, and you need to find him.'

'I'm sorry,' Tod replied, as if that were enough, as if that were ever going to be anywhere near enough. 'I'll take a note of your concerns and pass them on.'

'What about the texts? What about the attempt on my life?

My best friend's life? My baby's life? What's cutting brakes if not attempted murder? And why did I get a text late last night telling me that next time I wouldn't be so lucky?' Despite all the promises to myself, I had started to cry.

'Ms Shaw, I'm afraid you're going to have to leave the police work to the police. I've recorded your statement, and we'll contact you if we need any more information.' He stood. 'Thank you very much for coming in. Would you like me to see if I can get one of the officers to drive you home?'

He hadn't listened. He hadn't read the texts properly. He couldn't have. I should have argued with him, made him read them in front of me, but I think in that moment I had lost all heart.

'No,' I said quietly. 'Thank you.' I stood too and drew myself up as tall as I could, which was not very. 'I'll take a cab.'

I was on my own – that much was frighteningly clear. I was going to have to sort this out myself.

THIRTY-SIX

KIRSTY

KS/transcript #31

As we pulled up at the hospital, my phone started ringing. Tasha's face grinned from the screen, a cheeky thumbs-up in a photo I'd taken a few years ago. I struggled out of the Uber before I answered.

'Kirsty?' The background hum of an open-plan office. 'Are you OK? You sound out of breath.'

'That's the sound of a heavily pregnant quine climbing out of a cab. I *might* have absconded from the hospital.'

'*What?* Have you lost your mind?'

'Don't panic – I'm back now.' I scuttled – if a woman of my proportions could be said to scuttle; if scuttlers had thighs that rubbed together while scuttling – into the warm, where I breathed a huge sigh of relief. 'God, it's cold out there. I just popped over to the police station to give my statement.'

'But I told you they were coming to you!'

'Aye, well they didn't. And I couldn't wait any longer.'

'Kirsty!'

'Don't you give me a row. Dougie's already given me a row. I was one rude remark shy of punching that twat of a cop in the face just now, and meanwhile there's—' I stepped into the lift and promptly lost the connection.

When I re-emerged, my phone showed two missed calls from Tasha. I called back, waving at the sister, who was gesticulating wildly at me.

'Tash? Sorry, I got cut off.' I covered the phone with my hand. 'Sorry,' I said to the sister, attempting a light-hearted eye-roll and holding up my forefinger. 'Got lost. Just need to take this call. Sorry.' I turned my back on her and walked into the ward, towards my cubicle. The curtains had been drawn back, and there was someone else in the bed: a middle-aged woman strapped to a drip and looking very sorry for herself indeed.

'Shit,' I whispered to Tasha. 'I think I'm in trouble.'

'Kirsty,' Tasha said. 'I really don't think anyone cut your brakes.'

'Hold on.' I paced back out into the corridor, holding up a full palm to the sister in case the one finger hadn't sufficed. She was tapping her watch, her face stern. I gave her a weak smile, turned to the wall and closed my eyes. 'How do you know that?'

'Because we're not Thelma and Louise.'

'What? What're you... No one cut *their* brakes. They made a calculated decision to go over the cliff. Explain to me why I got a text late last night telling me that next time I wouldn't be so lucky.'

'You did?' Tasha had the decency to sound chastened.

'Aye. From the same number, which means from the same person who was warning me away from Joan using Joan's phone, which also means the same person who cut my damn brakes. Whoever it is killed both Joan and Reeny and is trying to kill me, I'm telling you.'

'Kirst. Stop. Slow down. You say something that makes sense then you say something else and it's bonk— I mean, you make these... these really big leaps. They've given an open verdict for Joan.'

'I know! And they're wrong!'

'Are they? Really? Do you actually *know* that? Maureen died of natural causes. If you ask me, it was a broken heart. It happens.'

'What are you on about? They weren't lovers.'

'I know, but they were best friends. They were both widows. And from what you've told me, they'd shared a lot, lost and found one another over the years. They were both in their eighties. Imagine if you and me had lost our partners and all our friends had died or were in homes or whatever... If you died, I'd be gutted. You'd be gutted if I died too.'

'I'd be mildly disappointed.'

Tasha laughed. 'There you go. You could die of mild disappointment.'

'A modest death.'

'A seemly death.'

'Are you telling me you don't want us to move in together once Scott and Dougie shuffle off the mortal coil?'

'I was trying to break it to you gently.'

There was a pause. Humour had saved us, and I was relieved. I couldn't fall out with Tasha, I just couldn't. I already felt like I was standing alone on a clifftop with the wind howling around me. All I could think about was the red Audi. Hughie Reynolds. Barry Sefton. Beautiful, elegant Joan floating face down in the water. Bright-as-a-button Reeny, forever asleep on that lovely egg-yolk couch.

'Joan didn't die by suicide,' I said quietly, with a firmness that was wavering by the second.

'There were witnesses,' Tasha said, so gently it made my eyes prick. 'A woman matching Joan's description was seen wandering about near the beach on Thursday, looking upset, talking to herself.'

'She came home that day. I saw her car.'

'But she killed herself sometime either late Thursday night or Friday morning.'

'Her car was still in the close on Friday morning. I think it was. Maybe it was Thursday. Oh God. But it definitely wasn't at the harbour on Saturday when I saw Stella. I checked.'

'These things are never a hundred per cent accurate. You have to let it go, matey. Please. For the baby.'

'But everything is linked. I know it is. I can feel it. Whoever sent the texts thinks I should know who he is, like it's obvious. I can't think of anyone who's obvious apart from Hughie. It's like he's daring me to say his name out loud or something. I think he thinks I can put the police on to him and they'll find out Joan's death wasn't quite so innocent. I'm willing to bet it was him who ransacked her place. I bet his fingerprints are all over that bungalow. I just don't know quite who I mean when I say *him*.'

'You never saw anyone in Joan's house, did you? There's no motive. There's no link.'

'That's you and the rest of the world think I'm nuts.'

'I don't, I'm just—'

'Oh my God, wait.' My head was pounding, blood pulsing through.

'Kirsty? What? Talk to me.'

'The registration number.'

'What about it?'

'Of the Audi. The red car. I was thinking it was 32 SA8. That's as near as I could get. But if you don't look at it through a mirror, it's 8AZ 23!'

'So?'

'It could easily be BAZ 23.'

'And?'

'Baz. Baz is short for Barry; 23 is the year of purchase. He must have bought it when he got back from Dubai in December. I bet you a hundred quid that car belongs to Barry Sefton.'

The phone line fell silent.

'Tash? You still there?'

'I am.'

'Don't tell me I'm being far-fetched.'

'I'm not. I'm thinking. Why would Barry Sefton be crawling round Joan's house? Unless...'

'Unless what?'

'Unless Joan did just slip,' Tasha said slowly, 'and Reeny did die of natural causes, and Barry Sefton was never crawling round them at all. Maybe he was crawling round you.'

THIRTY-SEVEN

KIRSTY

KS/transcript #32

A slick of sweat covered my entire body. My forehead was pressed hard against the wall of the hospital corridor, the urge to be sick rising. 'He was...'

'You never specifically saw him or anyone go into Joan's, did you?'

'No, he was on the road. But he was near.'

'Mate. What are you, two doors down?'

'Aye, but—'

'And he was opposite? So if this car does belong to Barry Sefton, and we don't know it does... I mean, I don't want to frighten you, but he could have followed you home from work, couldn't he?'

'OK. Yes. But—'

'Wait.' The sound of Tasha breathing came down the line. After a long moment, she said, 'I checked his LinkedIn. Did you?'

'Aye.'

'Well, he'll have been able to see you looked at it. And me. If he is Hughie, or at least not who he says he is, and the profile is fake, you're a threat because you work in the same hospital and you called him out. It's got nothing to do with Joan. It's you and you alone.'

'Why me?'

'Why do you think? He wants to shut you up.'

No sooner had I rung off than the doubts swam back. Tasha was right: Hughie was worried about being exposed as an imposter. A link to Joan was hypothetical, possibly a red herring.

But *someone* had moved Joan's car after she died. And that had precious little to do with anyone passing themselves off as an anaesthetist. *Someone* was pretending to be Joan when they sent those texts.

Yet again, I was alone, and I felt it bitterly. There was no point debating any of it with Tasha.

I wondered if there was any point talking about it to anyone at all.

Three hours and a slap on the wrist from my colleagues in Minor Injuries later, I was at home with Dougie, who was keen to make the peace and agreed to look again at the photographs of Barry Sefton.

First I pulled up the photograph from the LinkedIn profile. 'What do you think?'

Dougie took a swig of tea and lifted the phone out of my hand, giving or appearing to give the photograph due considera-tion. 'I want to say it looks like him. I want to make you happy. But honestly? I can't see it, babes. But I didn't know Hughie, not really. And it was a long time ago.'

I took the phone back and clicked on the hospital website, the staff photographs for the anaesthesiology department. 'This is a more recent photo. You can see it's the same guy, right?'

'That's him, aye. He's older than us though. Could he be Hughie's older brother? A cousin?'

'I had that thought, yeah. In among all the others. But Barry Sefton's the same age as Rosie's first child would have been,' I said. '*If* that child survived and *if* we can believe the dates on his LinkedIn. But he's too old to be Hughie. If, like you say, Rosie had another child later, that would make Barry Hughie's older half-brother and maybe Hughie's pretending to be him?' I didn't dare look at Dougie. I could just picture the disbelief.

The phone rang, thank God.

I picked up. 'Tasha?'

'I have updates.'

'I'm here with Dougie. Wait while I put you on speaker.' I adjusted the phone and laid it on the kitchen table.

'Right, so,' Tasha said. 'I've been on to my pal who works for the traffic police and she ran an ANPR for me. Don't tell anyone.'

'We won't.' I shared a smile with Dougie, the first since I'd got out of hospital.

'First things first, the officer assigned to our slow-mo car crash... Tod something—'

'Tod the Plod. Blonde. Supercilious expression. Face you'd never tire of punching.'

Tasha gave a brief laugh. 'Well, I didn't see him, but I'll take your word for it. He called to say forensics found nothing wrong with the brakes. No evidence of tampering. You had a leak in the brake fluid tank is all. It was just bad luck it ran out on a hill.'

'But the warning light had only just come on. Usually you get time to—'

'Hold your beans. I bring shocking tidings.'

'Go on.' I bit my lip.

'Back to the ANPR. The car *is* registered to Barry Sefton.'

I felt the chair thump against my back. Tears pooled in the

rims of my eyes, this time tears of relief – small relief, perhaps, microscopic, but relief all the same. I had been *right*. Finally, I had been right about something.

'You were right,' Tasha said, as if to confirm.

'I knew it.'

'You did. So... I did some more digging.'

'Oh aye?'

'*If* it's the same person as this profile, wait for it... Barry Sefton died in Edinburgh on the nineteenth of March 2009. He was... well, guess.'

'A consultant anaesthetist,' I almost shouted.

'Correct.'

Blood thrummed in my temples. 'He *died*? But—'

'Thing is, his date of birth is an exact fit with the LinkedIn profile.'

'Could it be a coincidence? There's got to be more than one Barry Sefton.'

'It could be. But this Barry Sefton worked at Edinburgh Royal Infirmary. It says on his LinkedIn he went to Dubai in 2010, but I don't think he did. I don't think we can rely on any of these dates. I think someone took over his identity later and did what they liked with it once his GMC records had expired. Whoever our guy is, he lifted Sefton's LinkedIn and took it to Dubai, adding to it and altering it over the years. When he came to Aberdeen, same thing. I'm just not sure why he picked a real person. Why not just make up a name?'

'Oh.' It was all I could manage. A quick glance up told me Dougie was as shell-shocked as I was.

'That's not all,' Tasha said, sounding very much like she was enjoying herself. 'I found a photograph of Joan's daughter, Rosie Wood, taken when she was a teenager. It was used in the appeal for information when she went missing in 1978. I'll WhatsApp it to you now, but again, don't tell anyone.'

A moment later, my phone pinged and the photo appeared.

The young girl had altered from the picture in Joan's bedroom – plucked eyebrows, thick kohl eyeliner, fair roots betraying black hair dye – but it was undeniably the same girl. Puberty had changed her features, shrunk her eyes, thinned her face. She looked vandalised, somehow, compared to that other photo. It was the first word that came to my mind. Like a once-loved doll that had fallen out of favour, been scribbled on, hair coloured in with felt-tip pens. She was harder, eyes missing their light or their spark or something. Their innocence maybe. The teacher, I thought. He had taken that spark from her, that innocence. Unwittingly perhaps, her parents had given the shame that belonged to him to their only daughter. She hadn't been able to bear it. She had left – horribly young, too young to know that the heat of any moment is best left to cool – and ended up who knew where. Dead before she was fifty, her parents left wringing their hands for the rest of their lives.

And something else, something that slowed my blood.

'She looks like Hughie,' I whispered.

'I saw the resemblance,' Tasha said. 'Which I suppose means she must look a wee bit like the man you thought was Hughie, do you see what I mean? Personally, I don't think there's much similarity, but you've seen him in real life. I think the most likely explanation is that Hughie stole Barry's ID and is pretending to be older than he is either to throw folk off the scent or to get them to take him more seriously.'

'But what the hell is he doing here now? And like you say, why not just make up a name? And why in God's name would he come here and risk being exposed?'

'That's what I'm going to try and find out.'

THIRTY-EIGHT

KIRSTY

KS/transcript #33

Minutes later, I was still sitting in the kitchen, nursing a fresh brew.

'My head is going to explode,' I said after a moment.

Dougie frowned. 'So *is* the guy you saw at the hospital Hughie?'

'Yes. I think so. I think he must be.'

'And he has something to do with Joan or not?'

'I don't know. I think so, but the guy in the hospital *is* the guy who owns the red car. And I'm convinced he's Hughie; I just have to figure out how...' I bit my nail. 'I think it's Hughie and he's posing as someone older so that no one will question his credentials. But why? It's all so confusing. Every time I think I've got it straight in my mind, I lose it again.'

'And you really think he did Joan harm?'

'I think... I don't know. I'm going to have to draw a diagram.'

Instead, I closed my eyes and listened to the rhythmic sound of Dougie chopping vegetables. The kitchen clock ticked. My tea cooled in its mug. I opened my eyes to find Dougie staring at me, the stare breaking into a soft smile. I smiled back. The events of the last week drifted down and settled around me like so many snowflakes. What did I think? I thought everything I'd thought all along, and nothing of what I'd thought all along, with some new stuff thrown in for good measure. All of it overlapped and contradicted and made perfect sense and no sense and was dangerous and benign, and suspicious and reasonable, and sinister and horribly, terribly sad.

All I could do was keep trying.

'I think,' I tried again, and, my God, my poor, poor Dougie having to listen, 'I think maybe the most logical interpretation, the calmest, most reasonable conclusion, is that long ago, this guy took himself a new life. For whatever reason, he wanted to escape his past, break the link with his family, so he took a dead man's name and all that went with it and left his old life behind. Then one day, years later, sick of being in exile, he gets himself a job back in Scotland. His roots have called him back, let's say. And if he's Hughie – well, we know Hughie cut and ran, back in the day. Now, if we want to make a link to Joan, maybe he knew her from when he lived here. Or maybe, if he isn't Hughie, he's Rosie's firstborn son. A lot of water has passed under the bridge by now. He's confident, successful. He's made something of his life. So maybe he decides to pay the granny he never knew a visit. It might have been well intentioned. He might have been skulking outside in his red car plucking up the courage to go and knock on her door.

'Maybe he never went into Joan's house. Maybe he did. Maybe he just wanted to tell her about her daughter, or maybe he wanted to present himself to her in a *look at me, didn't I turn out well* kind of way, thinking it would please her, give her some shred of family to be proud of.'

'Give her something to end her days with.' Dougie smiled sadly.

'Exactly. She'd been so unhappy. She'd suffered so much

loss. Reeny had all her photographs up in the house, you know? Her and her husband, her kids, her grandkids, high days and holidays, you name it. And meanwhile Joan just had that one picture of her and her wee girl in happier times. Nothing left of a life lived as best she could with whatever tools she had.

'So, say this guy goes there and tells her who he is. Say he does that. There he is, expecting a reunion, but Joan's prickly and suspicious. She takes fright. It's too much. And maybe, in an elderly woman with fading mental resources, the stress ends in tragedy. An aneurysm, say, or a heart attack. And once that tragedy happens, he panics. That's why he's been threatening me. He knows I know who he really is, and I can link him to Joan too, with the car. I don't know.' I let out a massive yawn, my vision clouding momentarily. 'I guess I just want it to be something kind. Behind the scenes, you know? I want to believe in a scenario in which Joan didn't suffer.'

I could feel the tears welling. When I looked up, I could see how hard Dougie was working to indulge me, how much it was costing not to tell me to stop, just stop and get some rest.

'Listen,' I said. 'Is it OK if I go for a lie-down?'

'Of course.' The relief was palpable. 'Can I bring you up a hot-water bottle?'

'No, it's OK. I'll put the blanket on. Thanks though. Love you.'

'Love you more.'

I climbed the stairs. My thighs ached. My back hurt. My slippers felt like they were full of lead. As for my head, it was a vortex. Questions, questions, questions. Questions without answers, circling around, looping back, crossing over. And still one person at the centre of it all: Hughie.

I know. It was a kind of temporary insanity.

Meanwhile, there was the fact that the baby would be here in a few short weeks. Earlier, I'd got an email from Wendy telling me I'd been officially signed off until after I gave birth.

Which was the right thing, of course, but it left me free to obsess about what the hell was going on. Looking back, I can see that if there was one thing I knew in that moment, it was that until I proved Hughie was behind everything, I would never find peace.

Is that why I did what I did? Yes. I can't explain it any better than that. All I can say is I had to know, and that by that point, knowing had overtaken everything else. It had become a form of madness in and of itself. Maybe that madness had been with me since the day Hughie left.

So that's when I did the thing for which all the anonymous armchair social media commentators have criticised me so much, although at least most of them drew the line at suggesting I deserved what happened to me.

It's funny, you know I'm a fan of these documentaries, and this would definitely be one of those moments when I'd have been shouting at the telly. *Don't do that. What the hell?* Et cetera. But for me, there was only one way to find the answers I needed, the answers that would let me get on with my life. I'd known it since I put down the phone to Tasha. It was why I hadn't been able to chat with Dougie a few minutes earlier. The fact was, I could no longer think about anything other than how Hughie could be Barry Sefton, or vice versa, and what his link to Joan was. And the one person who could give me concrete, one hundred per cent irrefutable answers was the man who had sent me those texts. I firmly believed that this was the guy who called himself Barry Sefton but who I knew as Hughie Reynolds.

But this is where we get down to the marrow of it, that soft, spongy matter of reasons hidden even to ourselves. Why I did what I did despite the possibility that Hughie or whoever he was *could* be a murderer. As far as I can know my own fraught, frightened and frustrated state of mind, I'd say I did it because I was *convinced* Barry Sefton was Hughie Reynolds and at that moment it felt like the only person who would believe me was him. I had to prove it – to myself and to the world – for my own sanity, for my past and for my present. For my baby. For my future. I couldn't tell a soul what I was about to do because I knew they would try to stop me. They would beg me not to do it. At that point, I think I even feared being forced into a psychiatric evaluation. I did worry about paranoid delusion, I did, but not enough to be dissuaded. And maybe this is the hardest thing of all to admit: at that moment, I truly believed he'd come here to talk to me. I truly believed that this was unfinished business between us and that we were going to finally have our conversation, once and for all.

So that's why I pulled up LinkedIn, and that's why I sent the message, and that's why I made damn sure I had a plan, despite the fact that deep down, deep in the heart of my eighteen-year-old self, I still believed Hughie would never harm me.

THIRTY-NINE

HUGHIE

HR/audio/excerpt #6

You're a brave woman, Kirsty Shaw, I'll give you that. I think by the time you sent that LinkedIn message, we both needed an ending. But even so, I was surprised.

Hello. My name is Kirsty Shaw.

I love that you gave your name. So sweet.

I am the heavily pregnant woman who thought you were someone else in the hospital the other day. I believe you know or have some connection to this person, an old friend of mine, Hughie Reynolds. I don't want any trouble, and I don't mean you any harm. All I want is to ask you some questions for my own peace of mind. If you can't tell me what I need to know, fine, but I would really like to talk to you face to face before my baby is born so that I can move on with my life.

Best regards, Kirsty.

I could hear your voice, KK, hidden in all that formality. How did you know to contact me on LinkedIn and not the burner phone? Did you know I'd thrown it into the sea by then? Or did you want to trick me into thinking you didn't know that the anonymous texter and I were one and the same? Whatever it was, by then my nerves were utterly shredded, and I'm sure yours were too. Maybe that's why you threw caution to the wind and effectively walked open-eyed into a trap you had laid for yourself.

I believe you know or have some connection to an old friend of mine, Hughie Reynolds.

Really? Was it possible you still had doubts?

I like to think you'd finally learnt to have the courage of your convictions and were trying to somehow play me. Make no mistake, Kirsty, despite everything, you have always known exactly who I am, from the moment you saw me in the hospital.

You just didn't know how I could possibly be me. And that's what did for you – your own dogged nosiness.

As for me, I was done hiding my identity from you. It really was easier to kill you by then, and that, like everything else that's happened, is down to you. I tried to warn you off. I never wanted it to come to this. I'm not a murderer! It's not what I'm about at all, as I've been trying to explain.

But frankly, you've been more annoying than a wasp at a picnic, and I think, actually, after all these years, it's a relief to tell someone everything, even if that means a death I never intended. And it feels right, somehow, that you should be the one to hear my story in full.

I replied, of course.

Aberdeen beach. Tomorrow. 4.30 p.m. Opposite Inversnecky.

Your reply, a succinct *OK*.

I thought a reference to one of our old haunts would dispel any last hesitations you might have. I love that you thought by meeting me in a public place you'd be safe. I love that you still had so little guile. I'm glad I didn't turn you into a cynical through-with-love kind of person. From what I've observed, you still got to live, while it lasted.

As I've said before, there is such a difference between those who live and those who survive. We see the world completely differently. I mean, come on, KK! Think! How many texts did I have to send? How many times did I have to watch your house? How hard would it have been for you to leave me alone and let me live my life?

This really is all your fault. You *rushed* me. And I hate being rushed.

One irony of many is that if you'd had the courage of your convictions, we wouldn't be in this mess. You'd have reported me directly to the police on the basis of fraud and that would have been it. Why didn't you?

And which part of you thought meeting up was a good idea? Is that your deluded determination to believe the best of people? Did you think we could talk it all through like grown-ups, reach a compromise? I think you're clinging to some forlorn and forgotten hope that I will sit you down and explain why I left. Maybe you're longing for me to say I still love you. Which, to be fair, is correct – the part about sitting you down and explaining, I mean. I will explain. I'm explaining now, aren't I? But of course I don't love you. Don't take it personally. I don't love anyone.

My explanation will be a shock. Let me warn you of that right now, up front. Whereas I have developed a keen sense of how someone like you might see things, it isn't like that for you. You feel people. I read them. For all your confusion about which feelings are yours and which belong to others – which is all empathy is, after all – you haven't learnt to *anticipate* the way others think. You're too busy identifying with them, putting yourself in their shoes, making excuses for shitty behaviour. You, Kirsty Shaw, like so many, plough on in the luxurious belief that people are more or less good, that they think more or less the same way.

Maybe that, that misplaced faith, is ultimately what made you a victim.

FORTY
KIRSTY

KS/transcript #34

At the seafront, I slowed the car. To my left, the crashing sea. To my right, the Inversnecky Café nestled in the parade. From behind, the familiar hoop of the Ferris wheel rose into a flint-grey sky, bright seating pods dangling from it like baubles. I could turn around, I thought. I could turn around and go home – to Dougie and to my life. But no. My life had changed. This man knew where I lived; undoubtedly he knew when I was alone; he could come for me at any time. Better to face him out in the open. Better to look into his cold eyes and hear him tell me he was Hughie Reynolds and explain to me why he had come back disguised as someone else.

I parked up and walked back past the arcade, through the funfair, to the beach. Opposite the café, a lone figure was leaning against the railings, looking out to sea. It was weird, because at a distance and with only that vague hunched shape to go on, I still knew with the terrifying certainty of the indoctrinated that it was Hughie, a boy I'd once known, a guy who for whatever reason didn't want me to know who he was or why he had come back.

I came out from the shelter of the candy-floss stalls and the burger vans into a face-freezing hoolie that howled along the length of the esplanade. Head down, I battled my way over the road. Hughie Reynolds clarified. He wasn't hunched – the hunch was a rucksack over the same expensive North Face puffer coat he'd been wearing when I'd seen him coming into the infirmary, the same woolly hat, gloves, good brown leather walking shoes. Unremarkable apparel, a uniform of sorts for the regular guy who lays no claim to style, whose only concern is practicality for an inclement climate. Closer now and in profile, he looked older still – double-chinned, jowly, baggy around the eyes. He was still staring out at the sea.

'Hughie,' I said, and he turned – whether this was an admission, I didn't know.

My throat closed. But he smiled and I saw the familiar overlap of his two front teeth.

'Is it you?' The words were swallowed by the wind. I pulled my hat down low to stop it from flying off and pushed my hands deep into my pockets.

'Kirsty Shaw.' His response answered my question, an anticlimax after all that had happened, and I felt myself sink. 'How the hell have you been?'

His eyes were beady without his glasses, his long nose bright pink from the cold. Unattractive. It was always about the charm. He'd left me rather than face his failure – this was the legend my parents and my friends had written in his absence. But in my most private thoughts I'd tortured myself with the belief that he'd left because there was something wrong with me. The way he had looked at me before he left, the disgust in his eyes. Now, years later, I could see it all so clearly. He was nothing more than a con artist, a fraud then and now. As Tasha had said all those years ago: he was a prick, pure and simple.

He'd had confidence, energy, verve. He'd been persuasive, dynamic, that was all. And when I'd rejected him, his inflated ego couldn't take it. The disgust wasn't aimed at me at all but at his own failure to get his way. Really, it was all so clear to me in that moment.

But was he a murderer?

'When are you due?' He nodded at the bump, a smile twitching at his lips.

'Any day now,' I replied, kicking myself for letting him lead. His easy confidence was all for show – empty, built on sand. I had the upper hand now.

'What do you want to know?' he asked, confounding me a second time.

'Shall we get a coffee or something?' I nodded to the café. 'For old times?'

But he shook his head. 'Let's walk.'

'I can't go too far, but OK.'

The wind was at our backs, blowing us along. For a time, we walked in silent challenge: who was going to speak first?

'So, you married Dougie?' he said.

'I did, aye.' I bristled. 'What of it?'

'Nothing. Just an observation.'

'I want you to tell me what's going on,' I said. 'Why are you pretending to be Barry Sefton?'

He clapped his gloved hands together, making me jump. 'You forget how cold it is here. Dubai was so gloriously hot. I can't decide which extreme I prefer. Do you remember rollerblading along here?'

I did, of course I did, but I wasn't going to give him the satisfaction. His Scottish accent was barely there any more, his words not ones he would ever have chosen. *Christ, it's fuckin' freezin'*, he would have said, before.

'You sound a lot posher,' I said. 'What are you, English now?'

'I'm... educated. Whereas your accent is identical. Still northern England with just the merest hint of Aberdeen. I'd expected you to be all *dinna ken* and *fit like the day* by now. You always were allergic to change. I'm more of a sponge, myself. I prefer to evolve. It's not good to close yourself off to influence, you know.'

For the second time, I bristled. He'd managed to insult not only me but the good people of the city I'd grown up in.

'Why are you using a fake name?' I asked without deigning to respond to his pathetic attempt at point-scoring. 'I'm not going to report you or anything. I just want to know.'

He threw up his hands. 'All right, all right!'

'This isn't some big joke, you know. It's people's lives.'

'I know. I know that. I will tell you. It's not what you think, trust me. That's why I agreed to meet you. I wanted to explain properly. It's all completely above board.'

We were walking past cranes now, warehouses, storage facilities, towards Footdee. It was quieter here, all but desolate, and my stomach cramped with tension. Why he had agreed to meet me when it would mean his unmasking was beyond me. But then why had I chosen to come here alone? We are mysteries to ourselves sometimes, I think now, in retrospect.

Maybe he was tired of pretending to be someone else just as I was tired of my mind torturing me with questions and contradictory theories. Maybe I thought he would trust me with his deception, as an old pal, an ex. For old times' sake. For who we had been to one another. He would ask me to keep my nose out of his affairs and if it was, as he said, above board, I would agree, at peace with the knowledge that I was right after all, that I *had* seen him that day, that I wasn't mad. And with that peace would come another settling: I would know that I wasn't mad back in the day either. Our relationship wasn't a mirage. It was real. I would know that he simply left me in a cruel and immature way, that it was no more than a teenage kid behaving like an arse.

'I don't care if you're using a different name,' I blurted. 'Names can be changed, quite legally.' I didn't even care that he'd stolen a dead man's profile, as long as his professional credentials were real.

'Of course it's legal,' he said. 'I needed a new start, that's all.' He smiled, his eyes warm, full of an old, forgotten affection.

I felt myself emboldened, and yes, maybe I felt safer then. This guy wasn't a killer; he was just Hughie. A chancer, a joker; maybe a bit of a rogue, but one who always made you feel like everything would turn out just fine. If you were lost, he'd find the way. If you ran out of cash, he'd sub you. If there was a problem, he had the solution.

'Let's get out of the wind,' he said, gesturing to the backpack. 'I've brought us some tea. *For old times.*'

We were almost at Footdee, just before the road takes a curve to the right. Despite everything, my mouth itched to smile. His rucksack often had some sort of picnic in it. He always did have a stash of something. Back then, I'd taken it for gallantry. I didn't know a single other guy who would whip out a tartan rug at a moment's notice along with a bottle and a couple of glasses; most of them barely knew how to speak to a lassie. It always seemed at odds with the orphan boy living with his foster mum, but I'd put it down to him having come up from Edinburgh, where in my teenage mind people were more sophisticated.

I was about to say, *no, let's go somewhere warm*, determined to set the agenda, but I didn't. He'd already turned away and was walking towards the wee steps that led down to the beach. This was my chance, I thought. My plan. I dug out my old phone, pressed record and shoved it half down my bra. Like that, I followed, caught up somehow in an old and familiar momentum. *Get in. I'll take you for a spin.* But this time I had a momentum all of my own.

'I need to get back soon,' I said, but he'd disappeared behind the wall.

I stood a moment, deliberating at the top of the short stone flight. I could leave. I could walk back to my car. I knew now that it was him, that I wasn't mad and never had been. That's all I'd wanted to know really. But I still had questions. And if I left now, I'd never know why he disappeared the way he did, why he wrote me that terrible note, and how exactly he was connected to Joan.

I found him sitting on a tartan blanket on the sand, his back against the seawall. From the rucksack he was pulling out a brushed chrome flask, and I remembered how he was always getting things from his school bag like some teenage magician: a wee baggie of weed, a hip flask of whisky, cigarette papers, filters, cans, packets of Monster Munch and Mini Cheddars when we got the munchies.

A memory assailed me: a basket for my seventeenth birthday, taken from the boot of his car. Inside, a cake, candles, a lighter. He'd driven us out to Cults forest. We ate cake and drank cava in the dappled shade of Scots pine and beech. It was the single most glamorous thing I had ever done.

'You always did like a picnic,' I said, lowering myself with some difficulty to sit beside him.

Here in the shelter of the wall, there was no wind. It was quiet, save for the percussive crash of the waves.

'Tea.' He handed me a white enamelled tin cup, steam rising from a blue rim. 'It'll warm you up.'

'Thank you.' I held my hands around it. I checked that he was drinking his before sipping, so I guess I must've been worried on some level. The tea was hot and sweet. We looked out to sea. It was hard to rid myself of the thought of Joan in that violent grey water. Impossible. Surreal too to be sitting here with Hughie, over a decade after I'd last seen him.

'Here.' He placed a woollen blanket around my shoulders. As with everything he did, it released a memory of him doing something like it before, putting his coat around me one summer's evening in the park after the sun had gone down. *You're shivering, KK. Here, take my jacket.* With the blanket around me, the shelter of the wall, the baby inside and the tea trickling its heat through me, I was warm enough.

'Go on then,' I said. 'I'm all ears.'

He sighed heavily. 'I'm not using my own name,' he said with slow deliberation, 'because before I came to Aberdeen, I had a criminal record. OK? That's it. That's the mystery.'

I tried to read his face, but his expression gave nothing away.

'As a laddie,' he went on when I said nothing, 'I was quite the tearaway. Then after my parents died, Aberdeen was a new start for me. But when I entered the profession, I needed something stronger, if you like. I needed not to be me. Back when we knew each other, I kept things about my past from you and your pals because I had to. And the same applied to my career. Not everyone lives a nice life.'

'I know that. Don't patronise me. I'm not some princess in a tower.'

The sea threw its white ruffles onto the sand. Rumbled backward in helpless, clinging retreat. Seagulls gathered overhead, screeching for scraps. The tea was strong, too sweet.

'I didn't want you shouting my name all over the hospital,' he said, quite conversationally, as if it were water under the bridge. 'Even though I've not done anything illegal, it's not something I'd want to share. Does that make sense?'

'Why come here? Why Aberdeen, where folk know you?'

He shrugged, his eyebrows rising, his head tilting to one side. 'A job came up. I didn't think anyone would recognise me.

I know I've changed. Deteriorated, more like.' He gave a brief laugh. I didn't contradict him.

'Are you even an anaesthetist?'

'Of course I'm a fucking anaesthetist.' Irritation cracked the polished veneer, leaked something of the old accent, the harder consonants, the barely perceptible rolling R. 'What? Do you think I go about randomly shooting drugs into folk?'

Folk. Earlier, he'd said *laddie.* Glitches in his assumed identity, tree roots breaking through tarmac. The public-school drawl was apparently struggling to hold on to itself. He's a chameleon, I thought. Always was. It's just that, when I first knew him, I didn't see it because he'd changed his colours to match with mine.

'So why now? Why come back now?'

'So many questions.' He laughed, though nothing was funny.

I scanned the beach, fighting the urge to shout at him to tell me what the hell was going on. Apart from the black squiggle of a windsurfer several groynes up, there really was no one as far as the eye could see. How quickly I had trusted the guy who had abused my trust so brutally. A drop of rain landed on my cheek. Another.

'I'm sorry I left the way I did,' he said.

I held my breath, electrified, but said nothing. My heart began to race. This was what I'd come here for. This was why I'd been so reckless as to come alone. Just the two of us, face to face at last, and he was going to tell me why.

'When I saw my exam results,' he went on, 'I felt like such an idiot. I knew I'd fucked it up. It was in my DNA, you see. I was pre-programmed to follow a pattern of behaviour, and I thought I could beat it. As I said, I didn't have the best start.'

'With your parents dying in the fire?'

'That was never true. Surely you all knew that?'

I pressed my mouth shut, suppressing shock. 'So... they're alive?'

'I never knew my dad,' he said. 'I have no idea whether he's alive or dead, and I don't particularly care. My mother died... well, she died by suicide actually.' He blinked over and over.

'I'm so sorry.' My skin tingled. Had I got it all wrong? Had I got *him* all wrong – then and now? Was the confidence not a confidence trick at all but the armour of a broken wee boy? That must have been heavy to wear, so heavy.

He shrugged, a sad smile playing on his mouth. 'What're you going to do? Life, eh? The hands we're dealt.'

I sipped my tea. 'How much sugar have you put in this?'

'Don't you take it any more?'

'Sometimes. It's fine. Don't worry about it. Just tell me what you did after you left. Why did you leave that stupid note? It was so cruel.'

'No excuses. I was a dick. I'm sorry.'

'Simple as that, eh?'

He nodded. 'Simple as that. I thought it'd be easier if you thought badly of me. I thought being angry would be better than being upset. I didn't want to break your heart.'

'Don't flatter yourself.' I gave a mirthless laugh. 'I was confused, that's all. Shocked. My whole family was. They were good to you, and you treated them like they were nothing. And me. I was barely eighteen. I didn't know people could behave like that.'

'Weren't you the lucky one?' he sneered. 'And you weren't a child. You were legally an adult.'

It was a strange thing to say. Another memory surfaced: the two of us in my room, the night before the exam results. His face above mine, his fingers wrestling with the buttons on my jeans. The sense of panic, hearing myself say, 'Stop. Sorry. I'm not ready.'

'Come on.' The urgency in his voice. The pressure. 'It's fine. You're legally an adult.'

Looking down to see he had undone his flies. The shock of it.

'When I saw you in the hospital,' he said, cutting through time and space, bringing me back to the cold seawall, the sand, the sea. 'As I said, I didn't think anybody would recognise me in a million years. Out of context, different name, a decade on...'

'I knew it was you,' I said.

'Of course you did. You never did know how to let things lie, did you? You were always such a nosy parker.' His voice had an edge.

'I wouldn't call it that,' I replied, apprehension flashing through me. I felt sick, I realised, like, really sick, like I was about to throw up. 'I like helping people, that's all,' I made myself carry on. 'It's my job to figure out when things aren't right and act accordingly. Lives depend on it. You should know that. You're using a fake name. What's to stop me thinking you're using someone else's qualifications? I will check, you know. Don't think I won't. Tasha's already looking into it.'

Why did I say that? To give myself a guarantee, I suppose. Maybe I realised I'd put myself in danger, though I had no idea then how much danger, of course. I guess the worst I was thinking was that he might turn nasty. I thought I knew him, you see. I can't believe I was stupid enough to think our history would protect me.

'I'm not working illegally,' he scoffed. 'I changed my name by deed poll because otherwise it would've been difficult for me to get work. Honestly, your imagination has run wild.'

'Barry Sefton's dead. He died in 2009. He was an anaesthetist at Edinburgh Infirmary.'

He had the grace to look surprised before composing his features into a vaguely supercilious expression. 'So what? It was as good a name to pick as any. By the time I was qualified, his records had expired. Not like he needed them.'

'But you went to Dubai with his name?'

He shrugged. 'No one had thought to take down his LinkedIn. I didn't steal anyone's identity. Not anyone living anyway.'

'But you stole his LinkedIn.'

'I borrowed it. OK, so I tweaked some dates here and there. Do you think the NHS has the budget to constantly check and cross-reference these things? You know better than that! Barry Sefton was long gone. I didn't do anyone any harm.'

'Did you kill Joan Wood?' I could barely hear my own question for the pulsing of blood in my head, barely say it through my parched mouth. I didn't stop to wonder why I was parched when all I'd been doing was drinking tea.

'Who?' he asked, looking me right in the eye.

'You know fine well who I mean. My neighbour. She was my pal. I cared for her very much.' To my absolute irritation, I was blinking back tears. 'I loved her.'

'The old woman who lives next door to you? Now why would I do that?'

'Next door but one.' My eyelids were heavy, drooping. I couldn't see straight.

I suppose he must have lifted the cup out of my hand. I have no memory of checking if he'd drunk his tea, but obviously I know now he hadn't, only pretended to sip it. I'd been so lost in my desperate need for information, I'd dropped the ball. About a second later, I felt his fingers hard and tight around my arm.

'Wha-a?' My tongue was too fat in my mouth.

He twisted me roughly. Overhead, a seagull shrieked and dived. Against the beach, the receding waves boiled. I tried to shout for help, but no sooner had I opened my mouth than I felt the soft press of a cloth. And a smell – sweet, cloying.

Then blackness.

FORTY-ONE
HUGHIE

HR/audio/excerpt #7

So here we are, Kirsty. KK. Old friends. Bookends. Rain trickling down the windscreen like... like so many broken-hearted tears. Here we are, revisiting old wounds on this dreich Aberdeen evening. Passers-by might see a lonely man come to contemplate his life. A husband come to pick up his wife from visiting a friend. A father, perhaps, waiting for one of his kids to run out from North Square after a playdate in Footdee. None of them will see the heavily pregnant woman bound and prone on the back seat.

Which is hardly relevant. There are no passers-by, not here.

I have to say, I thought the tinted rear windows were a bit much when I bought this racy little number, a present to myself for making it this far. But then I thought, what would Barry drive? And the answer of course was a high-powered person-alised-reg sports car.

I am nothing other than the identity I currently inhabit. Character is everything.

Which leaves us here. You, a woman of kindness and care,

safe in the identity you've inhabited all your life; me, caught between the past and present incarnations of my constantly metamorphosising self. I'm not sure why I've already told you so much since you fell rather gracelessly backward into my arms. It's not as if you'll remember.

But then again, you might. So I'm thinking maybe I did it subconsciously, a guarantee against the temptation of mercy. I can't afford a soft spot, even for you. The fake name alone is enough to finish me, and then there's the small matter of slipping Rohypnol into your tea before I knocked you out with the chloroform. Even a fake doctor would know that drugging and kidnapping a pregnant woman goes against pretty much everything Hippocrates stood for. I saw no one as we staggered to the Audi, but we can never be sure, can we? As for you, I have no idea what you'll hear or remember of this late hour in the countdown of your life. Not that it matters.

There is still so much to tell you. And it's so nice to have an audience.

You asked me before you succumbed to the drugs if I knew Joan Wood. I implied that I didn't, but I'm afraid that was one lie of many. I did know Joan really very well. I can't remember now if I told you that my name was originally Morris. Did I? Rhetorical question, I realise. You can't answer and you won't remember. I've tied your wrists with Joan's old tights, so hopefully they're softer than tie-wraps. I don't want them to dig into your skin. And before you start crediting me with kindness, as I know you'll be tempted to do, the fact is, I didn't want to leave any marks. If you follow your friend off the harbour wall, which I'm afraid you will, it has to look like you went in of your own accord.

This is all such a mess. I didn't intend any of it, and that really is the truth. But if you hadn't insisted on shouting my name all over the hospital, on stalking me online and on living so fucking close to Joan Elizabeth Wood, I could have gone slower. That's what I need you to understand. If you hadn't recognised me, you'd never have started putting two and two together. I could have written Joan a nice card to tell her I was in the area. I could have paid her a more socially pleasant call. I was planning to gain her trust over time, but when I realised that not only did you live within spitting distance, you'd also become one of those interfering little wifeys poking their noses into their neighbours' affairs, I knew time was something I no longer had.

This is what I mean when I say it's your fault, Kirsty. All of it.

Where was I?

Oh yes. Morris. Young Morris. The boy I used to be.

I think maybe I haven't mentioned him yet.

But let me take you a little further back. This would've been a year or two before Morris's mother died. Picture her passed out alongside her drug-dealing lover, the sofa shedding its synthetic stuffing onto the bare and filthy floorboards. Quite the tableau, I'm sure you'd agree.

Picture young Morris frantically searching his mother's handbag for cash to buy food when he discovers a letter. It is addressed to his mother. You might struggle to believe this, but Morris has never seen a hand-written letter before, certainly not one in a thick cream envelope. The envelope gives up an equally thick cream sheet of paper. In the top right-hand corner is a name and address written in flowery cursive handwriting. It is beautiful, actually, this handwriting, and Morris runs his bitten fingernails over its looping lines. The names at the top are Mr and Mrs Lachlan Wood. Morris feels his brow furrow. The surname is the same as his own. And why do Mr and Mrs Wood have the same first name? Are they his mother's brother and sister? No, that doesn't explain...

Dearest Rosie, the letter begins. *We write to ask after our precious daughter and very much hope you are all right.*

Daughter? There is a certain confusion for him in the phrase. Who is their precious daughter, and how does his mother know her?

We beg you to get in touch and let us know you are all right. It has been three years since we last received word. We ask with no obligation and no pressure, but please, darling, let us know.

The letter goes on. Morris's attention goes in and out. Not because the letter isn't interesting. In fact, it is fascinating, but he is calculating as well as reading and he is beginning to realise that *our precious daughter* and Rosie and his mother are all the same person. But it's all swimming about because Rosie has always told him her parents were dead and his father was never on the scene. It was just the two of them against the world. You and me, kid.

And yet here is a letter from her parents. And if Rosie has lied about her parents, has she also lied about his father?

Well. You can imagine the shock.

Folded into the letter is a cheque for five hundred pounds. Morris gasps at the sum.

Darling, the letter goes on, *please accept this cheque only as the loving gift it is meant to be. We give it freely and without conditions.*

They beg her to pay it in and wonder – so tentatively, although Morris doesn't know the word tentatively yet – if she might consider coming to see them. She can visit any time. They will pay her fare, a hotel if she needs space, although of course they would love her to stay in her old room. Their door is open. They will never stop telling her how dreadfully sorry they are for the way things turned out and wish they could turn back time and do it differently. They ask again – and here Morris's breath stalls in his chest – did she ever have the child? They understand why she has not answered this question and accept that it is none of their business. But they are getting old and Lachlan is unwell. If they do indeed have a grandchild, they would very much like to meet them, no matter the circumstances by which they came into the world. That is in the past now.

No matter the circumstances.

Morris bites his lip so hard he tastes blood. His grandparents appear not to know he exists. Circumstances. What circumstances? Rosie got pregnant after a one-night stand, a guy who quite literally came and went, never to be seen again. Is that another of his mother's lies?

You see, Kirsty, at this point Morris has no idea he is the son of a sexual predator, a rapist by today's standards, who abused his position of power in the most heinous way. He has no idea that Rosie's parents, being of the old-fashioned variety, transferred the shame of that violation almost wholly to her. But he is beginning to put together the pieces. Rosie's parents, his grandparents, are not dead but estranged. And he is the cause of that estrangement. You will no doubt have gleaned that Morris does not yet know the word estrangement either. His education has been, at best, patchy.

The letter is signed *Your loving mother and father*.

A pain tightens in Morris's chest.

'Your loving mother and father,' he whispers, tracing his fingertip now around the series of curls that make up the grandad and grandma he never knew he had.

While his mother snoozes off her opioids watched over by her attentive dealer and sometime lover, Michael Peterson, Morris googles Mr and Mrs Lachlan Wood's address on his stolen iPhone. Satellite images show an imposing three-storey granite town house with manicured shrubs and a wide wooden door painted duck-egg blue. White casement windows, though he does not yet know what they are called, nor does his colour palette extend to ducks and their eggs. What he does know is that his grandparents are respectable, well-to-do. They are rich.

God knows, he has been in plenty of houses like this, just not through the front door.

He pockets the cheque and hides the letter. His mother is so out of it most of the time, he can pay it into her account and transfer the money to his own without her noticing. Once it has cleared, he will buy a ticket to Aberdeen and get the fuck out of here. He will tell no one, not even Michael Peterson. Especially not Michael Peterson, who, despite being only a year older than him, is terrifying.

So. There's Michael Peterson, lying sprawled next to his mother on the dilapidated couch where we left him. But the thing is, Michael Peterson is never as out of it as he appears. Michael Peterson is not a slave to oblivion like poor lost Rosie Wood; he simply pretends to be for reasons too grubby to discuss. Sometimes it seems to Morris that Peterson wants his mother to be a slave not only to methadone but to him. Peterson has tight control over everything: his shady business dealings, his contacts in high and low places, Rosie.

Less than an hour later, Morris emerges from the bathroom and is preparing to go to work when the room darkens. He looks up to see Michael Peterson filling the doorway with a sneer. He is holding the letter. Morris feels a familiar flash of fear. Michael Peterson is not someone to cross. Morris can still feel the back of his head where Peterson shoved him against a wall last week.

'I've got the cheque,' Morris manages. 'I was going to pay it in for her.'

Peterson manhandles Morris into his tiny bedroom, stands over him while he retrieves the cheque from under the mattress. With Peterson's iron grip on the back of his neck, Morris admits his intention to travel up the road to find his grandparents. Thinking on his feet, he tries to frame his plans as a way of getting money for them all. He will smarten himself up. His grandparents will take him in and help him get the education he has missed so that he can make something of his life.

A second chance, that's all he's asking for. Once he's earning good money, he can send it home.

'We could buy a house,' he finishes, trembling by now. 'We can help Mum get clean.'

Peterson removes his hand. Waits a beat before bursting into a loud laugh that goes on and on and on. He laughs for so long he starts to cough. Morris begins to wonder if he's about to choke. At this thought, hope flares. But...

'They won't want a lowlife like you,' Peterson croaks eventually, wiping his eyes with the backs of his hands. 'Look at the fucking state of you.'

Morris doesn't speak right, Peterson goes on. He is not the right class at all. 'People like Joan and Lachlan Wood,' he says with relish, 'can smell poverty on a person like a mouse can smell cheese. And you, my deluded wee numpty, reek of it.'

Peterson has control of Rosie's account. He, not Morris, banks the cheque and spends all of it on drugs, which he sells on.

Morris is beaten but cannot let go. That wee glimpse of light was enough to make shadows on the wall, the silhouettes of two kind and decent people who have said they would like to meet him. At night, he dreams of a bedroom just for him, with white walls and fresh sheets that smell of lavender. He doesn't know what lavender smells like, but it sounds nice. In these dreams, Morris opens a wardrobe door to laundered clothes hanging in rows from those big wooden coat hangers you get in posh houses. A fridge in a country-cottage-style kitchen is filled with roast chicken legs and Scotch eggs and cold cans of Coke. There are no wraps on the coffee table, no syringes, no cockroaches.

Morris saves what he can, but his job pays little to nothing and progress is slow.

A year or so later, he reads of his grandfather's death. Lachlan Stewart Iain Wood was a judge, a respected person in the community, important enough to have made the obit page in *The Scotsman*. His daughter, Rosemary Wood, is mentioned as living in Edinburgh.

There is no mention of Morris.

By now, Michael Peterson is an almost permanent fixture, keeping his mother company as she rises to the surface of her addiction before he helps her sink down into its depths once again. Making himself as tall as he can, Morris tells Peterson that his grandfather has died. This is the moment. He will throw himself on his grandmother's mercy, and she will take him in. She won't care that his teeth have never seen a dentist, that his clothes are thin and cheap or that his hair needs a cut. She will only be overjoyed to learn she has a grandson. In her care, Morris will gain an education, and once he's on his feet, he will send money back to Edinburgh. A reunion can only benefit them all.

But Peterson is stealing antiques now – a sideline – and tells Morris there are much quicker ways to make money in this world.

'Only a fool would do it the hard way,' he scoffs. 'What're you even talking about? Education is for fools. Fools and the rich. You'd be better off going up there and robbing the place.'

Morris never thinks to wonder why, if Peterson is so good at making money, he is so often at the flat and not dining at one of the better restaurants in town or sipping brandy in some swanky members' club. Morris does not realise that education is the very thing Peterson wishes he'd had more than anything, that this deep and bitter desire is precisely why he pours so much scorn on it. It is only later that he will realise that Peterson's income stream is fraught with risk, that he spends his life second-guessing, dodging the long arm of the law, scared to death of incarceration. All Morris knows is that he himself doesn't want to be a criminal. He wants to be a person of standing and class, like his grandparents, not crumpled and shoddy like an empty crisp packet in the gutter. But when he tries to explain, again, Peterson laughs in his face. Because Peterson is too clever to show that he wants all the same things himself. If he admits to that, then young Morris will see he has nothing, nothing at all.

'If you so much as pack a bag,' Peterson almost whispers, leaning in close, his tobacco breath thick, 'I'll come for you. I'll make sure Granny Joan wants nothing more to do with you ever again. Do you understand?'

Morris nods.

Michael Peterson follows his threat by telling Morris he has to steal some tramadol from work. Morphine if he can get it.

'Just once,' Peterson promises. 'Problem with the supply chain, like.'

But once is enough to strengthen his grip into a stranglehold. Once is a trap, and Morris only realises it too late, and now there is no escape. At night, the darkness rushes at him. He rubs his eyes, makes purples and reds, fails to stop tears running into his ears.

Kirsty, if you were awake, you'd be weeping by now. But I would say wait. Because Morris's luck is about to change, as luck can sometimes.

Wait.

A few months later, young Morris is pushing a mop over the floors of the oncology department, unseen, unnoticed, invisible, when he is called to reception. There, two police officers, a woman and a man, are standing with their black-and-white hats held loosely at their sides. Morris walks towards them, swallowing hard. Please God, don't let his voice betray him. The detective constable asks if he is Morris Wood.

'Yes,' he says and tries to think how innocence might look.

'I'm afraid we have some bad news.'

The DC tells him in gentle tones that his mother and a man they believe to be Michael Peterson have been found unresponsive. An ambulance was called, but the paramedics pronounced them dead at the scene.

Morris closes his eyes.

'I'm sorry for your loss,' the woman says, placing a hand carefully on his arm. 'Let us take you home.'

Morris returns home in the patrol car. The police clear the neighbours from the walkways to give him his privacy. He enters the flat, to police, to death. Tearfully he identifies his mother and her lover. The tears spring from a complicated source. Down in the depths, in the gaping shell of his loss, it is hard to acknowledge the white, shining pearl: relief.

FORTY-TWO

KIRSTY

KS/transcript #35

Something was stuck to my cheek. I managed to get my eyelids to open, slowly, blinking over and over to unglue them. Leather, that's what it was. Leather car upholstery. The back seat. My hands were tied behind my back with something soft and thick. My feet were tied with the same. My lower back throbbed with pain.

Something had woken me – maybe the pain.

'There was no money for a funeral,' a man's voice said from in front of me. Hughie. That was what had woken me. A story. Someone telling me a long story about a guy called Morris. Hughie was telling me this story. I had the impression he and this Morris character were one and the same. There'd been drugs. Poverty.

I blinked, eyes desperate for moisture.

'Let me go,' I said, but my voice was little more than a croak.

'Oh, shut up, won't you? I'm trying to tell you my life story here.'

'You can't do this!' I tipped back my head, straining to see him. 'Help,' I shouted with everything I had. But it was barely above a whisper, and it was dark outside and there was no one, not a soul about. This could not be happening. It could not.

'If you shout, I'll give you some more chloroform. That'll shut you up. It's pointless anyway. There's no one here.'

I glanced all about me, eyeballs aching. I wriggled myself forward. My bag wasn't in the footwell. No surprise there. Oh God, what had I done?

'You have to let me go,' I said, hoping to hell the phone in my bra was still there, that it was recording. 'Dougie will call the police.'

'As I was saying,' he said, with such pomposity that if my hands hadn't been tied, I'd have punched him in the head, 'there was no money for a funeral, yes? For my mother and her lover.'

Lover, I thought. I had no idea who he meant. Had it been some sort of suicide pact?

'So. I emailed my resignation to Edinburgh Infirmary with immediate effect and left the cremation to social services.'

My brain was scrambling, digging out bits of what he'd told me. A mother addicted to drugs. Morris. A lover.

'There was no inheritance obviously. There never is for people like me. It's people who don't need one, who've had every possible advantage, who also get the fat inheritance. That's just the way things work.'

He was lost in his story, his expression in the rear-view smug and bored and rapt all at once. Hughie, then. An orphan. Morris.

'But that's why people like me are so resourceful, you see? Young Morris hitch-hiked up the road, determined to make a better future.'

'Wait,' I said, head spinning. 'You're Morris, yes? Who's Peterson?'

Hughie sighed. 'Yes. You really haven't been paying attention, have you?'

I'd been out of it. On chloroform and whatever he'd put in
the tea. But whatever he wanted to tell me, I suspected the
performance of it was more important. This wasn't really for me
at all. All I had to do was indulge him, help the time pass and
maybe...

'Young Morris planned to hole up in a B and B,' Hughie,
Morris or whatever his name was went on, so in love with the
sound of his own voice. With himself. 'He needed to clean
himself up. He wasn't addicted like Mummy, not even a social
user like Peterson. But it's impossible to live in a place like that
and not get smashed from time to time. So he throws the stash
into a bin along with his cigarettes. His grandmother is a classy
lady; she won't want filthy fags in the house, will she?'

His grandmother, I thought. Wait...

'Standing in front of a mirror in a motorway services bathroom,
Morris has a moment of revelation. He'd always felt unseen by
others, but right then it struck him how little he looked at himself.
He spent most of his time at work with his head down, cleaning up
other people's bodily emissions, doing jobs no one else wanted to
do. It was a shock to face the portrait reflected back at him. He had a
good set of shoulders; he gave himself that. He'd taken some clothes
Peterson had left at the flat. Not like he had any use for them now,
and they were about a million times better than anything Morris
owned – an Adidas hoodie, Carhartt jeans, Nike Airs, Calvin Klein
boxers. He'd left the Hearts shirt Peterson used to sleep in but
wished he'd kept a suit at his mum's. It might have been useful.

'From the neck down, it's not so bad, but from the neck up –
a different story. Morris's skin is pale but somehow pink at the
same time. It looks greasy even after he washes it with the
foaming hand soap. His eyes are red, ringed in purple, fingernails and the skin around them bitten to hell. Even if he stopped

biting, years of nicotine have stained his knuckles brown. He leans in and grimaces at himself. His teeth are a beige colour, scummy. Even he can smell his own rank breath, and it is disgusting. *He* is disgusting.

'He pays for one of those toothbrush and toothpaste sets you can get in these places and scrubs until his gums bleed. But it's no use. He could wash himself for a week, he could put on the smartest threads, but it would make no difference: Morris is grubby, a grubby human being.

'For the first time, he fears Granny Wood will not take him in.'

'Granny Wood?' I blurted. Did he mean Joan? My head ached. I was desperate for water, but Hughie kept on and on, almost crazed, lost in a labyrinth of his own making.

'I doubled my resolve,' he said. 'There's a phrase I would not have used at the time. I found a budget B and B in Crown Street where I holed up for a couple of weeks. It was hard to change old habits, but I bought ready-made salads, wholemeal bread that tasted like cardboard and, as Morris would have said then, *all that healthy shite.*'

He kept referring to himself in the third person, as if Morris were someone else. But they were one and the same. Weren't they? Yes, I was pretty sure. A lifetime of being an imposter had fractured him. I had been obsessed with finding out who he was, but now I realised it was possible *he* didn't know who he was. He'd lost himself somewhere amid all the aliases. It wasn't a labyrinth he'd made but a hall of mirrors.

'Morris drinks water by the litre,' he went on. 'Fruit juice, smoothies, you name it, he drinks it all. He drinks more water in those two weeks than he has in his whole life. And he sleeps. God, does he sleep! A lifetime of hypervigilance will tire a person. Twelve, sometimes thirteen, fourteen hours at a stretch. He wakes up wondering where the hell he is, who he is, what he's doing, before the fog clears and he remembers the big task ahead.'

'Do you have any water?' I pleaded.

Muttering curses, he bent into the footwell of the passenger seat. A moment later, a plastic half-litre bottle appeared. He opened it, twisted himself awkwardly around.

'Sit up then,' he said, his voice laced with impatience.

It took me a minute or two to shimmy myself into a sitting position. He held out the bottle. I leant forward. He tipped it to my mouth and let me drink. I gulped down the water, eyes closing in relief.

'Lie down. And if you make a sound, I will end you. You can have some more in a little while, but only if you listen nicely.'

'OK,' I said, nodding, humouring him. I wondered when the police would come. When Dougie would call them. Surely by now, now it was dark?

'So back to young Morris,' Hughie said, still in his authoritative tone. 'His skin clears. His eyes lose their red webs. His nails grow a wee bit, but the nicotine stains persist. Teeth are still far from white. He pays for one more week in the B and B. Buys a running kit with the intention of getting fit.' He stopped, laughing to himself before continuing. 'One jog around the block leaves him gasping for air and tasting blood, so he doesn't do *that* again. Being slim has never been an issue; he'd had barely enough to eat over the years and his ribs were xylophones at his sides. Unlike now, alas.' He glanced down at his belly and up again. I looked away from the cold bathroom-tile blue of his eyes. 'He buys some jeans he thinks an old lady will find smart and hits the barber's for an old-school short back and sides.

'And so, four weeks after he arrives in Aberdeen, young Morris knocks on that door in Ferryhill. An old lady answers and he sees Rosie drawn across her features, dancing in the hesitant movements of her hands.

'"Mrs Wood," he says in his best voice. He coughs into his fingers and remembers not to wipe them on his breeks. "You don't know me, but my name is Morris Wood. I'm Rosie's boy. I think I'm your grandson."'

I gasped. Blood pulsed in my ears. Hughie... Morris... *was* Joan's grandson after all. Rosie's son. All I could do was listen. Stay silent. I didn't want him to put me under again.

'Old Joan's eyes pooled with tears,' Hughie said with fake emotion. 'She'd been informed of Rosie's death from an overdose only a month before. She'd lost her husband to lung cancer not long before that. I gave her Rosie's death certificate as proof, offered up my bank card, a payslip from the hospital.

'"I've nae passport," I said. "Or anything like that. I've never been abroad, like, so..."'

'Joan,' I whispered.

'Joan, aye. Keep up.'

FORTY-THREE

KIRSTY

'Joan Wood,' I said. 'She's your grandmother? Was she... was she your foster mother?'

'Yes. And yes. Impossible, I know, but bear with me.'

I imagined it from Joan's point of view. Her only living relative arrives on her doorstep just when all is lost. Here is her one remaining shred of family, and he's come all this way. He's sought her out, and he's asking her to let him in. She takes him by the hand and leads him inside, of course she does, desperate to find out everything about him. He gives her a sob story. She asks him to stay. Days turn into weeks, weeks into months, spring into summer. He asks her to adopt him... is that what happened? Did Hughie fool Joan just as he fooled me, but in a much deeper, more insidious way? Thoughts swirled, but Hughie or Morris or whoever he was had begun to talk again, and I had no idea if I was recording. My head was an anvil, but I had to concentrate. I had to remember.

'By June,' Hughie started up, 'Morris and Joan are as wrapped up in one another as lovers. He persuades her to enrol him at the local high school, to let him gain the education denied him by his feckless, drug-addicted mother, not that he phrases it like that. They should call him by a different name, he tells his gran. They should tell the school his parents had been killed in a house fire.'

'So your parents didn't die in a fire?'

'For God's sake, why can't you listen? I've told you this, more than once. If you can't pay attention, I may as well sedate you again.'

'Sorry,' I said. 'It's just a lot to take in. What did you give me? What was in the tea?'

'Oh, just a little Rohypnol. It should have worn off by now. I suppose it might shock you to learn that your old friend agreed to such an illegal plan. Sweet little old lady, eh? Not so sweet, I'm afraid. Old Joan found herself *very* easily persuaded. I was her miracle. Her only blood.'

'Oh God,' I whispered to myself. Poor Joan. Her husband and daughter were barely cold in their graves and here was her grandson rocking up to take advantage of her loss, disguising himself as a lost wee boy who needed a second chance. Of course she agreed. She'd been blinded by grief, love and fathomless regret, and he used that to his advantage.

'I allowed Joan to be the mother she never was, you see? She'd failed her poor dead Rosie, and here was I, a project, willing to learn, desperate to be everything a child could be to a grandparent. Joan's grandson was given a double room and regular meals, an Xbox, you name it, a parental figure who actually gave a shit.' He paused, pushed his hands against the steering wheel so that his arms went rigid. 'Redemption. Safety.' He shook his head sadly, utterly caught up in the drama of himself. 'Love, even,' he whispered.

The whole thing was a performance. My hands curled into fists. *Dougie*, I thought. *Where are you?*

'Honestly, Kirsty,' Hughie said. 'That woman would've given me anything I'd asked for.'

'You took advantage,' I hissed.

'Now, now.' He laughed. 'Joan was only too happy to comply. She arranged the appointment with the head teacher! Mr Blythe, do you remember him? Mr Blythe, as it turns out, was not so ignorant of the school's history as to be unaware of a certain geography teacher getting a certain student pregnant back in the day.'

'Oh God.'

'I don't think *he* had anything to do with it,' he quipped with a flippancy that turned my stomach. 'By then, Joan had updated me on the real circumstances of my conception, you see, and it was some way short of immaculate.' Another flick of his eyes in the rear-view, edges crinkled with cold amusement. 'But I knew to keep schtum. So there I am, sitting silent as a stone while Joan tells Mr Blythe in slow, sad tones that Rosie lost that baby but went on to marry a businessman, William Reynolds, and was blessed years later with baby Hugh.'

So he *was* a later child, I thought. That explained it. Did it? I needed a painkiller. I needed to drink.

'Water,' I croaked. 'Please.'

Hughie sighed and opened the bottle. I shunted myself up, panting with the effort.

'Mr Blythe was only too willing to make amends,' he said as he held the end of the bottle, feeding me the water as if I were a goat. 'Especially after learning of Rosie's tragic death.

'*Of course young Hugh can enrol here at Aberdeen High, Mrs Wood.*' Hughie's imitation of Mr Blythe's slightly fey speaking voice was scarily accurate. '*We'd be honoured to have him. You and your late husband are well known to us; I was so sorry to hear of his passing. We look forward to seeing Master Reynolds in September.* Something like that.' In the rear-view, he shot me a smile that was more like a sneer.

'Blinded by love,' he went on. 'That was old Joan. Doted on me like I was her prince. She dropped her life for me, looked after me, bought me everything I ever asked her for. Driving lessons. A car. A holiday to Spain.'

'I thought you had a Saturday job?'

He laughed. 'God, no. Why would I do that when I had money on tap? And the beauty of it was, because what we were doing was illegal, Joan gave up all her friendships, her church, everything. All for our deception. She was prepared to do it as long as I played the adoring grandson. Don't get me wrong, I did my bit. I worked hard. I did my homework – at least until shadows of the old me crept in. As the end drew nearer, I could feel the threads of myself coming loose, unravelling me. I stole jewellery from Joan, one of Lachlan's watches. A carriage clock. I pilfered her savings. Call it my back-up plan. Call it once a thief, always a thief.' Again his eyes flicked up and met mine. 'Call it survival.'

'That's not survival,' I said. 'That's a con. You conned her!' I pushed and pulled at the ties on my wrists. But they didn't budge.

'The irony of it all,' he said, 'is that when I left in the night and took her money with me, she was forced to sell the big house in Ferryhill and move to something smaller. And if she hadn't had to sell up, she would never have ended up moving to your cul-de-sac and we would never have ended up in this mess, would we? Ironic or what?'

I could see his amused expression. I hated him. I hated him so much.

'I was absolutely horrified when I saw you coming out of your house. I'd thought it couldn't get any worse. A living night-mare, that's what you've put me through. Turning up like a bad penny, like a... like a fucking hawk!' He sighed, appeared to be fighting to calm himself down. 'But once you're gone, it'll be almost funny.'

'It's not funny,' I said. 'You're sick.'

'Now, now, don't be like that.' He pursed his lips.

All I could do was stay quiet and hope to God that Dougie called the police. They would check my messages, wouldn't they? Would they think to check LinkedIn? Tasha. Tasha would check.

'So,' Hughie went on. 'Poor young Morris is reborn as Hugh, soon to be known as Hughie. His young life has been chaos. Barely any school, no doctor, no dentist. I'm not sure I even had a birth certificate, do you know that?'

I didn't know how to answer, so I said nothing.

'Are you beginning to see?' he said, his tone increasingly frantic. 'Survival versus living? Two different worlds. You're too out of it. I get it. You're confused, reaching for the pieces to try and put them together. But you must be thinking the dates don't line up. How impossible it is that this story be true. Your friends have all told you, after all. It isn't him, Kirsty. It can't be. There's no way Barry Sefton is Hughie Reynolds.'

He turned to face me, one hand gripping the back of his car seat.

'But it is true,' he said, eyes glittering with a malice that made my heart quicken, my breath catch. 'It is the truest story you will ever hear. It's the story of a boy who grabbed his chance. Who escaped up the road into the arms of his broken-hearted granny. Overwhelmed by love, loneliness and regret, entranced by the promise of a blood relative to call her own, Granny Wood agreed to send Morris Wood to school as Hugh Reynolds, knowing it was illegal, knowing it was wrong, knowing that her grandson needed a false name.

'Because he was not fifteen at all.' His eyes narrowed, fixing onto mine. 'The year I started my Standard Grades, Kirsty, I was twenty-nine years old.'

FORTY-FOUR

KIRSTY

KS/transcript #37

My body filled with hot dread.

'*What?*'

'That's right,' he said, half laughing.

'But that's impossible. There's no way. You were...'

'I was what? In a school uniform?'

'No,' I said. 'No way.' His face above mine. His kiss. His hands. I tried to do the maths, but my head was mince. He hadn't been a teenager. 'You were a g-grown man,' I stuttered. 'When we... That's illegal.'

'Of course it wasn't illegal,' he mocked. 'You were of age. You were frigid, that's all, and now I know why.'

'You bastard,' I cried. 'You... pervert!'

'I am no such thing. We'd been going steady for a long time. Plenty of women have relationships with older men.'

'But I didn't know! I didn't know you were thirty!'

'Thirty-three by then actually.'

I'd begun to cry. I wanted to kill him. It was physical, an

animal reaction. My hands strained against the ties. I wanted so badly to punch him in his smug face until his nose bled and his eyes swelled purple. I hated him like I'd never hated anyone. I hated him with an intensity that frightened me. 'You... you bastard. That's... It's assault. You assaulted me.' His kiss. His lips on mine. I felt sick, so sick.

'Oh, come on. Hardly assault. You wouldn't let me, remember?'

My heart raced. My mind blackened, too many thoughts clouding. 'You're lying,' I said. 'You were a teenager like the rest of us. You falsified your LinkedIn just like you've falsified everything else.'

''Fraid not. Barry Sefton was the same age as me. I only used his profile because we had a... connection.'

'But we all believed you. It's impossible.'

'You'd think, wouldn't you?' He smiled. 'But remember, I didn't *tell* you anything, did I? I presented myself, that was all, in a school uniform so new it was stiff, the lovely tortoiseshell glasses fitted with plain glass, my trembling demeanour. None of you asked if my lenses were prescription, did you? No one asked me my age.'

'But the teachers!'

'Nope. Not one teacher, not one parent, not one child. Why would they?'

'Because... because...'

'My complexion? My thinning hair? What were they going to do, ask about the fire that had tragically killed my parents?'

'But you said your skin was damaged from the fire.'

'I didn't. I never said a word about my skin or my hair. I left you to draw your own conclusions.'

'You were twice our age! You were a grown man!'

'Now, now. Keep your voice down.' He laughed, his eyes mocking me in the mirror.

'But...' I couldn't form a sentence.

'Kirsty,' he said, as if bored. 'It'll be time for us to take a walk soon. You might feel a little groggy, but once we're at the harbour, the fresh air will bring you round. I'll give you a little something to take the edge off when the time comes.'

I looked about me, panting with distress. It was pitch-dark out. The car was hazy warm from the heater. *When the time comes...* What did that mean? Where were the police? Where the hell was Dougie?

Hughie – I could only think of him as Hughie – got out of the car. Freezing air rushed in, and I shrank from it. He slammed the door, then pushed his fists to his lower back and stretched. A second later, the back door opened. He'd been a grown man. He'd been nearly thirty when he arrived at our school. How? How was that possible? How had none of us seen? Tears were rolling over my nose, into my hair. Not hormones. Not empathy. Not happiness or love. These were tears of shock, a shock that was now turning to terror. Hughie Reynolds was at the car door, a cloth in one hand, a bottle in the other. He was going to kill me. I wasn't sure how I knew it, but I knew it. Had he told me? He hadn't told me he'd killed Joan or Reeny. But maybe he had. So much had been lost in the cocktail of chloroform and exhaustion. And anyway, I knew he'd killed them, in the same way I'd known everything from the start – in my gut.

His name was not Hughie Reynolds. It was Morris Wood. He was Joan's grandson. And when I met him, he'd been not fifteen but twenty-nine. Thirty-three when we'd almost slept together, when he'd recoiled from me, his face laced with disgust, when he'd sent me a letter he knew would devastate me. The skin damage wasn't skin damage. The thinning hair wasn't from a fire. They were age, pure and simple. The swagger was the confidence of a grown man, a man pretending to be a kid.

'I'm afraid we need to wait a while yet, but this should help pass the time.' He clambered on top of me, eyes crazy with cruelty. A second later, the sweet cloth closed over my mouth.

Morris Wood, I thought. Hughie.

Then blackness once again.

FORTY-FIVE
HUGHIE

People accept whatever is presented to them. I have always believed this, and I have never had cause to doubt it. Even before I saw your spotty adolescent faces, for years I had accepted my own life blindly, believing I did not deserve another. It was normal not to have clean school uniform, any school uniform, in fact. It was normal for no one to mention the idea of going to school, let alone take you. It was normal to long for the one free school meal, often the only meal of the day.

The Leith vowels leaked out from time to time. I heard them. Did you? What did you see, Kirsty Shaw? An orphan? Someone you could look after? A life to save?

That was presumptuous, wasn't it? I have never needed anyone, least of all you and your cutesy chocolate-box family. My foray into secondary education took not only initiative but a huge pair of balls. Can you imagine? Wondering every minute of every hour if this was the day the cops would turn up and say, *Oi, you're Morris Wood. You're a grown man!* On occasion, I've heard colleagues talk about imposter syndrome, wrestling with the trust placed in them and their opinions when sometimes they feel like they don't know what they're talking about. I allow myself the smallest smile.

You don't know the half of it, I think.

I don't consider myself an imposter, not really. I did the work. UCL is so enormous; there are so many students, and no one asks who you are. My colleagues were driving themselves into excruciating debt, and there I was, loaded with Granny's money yet getting it all for free. I knew I would need to know what I was doing even if I didn't need the certificates, the graduation ceremony, the stupid hat and gown thing. The certificates and references I could take care of myself. I had the ID. I had my old contacts. All I needed was the knowledge. Fraud met hard work. Fraud *is* hard work, to be honest. It takes an incredible amount of time, effort and resilience. A borrowed name here, a fake reference there. It's all about getting that first job. After that, you can build your own reputation. I'm a bloody good anaesthetist, Kirsty. I'm calm under pressure.

Did you know a lot of surgeons are psychopaths?

Anyway, all this to say I was born again. Sefton was a kind of talisman, a keepsake for good luck. I applied for a position at the American Hospital in Dubai. Things went well for a while. But just as in Aberdeen, my self-sabotaging instincts eventually kicked in; my roots dragged me back into the mud. I needed a rush. I had never had money. Now I had so much of it. But it ran through my fingers like water.

It irks me even now that having scoffed at my fellow students running up tens of thousands of pounds' worth of debt, there I was doing the same, albeit enjoying myself a great deal more. Like any other addict, I longed for the adrenaline. Four grand on a tailored suit, too many pairs of horse-leather shoes, too many high-end restaurants, too many holidays in destinations usually reserved for celebrities. The next morning, the self-loathing would descend, then the vows, the promises to do better, to curb my excesses, to stop. It's a circular thing. I knew that from my beginnings. Before I was ready to admit it to myself, I was up to my neck in the red, further credit denied.

All of which brings me round to your original questions: why come back? Why now?

Money, Kirsty.

I had no money. Joan did. Despite me taking her ISA, she still had the house to sell. And she was old, old enough to be handing it over.

I knew she would forgive me eventually for leaving the way I did. I would fall on my knees and tell her tearfully about my epiphany, the moment when I realised I had to return, to face what I had done and make amends.

I just needed time, as I have said. I thought if I secured a job, she would believe I was there to stay. I would tell her I had a girlfriend, that we were going steady, that we planned to raise kids here in Aberdeen. I would lure her for a second time with the promise of her own blood. And I knew there'd be plenty of change from the house. Enough to pay my debts.

I had not planned for her having altered her will.

Heartless, I'm sure you'll agree.

FORTY-SIX

HUGHIE

HR/audio/excerpt #9

This is where you come in, Kirsty. For God's sake, woman, I'd only been there a *week* when you spotted me. One week. It did not cross my mind that I would be recognised. I had, I knew, changed dramatically. Contrary to my school days, I now very much look my age. I thought no one would give me a second glance.

But we both know how that ended.

I'll be honest: finding Joan in such rude health was disappointing. She was eighty-one, for God's sake, and alone. After all she'd been through, she should've been hanging by a thread, but thanks to her attentive neighbour, she was thriving – another thing for which you are to blame, do you see? I had planned to take my time, help her along by degrees, Shipman style. But as soon as you called my name, the pressure intensified. I had to make my move.

Old Joan was shocked to see me, to say the least. When I'd managed to calm her down enough to let me into the house, she really laid it on thick with the recriminations. *I gave up my life for you. I gave up my closest friend, blah blah. I broke the law for you, and how did you repay me? You stole all my savings.*

'I didn't steal them *all*,' I said.

I must have raised my voice more than I'd meant to because she started shaking, cowering as if I was going to hit her. I am not a violent man. You can imagine how insulting that was. All that risk, all that courage, all those years in the service of becoming respectable and she treated me like the brown-toothed, nicotine-knuckled boy from Leith I had fought to leave behind.

'You didna even say goodbye,' she said, tears rolling down her face, shoulders still hunched as if to take a blow. 'I woulda left everything to you. But you disappeared. I thought you'd died. How could you do that to me? How could you?'

'Wait,' I said. 'What do you mean, *would* have left everything to me. Surely—'

'It's a' going to Reeny,' she interrupted, her voice shrill. And then, get this. This is the absolute peach of it. She said, 'And I've left the house to Kirsty.'

I had no idea who she was talking about in either case. I had never met Reeny, and as far as I was concerned, Joan had never met you. Back then, she'd been so careful to keep me from any of her friends, and I'd been very careful to make sure she never met any of mine. I assumed it was a different Kirsty. But the name rattled me nonetheless.

'You can't do that,' I said. 'I'm your grandson. I'm *family*.'

'You left.'

Defiance flamed in her eyes. But I saw doubt too. Maybe even guilt. Blood ties are not so easily cut, no matter what your family does to you.

I decided to revert to plan A.

'That's a shame,' I said. 'I came to tell you I'm back for good. I have a girlfriend. Her name is... Sheila; I met her in Dubai and we're getting married.' I let that sink in, but I could see she was still wavering. I would, I knew, have to push it one more notch. Maybe seeing you that morning had inspired me, who knows? 'She's pregnant,' I added. 'You're going to be a great-granny.'

Her eyes darted about as if there was a fly in the room. Defiance gave way to confusion.

'Joan?' I said. 'Granny?'

'I... I canna take it in,' she said. 'It's too much. How do I know if it's true?'

That was when I made my first mistake. I became agitated. I'm not sure why. Perhaps the fact that she'd cut me off after all I'd done for her? I suppose that must have hurt me somewhere.

I stood up. She remained in her chair, and I suppose I was towering over her. I didn't shout, not exactly, but my voice can be really quite loud when I become frustrated.

'You have to change your will,' I said. 'You must.'

She shrank back, her head hooked onto her neck like a vulture's. She looked a hundred. She looked terrified.

'Dinna hurt me,' she said. 'I never told a soul. Not a soul. Please dinna hurt me.'

'Of course I'm not going to hurt you! But now you've seen me again, and with a baby on the way, you'll be wanting to change your will. Otherwise... well, otherwise... Look, I don't want to have to leave all over again, and it would be such a shame for our child to never know her great-grandmother.'

Her mouth closed tight. She looked at me with what I can only describe as disgust. The callousness of the woman. I was beginning to understand why Rosie ran away and left her.

'I will not be blackmailed.' She spoke the words slowly and folded her arms. But she was trembling. I'd heard the shake in her voice, and she must have too.

I held on to my left wrist with the opposite hand as I had practised doing over the years and breathed deeply until my heartbeat slowed. Calm down, I told myself, over and over. In my head, I mean, not out loud. I could not let her know she was getting to me. I had to play it right or I would lose.

'If that's how you feel, then I'll go. I'm not going to stay here and be accused of blackmail. It was a mistake to come. Good-bye, Granny.' I walked out of the room. I opened the front door and waited a beat.

'Morris,' she called out, as I had known she would.

I slammed the door shut.

FORTY-SEVEN

HUGHIE

HR/audio/excerpt #10

I had hoped twenty-four hours to stew would bring her to her senses. Frankly, I was banking on it – and in my case, that is not just a figure of speech. Sure enough, the next day, she let me in.

'I've brought the new will for you to sign,' I said, striding into her sitting room. The smell of polish assailed me, transporting me briefly back to when I was a lad, or not quite a lad, in her care. 'It's in my professional name, Barry Sefton. That's all it is, Granny, a professional name. Nothing illegal this time.'

'I canna do that. It's no' right.'

I couldn't help but laugh. 'You can't do it? What, morally? Really? I think we both know you've done worse.' Anger simmered. I was still spooked after seeing you the day before. I had spent the night festering, and I was really too tired for Joan Wood and her bullshit.

'It's no' right,' she repeated. 'You're no' a good person.'

'Oh come on!' I'll admit I was shouting by then. I was a knife edge away from losing it altogether, and I should have read the signs but I didn't. 'After everything you've done?' I cried. 'I changed my name legally! You can't just cut me out because I made a mistake ten years ago. I'm back now, aren't I? I've said I'm sorry.' In truth, I could not remember if I had. 'I just need you to sign the damn thing and then we can arrange for...' At that point I realised I'd forgotten what name I'd given my imaginary fiancée. 'For m-my partner to come and visit. We can get to know one another again before the baby comes. We can be a family. Won't that be nice?'

But would you believe it, the old goat shook her head. 'I'll no' sign it.'

Undeterred, I took the document out of my bag and handed it to her, and said with as much menace-laced authority as I could, 'Sign it, or I'll make you sign it.'

'No.' She looked away, folded her arms.

'Gran,' I said, calmer now, at least on the surface. 'Come on now. Don't be like this. Or I'll leave town and you'll never see me again.'

'So leave. Good riddance to bad rubbish.'

I take no pride in telling you that this is the moment I truly lost it. All that careful planning and she wouldn't sign a fucking piece of paper. I needed it signed and I needed her gone, and all she could do was insult me. How dare she? I'd been prepared to take it slow, to edge her out of this world painlessly and with dignity, but the fact was, while she was alive and while her will had no place for me in it, I could not pay my debts. I could not live the life I'd taken such humongous risks to achieve. It wasn't fair.

The old red mist descended. I didn't know what was happening, I swear. I only knew once it had cleared and I realised I had hit her. I had hit her so hard she had fallen from the chair.

I crouched down, felt for a pulse. It was still there – faint but there. I stood up, my heart going like the clappers, and cast about, looking for what, I didn't know. A solution to a disastrous reflex. I stood for a moment breathing heavily and thinking little beyond *Shit*.

And then you rang the doorbell.

But I had no idea it was you. Not then.

In a state of panic, I rolled Joan's unconscious body under the front window, grabbed her phone from the coffee table in case she somehow managed to rouse herself sufficiently to call for help, although I sincerely doubted she would, and ran like a man dodging a hail of bullets out of the room. As the doorbell chimed again, I let myself out the back, pulse beating in my temples. Somehow I had the presence of mind to pocket the back-door key. I threw myself over the next-door neighbour's fence, cursing under my breath. It was supposed to be quick, clean and easy, but already I'd been recognised by you and now I'd assaulted an old woman and left her all but unconscious.

And she hadn't even signed the papers.

I edged around the neighbour's wall. If I'd known then how close I was to your house, to being seen by you again, of all people, I would have lost the plot entirely.

There was no one at Joan's front door. I ran down the neighbour's driveway and flung myself into my car, swearing, shaking, fumbling the keys into the ignition.

Imagine my surprise when I saw you, Kirsty, emerging from the side return of my grandmother's bungalow.

Two and two clanged four great bells in my head. *You* were the Kirsty from my granny's will. Somehow, in the cruellest twist of fate, you had become her beneficiary. You. Of course. I pressed my hands against the steering wheel and I roared.

And that's pretty much when I saw your cheery text on Granny's phone.

I bit the back of my hand until the pain brought me to my

senses. Typical, typical Kirsty Shaw, I thought. That obnoxious interference masquerading as kindness. Who the hell is my grandmother to you anyway? She's eighty-one, for Christ's sake! What is she, a *friend*? I fail to believe that, I really do. Who would be friends with someone over fifty years their senior? What is this need you have, have always had, to constantly make *connections* with folk?

Let me answer for you.

You need people.

It's exhausting. It's pathetic.

Why couldn't you have just kept to your own affairs? Why couldn't you have gone home for your dinner and left well alone? Can you see how this is all your fault? If you hadn't inveigled your way into my grandmother's life, I would not have lost my temper. I would not have hit her. And this whole mess could have been avoided.

Joan's phone had no PIN. No fingerprint ID.

I thought for a moment. What would a brittle old bird like Granny Wood reply to her doting neighbour? Once I had it, I typed:

I am quite well, thank you, Kirsty. There's no need to come to the house. Regards, Joan.

I was pleased with the tone. It reminded me of her telephone voice, back in the day. It seemed to do the trick. Your reply was as inane as your first message had been. I had successfully allayed your suspicions.

When I returned later that night, Joan was still alive but barely conscious. I knew she would not come back from this. Now I would have to find the old will and destroy it, not to mention deal with the immediate problem that if she were to die as a result of my perfectly understandable outburst, I had a crime scene on my hands.

Let's face it, I already had a crime scene on my hands.

I gave her a mild sedative, which knocked her out completely. Her pulse was barely there by now. I searched everywhere for cash. There was two hundred pounds in a shoebox in the wardrobe, but that was all – barely enough for a decent meal out these days. The will, I could not find anywhere. Neither could I find a single photograph of me, not even hidden away, not even in a purse or a jewellery box. I felt myself turn even further against her. She was heartless. Treacherous. She had lasered me out of her life like a common wart.

The rest you can imagine. Granny was woozy, unsteady on her feet, but as long as she was alive when she hit the water, I had a chance. I had to hold her up, which was more tiring than you'd think. The sea was rough. I gave her a last blast of chloroform and let her go. She won't have felt a thing, not one thing. No matter what you might think of me, Kirsty, I am not a monster. I take no pleasure in the suffering of others, and despite her betrayal, Joan had been good to me back in the day, and I owed her a painless death. Yes, I owed her that much. A firm shove was all it took. She will have died instantly.

Please can you stop groaning? Can you not manage a respectful pause for your old friend?

So. The North Sea has taken Joan. A shame, but hardly a tragedy. Plan B had to involve getting rid of this Reeny woman. There'd been a call from her to Joan's phone earlier that evening, which I had, of course, ignored. But now I was beginning to worry that Joan might have somehow told her about me paying her a visit the day before. Reeny would have to go. She was too high-risk. Besides, with her dead, her share of Joan's estate would go to me.

That was before I'd consulted my solicitor friend. In my frayed and jangling state, I reasoned that I could get in touch with the people who'd helped me become Barry Sefton in the first place and ask them to help me reinstate my original identity – at least on paper. If whatever Joan had left to Reeny would go to Morris Wood, so my flawed reasoning went, Morris Wood would come back from the obscurity to which I had consigned him. A body takes days to rise to the surface and my old contacts do not hang about. I had time.

Just.

FORTY-EIGHT

KIRSTY

KS/transcript #38

I could hear him, but I couldn't speak. My tongue felt fat, my lips swollen, my head a washing machine. It was all about money. Hughie Reynolds wasn't just a con artist but a psychopath. He'd murdered my friend and seemed to want to blame it on me. The details were fuzzy, but somehow he'd managed to cast himself as a victim.

'Looking back,' he was saying, 'I should have taken Joan's car that night and got a cab back for the Audi.'

I wasn't sure which night he meant. Thursday or Friday?

'My wits were disintegrating,' he said. 'I knew now that you and Joan were acquainted, but I still had no idea at this point that you lived two doors down.'

So it *had* been Joan he was after, I thought. But at the same time, I had the sense I'd had that thought before.

'A long con is one thing,' he said. 'A planned murder is another, but a violent crime committed in haste is something else entirely. There's no control. That's when mistakes happen.

All these years I had been so careful, and now I was cooking up all manner of hare-brained schemes. Despite what you may think, I am not some cold-blooded psychopath.' His eyes flicked up, met mine in the rear-view. 'It was all you. All of it was reacting to you and what I knew of your stubborn persistence, your tedious integrity.'

I'd been right. He was trying to blame it all on me.

'You reduced me to my grubby beginnings, Kirsty. Creeping about in the dark in someone else's house, wiping evidence. Going back to the itchy acrylic of survival is hard once you've got used to the cashmere of living. It's the whole Plato's cave thing, isn't it? I tried to leave the place looking like Joan had simply made a hurried departure. All I needed was her car keys and I was out of there.'

I lay in the dark, regret filling me inch by inch as he reframed every single thing I'd seen, everything I'd thought, all my theories, my wild hopes. His words fell and fell. And with each one, hope drained from me.

'If I'd been thinking straight, I would've taken comfort from the time I was buying myself. In a nosy neighbour's timeline, Joan left home sometime on Friday. As it was, I couldn't think beyond ditching the Polo, which I left up at Hazlehead Park. Leaving it at the harbour at that point risked raising an alarm. But I knew I'd have to move it to the harbour before the body surfaced, which was an inexact science at best. Sometime over the weekend... but when?' He laughed. 'Reacting is so horribly stressful. Far better to execute a proper plan.'

I glared at him, but his eyes were crinkled with amusement.

'You know what comes next,' he said. 'You. Putting another pain right up my ass. The texts, Kirsty. Constant. Just like the needy girlfriend I remembered. *Not seen your car for a couple of days...*' He was talking in a silly, mocking voice. '*Can you let me know you're OK when you get this?*'

I felt myself heat with rage. But I bit it back. It couldn't help me now. It would only make things worse.

'I knew if I didn't reply you'd be all over Joan's place like Miss fucking Marple, but no sooner had I whacked that mole than you were checking my LinkedIn! Dear God.' He shook his head. 'You should get some counselling, I'm telling you. It was stalking, when you think about it. All I could do was hope the profile would throw you off the scent for good. I just wanted to repair the damage you'd already done and get on with my life.'

'But instead you killed her,' I said. I was crying, but I didn't think he could tell, and he sure as hell didn't care. 'Are you going to kill me too? Is that your plan?' If I had to die, I could maybe stash my phone somewhere for the police to find. I could at least save others, if not myself.

'You have to believe me – I never wanted to kill you.'

I opened my eyes to what he must have thought was a contrite expression.

'That's supposed to make me feel better, is it?'

But he'd gone off again about the money, how he'd contacted some solicitor friend and found out that if Reeny died, her kids would inherit Joan's money. He was apoplectic.

'Can you believe that?' he said. 'My inheritance would go to some random woman's children! How fucking outrageous is that?'

'So you never had to kill Reeny,' I said, nauseous, heartsick and near-broken. 'You killed her for no reason!'

'Oh no,' he said. 'I still needed her dead. She was potentially in possession of knowledge that could put me away. As were you, except you didn't know I was linked to Joan, not then, and I didn't see how you could make that leap. Now I had two of you to deal with. Can you see the mess you caused?'

'Sure,' I said, with heavy sarcasm. 'This was all me.'

He banged the steering wheel. 'You were the reason my

nerves were in shreds! Honestly, when I approached Granny's house that night, I was practically *shivering* with fright.'

I had no idea which night he meant, but I didn't care.

'All these horrific scenarios were flashing through my mind's eye. Joan dripping wet and covered in seaweed, furious and out for revenge. But of course Joan was floating off Aberdeen Harbour.'

'You're a monster,' I muttered, but he had no interest in what I had to say.

'I was on my way out the back when I heard the key in the front door, and then the bloody doorbell went. I nearly died.'

My heart quickened. The vision of him there in Joan's house, just inches away; me seconds from discovering him. It was too awful to think about.

'I tried to close the back door behind me, but there was no time. I ran back to my car and drove it to the end of the close, lights off. I knew it was you. Who else would it have been? But still, I had to see. Sure enough, out you came, concern written all over your face. Were you enjoying it? I knew it was risky to send that final text, but I'd be getting rid of the phone so I made Granny sound cross, hoping you'd take the hint.'

I closed my eyes, the words swimming before me.

How dare you go into my house without my permission? Stay away.

The hurt I had felt.

'After that,' he said, 'Joan's phone followed her into the sea. There's a limit on texts in the afterlife, don't you know. It's in the contract.'

I was going to be sick. I groaned and let myself slide down, curling up as best I could. Everything hurt. Dougie. All I could think about was Dougie, about how if I ever got out of here, I would cherish every single moment we spent together.

'It's all such a shame,' he said. 'You were good fun once, if a wee bit earnest. But you wouldn't stop, would you? I was not functioning as highly as I like to do. I went to bed fully clothed that night and slept like I'd been shot.'

I kept my eyes shut, but I couldn't block him out. All I could do was lie there and listen to his garbage and try not to fall back to sleep. But my eyelids were so heavy. The car was so warm. I could feel myself drifting.

FORTY-NINE

HUGHIE

HR/audio/excerpt #11

As soon as they identified that body, I knew you'd be on to the police quicker than I could count a patient out under propofol. A good night's sleep had returned my powers, even though I was still very much functioning on adrenaline. I could control the narrative, I felt, as I scratched the ice from my car windscreen. All would be well.

But the brain fuzz came back, and that was your fault, going to the police station before Joan had even been identified, rushing me yet again. For several tense minutes as I watched you go in, I could not remember where the hell I'd left Granny's car. Time was of the essence. I knew you would have reported the old besom missing, and that would mean they'd identify her sooner and it wouldn't be long before they started looking for her car.

You led me to Reeny. I let you see my car on purpose. It was yet another warning you chose to ignore. I made sure she didn't suffer. As I've said, I'm not a sadist, only a survivor trying to hang on to my life with bloody, bitten nails. Chloroform followed by the kindness of a soft cushion, if you're asking. And yes, it was me who emptied your brake fluid. The days started melting into one here, Kirsty.

You were never going to drop it, were you? You sealed your own fate. You hounded me. You rushed me. You asked for this meeting. All I did was agree. And now here we are, hidden away in a car waiting for the dead of night. I wonder why they call it that? The dead of night. Soon now. And then I'll take you for a last wee walk along the harbour wall.

How can I possibly get away with it? you would ask if you were compos mentis enough to form a question. How can I dump your body off the harbour having already thrown my grandmother to the same fate and not end up locked away for life?

Well, let me spell it out.

Ready?

On being questioned, your darling Dougie will admit that yes, Kirsty had been super stressed recently. She was imagining being followed by a red car. She had started obsessing about her neighbour being kidnapped and murdered. She was seeing coincidences where there were none, creating ever more ludicrous theories out of thin air. She became convinced she'd seen her ex-boyfriend at work. She would not stop insisting it was him when everyone around her tried to tell her it could not possibly be. Tragically, she did not listen to reason.

Tasha will agree. Kirsty was convinced someone had cut her brakes, she will say. I told her it was all in her head.

The police will have evidence of your increasingly erratic statements, won't they? If I'm right in thinking you absconded from hospital, your final appearance at the police station will confirm everyone's fears – arriving dishevelled and deranged in the dead of winter, paper slippers on your feet. Madness!

Kirsty Shaw was a heavily pregnant woman, the forensic psychologist will explain at the inquest, who transferred repressed worries about her imminent maternity onto conspiracy theories without foundation concerning an ex-boyfriend from a decade before. Kirsty suffered psychological difficulties at the age of eighteen following a painful break-up from this boyfriend and his subsequent mysterious disappearance. Her pregnancy combined with her belief that he had reappeared awakened past trauma and led to an antenatal psychotic episode, which was identified, sadly, too late.

Don't be shocked. Medical records are so easy to come by if you know the right people and can pay the right price. Those who loved you *will* be shocked, of course. But when they look back, they'll see the signs were there all along.

But enough chatting. The time has come. The air is baltic tonight. Which is a mercy.

FIFTY

KIRSTY

KS/transcript #39

I heard the car door open. I kicked and squirmed, beyond
terrified. I tried to wriggle out of his grip, but it was no use; I
was heavy, cumbersome, and my wrists and ankles were tied.

He grabbed my feet, pressed my ankles under his arm. I
knew what was coming. Oblivion followed by a slow, groggy
awakening, my body filling with panic – for myself, for my baby.
I should have left well alone was all I could think. How could I
have got myself into this mess? Round and round in my head I
could hear my own voice wailing silently, *Dougie, oh, Dougie.
I'm so sorry.*

'Now,' Hughie said and tore a length of tape, which he
pressed over my mouth. 'Just for extra caution.'

I itched to peel it away, straining at the wrist ties. A moment
later, I felt my ankles loosen and separate. The next thing, I was
being dragged out of the car. My feet hit the tarmac. My lower
back screamed in pain. He grabbed my wrists and pulled me up.
I wasn't unconscious this time, only dizzy, as if drunk. But no

sooner was I on my feet than I fell against him, nauseous, reeling.

'Stand up, for fuck's sake,' he barked, his voice full of rage. He pushed my shoulders straight and held me roughly until I stopped swaying.

'What time is it?' I asked, but my words slid into one another, half muffled by the tape he'd put on too hastily and which was now hanging off at one side. 'How long have we been here?'

He must have understood me that time because he replied: 'Long enough.'

Holding me by the elbow, he made me walk, talking to me through gritted teeth. 'If you try and run, I will end you, OK? Here and now. Don't even think about it.'

We were on North Pier Road now. We staggered past Stella's place, and I turned, desperate to see her at the window, up with a restless baby, a midnight feed, something. Inside her cottage, a dim light glowed, but no, it was only the baby's night light. No one was awake. No one could see us.

We made our painstaking progress towards the end of the road, where the quayside opens up, the Silver Darling restaurant, the harbour. I was snivelling like a child, tortured by my own stupidity and by the cold death that was inevitable now. Dougie would lose me and our baby. This was my fault. I had done this.

Uselessly, I shook my shoulders, my cry for help pathetic, stifled.

He gripped me so hard I knew there'd be bruises where his fingertips had been. He was panicking, I thought vaguely. Leaving evidence. He didn't have things under control as much as he was pretending. 'If you do that again,' he hissed wetly into my ear, 'you'll get a blade across your throat. Makes no difference to me.'

I whimpered but walked on, back aching, legs chafing, mind

spinning. I couldn't stop myself crying, for Dougie, for Tasha, my pals, my parents, my team at work, for everyone I loved. For Reeny. For Joan. Dougie would be worried – but how worried? Enough to call Tasha? Enough to call the police?

More knowledge clouded in: Hughie's name was Morris Wood. He was Joan's grandson. Other things, so many things, all of them whirling about without ever staying still enough for me to see clearly. The wind blew through my clothes, my skin, into my bones. It was bitterly cold, no night to be out.

Joan. Oh Joan. Oh Reeny...

He said he was qualified, I thought. He said all he'd done was take a dead man's name, to hide a juvenile criminal record. This he'd said before, on the beach. The sweet tea. The tea was spiked. How could I have fallen for that? How could I have taken anything from him when I'd always known he had something to do with Joan's and Reeny's deaths? Why hadn't I listened to my gut, my sense of things? I had betrayed myself.

In the freezing darkness, his iron fingers around my elbow, he forced me onward. The more I came to full consciousness, the more everything he'd said on the beach sounded like lies. He could be a complete imposter. He could be injecting drugs without licence, without expertise. He could be a serial killer. He might have murdered hundreds. He'd give me something to take the edge off, he'd said before. Yes, he'd said that at some point, minutes, maybe hours ago.

Of course. The edge off my imminent death. He was going to push me and my baby into the water.

Dougie would be worried. Surely looking for me by now. *Come to the harbour. Come to the harbour, darlin'. I love you. I've let you down. I didn't take care of our baby. I'm so sorry.*

'Speak up or shut up,' Hughie spat. 'Stop groaning.'

I tried to shake him off, but he was too strong. Hughie. Not Hughie. Morris. Morris Wood. An orphan who fell on the mercy of his long-lost granny. Yes, he'd told me this too – in the car. Joan was his foster mother, the one we were not allowed to meet.

But why did he keep her a secret? I knew why. He had told me why, I was sure, because I could feel it like something rotten inside me, something I had pushed down. But I couldn't reach it, not then.

I know why now, of course. Our minds find strange ways to protect us; they do this so that we can survive the unthinkable.

I tried again to shout into the black and empty night, but the tape muted my words to a low, muffled sound that no one would ever hear. No one was awake. No one was peering through their windows. It was no time to be awake, no time to be out. We were at the quayside now. The Silver Darling restaurant all lit up. A lighthouse no longer. *Help, help, help, she cried.* Words from a lullaby my mum used to sing.

Funny what goes through your mind.

Hughie was retracing footsteps, footsteps from a week ago. Joan's.

FIFTY-ONE

KIRSTY

KS/transcript #40

'Walk,' he said.

I shook my head from side to side, up and down, gurning and grimacing, trying to work the tape free from my mouth. I bucked against him, attempting to shake him off. It was all in vain. He was too strong. My head was spinning. The harbour wall came in and out of focus. Inch by inch he moved me forward, his grip a wooden claw under my arm, painful on the tender skin, holding me up, pushing me on. I bent my knees and dropped down, an attempt to use my weight against him, but he was too strong.

'The more you fight, the longer this will take,' he said, shoving me forward so that I tripped. 'I'm sorry, Kirsty, but you're the one who's brought us here. You've cost me everything. Everything.'

'What? What are you talking about?' From my half-taped mouth the words were clear enough.

'Don't play dumb,' he scoffed. 'Don't insult me by pretending not to know that Joan left you her house. *My* grandmother left *you* her house. I couldn't get the will changed without her, and you made me kill her. You made me.'

I couldn't be sure, but it sounded like he was crying. Joan had left me her house? Had he already told me this? He was talking as if he had.

'I just needed more time.' He was snivelling now. 'But because of you, rushing me, always rushing me, I lost it, and then she... and then it was too late. I could have persuaded her! But no-o-o-o. You were there, of course you were, like the fucking interfering do-gooder you are. You literally robbed me of my inheritance, KK, and I'm sure as hell not going to let you rob me of my freedom.'

I'd rushed him? What was he talking about?

We had reached the end of the pier now. Ice twinkled underfoot. The black spikes of the North Sea. The hellish depths. Talking was no use. He had no interest in anything I had to say. The sea was below us, and it was as black as hell. The cold of it rose up, seeped into my bones. *Dougie. Oh, Dougie. I love you. I love you more than my own life.*

'I'm so sorry,' I wept. 'I'm so sorry. Oh, Doug. My baby. Mum. Dad. I'm so sorry.'

'Too late for apologies now. I'm going to untie your hands, but if you try anything, you'll be straight over the side with nothing to take the pain away.'

I nodded, whimpering under my breath. 'Mum. Dad. You were the best parents, the best, and I love you both so much. Tell my wee brother I love him. Dougie, you're my life. I love you.'

'Stop blethering and stand still.' He was in front of me, his eyes on mine. He was crying too. I had no idea why. 'I'm going to take the tape off. And then I'm going to give you some more of the sleepy stuff, and then that's it. I'm sorry. I'm sorry, but you did this. You did this. It won't hurt, I promise. I never wanted to hurt you.'

'My baby,' I cried, loud as I could, sobs racking me. 'Please don't kill my baby.'

Sirens wailed in the distance. From the esplanade, I thought, though I couldn't be sure.

He glanced towards the town, then ripped the tape from my mouth.

'Please. Don't do this. My baby.' My words were feathers in the wind.

His mouth was flat and grim as he rubbed at my face with the end of the cloth. He wouldn't look at me. He must be ashamed, I thought. He must know what he's doing is wrong. If he did, there would be a chink in his armour. I just had to find it.

'Please.' I gave it one last try. 'I'll give you the house. I don't want it. I have a house. I don't need two. I'll sign it over to you and say nothing to anyone. I promise. On my life, Hughie, I swear. On my baby's life. Please!'

He turned me roughly by the shoulders. All I could see was blackness. This was it. This was the end.

'Please God,' I whispered, closing my eyes, preparing myself. 'Let it be quick.'

Sirens wailed – louder, nearer. Helicopter beats thumped overhead.

'Fuck,' I heard him say as the sweet, cloying cloth pressed against my mouth and nose. I felt my knees give.

'Put your hands on your head.' A voice came from the sky then, robotic and all around us in the darkness. The chucka-chuck of the helicopter. The frightened scurry of the waves. 'Put your hands on your head. Now.'

Lights flashed, violet in the graphite sky. His hands fell away. I felt myself drop, the hard smack of the harbour wall against my knees. How beautiful those lights are, I thought. So beautiful.

FIFTY-TWO

KIRSTY

KS/transcript #41

I woke up. My eyes were stuck together, I remember that. I was trying to blink them open when I heard Tasha's voice.

'I think she's coming round.'

Tasha? Is that you? I said but then realised I hadn't. I couldn't open my mouth. It was stuck shut like my eyes. I could smell disinfectant. School dinners. And I could feel the dark thing, lurking. Something Hughie had told me, something so shocking my mind was keeping it hidden away.

'Kirsty? It's me, Tasha. You're in hospital. I'm here with Dougie. Your mum and dad are on their way.'

'Darlin'. Babe.' Dougie. That was Dougie, no mistaking.

Tears washed away the sticky feeling. I blinked. Slowly my eyelids unglued themselves. To creamy sunlight. To Dougie's beautiful face. To Tasha's beautiful face.

'Hiya.' My voice was a croak.

'Let's sit you up.' Dougie was fiddling about with the bed switch. A moment later, the bedhead buzzed me up.

'Greetings,' I said, and we all laughed – a bit pathetically, but you do, don't you, when you've been through something stressful. I mean, it was more than stressful, but you know what I mean.

Tasha pressed a plastic tumbler to my lips and told me to drink. 'Not too fast. Wet your lips first. That's it. Now sip it. It's nice and fresh. That's it. Better?'

I nodded as the cool water trickled down, wrinkling my nose at the Tupperware smell. 'Thanks.'

Dougie was crying. Tasha was crying. I touched my fingertips to my cheeks. I was crying too.

'Why are we all crying?' I asked, and we all started laughing again as well as crying, tears rolling down our faces. Their wide mouths were full of teeth, their eyes half closed.

'You pure gave us a fright,' Tasha said when we'd calmed down a wee bit.

'I got a message,' Dougie said. 'You said you'd been called in. I was so pissed off. Typical you, I thought. Going in when you'd been signed off. I was actually really cross. I can't believe that now. I can't believe I didn't figure out it wasn't you.'

'But then your friend,' Tasha jumped in. 'Stella, is it? She saw you being marched along the road. She'd seen you going down onto the beach earlier with some guy, but she thought it must be your husband.'

'I guess she's never met me, has she?' Dougie chipped in with a fat grin.

'She called the cops straight away. They must have put two and two together, what with you being a pain in their arse, because they blue-lighted straight to the harbour.' Tasha started to cry again. 'If she hadn't been up with the baby, she'd never have seen you.'

'Luna,' I said. Time slowed, paused for a moment so pure we fell silent. 'Luna saved my life,' I whispered into that silence. 'Stella's baby saved my life.'

We exchanged glances, all of us stunned.

I closed my eyes. My mouth and throat felt awful. Sore. A nasty taste. Stella must've been up feeding Luna. Must've seen me from the sofa though I couldn't see her through the window. I thought of the beach. The tea. The waves. The cloth over my nose and mouth. The back seat of the car sticking to my face. Him. Hughie. Morris. Morris Wood.

'I always say babies are miracles,' I whispered to no one in particular. 'Maybe she was saying cheers for helping her out into the world, eh? Oh God, I love you two so much. Sorry for crying. I can't stop. Hormonal, I guess.'

'Hey.' Dougie stroked my hair, eyes still shining. 'It's OK, babe. It's over. You're safe.'

Tasha was talking. I had the impression I must have dozed off.

'Rosie died of an overdose,' she was saying. 'Together with a guy called Michael Peterson. This is where it gets interesting. The records state that she left a son, Morris, born in 1979. So. I reckon Barry Sefton's real name is Morris Wood. At the time, he was working as a hospital porter, and I think he took Sefton's LinkedIn profile sometime after Sefton's staff profile expired, which it does after eight years.'

'Rosie was an addict,' I said, the dark thing pressing in, a shadow I could almost see. 'Hughie is Morris Wood.'

'Well hello again, Ms Shaw,' Tasha replied. 'Glad you could join us.'

I opened my eyes. 'Hughie is Morris Wood.'

Tasha smiled and patted my hand. 'He's not, hen. The guy who took you is Morris Wood, but he's forty-five years old and he's Joan's grandson, Rosie's son. Unless he was Rosie's lover.'

'No,' I said, but it was a protest, not an answer. 'It's not that.' My throat hurt like hell. The ache in my lower back was getting worse, the waves of pain more frequent.

'Just hear me out,' Tasha said. I wanted to argue so badly,

but Hughie's words were swimming about like wee fish in an aquarium.

'So what're you saying?' Dougie asked, squeezing my hand as if to say *don't worry*, thinking I was too tired, not realising I was simply trying to grab a hold of my bouncing thoughts so I could tell Tasha that I knew how this story went and it wasn't like this. 'How could he be Rosie's lover?'

'I'm saying there are a couple of theories at least,' Tasha said. 'People often go for folk who resemble them in some way. It's a familiarity thing. The man who took Kirsty is most probably Joan's grandson, like Kirsty said, come to claim his inheritance, *or* he's a lover of Rosie's come to, I dunno, maybe blackmail Joan or whatever, I'm not sure how.'

The pain in my back was making it impossible to think straight; it was like someone had the end of a broom handle to my lower vertebrae. I had to get Tasha to stop talking so I could get to the dark thing.

'When Joan threw herself in the water,' Tasha was saying, lost in her journalist's excitement, 'he must've realised you could potentially put him in prison.'

'So where's Hughie?' Dougie asked.

She shrugged. 'I have no idea. He said he was never coming back, and he didn't. Sefton's in his forties. Hughie's our age. He'd be twenty-nine, thirty at most.'

Twenty-nine.

The year I started my Standard Grades, Kirsty, I was twenty-nine years old.

The dark thing. At last. I could see it. I could grasp it like a rope. I could hold it even though it burnt through my fingers.

'It *is* Hughie.' I must've said it loudly because they both turned to me with shocked expressions.

'Babe,' Dougie said.

'No. Listen. In the car, he told me everything. He was old.

Back then. At school. He wasn't a kid. He's not twenty-nine now; he was twenty-nine then.'

Another wave of pain in my coccyx, too intense to ignore. I pulled up my knees, screwed up my eyes and tried so hard not to cry out. The bed was wet.

And that's when Dougie squeezed my hand tight and said, 'Darlin'. Babe? Your waters have broken.'

FIFTY-THREE

KIRSTY

KS/transcript #42

When I closed my eyes in that delivery room, all I could see was Hughie walking towards me down a hospital corridor, a corridor bleached white, light so bright, nothing else was clear. He was in scrubs, stethoscope draped around his neck, infiltrating my most private thoughts, where he had no right to be. I didn't want him anywhere near me, let alone in my head, but he was looking straight at me, a syringe in his right hand, and he was coming closer. He was young, with that funny thin hair at the front and tortoiseshell glasses and a smile that might mean mischief, might mean danger. I closed my eyes tighter and pushed him out, out, out.

'That's it, darlin',' Dougie said, holding my hand tight. 'You're doing brilliant. Keep going.'

Hughie came at me again, down that same hospital corridor white with bright light. I pushed harder, a great roar bursting from me.

'You're amazing,' Tasha said from the other side, pressing a cool damp cloth onto my forehead.

I closed my eyes and heard myself moan. Hughie was coming for me once again, syringe in his hand, murder in his eyes. I closed my eyes even tighter and pushed with everything I had left.

Hughie vanished. The corridor was empty. I opened my eyes.

'I can see the head.' Debs was there with us. She was newly qualified, grinning up at me as if to say: *Who's in charge now?* 'One more, boss. You can do this. One big push for me when I say so, OK?'

'I feel like a boxer,' I quipped as the contraction subsided, opening one eye and finding Tasha.

'You're as tough as a boxer,' Tasha replied, grinning, squeezing that beautiful cool water over my forehead. 'Tougher than a boxer. You're a bloody warrior, pal.'

But the contraction was back. I sucked at the gas and air as it came at me. Pain that wasn't pain, not entirely. Pain that was adrenaline and joy, courage and excitement.

I closed my eyes and went towards the pain. I was a warrior. I was me and all my female ancestors rolled into one. I was strength and light, blinding white light. There was no sign of Hughie. I had scared the bastard away. The corridor was empty, gleaming. I pushed then with a strength from somewhere beyond myself, strength I didn't have. The room was suspended, spinning in time and space, every person I had ever loved, every exam I had ever passed, every driving lesson with my dad, every shopping trip with my mum, every kindness, every hug, every kiss, every beautiful, unique, precious baby I had delivered. It was all with me in that moment. It was all in me somehow.

A cry pierced the air, so quiet and so loud, so strange and so familiar, so animal, so human. A blood call to every cell of my being. I opened my eyes, panting like a racehorse, tears already running down my face, my neck. Debs was holding up a pink and tiny creature, skinny legs and arms flailing, the tiniest fists of white-hot rage. My life, my everything, my wee baby.

My miracle.

'Congratulations,' she said, her face shining with sweat, her eyes with tears of joy and relief. 'You have a beautiful baby girl.'

'Thank you,' I managed before bursting into fresh tears.

'You're amazing.' Dougie kissed my head. 'Absolutely amazing. I love you.'

'I love you too.'

'I love you too.' Tasha was laughing and crying. She kissed my fingertips before backing away with a cute little wave. 'I'll let you guys...'

'Here we go.' Debs was lowering our baby girl to my breast. Her blood-warm skin pressed on mine. My own warmth, outside of me now, a tiny heart beating against my own. I looked into that screwed-up wee face that was new and ancient, ugly and beautiful, and felt the tide of love flush through me from head to toe.

'Hello, you,' I whispered as she curled her tiny fingers around my pinky. 'I am *very* happy to meet you, little one.'

'Her wee nails.' Dougie's voice was barely there, full of wonder. 'She's beautiful. Perfect.'

The door opened. The midwife in charge appeared. She must've been an agency midwife because I didn't recognise her. She grabbed the notes and glanced down at them before offering up a warm, wide smile. Her name badge said *Ann Shepherd*.

'I believe you're one of us,' she said, still smiling. 'How was it on the other side?'

'Amazing. Debs did a great job, really great.'

'I learnt from the best,' Debs said with a grin.

We all laughed. We would have laughed at anything right then.

Ann checked the notes again before looking up first at Dougie, then at Tasha. 'Sandra Douglas?'

'That'll be me,' Dougie said, blushing crimson through her freckles. 'Everyone calls me Dougie, like, so.'

'Well, congratulations to you too. You have a beautiful family. I wish you all the best.' Another smile, a brief nod and she was gone.

'We did it,' I said, looking up into the eyes of my beautiful wife.

'*You* did it,' Dougie said.

'We both did it. Oh God, I almost—'

'Don't say it.' Dougie kissed my head again and smoothed my hair behind my ear. 'Let's not think about any of that now. You're here and she's here and that's everything. I love you so much.'

I nodded. Dougie was right. We should just enjoy this moment. The rest we could pick our way through later. I had all the time to tell her the whole story. And Tasha. And I would. Once I got my head straight, I would. Hughie's words would come to me in flashes and eventually I would piece them together. The police would be able to fill in the blanks, and somewhere in that pile would be the truth.

But one thing was certain, even now: Hughie could not harm me any more.

'And do we have a name for this wee girl?' Debs asked us as they prepared to wheel me through to Postnatal.

I looked into Dougie's warm and shining blue eyes. 'I had an idea. How about Joanie?'

The shine spilled over and rolled in two wee raindrops down her cheeks. 'Joanie,' she said. 'Aye. I like that. Joanie Shaw Douglas.'

FIFTY-FOUR
HUGHIE

Dear Kirsty,

Kirsty Shaw. KK. You. You you you. You are enough to drive a man mad enough to punch a hole in the wall of his cell, do you know that?

I knew from the moment I saw you again that you would finish me. And you have.

I knew it was a mistake to ever come back here. And it was.

I hope you're satisfied. I hope you're happy, sitting all cosy and nice with your lovely friends and your loving family in safety and warmth and comfort. I bet there is so much love in your life. I know there is. I never told you in the car, but I parked outside your house and watched you and Dougie talking and laughing and hugging one another. That hug lasted for four and a half minutes. I know because I timed it. Who hugs for four and a half minutes? I've never had that. I never will. I've always known that I'm unlovable, from way back, when I was wee. Do you know why? Because my mother told me so. I was six when she told me to go and earn some fucking money, still six when she told me she'd never wanted children and that she wished she'd never had me, that if she hadn't, her life would've been so much better.

She could be very frank when she was in that kind of mood.

The thing is, I didn't come quite as clean as you think back in the car. I told you all my deceptions, of course. My identities, my names, my glamorous catch-me-if-you-can lifestyle. You might even remember some of my tale of survival. I did want you to hear the story of young Morris Wood and his piece-of-shit life. His no-good druggie mother. How he escaped adversity and came away up the road like a manky Dick Whittington determined to claw back something from his broken life. I suppose I wanted you to have some sympathy for me. Who knows? Maybe I wanted you to forgive me. Maybe I just wanted you to understand how hard it was to shake off the stamp of nature. That's from Hamlet, by the way. Just in case you were curious. I looked it up:

> Assume a virtue, if you have it not.
> That monster, custom, who all sense doth eat,
> Of habits devil, is angel yet in this,
> That to the use of actions fair and good
> He likewise gives a frock or livery

That aptly is put on. Refrain tonight,
And that shall lend a kind of easiness
To the next abstinence; the next more easy;
For use almost can change the stamp of nature.

I think the key word here is 'almost'. I think you'd have to agree that I tried my best to assume virtue, to be fair and good in my actions, and yes, this behaviour was my fancy frock for a while. For four whole years, in fact. I refrained like a champ, and the abstinence did get easier. Use almost did change the stamp of nature, but alas, the stamp proved indelible.

All of which is a kind of prologue to what I may as well tell you now. You'll doubtless find out at some point from the police that some of what I said in the car might not have been one hundred per cent true.

By which I mean some of it definitely wasn't true.

I painted a picture right enough. A scummy flat, a childhood scarred by hunger, anxiety, neglect. Young Morris, a good kid trying to stay on the right side of the tracks, thwarted on all sides, let down by his mother and her controlling lover-cum-pusher Michael Peterson.

That Morris was a good kid was true enough. But Rosie was not a bad mum, not as bad as I painted her. An addict, yes, but that came later, and she'd have done anything for that kid. I've never known anyone so determined to stand on their own two feet as Rosie. That girl had guts. Leaving her parents almost killed her. She became a survivor quicker than anyone I've ever seen. But it was a plummet no one could survive. Fifteen and pregnant, she arrived in Leith with some lowlife she'd met on the train and in her naïvety believed he wanted to be friends. That's what she told me anyway, a few years later. It's so long ago now, I don't really remember the details. She stayed on his sofa, I think, those first few days. He invited a few pals round at some point. Out came the gear.

But Rosie was determined to have her baby clean. She didn't take anything, not then. She did not get herself high and end up beholden to some pimp. She made friends. She was funny and kind and she had no edge to her, despite coming from wealth. Everyone liked her. They respected her and they respected her desire to do right by the kid. People wanted to do right by her. She had a way of making folk want to help her out. By the time Morris was born, someone had sorted her with a fake ID and somehow she got herself a flat. It was clean and tidy and Morris always had enough to eat. He always, always went to school.

She wasn't perfect. I'm not saying that. Far from it. But she cared for that boy, she did. She may not have registered him with the GP or the dentist, but she did get him into the local school. That much she managed. Made him his wee sandwiches and sent him on his way.

As for young Morris, he was no angel, but he was good enough. Skinny, tall, bright like his ma. When Michael Peterson came on the scene, Morris was too

young to realise that Peterson was giving his mother
junk, reeling her in with his dope and his charms,
making her dependent not only on the gear but on him.
Peterson was friendly. A big brother barely a year
older, full of life advice, advice gained from the univer-
sity of the street. You OK, bro? Let me know if
anyone's giving you hassle, yeah? The lads in the flats
never touched Morris once Peterson was on the scene.
They didn't dare. Peterson scared them all to death,
without any of them really knowing why.

But for all that I might have given the impression
Morris's childhood was somewhat less than a dream,
believe me, it was nothing compared to Peterson's.
Peterson's, well, I can't even put it into words. What I
can tell you is that when Peterson met Rosie, he fell
hard. That much is true. She was nice-looking back in
the day, before the drugs sucked away her cheeks,
erupted in constellations on the blue-pale skin of her
forehead. She was fourteen years older than Peterson
and was working in the Safeway as a cashier. He
admired that, that work ethic, that refusal to make
easier money at the cost of her soul. Peterson had
never worked a straight job in his life. To him, Rosie
was a woman of integrity, a better person. And sex is
a powerful enough force when you're an adult. When
you're a kid, it'll overwhelm you. Peterson was no virgin,
but girls his age were nothing compared to Rosie. It
was hard to know who was seducing who.

Morris tried not to see, not to understand, that
his mother was sleeping with a kid barely older than

him, a kid who he'd reckoned on being his protector, a kid who sold drugs for a living, whose business dealings were not to be thought about too hard. But it's tough to ignore someone who's pretty much living in your home, especially if that home is small and when the atmosphere changes by the day. Peterson dropped the big brother act. Whatever he was offering, it was not protection.

When the neighbours found out Rosie and Peterson had been found stone dead in the flat, they were not backward in coming forward. Rumours abounded. The pair of them were well known. That Peterson was always round Rosie's, they said. Always gi'ing her stuff, like. He was living there. Was he? Aye! Must be ten years now? A wonder she's still alive, all that shite he gi'es her. He was her pimp. No, he wasnae. Was. Wasnae. Boyfriend. OK, right, so, but dealer too. Dealer, aye. Lover. I'm nae one to gossip, but it's nae surprise they ended up killin' the'selves. Nae surprise, aye. Shame for the boy though, eh. A good wee laddie, that Morris. Hard worker. Always has a smile for everyone. What's he gonna do now wi' his ma deed?

Whatever.

The police cordon off the flat. Back you go. Away home now, nothing to see here.

Morris is at work. He's ready for the call, has spent all morning getting ready for it, in fact. He's got some expertise in the matter of narcotics. He's really not enjoying just how invisible he is there in that hospital, pushing his mop, but it's working to his advantage. From the shadows of menial service, he's watching the doctor slide the propofol into his adoring patient. Barry Sefton, his lanyard says. Consultant Anaesthesiologist.

A god.

But what is he doing really, this Barry? What's he doing that's so special, so clever? It's just dosing, at the end of the day, isn't it?

Because as you might have twigged by now, it isn't Morris at the hospital that day, but Peterson. Peterson who saw his chance when the news of Lachlan Wood's death came in, the chance of a proper education, the kind that normal kids have, kids who are loved and cared for, the chance to sleep in clean sheets, the chance to have enough, more than enough. Had not Morris himself explained to him that education was the key to leaving behind a life he loathed? Morris's plan would unlock the door to everything Peterson had ever wanted but had claimed so violently to shun. But Peterson cannot put the plan into action while Morris lives.

And so it's Peterson who is pushing that mop, watching, watching, watching the world through the blurry lenses of Morris Wood's prescription spectacles, Peterson who is marvelling that no one has noticed he isn't Morris. There's their shared age and colouring, sure, the shy, head-down demeanour easy enough to adopt, the brown hair styled forward this morning like Morris's, the glasses making Peterson's head ache, but even so, it's quite a shock to realise how little people look at those at the bottom. How much they look at those at the top. Oh, how they look. They gaze. They gaze as if star-struck at Mr Barry Sefton. And Peterson gazes with them.

And thinks: I can do that.

After all, it's no different from what he's just done this very night to a sleeping Rosie and her son, sliding needle into vein, pushing in the sweet milk of oblivion. It's not so different if you ignore the changing of Morris Wood's lifeless body into Peterson's designer clothes, the positioning of the drugged-up mother and son in a lover's clinch, the slipping of Peterson's wallet into the dead man's trouser pockets; if you forget to mention Peterson dressing himself in Morris Wood's scruffy attire that morning, slipping his feet into his rotting trainers, lifting his hospital lanyard from the hook in the hallway as he makes his way silently out.

If you brush all that to the side, it comes down to the same thing: dosage.

In either case, depending on the desired outcome, a mistake would have the most disastrous conse-quences. A mistake is life or death.

So. When Peterson sees the police waiting for young Morris Wood at reception, he knows that Rosie and Morris are dead of the overdose he himself admin-istered but that the police think they have found Rosie and her lover and dealer Michael Peterson. He knows there'll be no dental records because a life lived under the radar is not dotted with regular trips to have one's

S.E. LYNES

teeth scaled and polished. He's so tired of life on the wrong side of the tracks. It's fucking exhausting and the net is always closing. And there's no reverence, only fear.

You might wonder why I used the name Barry Sefton. Why not simply make up a name? Well, call me sentimental, but Barry was the anaesthetist I had watched in a state of awe, the man who had shown me so clearly who and what I wanted to be. It didn't take much to find him on his own. In some ways, the mop was a superpower: an invisibility cloak, if you like. Access all areas. Sefton didn't know what had hit him, other than, perhaps, the door to his locker, smack in the face. Spiked with precision by a man he didn't even see. Massive heart attack. These top jobs are so stressful. Really, they can kill you. Mr Barry Sefton had given me the gift of a golden epiphany; it was only right that I should keep his name alive.

Peterson is out of that changing room and already cleaning a spillage in Oncology when he hears his new name:

Morris Wood. Would Morris Wood report to reception, please? Morris Wood to reception, thank you.

FIFTY-FIVE
A YEAR LATER

My name is Kirsty Shaw.

I'm starting this journal on the advice of my counsellor. I was supposed to start it six months ago, but wee Joanie hasn't given me a minute's peace and there's been a lot to sort out. Anyway, she's gone for a nap and the house isn't too much of a bomb site, so I thought I'd give it a go.

I don't know what I want to say really. I feel a bit self-conscious writing this. Like, who am I even writing it for? Who cares what I have to say? But then I remember, this is for me. I've been told it helps to write things down sometimes, to get things straight in your mind.

I suppose if I think about someone reading this, that makes it easier. Like a conversation. I'll imagine you, whoever you are. I'm writing it like I'm talking to you. Hello! Maybe you've been through something traumatic too. Maybe you read my story in the papers or saw it on the news. Maybe you saw the documentary Out of the Shadows. I thought the lassie who played me in the reconstructions was very good. And they did a great job getting that strange wispy quality of Hughie's hair.

Those interviews took hours. I literally had to tell them the whole story. Every tiny detail, they said, especially my feelings. It was clever how they mixed clips of me talking with the dramatised bits, the clips from Dougie, Tasha, Gus, Callum and my folks, and of course the recording I'd made of Hughie in the car – I think they had to do some digital remastering on that, or some such clever thing. The muffled sound was actually very sinister when played over the scenes of the beach and the harbour and Joan's old house.

They probably only used about a fifth of what I said, if that. When I watched it, I was cringing behind my hands, and sometimes it was frustrating because they cut bits out that I thought were important. I looked so tired on camera. When it came out last month, I could see how much the whole nightmare had taken it out of me. I look a bit better now, thank God.

It did take it out of me, out of all of us. I had postnatal depression for a while, most probably owing to the extreme circumstances of my late pregnancy and Joanie's birth. As well as trauma therapy, Dougie and I went to couples counselling. We only needed a few sessions. That Dougie should have believed me sooner was one thing, but I could see why she hadn't, and besides, I had put myself and our baby in danger in the most irresponsible way. It helped that we both had stuff to bring to the table, and our love helped us both to forgive. Dougie is my person and I'm hers, and that's all we need.

As for Hughie – I still can't think of him as Peterson – I'm not sure I'll ever truly get over what he did. Sometimes, when I remember how deeply we believed him back in the day, it's still a shock. You just don't think a person could lie about something like that, do you? You'd never imagine no one would notice a grown man walking about in a school uniform. If I'd read a story about some bloke passing himself off as a teenager, I wouldn't have believed it. I might not even have believed it if I'd watched it on a true-crime documentary, like the one I ended up in myself.

But I lived it. And all I can say is that we had no idea at all. The fact that I was with a guy in his thirties when I was eighteen was a shock, of course it was, but it's in the past. The mystery of his disappearance and reappearance has been explained, and that, at least, has brought me closure. If I've done a lot of work with my counsellor, it's because I don't want to spend the next ten years pretending I've got over something when I haven't. I am learning to sit with the fact that I never will get over it but that my life will go on and I can be happy. I won't let Hughie take that away from me or my family. No way.

What else do I want to say to you just now? Maybe I would say that what happens to you doesn't define you. What happened with the man I thought was a boy didn't stop me from following my dreams. It didn't stop me becoming a midwife. It didn't put me off men or anything like that; I was already halfway to figuring that stuff out back in sixth year. So don't let your something bad stop you doing what you want. Don't let it define you.

For a long time, I thought Hughie's betrayal of me and my family was my fault. I thought Joan's and Reeny's deaths were my fault. I thought my kidnapping was my fault. If you've had something bad happen to you, maybe you think it's your fault too. But it isn't your fault; it's not something about you or something you've done wrong. I understand now that what other people do, how they treat you, belongs to them and only to them. That's not to say you can't be hurt or damaged, and it's good to acknowledge that damage and that you have feelings about it. Your feelings matter. You matter. But someone else's bad behaviour doesn't belong to you. I want to say that too.

I would also say it's worth dealing with things. It's painful but worth it. It was for me anyway. You've got to dig deep. You've got to bring that stuff out into the light and really look at it. It's hard work and it's very tiring. I thought I'd left Hughie

*behind, but in my sessions I came to understand that the sight
of him that day in the hospital caused a reaction that came from
an unhealed part of me. Just like that, I was back to that girl
who was still figuring herself out and who had trusted someone
only for that trust to be violated. I didn't realise at the time just
how deep that wound had gone and how much I had carried it
with me.*

*You can tell I've had all the counselling, can't you? Lol. I
even sound like a therapist.*

*You might think: but surely being kidnapped and almost
thrown to my death was worse? And in many ways, it was. Of
course it was. But anyone can see that was a terrible trauma, in
the sense that it's something everyone can understand. I don't
need to explain to myself or anyone else how terrifying it was.
But damage is not a simple thing. Who's to say what affects us
and what doesn't? What breaks us and what makes us
stronger? An offhand comment during childhood can set a
person's entire idea of themselves. No one else would understand why, but they know how they feel, and that's real to them,
and finding out why can be so powerful. I know that from the
group work.*

*Even Hughie (I still think of him as Hughie) in his letter
confessed that his own mother had told him she wished he'd
never been born, had never given him the opportunity to go to
school like a kid who is looked after and loved. Despite the
terrible things he did, I have compassion for the boy he once
was. Of course, I also know he's a brutal criminal who was
prepared to sink to unthinkable depths to hold on to the life he
had fraudulently built. For him, human beings were a means to
his ends; that's all they ever were. But whether he never had
empathy or whether empathy was blasted out of him by
mistreatment, that little boy is still in there somewhere. I
believe that. I choose to believe that.*

As I said earlier, you'll probably know all about it unless you've been living under a rock. You'll know that he – I'm going to call him Peterson – was found guilty on multiple counts of murder and that he will be behind bars for the rest of his life. Ironic for a man who believed he'd chosen to turn his back on crime.

I don't know what else I want to say really. This might be the world's shortest journal, lol! I can tell you that snow is falling outside my kitchen window. I can tell you that Joan's bungalow is under offer and that we're planning to give half the proceeds to charity but we don't know which one yet. I can also tell you that Dougie has gone to Herd's for sausages to make Douglas Saturday Stew, which is now an official family favourite. Her folks and mine are coming over later. The wood-burning stove is dancing away, the house is warm, and the snow is white and thick over the back garden. Wee Joanie will be up from her nap soon, and I will put her in her snowsuit and teach her to make snow angels and stare at the snowflakes landing on her nose.

Maybe that's all I want to say. To tell you about the snowflakes landing on my daughter's nose, about the stew I'll eat later with the family that I'm blessed enough to have. Life is a miracle. I have always thought it. I still do.

That's Joanie awake now. I'll pick this up tomorrow.

Take care of yourself. See you later.

A LETTER FROM S. E. LYNES

First of all, thank you so much for reading *The Perfect Boyfriend*. I hope you enjoyed its twists and turns and found it as satisfying as one of Dougie's Saturday sausage stews. If this is your first book by me, I hope you'll be tempted to read another. If it's your fourteenth, you deserve an award and a large drink. If you'd like to be the first to hear about my new releases, you can sign up to my newsletter using the link below. Your email address will never be shared, and you can unsubscribe at any time.

www.bookouture.com/se-lynes

I always try to share something of what went into a book's writing process. In this case, I was working on a twist involving an age-related fraud which takes place at a school, something that would have an emotionally scarring effect on a young woman's life and would be reframed years later in adulthood. Story is about catharsis and in this novel, Kirsty's painful journey ultimately brings about her healing, as pain often can. I was chatting about the idea to a Scottish friend who often finds herself being my sounding board. She told me a fraud like this had actually happened in the nineties in a school in Glasgow and that a documentary had been made about it. It was called *My Old School* and starred Alan Cumming. She sent me the link and I watched in fascination the story of a man who passed himself off as sixteen-year-old Brandon Lee in order to attend his own former school in Bearsden, aged thirty. The Scottish voices took me back to my time in Aberdeen, where my debut *Valentina* was set, so I decided to set the novel there. Eagle-eyed readers who have been with me since the start might have noticed the *Valentina*-related Easter egg I put in just for you – did you spot it? No? Well, you'll have to go back to the beginning and read it again!

Whilst I have not based this story on Brandon Lee, he and Hughie Reynolds do share aspirations to attend medical school, though the reasons for those aspirations are completely different, as is what transpires in both the past and the present timeline of this story. Hughie is not returning to his old school but starting afresh in a new city, a city he returns to years later with murderous intent, which was certainly not the case for the original imposter, whose real identity was uncovered whilst still at school.

I really enjoyed immersing myself once again in Aberdeen where I spent my younger days as a BBC reporter and producer, and where two of my children were born – in Aberdeen Infirmary maternity unit, in fact, the very place where Kirsty herself works.

The second strand of this novel was inspired by a news story about a lonely retired woman who went missing and was found by local fishermen drowned out at sea. This did not take place in Aberdeen. Police recorded an open verdict. Open verdicts are unsatisfactory because they acknowledge potentially suspicious circumstances without being able to nail down an actual crime. This means, of course, that they leave space for writers with dark imaginations...

I decided to bring these ideas together, develop them and see if they could be interwoven into a psychological thriller mystery. The answer came in the form of heavily pregnant Kirsty Shaw: midwife, good egg and crime documentary aficionado. Kirsty sees links where others don't and ends up unwittingly becoming part of a documentary all of her own. Hughie Reynolds aka Morris Wood aka Michael Peterson was given a dark and twisty background, which for me was a fascinating story in its own right. Leaving his inspiration point behind, I wondered why he would do what he did. Why would anyone? The fact is, people do the strangest things, their motivations often difficult to comprehend. For me, Hughie is a man embittered by his childhood, who believes, quite reasonably, that his potential was thwarted by the poor cards life dealt him. A man capable of great feats of planning and execution, his weaknesses – the temptation of the rich lifestyle and the status it affords, his arrogance and his inability to cope when things don't go to plan – hobble him in the end. Given where they took him, this is a good thing.

Like any other novel form, a psychological thriller has the scope to explore what makes us human. In the case of thrillers, I suppose these themes are most often explored through extremes of human behaviour rather than subtle misunderstandings. I try and investigate what is quiet through what is loud, if that makes sense. The Perfect Boyfriend is about many things – my much-visited touchstones of love and trust, relationships, loyalty, staying true to ourselves and what we believe, believing in ourselves and in our loved ones. It is also about community, another theme I find myself returning to again and again.

In her arguably overdeveloped sense of responsibility for others, Kirsty is in one way the mistress of her own fate, but it is her caring nature and tenacious community spirit that is her salvation in the end. She was under no professional obligation to visit Stella that day, let alone organise a vanload of second-hand furniture to help her get on her feet, but she did it because that's just who she is. Perhaps if she hadn't gone above and beyond, Stella would not have recognised her that night and would not have known something was very wrong. Or perhaps it was baby Luna saying thanks for helping her out into the world...

If you would like to contact me – and I do love to hear from readers – you can find me on Instagram and Facebook, occasionally X, links below. (I am alas too self-conscious for TikTok.)

Writing these words now, I am inspired by Kirsty's journal to tell you something small about my day. The sun is falling. I am hoping to finish this manuscript and hand it in tomorrow morning after a final check. My other half, Paul, has just this second poured me a glass of rosé, but I am not allowing myself to sip it until I finish this letter. I am hoping for crisps. I am hoping you are somewhere cosy and that you have enjoyed this story. I can tell you that I'm plotting the next book at the back of my mind, that I can't wait to start writing it and see what unfolds. Ah. The other half just brought some crisps. He's a keeper.

Take care,

Susie x

facebook.com/Lynesauthor

x.com/selynesauthor

instagram.com/selynesauthor

ACKNOWLEDGEMENTS

First thanks must go to my incredible editor, Ruth Tross, without whom Kirsty's confusion would have become the reader's utter bamboozlement. Ruth, you really did make this book so much better – and clearer! Thanks to my agent, Veronique Baxter, for being the third point in this creative triangle; I am blessed to be part of this solid structure of support.

Thank you to my copy-editor, Jane Selley; my proofreaders, Laura Kincaid and Becca Allen; my publicity manager, Noelle Holten; and all the many hard-working people at Bookouture, the most dynamic publishing house on the planet.

Big thanks to my friend and neighbour Ann Yates for an inspiration-sparking conversation over a cuppa one afternoon in 2023. Thanks to Fi Kelly for recommending the *My Old School* documentary. I was wondering aloud if I could pull off the big twist and she told me someone already had – in real life.

Thank you to my friend, midwife and ace giver of parties Wendy Burman, who helped me with the research, particularly the shoulder dystocia emergency. You may have noticed the midwife in charge in this novel has the same name...

To Bridget McCann, with me since the start of this journey, when she read aloud at the *Valentina* launch, my first – and so far only – book launch. Thank you for doing an Aberdeen sensitivity read to check the dialogue and any local references. This one's for you, pal.

Thank you to all the amazing bloggers, online book clubs and legions of readers who continue to support me and my work, at this point too numerous to mention without missing someone out by mistake. There are so many authors and so many books out there, and I am so grateful to still have a share of your time. I would not be doing this without you. I certainly wouldn't still be doing it without you.

Thank you to all my incredible author pals, a number that increases with each passing year through local meet-ups, talks and, of course, Harrogate. The crime-writing community is so generous and supportive, not to mention funny, and I still pinch myself that I'm allowed to be part of it.

Thank you to Mum, my first reader always; to my kids for not coming into my office unless you've broken a leg; and to my long-suffering other half, Paul, for helping brainstorm plots. And to Dad, whose highly selective fiction reading list includes my books alone – quite right.

PUBLISHING TEAM

Turning a manuscript into a book requires the efforts of many people. The publishing team at Bookouture would like to acknowledge everyone who contributed to this publication.

Audio
Alba Proko
Sinead O'Connor
Melissa Tran

Commercial
Lauren Morrissette
Hannah Richmond
Imogen Allport

Cover design
Aaron Munday

Data and analysis
Mark Alder
Mohamed Bussuri

Editorial
Ruth Tross
Imogen Allport

Copyeditor
Jane Selley

Proofreader
Laura Kincaid

Marketing
Alex Crow
Melanie Price
Occy Carr
Cíara Rosney
Martyna Młynarska

Operations and distribution
Marina Valles
Stephanie Straub
Joe Morris

Production
Hannah Snetsinger
Mandy Kullar
Jen Shannon
Ria Clare

Publicity
Kim Nash
Noelle Holten
Jess Readett
Sarah Hardy

Rights and contracts
Peta Nightingale
Richard King
Saidah Graham

Made in the USA
Columbia, SC
26 February 2025

54471457R00198